Past
FORWARD

VOLUME FOUR

Chautona Havig

~In Honor of Charles Dickens~

I have complained about your verbosity for most of my life—and I meant it. Pages upon pages describing room furnishings nearly drove me to distraction. However, did I not do the same thing with Alexa's wardrobe, or the nuances of Willow's life? I mean, technically, this series is one enormously long book—much longer than anything you ever wrote. So, despite my continued lack of appreciation for said excess verbiage, and the fact that I still don't respect you as a person, I tip my hat and apologize for my hypocrisy. Obviously, I have just as many issues with being a person of "many words" as you were.

Books by Chautona Havig

The Rockland Chronicles

Noble Pursuits
Discovering Hope
Argosy Junction
Thirty Days Hath...
Advent
31 Kisses

The Aggie Series *(Part of the Rockland Chronicles)*

Ready or Not
For Keeps
Here We Come

The Hartfield Mysteries *(Part of the Rockland Chronicles)*

Manuscript for Murder
Crime of Fashion

The Agency Files *(Part of the Rockland Chronicles)*

Justified Means
Mismatched (coming 2013)

Past Forward- A Serial Novel

Volume 1
Volume 2
Volume 3
Volume 4
Volume 5 (coming 2013)

Historical Fiction

Allerednic (A Regency Cinderella story)

The Annals of Wynnewood

Shadows and Secrets
Cloaked in Secrets
Beneath the Cloak

The Not-So-Fairy Tales

Princess Paisley
Everard

CHAPTER 105

Sunday afternoon, Chad snoozed. His crazy work schedule, the past few months' stresses, and the plans for the wedding all hit him at once. Mid-sentence, he'd just stopped talking. Completely. Willow watched him sleep for several minutes and then slipped from the living room.

Outside, she took a deep breath. She knew he needed his rest as much as she needed time alone to process the past twenty-four hours. She missed her mother. She needed someone to talk to and yet wanted no one around her.

Shrugging off her unsettled spirit, Willow marched straight to the washing machine and slowly loaded it with tablecloths, checking each for stains before she dropped it into the machine. In no time, the summer kitchen hummed with activity. She assessed the food situation, froze leftovers, and rearranged things to her personal preferences. In the greenhouse, she tended the plants, reordered the place, and found a few plates and things that had been stashed by someone.

Next, she folded tables and took them to the barn. There was a perfect place high above the kitchen to store them but Willow wasn't sure how to get them up there. Instead, she stacked them all in one stall and all of the chairs in another. She refused to attempt to climb a ladder pushing a table.

After the kitchen and yards were clear, she grabbed her tool belt and gloves, retrieved a roll of wire, and took off to fix the cut sections of fencing. Chad awoke to see her out by the road, wiring the fence back together in the afternoon sun. His chuckle would have confused her. Only Willow would spend the first afternoon of her honeymoon repairing fences when no animal needed them.

He pushed the screen door open and then paused. Maybe she needed a little time alone. Her world had been turned upside down in the last year, and in the past twenty-four hours—exponentially. His parents had worried about how their relationship would work, and Chad, once again, was amazed at how God definitely worked in their life to ensure everyone's good.

While watching Willow as she worked, Chad fumbled for his cellphone and dialed his parents' number. "Mom?"

"Chad! We didn't expect to hear from you so soon!"

"Is Pop there?" Marianne assured him that Christopher was with her and they had the phone on speaker. "I wanted to thank you guys for everything yesterday—especially when it was all up in the air. I was able to do my job because I could trust you to take care of everything else."

"Oh, Chaddie, you could have missed your own wedding!"

Christopher made hushing sounds. "But he didn't, he's fine. Just be thankful." To Chad he added hesitantly, "Everything ok there?"

"Sure, Pop. We—" Chad cleared his throat. "Well, we had kind of a long day yesterday— all those people, and then kind of a late night, so I took a nap this afternoon."

Marianne and Christopher didn't speak but their eyes communicated verbosely. "You all right, son?"

"Um yeah! I'm great, actually. Willow seems to have taken my naptime and put it to good use. The tables are out of the yard, she's probably washing linens, and right now, she's out fixing fences."

He could see them as if his phone was a camera. His mother's face showed disappointment, and his father had probably put an arm around her to comfort her. Was that a sigh? Probably. "I knew you guys would have the world's most unusual honeymoon," Christopher said.

"Yeah." He infused as much happiness as he could casually interject into his tone. This was going to be good. "Well, I should get out there and help her or she'll be antsy all night thinking about the work that wasn't done." Chad stifled back a snicker, as his parents said nothing. "I just wanted to invite you to come out any weekend—well, maybe not next weekend, but any time after that. We have enough room you know. Cheri can have 'her room' and the spare room mattress is comfortable, you know."

"We're not going to kick you out of your room, son. We can visit without staying overnight."

"Oh, no problem. You wouldn't be kicking me out of my room. I'm pretty sure Willow would have serious objections to giving up our bed." With that, Chad said goodbye and clicked the phone shut. What he would give to see his parents' faces right about then.

Chad slipped out the front door and started down the driveway, meeting Willow halfway. She smiled as she neared. "Afternoon, Chaddie."

Shaking his head at her, Chad took the tools and wire from her. "You could have woken me, lass. I'd have helped."

"You needed your rest."

They strolled up the drive to the barn. Inside, he dropped everything and pulled her close. "I am a very happy man."

"That was the goal," she replied impishly.

Chad's Argosy Junction CD played in his laptop as they ate dinner. Willow toyed with her salad, picking chicken pieces out and then dropping them back to the plate. "What's wrong?"

"I don't know."

As he ate his own salad, laden with leftover chicken from the previous night, Chad tried to imagine what could be bothering her. "Well, if you don't feel like eating, how about a walk?" Her shrug was less than encouraging. "Play a game?"

Chad didn't know what to think. Why was she so out of spirits? Had he offended her? Should he ask, or would that make it worse. Women got that way sometimes. If you didn't know why they were irritated that just made the situation worse. He glanced at her. No, Willow wouldn't be like that.

"Have I said or done something that bothers you?"

Her eyes flew up from her plate. "Of course not!"

She took a bite as if to assure him she'd be fine. It only unsettled him further. In desperation, he clung to the only thing that he could think might be the problem. "Um, would you rather I make up the bed in your mom's room?"

"No!" Willow stood and shoved back the chair. "That is, if you think that's best, then fine, but don't do it on my account."

"I'm trying to understand what is wrong, but I'm failing here."

"I don't know, I said. I wish I did so I could tell you, but I just don't know."

He carried his empty plate to the sink and reached automatically for a towel. The edge left the air in the kitchen as they worked silently together to put the room back in order. Once finished, the unsettled feeling shrouded Willow again, and Chad noticed immediately.

"I'll go milk Ditto."

"Why don't I do that and you relax?"

Chad started to protest, but the disappointment that crept into her face stopped him. "You're probably right. I think I'll take a shower."

While lathering and rinsing Chad prayed. As he dried off, realization dawned. He remembered Willow after his nap, during kitchen clean up, and the change that came over her as she strolled to the barn for Ditto's milk pail. He tossed the Dockers and button down shirt he'd brought to change into back into the closet and pulled on old jeans and a holey t-shirt.

At the barn, he met Willow carrying the milk pail. "So, what do we do on a spring evening? Hoe? Rake? Sow? Reap? If we reap, do we have to do it grimly?"

"You want to work?" A spark lit her eyes, but she quickly extinguished it.

"Isn't there a lot of work to be done around here?"

"Well…"

Draping an arm across her shoulder, Chad led her into the summer kitchen and began straining the milk. "Look, I think I know what is wrong."

"Well then tell me, because I'm going crazy."

"You're bored."

"I am not!" she protested hotly. "That's ridiculous."

"But you are. You're used to being very active, even if it's lying around catching fish. You're not used to lying around the house doing nothing. You've spent the past three weeks doing things that put you behind in your spring and summer work, and it's showing."

"But this is our honeymoon. Aren't we supposed to be relaxing?"

Chad poured the boiling water over the freshly washed milk pail and let it drip dry on the counter. He laced their fingers together, and pulled her outside into the evening air. "Some people go skiing, others go snorkeling or mountain climbing. Sightseeing is even exhausting. We're farming. So what?"

"Well, we do need..."

He listened as her mind went in a million audible directions. Among the things mentioned were another field for more alfalfa, more chicks arriving that week, the need to shear the sheep before the first of June, and a dog house for the new puppy. "Mother never allowed a doghouse. She said the barn was sufficient, but I always wanted a doghouse right under that tree, and I'd like to have one. You know how to build things."

"I can't believe you refuse to even try."

"I'm no good—"

His head shook as he interrupted. "Nope, not buying it. You said that about shooting, but you worked at it until you were good because you had to. Your mother wasn't there to do it for you, so you worked hard and learned it. Your mother always did well with wood, you found it hard, so you decided to let it beat you because it was less injurious to your pride."

Her protest died in her throat. She clamped a hand over her mouth and stared at Chad in dismay. "You're right. I can't believe it but you're right."

"Well, we can't build a dog house tonight."

"We can't plow up a field either. Too much work for so late. We can do that Wednesday. Tonight, why don't we work outside on flower beds, the garden, rotate the fields for the animals..."

13

Already, Chad felt lost, but his Willow was back. She folded the tablecloths from the line and handed him a new basket of wet ones. "Why don't you hang these and I'll walk around and see what we need to do first."

Until twilight, they worked. Chad rotated animals and picked weeds in her immense gardens. The space was twice the size of the previous year, and it took all evening to get all of the weeds and tomato worms out of the garden, even working as quickly as he could.

Meanwhile, Willow scrubbed down the porch, weeded the flowerbeds, and though it didn't look much different, felt satisfied as moonlight replaced sunlight. She stood up and dusted her hands, contented. "Well, that's a good day's work."

"Well, especially for Sunday—"

"Oh!" Willow's eyes widened. "Mother always thought we should limit ourselves once a week. She wasn't a strict sabbatarian, but she did think a day of less work was important. I just forgot it was Sunday."

"Well, we did enough. We wouldn't want to collapse in exhaustion—"

"Oh," she interrupted excitedly. "But I sleep best when I've worked hard all day. Crawl into bed, collapse, and don't wake up until the sun rises. It's the best sleep ever."

Chad's jaw attempted to drop, but he kept tight control over his stunned amusement. As they climbed the steps, he stifled chuckles, trying to think of a way to remind her of other possible plans for the evening. "I had other ideas..."

"Game?"

"Um—" As delicately as he could, Chad made several suggestions for how they could spend their evening, which caused Willow to blush and her eyes to grow wide.

"Again? We don't even know if it worked or not!"

"Worked?"

She stared at him with an unreadable expression in her eyes. "They now have ways to tell me if I'm pregnant in less than twenty-four hours?"

"Pregnant?" He knew he sounded like a parrot, but her words made no sense.

"That's kind of the point of it all, right? How can we know—"

14

"Oh, lass… we have to talk—"

Her laughter filled the room. Tears streaming down her face, she struggled for air between guffaws. "You—oh, your—your face."

"Why you little…"

Willow took one look at the expression on his face and ran. The hint of a limp as she thundered across the yard and vaulted the fence told him she was tired. He held back, waiting. She'd wear out soon enough, and he'd get her then. Several times, she stumbled as she glanced over her shoulder to gauge his distance.

At the pool, she jumped—shoes and all. Chad hesitated only long enough to kick his shoes and jeans off before he jumped in after her. "You can't get away from me, you know."

"Who wants to get away from you?" She winked. "Especially before we know—"

"I was so confused. I mean, I know you've had animals out here, so I—"

"I banked on that."

He dunked her—twice. She jumped on his back and tried to get him, but found herself landing several feet away. Willow surfaced, coughing. "How did you do that?"

Chad laughed and swam to the bank and found a place to climb out. "I don't even know. I—I just don't know."

"The water is cold."

He stood on the bank, staring down at her as she treaded water and gazed up at him. "So why are you still in it?"

"Because when I get out, I'll be colder and you'll just throw me back in anyway."

The sun would be down before he could get back with dry clothes. "So, do you want me to run for a towel or do you want to run with me to get a towel?"

After a few more seconds of observing him, she nodded to the rope. "Throw it in. I'll go with you."

To his surprise, she used the rope as an anchor to help her walk right out of the pool. "I'll have to swing out over it sometime."

Landing near his feet, she shivered and pointed to his clothes. "You might as well get dressed. There's no reason for both of us to freeze. C'mon!"

15

They half-ran for a few minutes until Willow slowed to a stroll. She slipped her hand in his and moved closer. "It's beautiful out here. I wish it were late enough for fireflies. We could have had an evening wedding with fireflies dancing around us like those twinkle lights Cheri put up in the greenhouse."

"Yeah, like that made sense. Who could see them?"

She laughed. "That's what I told her, but she wanted to do it. I forgot to take them down."

As they neared the house, she seemed to slow even more. Chad gazed down at her, concerned. "Lass, if you're not ready… if it was too much too soon…"

She didn't answer. Willow stopped midstride and turned, wrapping her arms around him. "I can't believe I ever doubted that you wouldn't understand—that you couldn't know how to make me feel safe. It's so crazy."

"I don't know what I'm doing. I'm kind of making this up as I go. I just can't stand the thought of you dreading—"

"It's not that, Chad. Not at all."

"You're hesitant to go back. I can sense it."

Again, she didn't answer. Frustration filled his heart and anger welled in his spirit. Fury at the men who had done this to her without ever speaking an unkind word or touching her in any way overwhelmed him until he feared she would notice. Two dead men and a woman in jail had warped her before she was even out of the womb. He should feel grief or compassion for the likelihood of their lost states. All he could muster was relief, knowing that the God of mercy who would have saved them was also a God of justice.

"Remember what I joked about?" she asked at last.

"How could I forget. I have to tell my dad about that, you know. I just have to."

"Go ahead. I don't care."

Several more long seconds passed. She did not speak. "Lass?"

Again, she hesitated. "Well, if I really thought that—just pretending I did—" her eyes rose to meet his. "Would that make it good or bad that I would have been hoping that it didn't quite work yet?"

16

CHAPTER 106

A very different Willow left the sheep ranch outside New Cheltenham, cuddling a puppy and trying out names on her. Chad remembered getting Saige, and while Willow hadn't been ambivalent toward the dog, she had not shown nearly as much interest in that pup as she did in this one. Fluffy ears and puppy breath kept her mind and hands occupied for the fifty miles home.

"She's a black and white dog…"

"That's astute of you."

Willow shoved him playfully. "Knock it off. I think I'm going to name her Portia. She's as black and white as Portia's interpretation of the contract in *Merchant of Venice.*"

"Shakespeare. You would."

The pup curled into her lap and settled down for a short nap. Every mile that passed seemed etched in the story of their new life together. Somehow, a change had washed over their relationship, and yet everything was also the same. Had they tried to explain it, he suspected that they both would have failed.

At home, the pup bounced around the barn as Willow pulled out the cultivator and then collapsed in exhaustion on a pile of straw. Chad followed her to the field she planned to "plow" and smiled to himself as she cheered at the softness of the earth. "That rain last night helped me sleep well, and now look what it's done. We have easy soil to turn over."

He'd never seen anything like it. A large wheel propelled

prongs that dug up the earth as she pushed it along wheelbarrow style. Chad was sure it was never intended to replace a regular plow, but of course, Willow and her mother had no way to get gasoline for fuel-powered machines. After seeing her fight and struggle across the short side of the field for several minutes, he called her to him.

Uncertain of how committed she was to her old-fashioned ways of doing things, he jammed his fists into his pockets and stammered ineffectively a few times. "I was thinking—"

"Chad, what's wrong?"

"It's killing me to watch you work yourself like that. You could plow that whole field in a few hours instead of a week if you had proper tools."

"What's wrong with my cultivator?"

Frustration nearly overcame him but he kicked a dirt clod with his shoe and continued as calmly as he could manage. "It requires so much of you, Willow. You'd be done with that row by now if you had a motorized one. It'd save so much time and hard work—"

"But what would I do with all that time I saved?" The question was more of a tease than a serious inquiry.

"Spend it with me, for one thing. You could just double your production with half the work." As a concession to her lifestyle, he added, "If not motorized, then we at least need two of those things so we can take turns breaking ground— one 'plowing' and the other following behind. I assume it's going to take more than one pass..."

"Where can we find one of these motor ones you're talking about? Maybe we can use the motor for the first pass and then mine for the second."

Excited, Chad hugged her and pulled his keys from his pocket. "I'll find one to rent. We can see if you like it." He kissed her briefly, jogged toward the barn, and retraced his steps. "I think that was a little weak..."

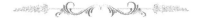

By the time Chad arrived with a tiller, Willow had made two full passes across the field. She watched as he started the tiller and slowly, yet much more quickly than she'd managed, made a full row across the field. After about twenty feet, she grabbed her tiller and followed. Chad was right. It was much easier to follow after the machine broke the ground first.

At lunchtime, Willow, covered in dirt and sweat, scrubbed in the summer kitchen, made two huge sandwiches, and poured the last of the lemonade into glasses. Seated on the back porch, feeding scraps to the pup, she turned to an exhausted Chad and began discussing the tiller. "Ok, so how expensive are those things? Would we need to own one once this is tilled? It should be easier to do next time, right? What about—"

"Whoa, lass. We don't have to decide to buy one of these things today."

After another bite, Willow continued her vocalized thought processes. "Well, I keep thinking of the gas. It would become expensive to use it for something so easy to do—"

"Easy? It's brutal. I almost ached just watching you force that thing through the dirt."

"It's work. Work is hard. I don't understand why it's so bad?" The confusion in her voice was familiar—and genuine.

Chad's fists found his pockets again. "Willow, we were brought up in entirely different worlds. Where you did whatever was necessary, no matter how physically taxing, my friends and family looked for the path of least resistance to get the same job done. You made your candles; we bought ours. You hand tilled your acres of soil, we rented one of those things for our flower beds."

"And worked more hours somewhere else to pay for it?"

He shrugged to show that he wasn't angry at her. Her observations were valid and he found that as he considered it, accurate. His father had traded one kind of work for ease in doing another. Both were still work, and his father had chosen the work he enjoyed most which was exactly what Willow did every day.

"You're right. I think I understand now."

"Well," she said rinsing her glass in the sink and washing her hands. "I don't. That's ok, I'm getting used to it."

Pulling Willow to him, Chad wrapped his arms around her. "You're right. Dad did the work he preferred in order to

19

make work he didn't enjoy easier. You're doing the work you prefer. I wasn't brought up to enjoy it, so I naturally try to find a way to make it easier."

It was a huge breakthrough in understanding for both of them. As much as they enjoyed their relationship, some aspects still required both of them to step back and consider that there were other ways to see things. Neither way was necessarily superior, but what was familiar was usually preferred, and their comfort zones were on nearly opposite poles.

"I think it's simple," Willow finally said.

"Oh you do?" Just as he realized that she might feel patronized by the amusement in his tone, she spoke.

"Of course. When I'm working alone, I do what is familiar and comfortable for me. When you work with me, you do what you do however you prefer to do it. Why should either of us overhaul anything? Doing both worked for the field. It'll work for other things too."

Chad grabbed his gloves and pulled them on as he led her out of the barn. "Why didn't someone tell me I was marrying a practical genius?"

"Simple."

He eyed her warily. "Oh?"

She took off running toward the field. "They didn't want you to be jealous!"

Willow heard the bathwater running upstairs and smiled to herself as she fried chicken. It felt almost like "old times" when she'd make dinner while Mother bathed. How Chad could stand laying in water that slowly grew cold, she'd never understand. Her hair, still dripping after her own shower, soaked her shirt as Willow rolled her shoulders, stretching out the kinks that occasionally tried to form in them.

The kitchen felt warm. They'd have to eat on the porch. Willow had long noticed that Chad felt the temperature extremes differently than she did. What she considered comfortably warm or cool were hot and cold to him. She tossed a salad, sliced bread, and jumped as Chad's arms wrapped around her waist.

"That was sneaky!"

"And after the mud clod fight, you deserved sneaky."

"How was I supposed to know you'd never had a mud fight?" The innocence in her tones didn't change the mischievous look on her face.

"I can't believe you and your mother used to do stuff like that. At your age!"

"Mother said we shouldn't give up our favorite fun just because the calendar told some people we were too old for it."

Chad popped a cherry tomato in his mouth and collapsed in the rocking chair exhausted. "Mother was right."

Willow turned, her eyes slowly filling with tears. Deep sobs welled inside her and then wracked her body. She sank to the floor in front of the kitchen sink lost in grief.

"Wha—" Chad flew across the room, his alarm barely reaching her consciousness.

For several minutes, he held her, hushed her, wiped her tears, and then held her some more. Nothing he said or did helped to calm the emotional torment that swallowed her. The chicken burned; Chad tossed the pan in the sink, and still Willow curled into a ball, her back to the sink, and sobbed until her heart was empty.

"I'm—" she choked back tears. "I'm sorry about the chicken."

"What's wrong, lass?"

Willow knew he hated seeing her like this. She hadn't cried like that in months—not around him anyway. "It's silly. I feel so stupid." New tears, quiet ones this time, spilled over her cheeks splashing onto his hands.

"I still don't understand—"

"You didn't say *your* mother this time. You just called her *Mother*. It felt like you finally became a part of my family too instead of the other way around." She blushed at his look of incredulity. "I told you it was silly."

"I can't take credit for anything. I could just as easily have said 'your' again. I never meant to sound distant—"

"You didn't. This just felt like she was 'our' mother now instead of just mine—like Marianne feels like 'ours.'"

"I know I would have loved y—Mother, but Willow, I

21

never knew her. I often think of her as just 'Mother' but other times…"

"I'm sorry," Willow jumped to her feet brushing away her tears. "I know it's crazy, but I always feel like I'm continually taking and never giving anything."

"You gave me you. What more could I ask for?" He stood and brushed her hair away from her face, his heart aching at the sight of her puffy eyes. "We'll get to know your grandparents, aunt, uncle, cousins—you'll see. I got a new family too. You just don't know them that much better than I do is all."

She gave him a halfhearted smile. "I also gave you a charred meal. Every bride's nightmare, eh?"

"How about a trip to town and dinner at the Coventry?"

"Deal."

Chad waited until she stood and then added, "And then when we get home, I'm going to whip your bum in Yahtzee."

"Don't you mean…?"

Chad snatched the kitchen towel and snapped it after her as she raced toward the stairs. "Get up there and get changed, woman!"

CHAPTER 107

Early Wednesday morning, before the sun forced its way over the eastern horizon, Chad rolled over and his arm curled cozily around—nothing. Subconsciously, he knew something was wrong, but it took him several minutes to fight his way out of sleep and back to the land of consciousness. Willow was gone—her side of the bed, cold.

He shivered at the cool air that hit his arms and legs as he crawled from the covers and wrapped the robe from their personal shower around him. Chad remembered her hanging it on the wall next to his side of the bed, assuring him he'd need it. He had told her she was crazy but here he was, wrapping it around him, shivering. The open window sent damp breezes into their house.

Their house. Already he'd begun to feel possessive of her property. Was that good? As he jogged down the steps to the living room, Chad pondered the question but came to no conclusion.

She wasn't in the living room, kitchen, or library. He glanced out the back door but saw no lights in the barn. The front porch looked dark as well, so he wearily climbed the stairs again checking the craft and newly decorated "sitting room," but Willow seemed to have vanished.

"Willow?" Why he called quietly, Chad couldn't explain— even to himself. In their room, he stared hard out the window trying to discern if the lump by the oak where her—their mother was buried was the gravestones or if Willow had gone out there again. He couldn't tell.

With a sigh, he pulled on his shoes, sans socks, and dragged himself back down the stairs. In this mist, she'd get sick if she fell asleep out there. He then laughed at the thought. If anyone wouldn't get sick, it was Willow. She never got sick. She'd once told him she only remembered being ill a few times in her life.

As he stepped out the front door, he stopped. There, sleeping comfortably in the swing with her mother's journal on her chest, lay Willow. A quilt covered her, but to Chad, she looked cold. Although he hated to wake her, the idea of her sleeping on the narrow swing, rolling off, or getting chilled was too much for him.

He shook her gently. "Willow, lass, wake up."

"He's good to me, Mother," she murmured in her sleep. "You would like him."

The hollow tones in her voice told him the ache of Kari's loss was still rooted in Willow's heart. She must fight the pain constantly and, he realized miserably, probably for his sake. "Lass, come on. Let's get you inside."

"I want to stay out here, Mother. I feel closer to Jesus in the night." She mumbled the words in a whisper, making it nearly impossible for Chad to hear them.

Not knowing what else to do, Chad went inside, grabbed her wool afghan from the chaise, and draped it over her. He brushed her cheek with his thumb, staring down at her before he picked up the hand-tied "journal" and carried it upstairs. There was something lacking in these copied journals. He needed to see if the Chief thought the originals were safe at home again or not.

Upstairs, he tossed and turned. How had he grown accustomed to having her close after only four nights? Finally, in desperation, he lit the lamp and read.

January, 2001

I'm broken. I knew this day would come. I knew eventually she'd resent me or worse. Today when I planned a trip to Rockland to discuss her majority with Bill, she asked to go. I refused. Why am I so unreasonable—why do I let my fears overcome me? Why can she not see that I wouldn't do

24

this unless I thought it was best?

She attacked me. I want to say I have no idea where this venomous side came from, but I know it would be dishonest. She got it from me, and if it can be passed along genetically, I assume from Steve. The things she said—I can't repeat them. My heart was broken. I take that back. My heart is broken.

How long will it take her to forgive me? How long will it take me to forgive her? Is this it? Is this the beginning of the end of this idyllic life I tried so hard to create? Can we ever get past this?

I can't stand it. She won't look at me. I can't speak to her. We work together in silence and avoid that togetherness as much as possible. Did I blow it? Should I have reconsidered the adoption scenario?

No! It was the right thing to do. Oh great. There's a car coming up the drive. I need to go run off a salesman, missionary, or some other obnoxious trespasser.

Well, I didn't get back to this for a few days, and I'm glad. Willow apologized, as did I. I told her that the next time I go to town, she's welcome to come, just not this time. I wanted her to make the decision to go because she'd thought it out clearly, not because I made forbidden fruit acceptable. She seems fine with it.

Willow just came in and apologized again. She seems broken over her ugliness. It was truly horrible. The things she accused me of doing were vile. I think she's been rehashing the conversation in her mind and realizes how it cut my heart.

Her repentance is beautiful. I know I'm a mother and that I am probably unreasonably biased toward my child, but when I think of the people I knew when I was her age—when I think of me at her age, I see justification and anger when confronted with my sin. If not confronted, I was ambivalent. I didn't care. I brushed it aside and ignored the searing it did on my heart.

Not Willow. My girl doesn't do that. She sins—she's human, but she repents, whole-heartedly. There is no justification. There is only acknowledgement, contrition, and confession. It may take her a while to see it, but once she does, it's over.

I love her. I try to imagine her in the so-called "real world," and I cringe. It'll destroy her. It'll ruin the woman that God has molded out of His clay. She'd be seared— hardened. Her conscience—how could it remain so tender when constantly beaten by the ugliness of this world?

Men would be drawn to her, and yet they'd mock her. She'd trust them and then be crushed by their insensitive ugliness. Even a kind man like Bill wouldn't understand her.

Bill. I wonder about him. Why hasn't he married? What horrible things do I not know about him? When Willow had that crush on him, I worried. Now I worry about what happens over the next few years. She's growing into a woman. It won't be long before he won't see her as a child. Will he take her away from me? He's not blind, he's not stupid; what will I do?

Oh how ridiculous. I'm borrowing trouble and being fearful. He's watched her grow up. If anything, he'd see her as a little sister to fix up with some kid at church—which would be even worse. I need to make sure that home is the most wonderful place to be so that she doesn't develop the desire for anything else.

If all else fails, I'll buy her some of her blasted sheep. She can spend a few years perfecting her sheep and spinning skills and maybe by then, I'll have something else to interest her. I could always insist that she learn woodworking. After all, eventually I'm going to get old and find it hard to do some of these things.

She just brought me peach tea. She hates the stuff—even the smell of it but she did it for me. Lord, I don't deserve such a wonderful daughter.

Chad closed the pages and laid them on his nightstand. He understood Kari much more than Willow ever would. Her concerns about men—she'd even considered the possibility of Bill. How wrong she'd been. Chad remembered the pain in Bill's face as he shook hands at arrival and their leaving. The waltz—Willow had sought him out and danced not realizing how much it hurt him to do it.

She'd been right about one thing. Willow was wonderful. The more he thought of it, he realized that everything he

26

thought he'd ever wanted in a wife—Willow had. "She is wonderful Lord, and like Kari, I don't deserve her."

Rain pounded the roof and earth. Willow stared out the window and Chad stared at Willow. Such a ridiculously exciting moment in their new marriage.

"Bowling?"

Willow shook her head The idea sounded revolting. "No thanks. I'm tempted to let the puppy in."

"You'll regret it."

"I know."

He'd hoped she'd relent and agree to let Portia inside. Chad hated the idea of that poor puppy out in the cold and the rain. The stupid animal kept sitting in the yard howling for someone to rescue her from herself. "What about a movie? There's an action movie in Fairbury right now..."

"I don't want to get sick. I think all that moving around on that huge wall would make me sick."

He'd never seen her bored like this. It was hysterical. "Well..." His mind raced with ideas from roller skating to museums. Finally he jumped to his feet. "Get your shoes on. Let's go to the Aquarium."

"What is it? I mean, I know what an aquarium is—we almost got one once—"

"Well, the Rockland Aquarium is huge. It has fish from all over the world. There are actual sharks and octopi and even penguins."

Rockland Metro Area Aquarium and Water Park loomed before them. Chad led her eagerly to the door, talking about all the shows he'd seen, an overnight class trip, and the special exhibits that came from time to time. "The water park is cool, but it's only open in summer—except for rainy days. Closed on rainy days too," he chattered as he urged her inside toward the exhibits.

At the first wall of glass, Chad met the Willow Bill saw when she first arrived in Rockland, but he didn't realize it. Her eyes widened, her breath became shallow, and then she froze. He wandered back and forth, admiring the various fish, pointing out unique specimens, and looking for hidden ones. She never moved. Oblivious to all but his delight with the fish, Chad enjoyed himself until he came back to her side and took her hand absently. The coldness of her fingers surprised him.

"What's wrong?"

"Is it safe?" She couldn't believe she was having this conversation again.

"Is what safe."

"That wall," she whispered, shuddering at the mental image of the glass giving way and drowning a room full of people.

Chad pulled her close to him turning her away from the wall and through a doorway. "It's safe. Thousands of people come through this room every week. Not once has that glass even cracked."

"But the second law of thermodynamics—"

"I know," he agreed soothingly. "But no one said that the decay was rapid. Look how well preserved the earth is after six thousand years. Look at that tree in California, Methuselah. It's been around since the time of the flood, and it's still standing. It's dying like everything else but it doesn't happen overnight."

She nodded. This she could understand. "How will they know when it isn't safe? Will they know before someone is hurt?"

She tried to glance back at the wall of glass, but the darkness in the aquarium made it mercifully impossible. At the jellyfish tank, Chad pointed out the sizes and colors of the translucent creatures, and though she could sense his blatant attempts to distract her, Willow appreciated it. By the time they reached the penguins, she was so delighted by their odd waddles, that her fear dissipated.

Alas, Chad forgot the famous Rockland *Under the Sea* exhibit. They followed a tour guide through the archway and into the dome of the exhibit. At first, Willow was as awed by

28

the incredible sights of the water around her, but when a small shark swam straight for her, she screamed. Her voice, echoing through the room, pierced the ears of everyone and frightened several small children. Their wails, combined with her panicked screams created instant chaos.

She found herself wrapped in Chad's arms with her head buried into his shoulder. Slowly, he backed them out of the room. Her screams ceased the moment he pulled her from the tunnel leading to the exhibit.

"It's ok," he murmured sitting down and pulling her closer. "It's just a room. I forgot about it, or I would have warned you."

"There are children in there," she sobbed quietly. "How can they risk it?"

"People work for peanuts giving those tours and cleaning the glass; do you think they'd do that if it wasn't safe? Is the little bit they are paid worth the money if it's dangerous?"

"They're stupid." Chad's chuckle sent her upright, glaring at him. "What is so funny?"

"You just make my heart happy. Even when you terrify small children."

"I— I didn't. How?"

"Well what did you think would happen screaming like that?"

"I screamed?" She remembered panic. She'd frozen in place; she was sure of it, but Willow had no memory of screaming. "I never scream."

"Want to try again?"

She shook her head. "I really just want to go. Please—" Her voice dropped to a whisper. "I can't get the image of that shark swimming right at me out of my head."

Once outside, Willow glanced around her smiling at the tall buildings. "I never thought I'd be so glad to see those huge things. I love those buildings now."

"Well, where to? We're in town—"

A smile broke out over her face. "I want to go to the fabric store where I bought the fabric for the girls' dresses. I want to give the man who helped me a tip. He was so kind."

Chad shrugged and accepted the address she passed him. "Do you have a card?"

29

"For what?"

"Well," Chad explained patiently, "most people get embarrassed if you just hand them cash, but if you put it in a card that says thank-you, it's just different."

On the way to the fabric store, Chad pulled into the parking lot of Rite-Aid. "Let's get a card here."

"At a drugstore?"

She should not have been surprised to step into a store and find rows upon rows of cards for every occasion. New job, new baby, retirement, birthday, wedding, sympathy, graduation—they had it all. A four-foot wide section intermingled thanks and sympathy together.

"Something small," she murmured as her fingers skipped over the tops of the cards.

"Why small?"

"Because if it's embarrassing to receive cash, it'll be embarrassing to receive a large envelope—it'll be conspicuous."

His smile was his only response. She'd done something right. That pleasure that his approval brought her—nothing felt better.

"Hey, this one is nice. I think he'll like it. It has lilacs on it."

"Um, lass, flowers are usually better for girls. Guys like boring or something more masculine."

"But he loved the flower choice. I think he'll like it. I'm ready. Let's go."

Twice on the way to the fabric store, Chad commented on the card, but Willow ignored him. Josh would love it. As he drove, she struggled to write the card without destroying it. Stoplights became her friend until she signed it—Willow Tesdall.

"That's something I like seeing."

"Me too. I've never written it with Tesdall before. I almost forgot."

"Most people would have," he agreed. "You just don't write so fast that your head can't keep up with you."

She hurried from the truck, practically dragging Chad into the store and up to the first empty register. "Is Josh working today? I need to speak to him if I can."

30

"Well," the cashier said lazily, "I think he just got off..."

"Can you page him just in case he hasn't left yet?" Chad's voice was firm but agreeable.

"Well—"

"Thanks, we'd really appreciate it."

When Josh burst through the double doors, Chad nudged her. "Is that—"

"Josh!" Willow rushed forward smiling. "Do you remember me?"

"Daisy yellow. Your wedding was just a week or two ago wasn't it?"

Willow's eyes grew wide. "Wow! You remembered!"

A passing employee laughed. "We call him the elephant."

Her eyebrows drew together as she tried to understand. "Why? He's too scrawny to be an elephant!"

"People like to say that elephants never forget, lass. She's saying he has a good memory," Chad whispered.

"Oh! Right. I remember that. Sorry." She started to hand him the envelope. "I brought you a card. The dresses were just perfect and you were so helpful."

Josh looked around uncomfortably. "Want to get a coffee with me?"

Willow smiled and pulled Chad forward. "That'd be great. You can meet my husband." Her throat swelled—her *husband*!

"It's nice to meet you," Chad said. "We'd love to get coffee with you."

"Oh!" The man's gestures were the same effeminate movements that had interested her the last time. Before she could introduce Chad, Josh added, "You are a lucky man. Come on, I can't wait to hear everything."

Outside the store, Josh led them down the street, around the corner, and into an old café that had definitely seen better years. "The coffee isn't gourmet here, but it's good and it's hot." He waved at the waitress at the counter. "When you have a minute, Wendy."

Chad pushed Willow's card across the table. "Willow told me how helpful you were. I really appreciate it. I was afraid she'd be overwhelmed in a store like yours."

"I could tell she'd never been in one." He grinned at

31

Willow. "You know, if you hadn't said bridal, I would have asked you out right there. You were the most interesting person I've met in a long time."

The look of shock on Chad's face surprised Willow and amused Josh. "I thought—"

"I'm not surprised," Josh agreed. "Before Barney over at the mission introduced me to Jesus..."

Chad grinned at Willow and said, "This is going to be beautiful. I can tell."

"I don't understand."

Josh looked at Chad surprised. "She didn't think—"

Chad shook his head. "She's never been exposed to—"

A wistful tone entered Josh's voice. He looked into Willow's eyes and reached one hand across the table to squeeze both of hers. "You have no idea how absolutely blessed you are."

Confused, Willow listened as Josh told of his lifelong love of fashion, interior design, and beauty. "People always assumed—I guess I can see why, but—" He sighed. "If you hear it enough, you start to believe it—or at least believe you don't have a choice."

Curious, Willow's eyes darted back and forth between the men, pausing on Chad as he said, "You felt trapped and assumed that others knew more about you than you knew yourself?"

"If it looks like a duck, walks like a duck, and quacks like a duck—"

"It couldn't possibly be a person who likes to wear duck costumes?" Compassion and surprise flooded Chad's voice. "When did you realize it wasn't what *you* wanted?"

"When Barney treated me like something worthwhile. He loved me, told me about Jesus, and didn't preach at me about my lifestyle. I finally had to bring it up."

"What'd he say?"

"Nothing. He said that when Jesus indwelled my heart, He'd help me do whatever Jesus wanted me to do. He could have shown me the Bible. At that point—" Josh's slight lisp grew slightly more pronounced. "I would have grabbed at any excuse—"

"I'll bet that's why he didn't," Chad commented. He was

impressed. Without a doubt, Chad knew that one of the first things he would have done would have been to encourage Josh to repent.

"Right. I was looking for an out for something I hated anyway. I don't know if I would have ever truly repented if he would have pushed right then."

Willow listened confused. Josh and Chad seemed to understand each other perfectly, but she didn't have a clue as to what was such a big deal. Though tempted to interrupt and ask, she wisely decided to wait. Chad could explain later. Josh seemed to need to talk.

"Of course now," Josh continued, "I'm an outcast with the old crowd, the girls at church see me as something they can't quite trust, and I feel as alone as I ever did."

"But with Jesus—" Chad began.

"You're never alone."

Unconsciously, Willow began humming the old hymn, *"... no never alone, no never alone. He promised never to leave me, never to leave me alone..."* Josh squeezed her hand again. "Exactly. Someday I'll meet people who are as comfortable with me as you and Willow— and even Barney—"

"I bet you know my sister." Chad hesitated even as he spoke.

"What's her name?"

"Cheri Tesdall."

Josh's eyes lit up. "She was the first person to invite me to one of those singles things that happen around different towns. I knew she was going with some other guy, but just knowing *someone* wanted—*me* to go—"

"I'm just glad she's not one of the ones who rejected—"

"Cheri wouldn't! Chad, how could you think that! I think Cheri would like Josh if she wasn't so wrapped up in Chuck." She blushed. "Well, I mean she'd like him anyway, but I thought she'd appreciate him more personally if her—" Willow stopped herself. "You know what I mean."

They stayed through dinner, ate dessert, and continued to talk. After half a dozen glances at his phone in the past ten minutes, Josh jumped up and insisted he had to leave. "I'm supposed to play the piano tonight for the children at the mission. I have to go."

Chad pulled an old receipt from his wallet and wrote their phone numbers on it. "Call us. Anytime. Come visit. Come to church with us. Maybe what you need is a broader group of friends, and we'd like to be the first to invite you to Fairbury."

Fighting back tears and an even heavier lisp, Josh waved and dashed out the door, thanking them as he went. Willow hardly noticed; her eyes were focused on Chad. He seemed upset. "Are you ok?"

"Just disgusted with myself."

"Why?"

"I don't know how to explain it," he began. "I feel like the very people who probably caused those self-doubts in him. People like me—we caused his pain." Chad toyed with a straw wrapper. "I wonder how common that is?" he wondered to himself.

"How common what is? What *were* you guys talking about? What *are* you talking about?"

Chad sighed. "Didn't you notice anything unusual about him?"

"Well," she admitted, "he's a little girly, but I expect it's just because he works with fabric, and the few men I know don't. He probably spends a lot of time with women or something."

"It's something like that. Mind if I explain some other time?" Chad stood and grasped her hand helping her from the booth.

"Sure. Or I can ask him—"

"I'd rather you didn't," Chad insisted sadly. "I think you'd make him uncomfortable."

"I think," Willow said remembering the walls of glass and water, and the afternoon's conversation, "I think people overcomplicate things. Let's go home."

CHAPTER 108

The shearers arrived on Friday. Willow hung over the fence, fascinated with every movement. It took almost no time for the two men to produce two full skirts. Willow nudged Chad. "Ten minutes—from start to finish, two fleeces in ten minutes. I've got to learn how to do that."

"Really? You want to do that? It looks like a hassle."

"Looks fun to me." She called out a few questions and turned to Chad, excited. "Did you hear that? A shearing school in New Cheltenham! I want to go."

"Then you'll go." Despite his personal lack of interest, her excitement appealed to him. "I love how into all this you get."

"Even though you think I'm nuts."

"You are. I agree with Mother on that one. Sheep are stupid and obnoxious." He nudged her boot. "Kind of like chickens."

"They're tasty like chickens too."

"How would you know?"

Willow giggled at the gawky-looking sheep before answering. "Had it with Bill at that restaurant the day you made me wear my slippers to town."

"They were flip-flops."

"I felt like I was walking around town in my pajamas."

Chad shook his head. "I remember thinking you looked amazing."

"You acted like I looked ridiculous." She winked. "That's

probably because you wanted an excuse to stop coming."

"I did." He winked back at her before adding, "I've never been more happy to be wrong."

"Me too."

"What were you wrong about?"

Willow laughed. "No, I've never been happier for you to be wrong."

"That's it. They don't need me, you're insulting me, I'm going to go inside."

"I'll be in when they're done."

Books on shearing, cleaning, carding, and spinning littered the kitchen table. For three days, she'd stacked them out of the way before each meal, dragging them back as soon as the plates were cleared. She had wool now. What good would wool be without a spinning wheel?

A glance out the door told him he only had a few minutes. Scrolling through his phone, he looked for numbers of yarn shops all around the Rockland Loop. He consulted her book, asked questions, and took notes of what each shop had in stock. By the time she climbed the steps, still waving at the departing shearers, he thought he had a plan.

"What're you doing?"

"I have here a list of every type of spinning wheel I could find within driving distance. What do you think about us going to get one? What good is that fleece without something to spin it with?"

His eyes closed and he laid his cheek on her shoulder as Willow slid onto his lap at the table, poring over his notes. It hadn't been that long ago that the movement would have been instinctive—instinctively friendly. This was different, and every time she made those little gestures, it filled his heart with gratitude. Only the Lord could have effected that change in her. Only the Lord.

Saturday morning, Chad sat at the table, amazed as he remembered the week he'd enjoyed with his wife. *Wife.* Had it really been just a year since he'd prayed that the Lord would take Willow out of his life? Had he really resented her as much as he remembered? Seeing her as she pulled muffins from the oven, scooped eggs and "breakfast steak" onto his plate, humming contentedly, he almost couldn't remember why he'd rejected her for so long—almost.

He had almost expected something to go wrong—some kind of awkwardness or argument to upset the balance of their relationship—but it didn't happen. Each day had its new experiences and opportunities for misunderstanding. They'd never spent that much concentrated time alone together. During her injury and his, there had always been times apart. Willow liked her solitude. Still, even amid the newness of marriage, their comfortable camaraderie never wavered.

Chad smiled across the table. "What are you going to do today?"

After a bite of her eggs, Willow shrugged. "I've been neglecting the chickens. I think it's time to do some more butchering. I've got those new chicks coming in so..."

"Great day to go back to work."

"I waited for it..." she teased. "I considered offering, but I'm too selfish. I want the blood—the guts—"

He jumped up and carried his mostly-empty plate to the sink. Kissing her cheek, he dashed out the door calling, "See you tonight."

She hurried to the front porch and waved as he drove down the drive— another first in their life. As the truck brake lights disappeared, Willow gave one last glance at the empty drive and hurried to clean the kitchen before her afternoon of chicken slaughter. She wanted it all done and every trace gone before Chad came home from work.

Her eyes widened as she opened the cupboard. Her fingers slid down the stack—*stack of plates*—as she put the breakfast dishes away. Eight plates. Eight bowls. Eight mugs, glasses, small plates. The silverware drawer had silverware in a tray inside. No more forks, spoons, and knives in a mason jar next to the plates. There were enough utensils and dishes for the entire family.

Sobs wracked her body—again. When would the little changes stop affecting her so deeply? As she lay curled on the mat in front of the sink, her hands wiping ineffectually at her eyes, Willow tried to pray. Words and thoughts failed. In the deepest part of her heart, hidden under the secrets in her soul, a small part of her was comforted by that pain. It meant she had not forgotten Mother or their life.

Willow awoke half an hour later, refreshed. It took a moment to realize just what she was doing on the floor, but when the memories flooded her again, she felt comforted. "Thank you, Lord," she whispered.

Chickens. Time to butcher chickens. She changed clothes and jogged down the back steps to the barn, setting up her butchering station. Portia raced between her legs, charged the coop fence, and barked at the slightest movement. "Well, girl, your herding skills are excellent, but I do not want my chickens herded! Go!"

Portia did not go. She chased again, until Willow, frustrated and ready to lock her in the cellar, tied the yapping bundle of fur to the front porch. Although the chickens weren't any more cooperative, Willow didn't care. She grabbed the first bird, wrung its neck, and carried the animal to the barn. In nearly record time, she had the birds skinned and ready to process in the kitchen. Once she plucked and gutted the last two birds, she would be done.

The clock showed five-thirty by the time she finished the butchering, fed the animals, milked Ditto, and put away the rest of the tools. She grabbed her favorite skirt and top, a towel, and raced for the shower. After the day's work, she looked forward to relaxing in the porch swing until Chad got home.

Showered, dressed, hair braided—refreshed. Willow strolled out to the summer kitchen to give the chicken a final baste before she walked around to the front of the house and untied the puppy. She grabbed the journal she was currently reading and Portia's favorite bone and settled into the porch swing, kicking the bone across the porch. While she found her place in the journal, the puppy bounced after the bone, grabbed it, growled, rolled and made a puppy nuisance of herself over it. Willow read.

June 2001,

I realize that I need to stop treating Willow as my child. I mean, she is my child but she's an adult now. The law can say what it wants, but she's been an adult for many years already. I think I need to ease her into a different way of interrelating. I'm not sure how to do it.

I have tried to remember what mom and dad did. I don't know. It seemed as if one day I was just there and had been for ages. One thing that I am certain of—she needs a solid idea of what work comes when, so she can plan her own time and not rely so heavily on me. I just don't know how to do it.

She could do it. If I dropped dead right now, she'd be fine, and that's always been my focus. I need to focus on how to live as two adults together rather than as just mother and daughter. I don't know, maybe I'm overcomplicating things. There has just always been this implied authority in our relationship, and well, I'm not sure it's appropriate anymore. At her age, I would have resented it I'm sure.

I need to condense our work journals. I need to encourage her to choose what she wants to do rather than delegate. I can make this happen. I must make this happen, if I hope to keep her happy here.

Chad's truck bounced across the driveway and into the yard. Portia raced for it, sending Willow and Chad both into mock cardiac arrest. Willow swallowed hard, remembering how Othello had stopped Saige from nipping at them. He had been a good dog.

"Next time I drive up, hold her back until I turn off the truck. Maybe if we don't let her go until the truck turns off, she'll learn to wait for it," Chad called before grabbing an arm full of uniforms from the passenger's side and slamming the door behind him.

"What if it's two in the morning and you don't see her?"

"Better lock her in the barn at night until she's bigger."

Willow made a face. "So much for a guard dog."

Chad reached her side and pulled her close. "Hey. I missed you."

She grinned. "And you were glad to miss me and all the chicken guts too."

"Ew. What's for dinner?" he interrupted, grabbing her hand and pulling her into the house. "I've got to get these upstairs and change."

"The chicken is probably done…" She waited expectantly.

"Ew! Really? How can you stand to eat one of those things after wallowing in their innards all day?"

"Probably how you can stand to drive somewhere after work when you've been driving all day." She retorted, feeling utterly smug.

Chad gave her hair a tug as he climbed the stairs. Willow waited a moment, heard the drawers opening, the linen closet bang, and then the bathroom door shut. Impatiently, she drummed the newel at the base of the stairs. The bath water turned on and she took a step. She waited. Another step. As the sound of the metal curtain hooks slid across the rod, she hurried into the kitchen and listened contentedly to the familiar sound of bathwater running as she finished her dinner preparations.

"The Lord gives, takes away, and then gives again. Blessed be the name of the Lord," she whispered.

As Chad bathed, he debated. There were two things he knew that they needed to discuss but on his first night back after work? Tomorrow was Sunday, though—the debate raged inwardly. Grabbing his shoes and socks, Chad headed downstairs, praying for guidance as to know when or if to mention anything yet. Perhaps a call to Luke or Pop before he broached any difficult subjects was in order.

"That smells wonderful. I am starving."

"I thought you would be. A frozen burrito from the convenience store for lunch?"

"How'd you guess?" Chad accepted his plate and held her chair.

"Oh, you're a creature of habit." She sat down and murmured, "Thanks."

"Well, what's on tomorrow's agenda?" Chad tested the waters.

"Don't you have until two?"

"Yep."

Willow grinned. "Well, then surely we'd have time to go to church and get you home in time to get fed."

Chad nodded. It was enough. He'd worry about money issues later. "Sounds like a plan."

"Chad, what's wrong?"

"I've just got a lot on my mind."

"Care to share?"

Chad hesitated. Maybe it was the right time. "I wasn't sure how you'd feel about coming to church when I had to go to work right afterward."

"But you always go to church if you're off work. Why wouldn't we?"

"Well," he prayed for the right words and then felt silly. This was one of those times where he knew he'd look ridiculous for making mountains out of molehills. "I just know that you don't always go, and I was borrowing trouble. I thought you might resent me for wanting to go."

"Why? I like to go to church too and even if I didn't, two hours isn't going to ruin my life." Her face was a comical study in confusion.

"Like I said, I was borrowing trouble. I've never asked why you don't always go, so I just made assumptions with nothing as a foundation."

"Well, you could ask and then you wouldn't need assumptions."

He could almost see her thoughts. She thought he was being ridiculous—and was probably right. "Ok, why don't you go sometimes?"

"Lots of reasons." Willow held up a hand and ticked off fingers for each one. "I forget. I don't feel like walking. I have something to keep an eye on here. I need a few hours alone with the Lord, and it's a convenient time for it. I know you're not going to be around to bring me home, and I don't feel like turning down half the church as I try to get away..."

"Ok, ok." It was now or never. "I wonder, how often have you read Hebrews?"

"Several times a year for most of my life."

With a deep breath, he plunged forward. "So what do you make of the verse that says not to forsake the assembling of yourselves together?"

"Well, obviously that Chris—" she paused. "Wait a minute. Are you saying that you think I am wrong not to go to

41

church every week?"

Chad stammered. The word every pounded in his brain. Had she left out every, he could have easily answered yes. Now if he qualified it, he'd look like he was waffling. "I'm just wondering what value you place on assembling with God's people."

"Well, if I show up on semi-regular basis, how on earth can that be evidence of forsaking?"

"It isn't. I was just asking—" He knew he was being a coward. Chad took a deep breath. "What about Acts?"

"What about it?" Willow's curiosity kept her from feeling attacked much to Chad's relief.

"Well, the Christians met from house to house daily. They had the Lord's Supper weekly. It might not be commanded, but doesn't it look implied?"

Willow shook her head as though to clear it. "I don't understand what you're saying, Chad. I think you want something from me, but every time I try to ask, you divert the question."

"I just think that, scripturally speaking, there is strong evidence for making gathering with other Christians on a regular basis a priority in our lives."

"So, you think that whenever you're off of work we should be there?" She nodded. "I'm good with that."

"I'd like," he added hesitantly, "to know that whatever part of our family can be there, will be there, every week."

"You want *me* to commit to going every week?"

He nodded. "For the most part, yes. I think it's important."

She didn't answer for over a minute. Just as he started to ask her to pray about it, she sighed. "Ok. I don't make promises when it's raining or freezing out, though."

"You could learn to drive—"

"No thanks." If there was one thing that Willow held no interest in, it was driving. It made no sense to Chad, but he accepted it— usually.

Several minutes passed with little more than the clinking of silverware on plates to fill the quiet of the kitchen. "Chad?"

"Mmm hmm?"

"Why didn't you just tell me you wanted me to go? Why all the questions and hemming and the hawing, or whatever you call it. I don't get it."

"Well, I didn't want to ruin my first night home after going back to work, but tomorrow is Sunday…"

"But, still, I don't understand. Why the hoops? Why not just ask or tell me?"

He took a deep breath. Kicking himself for not realizing she'd notice his discomfort, Chad shrugged. "It's just that when people suggest that consider doing something different than you've always done, or worse, imply that you could be wrong—well, you don't take it very well. I didn't want an argument."

"Ouch."

Chad grabbed his plate and went to refill it with more chicken. "This is really good. More tender than the last ones."

"It's younger. I waited too long to kill the other ones." She smiled up at him as he sat down again. "Chad, I'd rather have an argument than to know you want to say something but don't think I'll like it."

"And I'd rather avoid arguments all together. You don't mind the conflict as long as it's resolved. I hate it. I hate conflict." He sighed. "Willow, I just don't like to bring up subjects that'll make things awkward between us. I like it when everything is right, and I hate it when we're out of sorts."

"Am I really that bad?" She smiled at him again but it didn't reach her eyes.

"Willow, the last time we had a discussion about something we didn't like, you were ready to call off the wedding."

"I guess I am," she admitted, her tone a little terse. "I wasn't trying to be difficult that time. I was trying to—"

He sighed. "That was a low blow. Sorry. That one was completely my fault, and I had no business using it as an example. How about 'no kids if I have to educate them like this?'"

"I guess you're right. Mother and I must have agreed on more than we thought. We never—" Her eyes grew wide. "Oh, Chad. I did that to Mother too! When I didn't get what I wanted, I stabbed her in the heart." Tears filled her eyes and she jumped from her chair. Chad started to follow, but she waved him back. "I need a few minutes."

He watched confused as she left the house and strolled across the fields toward the stream. "Lord, what just happened?"

Late that night, after they'd been sleeping for hours, Willow crept from the covers and padded downstairs. Chad heard the creak of the screen door and sighed. He tossed the blankets from him and followed. Everything had seemed fine, why was she now so unsettled?

"Willow?"

She turned and smiled. "Hmm?"

Chad pushed the door open letting it bang gently behind him. "You ok?" He sank to the step beside her and pulled her to him. "I'm worried about you."

"I was just thinking."

"Have you always come out here in the middle of the night?" Chad didn't remember her wandering last year.

"Usually. Mother said she found me in the porch swing as often as she didn't when I was little."

"Didn't she worry about you wandering off somewhere?"

Willow shrugged. "Not that I can remember."

"What do you think about when you come out here in the middle of the night?"

"It's when I feel closest to God. It's when that 'still small voice' seems to pierce my thick skull. I love praying in the dark and the stillness."

"Want me to go?" Chad's voice was little more than a whisper in her ear.

"Never."

CHAPTER 109

Becca Jacobs tentatively exited her car and glanced around her. It hadn't seemed too intimidating when the farm was crawling with other guests, but now, here alone, she felt awkward and uncertain. Was she truly welcome? She must be, but then...

"Becca! Back here. I'm just hanging the last of the laundry." Willow's voice called to her from behind the house.

"Hey. I hoped you still meant it—"

"Of course! I'm glad to have you here. Have you ever made candles?"

Becca's eyes widened. "*Make* candles?"

"Well, you will now. I gave away most of my candles during the power outage this winter. I'll need more before long."

As Willow led her to the summer kitchen, curiosity filled her. "So why..." Becca hesitated. It was none of her business.

"What?"

"Well," with a sigh, Becca plunged forward. "I just wondered why you don't use electricity instead? It's a lot less work but—" she winked. "I admit probably not as much fun."

"You're one of the first people who has even hinted that there might be an advantage to making candles." She grabbed the candle wicking, tying it to her dipping sticks as she spoke. "We like having the simplicity that comes without having easy access to electricity. I mean, it's easy access—I just have to flip the breaker—but we aren't tempted to stay up too late, watch too many movies, or even stay up too late because they aren't available. Why buy a TV if you don't want to watch it very often? Why stay up late doing more things that you don't need?"

"Why not?"

"Well," Willow agreed, "You have a point. There's nothing wrong with doing any of that. We just never wanted to, so we took away the temptation. Well, Mother did. She did it at first because she knew she needed to make it hard to do what she was used to doing in order to retrain her palate. Then it was just our life."

"It sounds beautiful. Like Laura Ingalls without the hardships."

Willow handed Becca dipping sticks. "Just dip slowly and raise. Dip in the water to cool, raise. Repeat." She demonstrated as she explained. "You're right. We are like Laura Ingalls but without the hardships. I had a wonderful childhood. Honestly, I like to tease Chad he married me for my childhood."

"He's so in love with you."

Uncertain eyes glanced at Becca. "What?"

"Chad. I could see how much he loves you at the wedding. It was a hard day for him, wasn't it?"

"Why do you say that?"

"I don't know. I'm crazy I guess but it seemed like he was nervous about something."

"He was—I'm a scary prospect," Willow teased.

"How did you meet Chad?"

With a rueful smile, Willow answered as simply as she could. "He was the officer on duty when I reported Mother's death."

"Oh I am so sorry."

"No, it's ok. It's a natural question. Who meets their husband over a police counter?"

Becca held up her candles. "How are these?"

"Excellent! I think you have a knack for it."

"So tell me more about you and Chad," Becca persisted.

"Like what?"

With a mental list of dozens of questions, Becca launched into the first ones that came to mind. "When did you fall in love with him? What is his best quality? Are you planning to have many children? What was your favorite date?"

"Well, you don't ask much, do you?"

"I just got started!" Becca laughed nervously.

"Well, which first?"

"When did you knew you were in love with him?"

Willow smiled apologetically. "I'm afraid my answer is going to be less than satisfactory. You see, I'm not in love with him. I love him of course," she hastened to add. "But from what I read and what several people have told me, I'm not 'in love.' Yet."

"How could you marry—"

"He's my best friend. How could I not?"

This was logic that Becca couldn't argue. "I suppose. It would make things easier." She hesitated. "It's like at Adric's. With what we're doing..." Becca paused. Maybe taking about her situation wasn't appropriate. After all, what she thought of how her month was going was not just about her.

Compassion flooded Willow's face. "I think you're very brave. To move into a man's home, trust him with your safety and your heart—that takes courage that I don't have."

"I—" surprise stopped her. Courage. It wasn't a word Becca would have chosen but described as Willow did, it had taken courage. "I guess I can see that. But then, Adric turned out to be such a wonderful man."

"From what I could tell, he seems like exactly the kind of man I would have looked for had I gone looking."

Willow's words swirled in Becca's mind as she tried to process them. Adric seemed nothing like Chad, and yet Willow was right. Adric was exactly the kind of man she'd prayed for since her unfortunate "marriage" failed. The thought confused her. "Isn't it odd that you made a friend and married him without worrying about love, and I'm spending a month with a man I don't know trying to find love without a friendship?"

"I think it's two roads to the same destination. I imagine both have smooth spots and both have ruts like my driveway gets sometimes, but it works." Willow smiled. "Tell me, what are the chances you would marry Adric if everything continued going as it is going today?"

47

"Honestly, after talking to you today, if he asked me to marry him tonight, I'd probably say yes. He's growing fond of me—I can tell. I know he'd be good to me and he is the kind of man I could be happy trying to help. Yesterday I would have said, 'I hope I fall in love with him or someone like him, but you've really changed how I think."

"I didn't mean to." A panicked tone grew in Willow's voice.

"Well, I'm glad you did. I might have given up on a great guy, because I assumed I needed something that I don't. Look how happy you are! Look how in love Chad is— If it can work for you, why not me?"

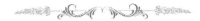

"I didn't know what to say," Willow said sleepily. A year before, Willow would never have imagined talking to Chad about their love life at two in the morning as he crawled in from work. "I told her it wasn't like that—that neither of us are in love like that—but she didn't understand."

Chad led his wife out of the kitchen and up the stairs. "Aw, lass, but your friend is right," he assured her as he pulled the light summer blankets over her as she crawled into bed.

By the time he returned from his shower, Willow was fast asleep. He leaned against the dresser and watched her as the moonlight shone across her face. The light reflected the peace in her expression, and yet there was the slightest wrinkle in her brow as though there were questions unanswered in her mind that troubled her.

"You have no idea, lass. You have no idea."

At ten o'clock Chad crawled from the covers disoriented. The room was darker than he thought it should be, until he realized that she'd made new shades that blocked out the light entirely. Chad spent a few minutes trying to discover how to raise them until the obvious answer made him chuckle. "Only Willow would make shades that you hand roll up and hook onto the top of the window," he muttered to himself.

In the bathroom, he was tempted to ignore the dark stubble that turned his jaw line into sandpaper, but remembering Willow's involuntary grimace one morning the previous week, he grabbed his cordless razor and carried it into their bedroom. As he retrieved jeans and a t-shirt, he removed his recent growth. Who knew what she'd have them doing that day?

Becca's laughter greeted him as he entered the kitchen. "I can't believe it worked!" Becca blushed. "Hey, Chad. She let me stir and look!"

Chad obediently looked in the large enamel pot and nodded as if he understood what he saw. "Excellent. You having fun?"

"This is the most fun I've ever had in my life. I can't believe how at home I feel doing all this stuff that I didn't know anyone did anymore."

Willow handed Chad a cup of coffee and a muffin. "She's good. I could leave her the recipe and go work out in the garden and come back to a perfect set."

"Then, can I steal you for a minute or two?"

Outside, Willow leaned against the porch, staring up at Chad. He leaned one arm over hear head on the same post, playing with her hair. "I've got bad news, Willow."

"Do I want to know?"

"Probably not," Chad admitted, "but you should know anyway. Lynne Solari's trial..."

She nodded. "So what you're trying to tell me is that the trial is going to start soon?"

"Next month. She has the best lawyers, but the evidence is undeniable. According to the D.A., she is not allowing her lawyers to call you to the stand."

Willow's eyes widened. "Wow. I didn't know that was an option."

"He told me he might call you in for a deposition, but he doesn't think he'll need you in court."

Shaking her head, Willow protested. "I don't want to do that."

"Well, you won't have a choice if they subpoena you."

"What do you mean, 'won't have a choice?' I don't want to go to court. I don't want to talk about it."

"Well," Chad hadn't realized that Willow didn't understand this part of the law. "They can compel you to come and testify."

"How? Will they torture me? What kind of country is this? I thought we had protection from this kind of tyranny!" Tears of frustration filled her eyes and threatened to overflow. She brushed them away impatiently. "I don't want to have anything to do with it."

"They'll find you in contempt of court. You'd be fined and probably jailed." Chad lowered his voice, running a finger along her cheek. "It'll be okay, lass. The D.A. said he didn't think he'd need you in court. He just wants a deposition."

A stubborn look filled her face. "Then I'll pay the fine and sit in jail until they realize that they can't make me testify."

"They can keep you there until you do. Which means," he added with the slightest hint of an edge to his voice," that I'll be left without a wife, doing all the work around here, your crops will die, the animals will suffer, and we won't be prepared for next winter—if you're even out of jail by then. You'll have a criminal record which, in this area, would probably kill any chances of my becoming an elected sheriff."

"It's just not right!" Willow's eyes flashed as she realized the helplessness of the situation. "I don't want to get involved."

Chad slipped his hand in hers and led her slowly back to the barn. "You may not be. We don't know." He paused by the kitchen door and wiped away a stray tear with his thumb. "On a brighter note, your grandparents want us to come to dinner on Sunday. Joe switched with me so we could go."

"But you'll miss church then!" Willow's eyes looked confused. "I don't understand you. One day church isn't an option and the next it is."

"Family is important too, Willow. Your uncle and his wife and daughter will be there. I don't know about the boys. I said I'd call this afternoon if we can make it."

"Well, we can make it, but—"

"Good. I'll call them right now. Are you guys going to work on that wool after the soap?"

Willow shook her head. "I thought about it, but then I remembered Jill saying something about soap sleeves, so I think we'll drag out the paper and paints and things and make covers for the soap. We can work on wool tomorrow."

"But Josh is coming—remember?"

"Well, he can watch while we talk. You guys can go fishing or something if he's not interested."

Chad's laughter startled Becca as she poured soap into molds. "Willow, I don't think Josh is the fishing kind of guy. I think he'd find it pretty disgusting."

"Who wouldn't like fishing?"

"Guys like Josh are um—well they're more interested in artsy things. Some don't like the outdoors much—"

"Oh, so Josh is like Bill. I see—"

"Um..." Chad hesitated. Should he even bother explaining? "Let's just say that Bill wouldn't find that a very flattering comment. I'll show him your books and craft room and maybe take him on a tour of the town if he's not interested in wool. I can see him being very interested in spinning so who knows."

"Chad?"

"Hmm?"

Willow reached up, pulled his face closer to hers, and met his eyes. "Sometimes you make no sense."

He kissed her nose and opened the kitchen door. "Why don't I go bring down that paper stuff for you while you guys finish the soaps?"

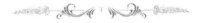

"So what does Chad do all day? I mean when he's not working?" Becca suddenly felt stupid. He worked all day or night—what else did the guy need to do.

"Well, when he's home, he takes care of the animals most of the time. Anything I need harvested he's good at, and he did the new field plowing for me. He's probably going to be the woodworker around here too."

"So will you do more of your own animal breeding and

butchering now that he's around?"

This wasn't something Willow had ever considered. The problem with having a predictable routine was the inevitable tendency toward a rut. "I don't know. I'll have to talk to him. Perhaps he'd rather do that."

"I was thinking this'd be a cool place for school field trips. You know, the kids could come and see you make soap and candles, milk a goat, spin some wool, bake bread in a woodstove, can food—it'd be almost like one of those living museums."

"Do you really think anyone would be interested in seeing something like this?"

"If you had regular tours, I'd find the ones most appropriate for my older daycare kids, and I'd bring them out one summer day. You could have hayrides and picnics..." The dreamy tones to Becca's voice told Willow that her guest was romanticizing her life.

"How would I show the work involved though? Making soap is fun—candles too. But this is all work. Sunup until sundown from around February, thanks to the greenhouse, through October at the least. It's hard work. How do you take away the romantic idea that it's just playing Laura Ingalls three hundred sixty-five days a year?"

Concentrating on Willow's words, Becca shrugged. "I'm not sure. I mean, it'd be a lot of work giving those kinds of tours, and if you don't have time to spare, it probably wouldn't work."

"I'll talk to Chad. He's always saying that children should all have my childhood. I disagree. I think that if everyone had the same kind of childhood, the world would be a very uninteresting place. But, maybe he has a point about everyone experiencing a taste of it, just as I'd like my children to taste the occasional day in the city going to museums or the zoo."

Becca held up another finished soap sleeve and smiled. "I like them. Why is it called Walden Farm instead of Finley or Tesdall?"

"Chad named it for Mother. She loved Thoreau's 'live life deliberately' and 'sucking the marrow out of life,' and that's what this farm was about—enjoying every moment of every day to its fullest. So he thought we should name it. I think Bill is working on changing our holdings over to some kind of corporation with that name too."

The living room clock struck four-thirty. Becca's eyes widened in surprise, and she quickly began clearing her paper mess. "I have to go. Gram is going to be wondering where I am, and what I'm doing. Adric gets home in a little while."

"How is it going? Are you hoping to keep seeing him next month too?"

"I think I will. He's being very—oh, I don't know the word. Attentive perhaps. He's good to me; he's a little affectionate, and from the way Lily was talking, he hasn't done that yet. Sometimes I think I see something in his eyes that tells me he's even more attached than he says, but I don't know. I'm just so happy that it looks like there's a chance, you know?"

"Well," Willow teased, "Don't keep the man waiting too long. There's another gal from next month just waiting to step into your shoes."

"Don't I know it," Becca agreed ruefully. "It makes me sick to think about it, but if I'm who the Lord wants for him, I guess I need to have a little more faith."

CHAPTER 110

Willow pounded beef while Becca stirred the sauce on the stove. "Now when those flavors taste right, let me know."

"What is the purpose of the beef again?" Becca had never heard of "pizza" like this.

"Well, the first pizza Chad bought me was mostly bread with a little sauce and a lot of cheese. Almost no meat— nothing to stick to your ribs until the next meal. So I put a thin slice of beef over the bread before I add the sauce."

"Have you thought about Italian sausage instead of beef?"

Shaking a bottle of olive oil, Willow shrugged. "I've never had Italian sausage, but Chad bought me this olive oil. He says it'll taste better on the bread than the butter."

Chad entered the kitchen with a basket of greens and a few well-ripened tomatoes. "I didn't remember if you wanted the green onions or not."

"Yes. But if you didn't get them, don't worry about it. It'll be fine without them."

He held up a bunch triumphantly. "Score! I remembered it all then."

"I can't believe you guys have ripe tomatoes from a *garden*!"

"Greenhouse," Willow corrected. "Now that I have the greenhouse, I can have ripe tomatoes all year."

Beef pounded, Willow scrubbed her hands and then began washing the lettuce. She paused, examining it closely.

"Is this lettuce from the garden?"

"Well, it looked ready, why?"

"Loopers. I've got to get out there and soap them before we get eggs. I'll do that before dinner." Willow quit rinsing the greens and immediately left for the barn.

"Loopers. What are they?"

Chad shrugged and started washing the leaves looking for whatever had bothered Willow. "Becca, your guess is as good as mine. Apparently it's something we don't want in the garden though."

Willow arrived with a large spray bottle and filled it as Chad washed. Then she dropped a large squirt of dish soap in the container and shook it vigorously. "Don't let me forget Chad."

"Why not do it now?"

"Best to do first thing in the morning or late afternoon. That's when the obnoxious critters are out."

Becca and Chad exchanged confused and amused glances. Willow took the scrubbed greens and tore them, filling a large wooden salad bowl with them. Deftly, she chopped tomatoes, onions, radishes, and cucumbers. Before she could ask Chad for the croutons she'd made at breakfast, a car crunched in the driveway.

"I think Josh is here. Why don't you go get him?" Willow waved Chad out the door and pointed to a bowl on the top of the stove. "Becca, can I have that bowl please?"

By the time Chad ushered Josh into the kitchen, Willow and Becca were assembling the modified pizzas, ready to pop them into the oven. Willow noticed beads of perspiration on Chad's forehead and a growing line of them across Josh's upper lip and groaned inwardly. It might be time move to the summer kitchen already.

"Chad, why don't you go get one of those tables and some of the chairs from the barn and put it all up on the back porch. We can eat out there where it's cooler."

The look of relief in Chad's eyes told Willow she'd made the right move. "I'll do that." Before he left, he turned to Josh. "Oh, this is Becca Jacobs. She's here visiting a friend on the farm that backs ours."

Becca rinsed her hands, dried them on her apron, and

turned to greet Josh and froze. "Oh, I'm sorry." She extended her hand smiling. "It's very nice to meet you."

"It's nice to meet you too." Josh looked at their hands, his feet, back over at Willow— anything to avoid meeting Becca's eyes. Willow didn't understand what was wrong with them.

"Hey Josh, mind giving me a hand with the chairs?"

Once the men were outside, Becca turned to Willow, confused. "I didn't expect your friend to be—"

"Be?"

The girl flushed. "Well, I don't mean to be offensive. You just don't expect to meet someone... like him out on a farm." Her face went deep red. "Oh, that sounds just awful. I didn't mean to be—"

Willow interrupted. "He's a little girly, isn't he? Chad said something about him being more like my friend Bill than the Tesdalls. Bill is kind of a sissy when it comes to the farm and Chad thinks Josh will be too."

"Where did you meet him?"

"He was the one who helped me find the fabrics for the wedding. He has amazing fabric and fashion sense. I thought it was odd at first, but then I remembered mother talking about men like Monsieur Worth and more recently Christian Dior, and I realized that men have always been interested in women's fashions and things."

A voice from the doorway interrupted them. "Thanks Willow. Not everyone understands that."

"Oh, Josh—" Becca blushed furiously. "I had no business discussing you like that. Willow didn't bring it up—"

"I don't mind. People tend to find me a bit of an enigma. I'm not what they think—" he paused letting the words sink in and register. "—and I'm not like a lot of other men so they don't know how to categorize me."

"Well," Willow said testily. "Perhaps people should quit trying to categorize everyone in the first place."

"Perhaps," agreed Josh and Becca in unison. Josh continued with an amused smile, "But it's natural to want to know where you stand in relation to everyone else, so you categorize. It's just human nature."

Willow slid the pizzas from the oven and arranged them on a platter. "Ok, time to eat." She tossed her apron onto the counter and grabbed the platter and salad bowl, nodding at plates and silverware. "Can you guys grab those?"

Willow and Chad said little during lunch. Instead, they watched their guests. Becca and Josh joked, laughed, and, it seemed to her, forged a nice friendship. Considering they both lived in Rockland, that seemed like a good thing.

"So, we were going to try to card wool today," Willow began after everyone declared themselves overfull. "What do you think Josh—too crafty for you?" An excited look grew in her eyes. "You and Chad could go out with the paintball guns!"

"I think—" Josh began giving Becca and Chad amused glances that left Willow in a state of utter confusion. "I think I'd rather see how wool carding works."

Willow jumped from the table eagerly. "Let's get the dishes—"

"I'll do them, Willow, you guys go get your wool stuff and have at it." Chad kissed her cheek and pushed her toward the door. "Go, woman!"

"I'm under orders, I guess."

While Chad washed dishes, cleaned the kitchen, and pulled the chicken from the icebox, readying it for a slow roast on the grill, Willow, Josh, and Becca congregated in the living room. She passed out towels, handed everyone a wad of washed fleece and referred to her notes. "Ok, it says pull the locks from the fleece. You're supposed to separate them into individual locks that aren't interlocked with the rest of the fleece—I guess."

They all worked until Willow thought she had a large enough pile on the coffee table. "Ok. Who wants to keep separating?"

Josh insisted he do it. "I can't mess this up. You guys do whatever you need to do."

"Ok, Becca, now we take these locks and we separate them. The instructions say to pull them apart sideways. We're supposed to discard any really short pieces or if there is any leftover 'dirt or debris.'"

"I can't believe you're just doing this without any kind of instruction." Becca's voice was heavy with admiration. "I'd be afraid of ruining an expensive fleece!"

"This is how the Finley women learned everything," Chad called from the kitchen. "If they don't already know it instinctively, they just teach themselves."

Willow shrugged. It made sense to her. She couldn't understand why anyone would refrain from doing something just because they didn't know how. If everyone did that, no one would learn anything. Seeing them waiting for her reply, she said as much.

"Wow."

Josh grinned at Becca's response. "I've come to the conclusion that 'wow' must be the most commonly used word around Willow."

"Got that right!" Chad's voice boomed from the kitchen.

"You oughtta know!" Josh shouted back, winking at Becca.

Becca smiled back before asking, "So now we just separate all of these?"

"Yep. Once we get enough, I'll play with the card paddles. I got two sets because I thought *Chad would be helping.*" Her words grew louder as she teased her absent husband.

"A guy offers to clean the kitchen and all he gets is complaints, complaints, complaints," came his voice from the kitchen.

Becca and Josh exchanged wistful looks as Willow jumped and dropped the wool from her lap. She raced to the kitchen where it became obvious, even from the living room, that a serious tickle fest was in full swing. "Can you believe how amazingly happy they are?"

Josh shook his head. "By the time I got done helping her that day in the store, I really wished that he'd dump her at the altar and she'd try to return the fabric. I *so* wanted to ask her out."

"Really?"

"What guy wouldn't want to get to know someone like Willow?"

She hesitated and then risked complete honesty. "A guy who was concerned she'd take his interest the wrong way."

"Well, that guy wasn't me. I was interested all right, but once I met Chad—I knew. He's perfect for her. Drat it all."

Josh watched as she carefully separated lock after lock, ignoring the banging of the screen door and the squeals that now echoed around the house outside. "So they said you're visiting a friend here. Where are you from?"

"Rockland."

"Really? Wow. What part?"

"Old residential on the south side. Near Madison Park."

Josh's eyes lit up. "Really? I'm not too far from there. I moved back in with my parents after—" He hesitated. "After I escaped a lifestyle that I never really wanted."

"I wondered," she admitted quietly.

"I know. You were more tactful than most. I appreciate it."

Becca struggled with unasked questions until Josh assured her he didn't mind if she asked them. "I really only have one but it's just none of my business."

"Assume it is and just ask."

"Why did? I mean, if you didn't want it in in the first place—"

"I felt trapped by expectations. Everyone said that I was gay. Eventually, I believed them, and then once in that life, I felt even more trapped than ever. Then I met Barney—he's the pastor—"

"Barney? He's my pastor! You go to the mission?" Becca saw her surprise mirrored in Josh's eyes.

"I don't believe this. I've never seen you there!"

Chad and Willow stood outside the screen door hesitant to listen but even more hesitant to interrupt the conversation within. Finally, Chad led her away from the door, down the steps, and around the barn to the tree swing. "Let them talk. I think something is there."

"Something?"

"He's interested, and she's not immune to it."

Willow's eyes widened in horror. "But Adric—"

"She has no obligation, Willow. Would you want her to choose Adric over someone she prefers just because she signed up to get to know him?"

Sighing, Willow shook her head and jumped on the swing. "No. I just don't want to see anyone get hurt."

"Someone is going to get hurt. Before all of this girl-of-the-month stuff is over, *someone* will get hurt. There's no way to avoid it."

"Then why do it Chad? Why put people through that?"

"Everyone is willing to risk it on the chance that they meet the right person." He hesitated. Willow came from such a different worldview than he did. Would she understand? "I would have probably tried something like that eventually—if the opportunity arose. I'm not an outgoing person. I'd had so much trouble with girls—well girl—already, that having someone pre-screen, having recommendations from their pastors—" he shrugged. "I think at Adric's age especially, I'd have done it in a heartbeat."

"So are Josh and Becca just interested because they have things in common—church and stuff, or is there something else there that I'm missing."

Chad smiled as he pushed her higher. "Get ready for a very confused young woman. There's more to it than that. She's so concerned with making everyone happy—this is going to tear her up."

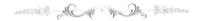

By three o'clock, Becca and Willow carded in a semi-rhythmic flow. Chad and Josh spent their time pulling locks, separating them, and joking about everything from Willow's naïveté to the natural way Becca took to Willow's lifestyle. Willow and Becca occasionally sent balls of wool in their direction as if wool fluff could possibly stop the barrage of jokes and teasing.

The wool flying through the air reminded Willow of North and South. "'I have seen hell and it is white. It is snow white.'"

"What?" Becca looked at Chad as if Willow had lost her mind.

"It's from a movie my mom got her." An impish glint filled Chad's eyes. "She *loves* that movie—she *really* loves the ending best though."

"Civil War?"

"Oh, no!" Willow protested. "Northern vs. Southern England—not the War Between the States."

61

"Did England have a Civil War too?" Becca's eyes grew wide.

"Cromwell in the mid-sixteen hundreds. But technically the United States—"

Chad interrupted. Debate over historical semantics was not likely to be a popular topic of discussion. "It's about the difference between agricultural southern England with its gentility and proximity to London verses the northern industrial cities like Manchester."

"Sounds an awfully lot like the United States." Josh's surprise was echoed by Becca's nod.

"Well, there are similarities of course, but the British class system was much more ingrained so there were deeper clashes than you found over here," Willow explained. "The movie is amazing. You see the strengths and weaknesses of all lifestyles. You can imagine it but seeing it on the screen— it's just overwhelming."

As Willow was speaking, Chad stood, retrieved his laptop and the movie, and flipped on the power switch. Within minutes, all four were lost in a world of cotton, mills, gentility, and abject poverty. Willow carded and rolled nearly automatically now. Her eyes rarely left the screen as she worked the paddles back and forth, rolled the batt, and carded again.

Chad, on the other hand, observed everyone else as they watched the scenes scroll by on the computer screen. Willow was immediately lost in the nineteenth century world of cotton and industrialism. The incongruity of her hand carding wool while watching a movie on a laptop in the middle of her normally electric-free house struck him. Even more than that, the constant attraction between Josh and Becca kept him entertained until the clock struck four-thirty.

"Oh, I have to go. Gram is probably working on dinner already and—"

Josh's face fell. "I didn't realize— Well, I can see you in Rockland at church I guess."

"Sure. I'll be back this Sunday. We leave Saturday."

Willow picked up on the awkward strain and to Chad's surprise and amusement, delved into her first attempt at matchmaking. "You'll come back tomorrow though, won't you

Becca? We were going to try out the spinning wheel—"

"Of course!" Becca was already cleaning up the area around her trying to reduce the mess she'd created as she worked.

"I'll get that for you Becca," Josh insisted. "Let me walk you to your car."

Willow smiled knowingly as Josh led Becca out to her car talking quietly as they walked. "You're right. They're so cute too."

"You are incorrigible."

"How?"

Chad nudged her knee smiling knowingly. "That was a 'Josh, don't you want to come back tomorrow' hint if I've ever heard one."

"Well, he should know she's going to be here so when I invite him back, he knows—"

Chad's laughter echoed through the window and out to Becca's car. "It was nice meeting you, Josh. I'm looking forward to seeing you at church."

Chad and Willow sank back onto the couch as they saw Becca nod and Josh slam the door shut for her. "They're going to hit it off beautifully," Chad murmured.

"Silly, they already did."

"Did what?" Josh's sounded excited as he entered the door.

"You two seemed to hit it off..." Chad commented.

"She's amazing. I can't believe we've gone to the same church all this time—"

Willow's quiet voice interrupted gently. "From the way you've spoken about your life, I didn't think you were ready to meet anyone special before now."

"You're right. I wasn't. I'm not sure I am now, but I can't stand the idea of not getting to know her better."

With a sidelong glance at Chad, Willow picked up her carding paddles. "So do you have to work tomorrow?"

"No, I'm off again, why—Oh."

"Well, if you find yourself looking for something to do, we're going to try our hand at spinning tomorrow, and there's lots of wool left to pull and separate..."

A huge grin split Josh's face and the excitement in his

voice made his lisp all the more pronounced. That's so nice of you. Are you serious?"

"She's been showing up around ten."

"I'll be here. Thanks."

Moonlight flashed across their bed as clouds covered and then drifted away from the moon. Willow lay awake and unmoving knowing that she often woke Chad when she slipped downstairs for her trysts with the Lord. As carefully as she could, she turned on her side and tried resting quietly that way but still felt restless. Chad's voice came sleepily in her ear.

"Go downstairs if you like. I'll see you in the morning."

She turned to find his face centimeters away from hers. "I'm sorry. I tried not to wake you up."

"You didn't. Nature calls. But I could tell you weren't sleeping and I guessed why. Now go downstairs and commune with nature or whatever it is you do."

"The Lord, goof," she commented as she slipped out from under the sheets. "I commune with the Lord."

Chad watched her jog down the stairs and listened as the screen door opened and then the soft "whap" as it shut behind her. "Lord, she's such a multi-faceted person. Every time I think I understand her, there's something else to discover. I'm starting to think that she's going to look at me in a few years and think, 'I married him. Why?' Don't let that happen— please."

With a sigh, he slipped from the covers and shuffled toward the bathroom. "Oh, and remind me to avoid coffee before bed? I really am tired of these late night trips."

CHAPTER 111

Josh arrived at nine thirty-five. Willow attempted to stifle snickers as he confessed that he'd driven to Brunswick and back before he decided that wasting gas was not worth the salve to his pride. "Well, come in. I've got bread baking."

"That's what smells so good—hey, I have a question for you."

"Shoot."

"Do I have to confess to Chad that I showed flagrant disregard for the speed limit on my way here?"

Willow's grin embarrassed him. "Not unless he asks..."

"I like you."

She shook her head. "I think you have another female in mind."

"I was thinking about her last night. I can't believe I didn't realize it, but I've seen her. She works in the kitchen on Sundays after church. I've seen her when I escort the kids to the dining hall for lunch."

"Well," Willow said smiling. "I think you should go out and take her for a walk. I'm stuck here, and apparently she's here early."

Josh hurried from the house and almost reached Becca's car in time to open the door. "I'll have to be faster next time."

"You're here! I thought—"

"They invited me back and well I—" Josh hesitated. How do you tell someone you've barely met that you drove back at break-neck speed in order to see you again without sounding desperately pathetic.

"I'm glad you came." She whispered the words, her expression pained.

"What's wrong?"

"Maybe I can explain later. I should go in—" Becca gestured toward the kitchen as if to say, *"don't you want to come in too?"*

"Actually, Willow suggested we take a walk. Something about her bread."

They started toward the field where the annual "Dinner" cow and the sheep grazed. He didn't care to admit it, but the sight of the large animals unnerved him. "How dangerous are cows anyway?"

"Willow says they're safe. They pretty much leave everyone alone, but we only have to cross that corner. We could run for it before they got to us if we had to." Becca's voice held a trace of mirth.

"Stop laughing at me. I've never been around big game—"

"I'm pretty sure sheep aren't considered big game."

Once near the stream, the couple continued to amble along the banks, rarely speaking but communicating much. Finally, Josh's curiosity overcame him and he sat down in the grassy shade of a tree. "Ok, so you said you'd tell me what's wrong."

"Do you know why I'm here—who I am visiting?"

"No, you—no one ever said."

Blushing, Becca made herself comfortable against the trunk of the tree facing Josh. "It's kind of a church sponsored 'Bachelor House.' I'm here for a month to see if the guy is the one for me."

Josh took in her words. It sounded surreal and far-fetched. "As in like the TV show with a dozen half-dressed women and hot tub orgies?"

"No!" Becca's face flamed even deeper scarlet. "Nothing like that. We have a chaperone— my Gram actually, and he's kept himself physically respectful. Well, that sounds awkward. He's been great really."

"So you stay for a month, and then what?"

"I go home. Actually, I go home on Friday."

Josh didn't miss the relief in her voice. "Not working out?"

"Well, actually, before yesterday, I would have said it was going well. Now I'm all confused."

"Did something go wrong?" Josh ordered himself not to pray, *"Please say yes."*

"I met someone else." Becca's voice was such a quiet miserable whisper that Josh wasn't sure he'd heard her right.

"You met someone else?"

"Mmm hmm."

"What are you going to do about it?"

"I don't know." Disappointment filled her tone. "I don't want to be foolish and waste what really was the most wonderful month of my life, but how do you ignore strong attraction for someone else?"

"Strong attraction, eh?" Josh's voice sounded nearly giddy and his lisp grew more pronounced.

"You're not helping."

"So what's the real question?"

Her shoulders slumped. "What would you think about a woman who invests herself in one man for a month and is ready to turn her back on all that work she put into a relationship after just a few hours with someone else?"

"What kind of commitment did you make?"

"To come, get to know him, and decide if I want to continue talking to him after I leave. If he asks, I say yes or no."

A grin split Josh's face. "So, in other words, this is like a really long blind date with no expectations, just hopes."

"That's one way to put it." She waited impatiently for him to answer and then urged again, "So what would you think if you were a guy who spent a month with a woman and she turned you down at the end because she thinks another guy is interesting."

"Well, now that I know there is no real commitment, I hope I'd be happy for her."

"But once she walked, that'd be the end of it," she said for him. "You wouldn't take a chance on her if something went wrong later with the other guy."

"Depends on how much I liked her. I'd rather her find

out just how interested you are in him before you invested more in me and then realized after a long time that you were still into someone else."

"This went from she to me awfully quickly," Becca joked. "So, am I being way premature?"

Josh studied his hands. When she started to speak, he stopped her. "I asked you out already, if you remember."

"That's no answer." A bite to her words made her blush. "Sorry. I didn't mean to snap. This is just really hard."

"I don't want to interfere in your—" Josh searched for a word, "thing but..."

"But what?" Her face lit up. "Oh, you mean you're not ready? I mean, I totally understand—"

"I wasn't until yesterday. If you had asked me, I would have been adamant—no romantic entanglements. Period." A smile grew slowly across his features. "But I was wrong."

"Were you?" A grin grew until her eyes fairly sparkled.

"What is this guy like?"

"Everything I ever thought I wanted in a husband and more."

"But you are willing to risk throwing it away on someone you have only spent an afternoon with?"

"I'm not willing to risk throwing away what I've been hoping for on the wrong man."

Chad arrived at two o'clock and found his wife and guests laughing at her attempts to use the spinning wheel. Her hands worked to hold the wool, pull, and still work the treadle. She had managed to create thick yarn with occasional clumps. Splicing the yarn was trickier. Becca and Josh spent half of their carding time giggling over the quirky way Willow stuck her tongue out of the corner of her mouth as she tried to twist the fibers back into the broken yarn, as yet another piece broke.

So concentrated was Willow on her work, that she didn't hear Portia yapping happily, the screen door slam against the doorjamb, or the titters of Josh and Becca at the look of amazement on Chad's face.

He bent low near her ear and murmured, "How are you doing, lass?"

Willow jumped, her hand flying into the air and whacking Chad's chin as she did. "You scared me!"

"Well, I made enough noise coming in…"

She put down her wool, stood, and walked to the kitchen to make him a sandwich and reheat a bowl of soup. Chad's face furrowed in concern as he noticed a slight limp in her step. He pointed at the wheel. "How long has she been using that thing?"

"Only since around eleven or so. Is there a problem?" Chad's face left Becca feeling concerned as well.

"She over did it—repetitive motion. Her muscles and nerves are probably killing her."

"Why—"

"Accident last summer. She spent a lot of time in therapy, and I'm guessing that motion isn't one she practiced."

He left them staring slack jawed at him and went to bully his wife into a chair while he fixed his own sandwich. "Lass, I've got it. Sit."

"I'm fi—"

"You are not. Your leg is killing you, I can see it."

Willow shook her head protesting. "It's just unused muscles. I'm fine."

"I can see pain in your eyes. Rest. I'll rub that calf as soon as I get some food in me."

The front screen creaked and then banged shut. Willow retrieved the oilcan from the pantry and walked to the living room before Chad could stop her. Within seconds, the screen no longer squeaked. He tried not to let his frustration show. He relied on that squeak to let him know where she was and what she was doing.

"How are things going with those two?"

She gave him a smile he usually only saw in the most intimate of moments. "Do you think she'll let me make her dress? I'd love to try to make a wedding dress."

"Seriously? You think—"

"They remind me of us—but different. There's this electricity in the room whenever they're there. I don't know

69

how else to describe it." She paused trying to find words she couldn't imagine. "Like—like—you know, when you shuffle across the house in your socks in winter and then touch the doorknob. That."

"Static electricity."

"Yes!" she exclaimed relieved. "That's what I mean. It's in there, with them, all the time. It's fascinating."

Chad didn't want to disappoint her, but he could see her building romantic hopes for her new friends and didn't want to see her hurt. "You know, sometimes that's all there is—it's called attraction, infatuation. It doesn't always grow into anything more substantial."

She nodded sagely. "I can see that. Endorphins. That's what Mother called them. She said that they controlled happiness, crushes, and something else. I can't remember."

"Crushes?"

"It was when I went nuts for Bill that year when I was fifteen. She explained it all, and I saw that it was just a natural chemical reaction that God built into—"

"Enough. I can't stand to hear it," Chad said wearily. "Your mother was so amazing in almost every area of her life, but when it came to male-female relationships, she knew how to strip the God-given joy out of things."

"Well," she retorted giving him a playful look that he recognized all too well. "I learned a lot from her, but I've had other teachers in my life too."

"Just give me that calf and let me try to work out the kinks before it turns into a sore mess and a Charlie horse," he growled.

"Oh, my leg isn't kinky. It's just tired."

Chad rolled his eyes heavenward and shrugged at the Lord. "What can I say, Lord? What can I say?"

After dinner, Chad brought up the mail. In it was a large package from Boho full of fabrics for the following spring. "They sent you more fabric? Didn't you just finish with fall?"

"Lee says that they're trying to get on a normal schedule. Apparently, they try to be a full year ahead of current time. If they're selling spring/summer now, they want spring/summer done for next year too."

Before Chad could give his idea on that score, the sound of tires crunching in the yard interrupted them. He glanced out the window and groaned. "Adric and Becca are here."

"Wha—"

"I think Becca needs some advice, and from what I can see, Adric looks a little lost." Chad tugged gently on Willow's braid to bring her eyes to meet his. "I'll take him if you can handle her."

"It's a deal. Oh, and I intend to do some crying later. I feel it already. Thought you should know."

"Duly warned, milady," Chad acknowledged with a goofy sweeping bow.

"That's lass and don't you forget it."

"Yes'm—hey, Adric. Good to see you guys!"

Adric opened the door for Becca and ushered her inside. "Becca needed—"

Before Adric could finish, Becca with tears streaming down her face, rushed at Willow and threw her arms around her. "I'm so confused."

"Come on, Adric, why don't we go take a walk and let the women talk."

Willow, not knowing what else to do, led Becca to the couch, wrapped her arms around the weeping woman, and just held her. The minutes ticked by until Becca quieted to an occasional sniffle. Willow reached around her and retrieved a box of Kleenex."

"I thought—" Becca sniffed again, "I would have assumed you'd be big on handkerchiefs."

"I am. Chad isn't. He compromised a lot to move here... you know, no electricity, lots of hard work, goat milk, which he hates but drinks because he doesn't want to hurt my feelings..."

"He hates the milk?"

"From the faces he makes when he doesn't have his guard up, he hates it. Doesn't mind the butter, cheese, yogurt, or ice cream but the milk..."

Becca gave a half-hearted laugh. "That's funny."

"Something isn't funny in your life. Am I crazy to suspect

71

it has to do with Josh and Adric?"

Becca's eyes filled with fresh tears. "Am I insane? What is wrong with me? I have a wonderful man who is genuinely interested in me. He's everything I ever wanted. He has invested in me this month, and I know he's going to want to keep corresponding..."

"But you find Josh attractive."

"I find Josh attractive," she admitted. "What do I do?"

"In five years, if you are married to Adric and things are going badly for whatever reason, will you wonder and regret not at least seeing if there was anything to consider with Josh?"

Willow's question wasn't what Becca expected but immediately, it gave her the answer she needed. "I'd regret it before trouble hit if I couldn't stop thinking about him."

"If Adric is the reasonable man that I think he is, he'll understand. He'll be hurt—definitely. He might not even realize he'll understand, but he will. If you spent time with Josh for six months and then decided he wasn't for you, and Adric still hadn't found the right woman, I think if you contacted him, he'd be willing to at least meet to discuss it."

"But isn't that kind of using him?" Becca's pleasing tendencies were tearing her apart.

"Not if he knows up front. Not if you don't string him along while you get to know Josh. From the way you've described it, he'll ask to continue correspondence, and you can choose yes or no. Tell him no and tell him why. He'll know you won't be playing with fire while pouring water on it at the same time."

A strange look filled Becca's face. "I have no idea what that means, but I get the gist—I think."

"Something's wrong Chad, I can sense it. I'm not the most intuitive man, but it doesn't take one to see the difference in the past two days."

"This is a difficult process. I imagine for women, it is even more difficult—all those emotions..."

"I know it's crazy, but I started to care. I'm not head over

72

heels but—"

"I know exactly what you mean. It's what I felt for about two or three weeks before I fell in love with Willow."

"When did you know?" Adric's voice seemed simultaneously resigned but curious.

"The Friday before the wedding when you came over to talk to her about the property situation."

"Huh?"

Chad grimaced. He still felt foolish over his illogical flash of jealousy. "You were out here talking to her and she was so concerned about you, your situation—I watched the two of you and I'm not stupid, she's an appealing woman."

"So jealousy pushed you over the edge?" Adric's voice was filled with amazement.

"Something like that."

"You know—I mean, I hope you know—that I'd never—"

"I knew. I just realized, at that moment, that my irritation with a pesky woman that had grown into brotherly affection had moved beyond tentative caring and into a love I cannot describe but am thrilled to have."

"That's what I keep waiting for, but I'm not so sure—"

"I don't know," Chad began hesitantly, "if it's the right thing to wait for or not. I just don't know. I do know that we would have had a glorious life if neither of us ever lost our heart completely. You don't need it to be truly happy. I'm just blessed that I have it."

Adric kicked at the dirt for a minute and then told Chad about a man he'd met in Ferndale. "Allison, from April, she took me to her Saturday morning Bible study and there was this man there—Silas." He paused remembering the story and amazed at how much he desired what Silas had while thinking the man was crazy.

"Silas met this girl—a lot younger than him. Not just in years but maturity wise, you know? She's so far beneath him it's not funny, but he loves her. I've never seen anything like it. She left him; he took her back. She goes out with other men; he waits. Until the day she marries someone else, he'll never quit hoping and trying."

"And you wonder if that's rare or worth holding out for." It wasn't a question. Chad understood the appeal of

73

something so deep, but couldn't encourage it. "I don't know if Becca is the one for you or not. I do know that if she is, or if this Allison is, or any of the other women you've met, it won't be *just* because you can't stand not being with her. I think that's probably a little rare—especially for a man."

Adric nodded. "You're right. It was amazing to watch, but—"

"I will say that I'd rather marry someone I know I can trust, respect, and enjoy spending my time with even if I didn't have the crazy mixed up love for them that I have for Willow, than to marry someone who after twenty years, makes me wish it was over rather than wish for another twenty."

They wandered through the greenhouse, out to the gardens, over to the pasture where the sheep enjoyed an evening trough of liquid refreshment, and then back toward the house. As they neared, Adric paused, his jaw working so much that his teeth ground together mercilessly. "Do you think Becca is going to turn me down?"

"For what, marriage?"

"No, to keep corresponding. Something is wrong. I'd just like to know what I did wrong."

Chad chose his words carefully. "I don't know that you did anything wrong, man. Even if she isn't the woman for you, aren't you glad you had a month with her?"

"I am but—"

"Then be thankful for your month and forget about what you can't control. Trust the Lord in this one. Trust Him."

"You've got to be a good ten years younger than me, Chad. I'd give anything for that kind of faith." The exhaustion in Adric's voice was very telling.

"You have it. You're just weary. Rest in the only One who can give you true rest as your brother-in-law always tells us."

As Adric and Becca drove away, Chad and Willow waved from the front porch. "Is she going to turn him down?"

"Yes." Regret hovered around Willow's single word.

"He's going to be so disappointed."

"I wonder if she knows that Josh switched work days with one of the ladies from the store."

CHAPTER 112

Willow held her phone away from her, one hand covering her mouth, and her eyes closed tight. She was tempted to refuse. After all, if she did, maybe the D.A. wouldn't subpoena her. It might happen, right? She remembered Chad's words and hesitated. Was it disrespectful to balk at something that she knew Chad wanted her to do willingly? He asked so little of her, and while technically he hadn't asked her to give her deposition willingly, she knew he hoped she would. With a deep breath, she opened her eyes, held the phone back to her ear, and sighed.

"I'm here. I'll come whenever you need me, but I want to make it plain, I won't be volunteering any information. I'll answer your questions, but I'll not elaborate."

"You don't want to testify against the woman responsible for all your trouble last winter?"

"She's not. Her husband is and he's dead."

"And your grandmother," the D.A.'s assistant said firmly, "killed him."

"I'm aware of that, but since I have hardly spoken to the woman, I don't see how that is relevant to me. I'm only cooperating out of respect for my husband and his job. If I were single, I'd rot in jail before I testified."

"I see." The tone of the D.A.'s assistant told Willow that the woman didn't "see" at all.

"When do I need to be there, and how long should I expect it to take?"

"Monday morning, eleven-thirty. We'll break for lunch at one o'clock. Depending on how well it's going, we could be done by then or have several more hours. It really depends on if the defense attorney perceives you as an asset or a liability."

"And," Willow said wearily, "if I do this, then I don't have to go to court?"

"Probably not, but you never know. Sometimes people get called, sometimes not. But if we don't get a deposition, you *will* be called to testify in court."

"Then I'll be there. I'll see you Monday morning. Bye."

Willow slid the cover over her phone with more force than necessary. Leaving her baskets of freshly picked produce sitting at the edge of the garden, she slowly wandered toward her mother's grave, talking to Portia as she went. Portia, somehow, had become the replacement for Othello that Saige had never had the chance to become.

"Portia, girl, I don't know about this. I don't want to do it, but I want to disappoint Chad even less. What would Mother do?"

The dog looked at her innocently as if to say, *How on earth should I know?*

"Othello?" Willow sank to the grassy mound next to her mother and scratched Portia's ears as she rambled her thoughts aloud. "What do you think? What would Mother do?" She giggled. "Of course, if I ask you, why can't I ask Mother? I feel like that bookkeeper in the movie about the bookstore owner—asking the mother what they should do."

Chad saw her there several hours later as he turned into the driveway. She lay curled on the ground, sleeping under the shade of the tree with Portia chasing butterflies nearby. At the sound of his wheel on the driveway, Portia raced for the fence excitedly.

As he leapt over the fence and strode to Willow's side, Chad's face slowly furrowed in concern. Why was she out here? Willow rarely visited the grave unless bothered by something. What was she planning?

He sat beside her, brushing escaped tendrils from her braid away from her face and watched her sleep. Though it made him feel strange and sometimes foolish, Chad loved to watch her sleep. He'd always heard how parents enjoyed gazing at their sleeping children and thought it sounded almost creepy but not anymore.

A glance at his watch told him he'd better waken her. Jill would arrive any minute to pick up the produce, and Willow wouldn't want to be caught asleep. "Willow?" He shook her shoulder gently. "Come on, lass, it's time to wake up."

Willow stirred murmuring sleepily, "Hmm?"

"Jill will be here soon. You fell asleep." His hand trailed along her cheek and then tugged on her ear playfully. "Come on, you can do it."

"I don't want to get up. It's nice and warm here." The words were mumbled and clearly not fully consciously spoken.

He had to wake her up, but how was another story. In the house, he'd have dumped water on her head, but somehow he couldn't bring himself to do that out here. Finally, he picked her up, set her on her feet, and held her there in a bear hug until she slowly opened her eyes. "Hey."

"Hi," she murmured sleepily. "What a way to wake up, eh?"

"It's almost time for Jill to—"

Full consciousness arrived instantly. "Oh, no!" She started to run toward the barn but Chad caught her hand.

"The truck, Willow. It's faster and it'll give you a minute to wake up."

"Right."

He glanced at her sideways as they rolled toward the yard. "What were you doing out there?"

She sighed. "Coming to grips with my deposition on Monday."

"You decided to do it?"

"Well I thought I didn't have a choice." The dismay in her voice hadn't left.

"Well, you can refuse a request—just not a subpoena."

Willow nodded, resigned. "That's what I thought. I don't want to make it hard on you so—"

"You did it for me?"

"Of course!" Her indignation would have been comical if he hadn't found her actions so endearing. "If it was just about me, I'd let them throw me in jail indefinitely."

"Sweet sentiment, lass, but you'd go insane in a prison and beg to be allowed to testify." He opened her door and smiled down into her eyes. "But I love that you think you would and that you did something so sacrificial for me. I know how much this is costing you personally. Thanks."

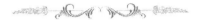

Willow expected the deposition to be a lot like her court hearing regarding her birth, but it wasn't anything like that. They sat at a table in a conference room at the courthouse. A young man with a stenograph machine sat at one end of the table, and Willow sat at the other with the defense attorney and the D.A. on either side of her.

All feelings of informality disappeared when the D.A. began reciting the purpose of the deposition and the case. The words, "The state vs. Solari" effectively killed the last remnants of her self-possession. Panic rose in her throat leaving bile in its wake. She reached for her tote bag and withdrew a bottle of water.

"May I?"

The D.A. unscrewed the top for her, satisfied that it was untampered with, for reasons that Willow couldn't comprehend. "Certainly."

"Ok, please state your full name and address for the record."

"Why my address?"

Willow's question set the tone for the rest of the deposition. Some questions were indicative of her perception of breached privacy while others were merely curious. The D.A. and defense attorneys acted split between irritation and amusement during the entire proceeding.

"You went to his office on what day?"

Willow's answer was swift. "December 7th."

"And how are you certain of that date?" The D.A.'s voice sounded bored.

"Because we celebrated my husband's birthday that evening."

"Did you make an appointment?"

The questions came in a slow steady pace. Most seemed

78

inconsequential to Willow. Who cared what Steven Solari had done to her? How was that relevant to the case against her grandmother?"

"When did you first speak to Lynne Solari?"

"She came to my house pretending to have a disabled car."

"Pretending—please define that," the D.A. requested quickly.

"Actually, she did have a disabled car. She disabled it so she'd have an excuse to come to the house. She admitted it once I confronted her with it."

"She actually said, 'Yes, I made this up to come out here?'"

"Not those exact words but very nearly, yes. She apologized and said that she just wanted to see me now that she knew I existed."

The D.A. nodded as though picturing the scene in her mind. "And when was this?"

"Approximately one week after I went to Mr. Solari's office." Weariness grew in Willow's voice. Her mind was growing muddled.

From questions regarding the attempts to terrorize her to detailed accounts of her every meeting with both of the Solaris, Willow's memory was tapped with every kind of question. Occasionally, the D. A. would respond with a rebuttal query such as, "Are you aware that Ms. Solari asserts that she did not attempt to deceive you about the reason for her visit?" Willow's replies were swift and confident. "I think you should question Officer Chad Tesdall as to the accuracy of my statement. I said she confessed her scheme, and she did. He heard the conversation."

Once the ordeal was over, Willow stood, shook everyone's hand, and then turned back to the District Attorney. "Ma'am, I have to tell you—I do not want to testify. I can't imagine how I would be helpful. Please don't put me in that position."

As they watched her exit the room, the reporter, the lawyer, and the D.A. all said in unison, "Wow."

Willow overheard them and rolled her eyes.

Wednesday, Willow woke up vomiting. She barely reached the bathroom floor before she retched uncontrollably. Unable to remember exactly when the last time she'd vomited was, and feeling exceptionally weak, her heart sank. By the time she'd decided to call Marianne for ideas of what to do, another wave of nausea sent her racing for the toilet again.

Ditto cried for relief before Willow crawled downstairs. She made it to the barn just in time for her to heave into the milk pail. A glance at the phone charger told her Chad had left the phone beside her bed before he went to work. She didn't know how she'd get back up those stairs, but she had to try.

Another wave of nausea hit in the middle of the yard. She curled into fetal position on the ground, her arms wrapped around the milk pail for dear life and prayed that the Lord would either kill her now or send someone to help. To her utter disgust, she not only lived but no one came. Still, she kept up the running prayer until she managed to crawl back upstairs and into bed.

Keeping the milk pail close, and berating herself for not grabbing a clothespin to block out the smell while in the barn, Willow collapsed on the bed and hit the button to dial Chad. His voicemail irritated her enough that had she had the strength, she'd have thrown the phone through the window. "How did mother handle illness all alone?" she wailed miserably.

The phone rang and Chad's name flashed across the screen. Just as she clicked it open to answer it, another attack hit her. "You ok?"

"Do I—" she retched once more, "sound ok to you?"

"Oh, lass, I'll get someone to come in for me and be right there."

"Can you do that?" Willow's voice sounded doubtful.

"I can do that. Hang in there until I get home."

Only the sounds of Willow's illness crossed the airwaves until she finally whimpered, "Hurry—please?"

Chad immediately dialed the Chief. "Sir, I've got a problem."

"Waverly call in sick?" The new officer had called in

twice in the past month.

"No. It's Willow. She's vomiting and she called for help. I'm sorry sir, but she wouldn't call unless she couldn't function."

"Forget that, son," the Chief contradicted, "that woman wouldn't call unless she was at death's door. I'll come in early. You get home."

Chad was already walking as briskly as possible toward the station. Aiden Cox stared slack-jawed as Chad passed him, sans helmet, on the scooter—again. It registered somewhere in the back of his mind that he should do something about that boy, but he couldn't remember what. He tossed the keys at Judith and raced back out the door, ignoring her indignant retort.

Chad heard her before he saw her. How one body could continue to retch the way hers did both amazed and terrified him. "How many times do you think you've gotten sick?"

Between dry heaves, Willow gasped, "About five or six when I first got up—it's all over the bathroom floor. I couldn't clean—"

"I'll get it," he reassured her sounding much more confident than he felt. "Just rest." Then he saw the milk pail. "If you only got sick five or six times—"

"No, that was just when I got up. Then a half a dozen times in the kitchen, a few times in the barn, and a dozen times or so since I got back upstairs, but there's nothing left. It just keeps trying—" Another wave hit her.

Chad held her head, smoothed her hair, and tried not to lose his own breakfast as he watched her body fight to rid itself of nothing. There was just nothing left. Another whimper escaped. "I begged to die, but God rejected my application."

A low chuckle rumbled over her. "I'm glad He did. I'm very glad He did."

They talked between waves of nausea. Time passed with aching slowness. Chad didn't know how he managed to hold back his own gag reflex as she grew sicker and sicker. "What did you eat last?"

"The grilled chicken we had last night, salad, milk, etc."

"In other words," he sighed frustrated. "Everything I

ate."

"You don't feel sick?" She prayed he wouldn't get it.

"Nope… only when you toss your cookies."

"But I didn't eat any cookies." Confusion in her face was so comical, Chad burst out laughing.

"It isn't funny—" she began before another wave of dry heaves attacked. As she fought to gain control, an idea hit Chad.

"When was your last period?"

"What?" she gasped between heaves.

"Your 'monthly.' When was your last—"

"I—" she took deep breaths trying to control the deep urge to hurl once more. "I can't remember for sure. I think I was due last week though."

A grin split his face. Torn between guilt and excitement, he said, "I think you're pregnant. Morning sickness. I'll get you some water and then drive into town for some crackers. I think that's what women eat. I'll call Mom."

Willow turned the most disgusting shade of green. "Pregnant?"

"It makes sense. You're late, you're puking—"

"You puke?"

Chad shook his head at her. "Surely you've heard or read of morning sickness."

"Yeah," she whimpered. "I just thought it was fatigue and swelling or something. Animals don't vomit." There was the merest trace of indignation in her weakened voice. "I'm thirsty, but I'm terrified to try to drink."

He brought her a glass of water and suggested she rinse her mouth with it. "Spit it back out. Don't swallow. At least you've moistened things. We'll work on taking tiny sips of water or something when I get home. I'll be right back."

With the gentlest kiss to the top of her head, Chad raced down the stairs, out the door and then stopped. He thought he heard her voice. Uncertain, he retreated back into the house, up the stairs, and paused in the doorway. "Did you call me?"

"Ditto," she wailed. "That poor goat—the chickens—"

"I'll get them when I get back."

"I feel a tiny bit better. Get them now." Willow's eyes pleaded as she spoke.

"I'll get 'em, and then I'll check on you before I go."

"Thanks."

In the barn, Chad grabbed a pail and raced to Ditto's stall. Without pausing to wash the teats, he milked the goat in record time earning him a few butts and a kick, but Chad hardly noticed. In the summer kitchen, he realized that the milk was contaminated. They couldn't drink it. He started to pour it down the drain and then thought of the soap. Maybe it could be saved for soap.

The stove was empty. No boiling water waited for him to scald the pail. With a sigh of frustration, he grabbed a kitchen towel, tossed it over the pail, and forced it into the fridge. He'd deal with it all later.

Willow slept with one arm curled around her pail by the time he climbed the stairs once more. He paused. Should he rinse it and clean up the bathroom before he went to town or after? The stench in the room grew worse by the second. He slipped the pail from her arm and took it to the bathtub trying not to breathe as he stepped over the mess on the floor. Once clean and free of odor, he stepped out of the bathroom, closed the door, and replaced the pail back in the crook of her arm. With her door shut, and the bathroom door shut, the air in the room smelled reasonably fresh again.

Chad raced back downstairs to his truck. Guilt tried to worm its way into his heart, but he was too excited. Pregnant! A baby! Chad couldn't believe how blessed he was. A wife and a child all within a month! Well, he had a few more months of course, but still! They were going to have a baby.

At the end of the driveway, he braked hard. Pulling out his phone, he dialed home. "Mom? What do you give a vomiting woman for morning sickness?"

"Well, saltines are good, and broth—oh, wait, did you say morning sickness?"

"Yes! Willow woke up puking, and we just realized that she's a week late!" The pride and excitement in Chad's voice made him feel ridiculous—and he almost cared.

"How bad is it?"

"She's resting now but she spent a long time emptying a very empty stomach. I need to get something in her that'll stay."

"Get some Jell-O too. It's gentle and it's comfort food. Oh, and 7-Up. Don't get Sprite or Slice; get 7-Up. It just works."

"I like Sprite," Chad contradicted.

"Get her—"

Chad's laughter interrupted. "7-Up. I got it. Anything else?"

"A pregnancy test. You'll want to be sure."

He leaned his forehead against the steering wheel. "Is it important today?"

"Well, I know I'd want one as soon as possible just to rule out something like food poisoning. I mean, she's late so it's pretty much a given, but it can't hurt—"

"I have to go to Brunswick then. It's twice as far both ways." Chad's voice sounded uncertain.

"Why?"

"Mom! This is Fairbury. If I buy a pregnancy test in town, they'll have her baby shower planned before she pees on the stick!"

"I'm surprised they carry them then," Marianne retorted dryly.

"You're right. I bet they don't. Good thinking. Gotta go, Mom, I need to be back before she wakes up puking again."

Chad could almost see her as she smiled to herself and blithely punched the numbers to her husband's store, while he tore down the highway toward Brunswick praying that he wouldn't meet Joe returning from a transfer. No luck. Just as he rounded the bend where he'd totaled the cruiser months earlier, he passed Joe and waved.

Within seconds, Joe was behind him lights flashing. Chad waved his arm out the window, but Joe kept coming. Finally, Chad pulled over and pounded the steering wheel. Joe reached the window by the time Chad managed to keep his hands gripped to the wheel instead of trying to pulverize it.

"Hey, Joe, I know. Give me a ticket and let me out of here, although," he added with a growl, "technically we're out of city limits here."

"What—Chad! You're supposed to be on beat!" Joe was not amused.

"I need to get stuff for Willow. She's sick, and I need the

84

pharmacy."

Joe shook his head. "Keep it to a reasonable level man. She needs you to get back too."

"You're right." Chad hesitated. He felt almost obligated to explain his mission, but he didn't want the news all over town before he could enjoy it with his wife for just a little while.

"Hey, I'll be praying for her. Do you guys know what is wrong?"

"Yeah, we think so but we need to be sure. See you later. Thanks, Joe." Without another word, Chad punched the automatic window button, turned on the key, and once Joe stepped away from his truck, eased onto the highway and drove the rest of the way just barely over the speed limit.

Willow awoke feeling weak, hungry, nauseous, and with the terrible urge to use the bathroom. Unsteady on her feet, she grasped the bed and dresser with one hand while clutching her milk pail with the other. A glance inside the bucket surprised her. It was clean. It didn't smell.

A smile spread across her face. "He cleaned up for me. What a man."

She stood confused at the closed bathroom door. Why was the door closed? Willow knocked. She rattled the knob. As cautiously as she could, she pushed it open, calling for Chad. Silence greeted her. She took a step forward and froze as she realized her mistake. Her foot slid through the previous contents of her stomach, sending her careening across the bathroom. She slammed into the edge of the tub and groaned.

"Ow!" Tears sprang to her eyes as her head impacted with the cast iron. "Oh man." The room spun, her hand groped for the milk pail and grabbed it just in time.

Sounds of feet on the stairs sent her into fresh tears. "Chad?"

Chad, hearing he commotion upstairs, had dropped his bags just inside the front door and bolted upstairs. The sight of Willow sprawled across the vomit streaked bathroom floor, holding her head in one hand and her bucket in the other, made him wince. "Oh, I'm so sorry. I almost cleaned it up and then I thought I could get back faster and clean it even if you were awake. I—"

"I'm coated and it's making me feel worse."

Chad grabbed two towels and mopped up the worst of it. Quickly, he helped her out of her sodden pajamas and into the tub. While she soaked with bucket in hand and whining about the disgusting practice of sitting in one's own filth, he raced downstairs with the stinky laundry gagging any time he was forced to take a breath. He tossed the towels in the washer, dumped a scoop of dripping laundry soap into the machine, turned it on "normal wash," smelled his shirt, peeled it off, dumped it the tub, and raced back inside.

Willow was almost asleep by the time the tub filled. He brought her water, crackers, and sat on the floor beside the tub wishing he'd thought to buy some ammonia. "Bleach! That's what the floor needs. Bleach. Be right back."

All morning and into the early afternoon, Chad brought her something to drink, something to munch on, dumped her milk pail, and then sat beside her on the bed, stroking her hair and praying for her. As the day passed, he grew worried. What would they do if every day was this bad? What if it kept going for several weeks or even the whole time? He'd heard of that.

His phone vibrated in his pocket sending him downstairs quickly to answer it. "Mom?"

"How is she doing?"

"Better, I think. She's kept down her last few crackers and the Jell-O. The broth was a nightmare."

"Does sound like it—did you get a test?" Marianne tried not to sound as eager as she felt.

"Got a test, but we haven't taken it yet. We've been talking. She's so excited—when she's not puking anyway."

Marianne's sigh filled both their hearts with delight. "I'm going to be a grandmother! Isn't she going to be the cutest pregnant mother ever?"

"Mom, you *are* a grandmother—you'll just have to wait to meet your grand-something."

"Child. It's called a child, Chaddie. Oh, do you want a boy or a girl?" Her excitement became infectious.

"Both?" He laughed with her. "Actually, whichever is most likely easier for a first baby." He tried to do the math and couldn't think. "When do you think the baby is likely coming?"

Murmuring as she counted, Marianne finally said, "Mid February to the first of March I think."

"Valentine's Day."

"Or if she goes overdue, you could be talking St. Paddy's Day."

"That's forever."

Her laughter turned to howls. "Son, you sound about six years old."

Willow stirred. "Gotta go mom, she's waking up. I'll call after she takes the test. Can you scout around for doctors in Brunswick?"

He whispered his love, and then hurried to Willow's side. "How are you feeling?"

"Weak, thirsty, and hungry."

"How's the nausea?"

She shrugged. "I can tell it was there, but I think it's gone."

"Well," he chuckled, "I hope you don't have it that bad every day."

She stared at him in horror. "Every day?"

"Some women—" he didn't have the heart to tell her. "Have it more than others."

"I'd better be done." The finality in her voice was comical.

"Mom is calling around for a doctor. If it keeps up, they have medications that can help."

Willow didn't answer. She was already asleep. Frustrated, Chad carried the box of pregnancy tests back to the bathroom, opened it, and placed one wrapped test on the back of the toilet. He stood in the bathroom doorway, hands stuffed in his pockets, and stared at it.

When his feet ached, he forced himself to go downstairs. "You're acting like an idiot, man. Go feed the chickens and get eggs—" The thought of eggs made him smile. First baby chicks and now baby humans. They'd have to start breeding goats, cows, and sheep next.

His eyes widened at the direction of his thoughts. "Oh,

87

ick. I'm *not* going there. We'll stick to breeding humans. Wait—" Chad shook his head. "That sounds even worse."

CHAPTER 113

She stretched, yawned, clutched the bucket, and then relaxed. No wave of nausea followed, but her muscles felt weak and her mouth tasted as though something crawled inside and died. Willow crawled from the bed and stumbled into the bathroom, eager to brush her teeth. Minutes later, she flushed the toilet and saw a plastic wrapper and a folded paper pamphlet.

Not until she was cuddled against her pillows sipping on 7-Up and resting did she realize the purpose of the wrapper and pamphlet. She read all instructions carefully, reread them, and was on a third pass before Chad found her flipping the paper back and forth curiously.

"Hey, did you test?"

"I'm reading. Did you know that the other side is in what looks like Spanish? I saw diez. I think that's ten and on the other side the same paragraph says something about not reading it after ten minutes."

"Most medications and instructions come in English and Spanish." He hesitated searching for the right words. "*Estados Unidos llega a ser una sociedad bilingüe.* Or something like that. I'm rusty."

"Say it again. That's beautiful!"

Chad repeated the words slowly watching comprehension dawn as she listened. "I heard States United society bilingual. You said something about the United States being a bilingual society."

89

"Very good. I actually went with a fairly literal translation of 'the United States is becoming a bilingual society.' I'm sure it's not correct, but I was always better at translating than at communication."

"When did you learn Spanish?"

Chad shrugged. "Two semesters in high school, two more in college. I thought it'd help on the job, and it's easier to learn than Japanese, Korean, or Russian which are the other four most spoken languages in the greater Rockland area."

"I can see why it's easy to understand anyway. It's very similar to English. I mean I knew it was to a degree—Latin is at the core of both languages, but the songs I've heard in Spanish were never as easy to understand as what you just said."

"Well," Chad admitted, "It's not all that simple, but compared to Swahili or something—"

"Why would you learn that? Is there a large population of Swahili speaking criminals in the area?"

Her question would have seemed sarcastic to the average person but Willow was curiously serious. "No. That's just a joke. So are you ready to try the test?"

"It wants me to—" Suddenly, Willow understood her mother's distaste in discussing personal bodily fluids. In general, things were fine. Personalize them and well, she'd either gotten self-conscious for no reasonable reason or she was becoming her mother.

"Yeah, I know how they work."

"Really? Then why leave me the directions? Why not just tell me?"

Chad stared at her oddly. Was she teasing him? Was she serious? Was she curious? The whole scenario was bizarre. "Well, you tend to like to read things for yourself..."

"I do. You just usually tell me how it works, and I wonder why you don't want me to read the instructions, and this time you didn't."

He stared to protest but the truth of her words effectively corked his reply. He did tend to set instructions aside and tell her what he thought they said. He hadn't picked up on it but Willow sure had. "Next time, ask for the instructions. I wasn't doing it consciously."

"You haven't steered me wrong yet. When you make me take twice as long as necessary to do something, then I'll start asking to read the instructions." Before he could reply, she tossed the paper at him. "I used the bathroom before I read it, and I have very little liquid to absorb as it is. I need to drink for a while."

Chad rolled onto his back and stared at the ceiling. "Where do you think we should put a baby? In Mother's room or in the one you just fixed up?"

Willow curled next to him resting her head on his chest. "I don't know. I'll have to read which is best and see why mother chose this room for me and her room for her. There might be a reason."

Willow covered her mouth to stifle a giggle as Chad stood in front of the bathroom window rocking the pregnancy test back and forth trying to get a clearer reading. "It's not going to change. I think I did something wrong."

"What can you do wrong? How hard is it to pee on a stick for goodness sake!"

"Well, maybe for a man it's not so hard but women are shooting blind you know!" The indignation in Willow's voice did little to hide her amusement.

He threw her an impatient smile and shifted once more. "Well, I think there's a line in that control window, but it's so faint I can't tell. The other window seems to have a line too but it's also faint so I can't tell what is going on. I think you need to do it again."

"Well, then we'll have to wait a while because I need a nap."

Chad glanced at his watch, confused. She'd hardly been awake for an hour. It was almost four o'clock, and she'd slept most of the day away. He'd never heard of that kind of somnolence as a symptom of pregnancy, but what did he know? Tucking her into the bed, he positioned the bucket nearby just in case. "Get some sleep. I'll go buy the soup du jour at the deli. It'll be easier on your stomach for dinner than anything I can make, and it'll taste better than canned."

91

"Mmm hmm. Thanks," she murmured, half asleep already.

On the porch, Chad dialed his mother. Her excited voice sent him into panic mode. "Mom, stop! I don't know. She took the test and it was a dud or something. You're supposed to see lines in two windows and if I held it just right with my right hip cocked and my tongue sticking out, I think I saw a line in each window, but for all I know, it's just the light shining on whatever chemical makes up that line in the first place."

"Well, she can take another one. Did you buy two?"

"I bought two boxes so we'd have a spare but there are three in each box. Honestly, Mom, why three in a box? Do they really need to triple confirm?"

"I think it's so if you're negative one month, you don't have to go back over and over."

The disgust in Chad's voice was comical. "I think it's so they can sell the duds and blame it on the consumer. Willow immediately said she thought she messed up the test."

"Oh, what did she do wrong?"

"Come on, Mom, how hard is it to pee on a stick!"

"Well Chad," she began patiently, "really. Remember how you and Chris used to drop Cheerios in the toilet and try to aim for them. Girls couldn't do that. They'd be shooting blind."

Chad stared at his phone. "Have you been talking to Willow?"

"No, why?"

"She said the same exact thing. It's like déjà vu. I feel like that kid in *A Christmas Story*. Is everyone going to tell me she'll shoot her eye out?"

"Oh honestly, Chad. You are being silly! Now why don't you just go make her a nice bowl of soup—"

Chad interrupted quickly. "Actually, that's why I'm calling. I'm on my way to buy some at the deli. We don't have anything light enough for a weak stomach."

"You're calling about soup?"

"No, I'm calling," he tried again with practiced patience. Why wasn't his mother following the conversation better? It was as though she'd lost her mind at the hint of babies or something. "Because she's asleep again. She's slept most of today and all last night."

"Well, some pregnant women do that. I remember Libby saying she slept away the first four months of her pregnancy with Corinne."

"We don't even know if she *is* pregnant, Mom!"

Marianne reminded her son that after any stomach bug, he'd always slept most of a day away while he recuperated. "She'll either be fine and pregnant or fine and ready to handle a miserable late cycle. It's pretty much either-or on that one."

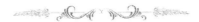

At two a.m., Chad strolled into the police station, trying not to worry about his wife, thanking the Lord for the unlikelihood of a drunk tourist, and counting the hours until his lunch break. "Hey, Waverly. How're you doing?"

"Fine, but what are you doing here?"

Chad pointed to the board where his name had been written, erased, and Waverly's filled in. "You worked for me yesterday. Go home."

"No. Your wife is sick. You go home and get some sleep before you come down with it. That bug is awful."

Oh how Chad wanted to deny it was the problem. He couldn't wait until he could tell everyone that his wife was having a baby. *"Ugh,"* he mused to himself. *"You sound um... paternal! You're only twenty-six man, get a grip."*

"Chad?"

He glanced back up into Waverly's concerned face. "Huh?"

"Go. Home."

"I can't do that to you."

Waverly placed his hand on the phone. "Do you go home now, or do I wake up the Chief and tell him you refuse to obey orders."

"Since when do I take orders from you?"

"From the chief, you moron," Waverly spat exasperated. "Get out of here, or I'm calling and you can deal with Sir Sleepless."

"Sir Sleepless?" Chad couldn't help mocking him.

"It's two in the morning, and I've almost worked a double

93

shift. What do you want from me?"

"You to know how much I appreciate it. Thanks, Brad."

At four, Willow finally dragged herself from the bed, grabbed the instructions, and padded toward the bathroom. Chad barely stirred. Though woozy from lack of food and fuzzy from too much rest, Willow felt nearly well. She grabbed test number two and reread the instructions carefully. Instructions for saved urine seemed easier so she retrieved a pint canning jar from the pantry and followed directions step-by-step.

The clock never moved so slowly. As the thought flitted across her mind, Willow realized that it was also a strange thought. How would she know? She'd read the comment repeated times and finally understood the meaning in more than a theoretical sense, but the fact of the matter was, she rarely noticed the passing of time unless it was one of those odd occasions when she realized that something was unusually swift. This was the opposite feeling. If it could go any slower, time would cease.

Finally, the clock in Mother's room insisted that ten minutes had passed. She picked up the test and examined it carefully. In the "control window," a nice bold line stood out from the damp background. In the "results window," nothing. She wasn't pregnant. Chad would be so disappointed.

Laying the test on the sink where he could see it and tucking the instructions behind the faucet for easy reference, Willow crept slowly downstairs, out the back door, and sat on the porch whistling softly for Portia. "No baby, girl. I couldn't imagine so soon, but then again, when we bred Dandy, it only took the once so…"

Portia rested her head comfortingly on Willow's leg. Together, woman and dog, sat on the back porch of Walden Farm, and while the woman imagined life with a tiny baby, a toothy toddler, or an inquisitive child, Portia slept dreaming of chasing butterflies that turned into steak. Or at least, that's what Willow assumed.

CHAPTER 114

Being as observant as most males, Chad's hands were washed, dried, and he was on his way out the bathroom door before he glanced at the back of the toilet. The test was gone. He hurried into their bedroom and eyed the bedside tables, but nothing was there. Back to the bathroom, he glanced in the trash and found the wrapper but no instructions and no used—the test at last.

Comparing instructions to test, it was obvious to Chad that the test was negative. Disappointment washed over him. He'd been so sure. Why was she so sick if she wasn't pregnant? Willow was never sick and had little opportunity to catch anything anyway. The sound of the back screen door banging softly against the doorjamb told him she was up and dealing with her own discouragement.

She sat on her heels stuffing the stove with wood and mumbling something under her breath. "You're awake."

"I think we're a pair of geniuses. I was just about to make the same observation." Chad's heart constricted at the pain in her eyes, but he didn't move closer. "Lass, it's not the end of everything. There's always next month, or the next, or even next year or so."

"You were so excited..." She reached for another handful of kindling. "It feels like I failed—"

Chad's hands, on their way to his pockets in his characteristic frustrated stance, reached for her instead. "Oh Willow, I'm sorry. I didn't want you to feel like that! I jumped the gun. I've never seen you sick so I just assumed—"

"But I'm late. I am sure of it. Normally I don't pay really close attention, but your mother said something about our wedding date needing to fit around it, and I wanted to surprise you so—" She buried her face in his shoulder.

She sagged in his arms limply. "I'm dizzy…"

Chad hoisted her over his shoulder and carried her to the couch. "Put your head between your legs and breathe normally."

"What happened?" Her voice was a little weak and confused.

"You said you were dizzy."

"That's right." She glanced back up at him but shoved her head back down between her knees. "I want to lie down."

As he rolled the quilt from the back of the couch into a ball, Chad began thinking aloud. "Maybe you're dehydrated. Have you been drinking enough?"

"I've not been able to keep much down, if you'll remember."

"I wonder if I should take you into the clinic…" His voice trailed off in the general direction of his thoughts as Chad considered their options.

"Maybe," she said obviously feeling better having lain down, "you should consider getting me something with which to hydrate myself first. Water works."

Absently, Chad poured her a glass of water and brought it back, stuffing a straw in it as he handed it to her. "Drink up."

"It's stuffy in here."

Her complaints brought a smile to his face. Willow must be feeling better if she noticed stuffiness of all things. While she rested, sipping water and resting her eyes, he threw open all of the windows, knowing that with the coming storm, he'd just have to close them again later. "Is that better?"

. "I smell a storm."

"Yep. The forecast is for heavy winds, rain, and possibly hail."

"Hail?" She sat up abruptly looking visibly woozy. "It gets cold in here when it hails. We'll need more wood for upstairs tonight."

96

"I'll get it. You rest."

"Can you open the windows up there too? The breeze just before a storm smells so good…"

With shades drawn to keep the sunrise from slowly filling the room with sunlight, Willow crept from the bedroom, closing the door behind her. Downstairs, she opened the front door and groaned at the sight of her front yard. Tree branches littered the grass; one large one had crashed through the porch railing, and some of her flowers were battered beyond recognition.

Chad opened the back door an hour later to find the chickens pecking at the seed in the yard, Ditto in a freshly cleaned stall, and Willow dragging tree branches behind the barn. As he watched her, his hands found their way into his pockets and the crease between his eyebrows deepened. She looked tired—exhausted really. Every move, every step looked labored.

He hurried inside, filled a glass with water, and brought it out to her. "I'll finish that one; you go sit on the steps and drink up."

"But—"

"Lass…" His tone was one he'd only used once before—when he'd ordered her from his parents' house that winter.

"I'm going, I'm going."

She sat long enough to empty her glass and then pulled her gloves back onto her hands and started pulling debris from the flowerbeds. They worked for another hour. Chad detached the railing from the house and dumped it in the back of his truck. "I'll go get another one later."

"I'm hungry." Willow sank into the porch swing exhausted, weak, and thirsty.

"You," Chad called as he went inside for the couch quilt, "you need your rest. I'll go get a new rail top and be back in no time. I'll grab something for us to eat on my way back."

Willow pointed at the empty glass and promptly fell asleep. Chad refilled it, set it on the ground next to her, and watched her sleep for a moment before he jogged to his truck and drove toward Brunswick. His watch told him he had just enough time to get there, get the materials, and get it fixed before he had to change for work.

His phone rang. "I just left you sleeping!"

"I heard the truck start. Listen, I was thinking. Can you get me some red exterior paint?"

"Red?"

Her impatient voice snapped back, "Yes red. You know, the color of tulips and candy canes?"

"Whatever for?"

"I really loved Aggie's door, but I thought I couldn't have one because the screen would hide it. Why go red if you can't see it, you know?"

Chad nodded absently. "Ok..."

"Well, if I paint the screen, I get that bright and cheerful door after all. A gallon will probably be too much but it'll be good for touch ups.'

"Red. Got it. Anything else?"

She smiled to herself. "Do you remember last summer when I had a bad day and you brought me some chocolate thing?"

A grin spread slowly over Chad's face. "I do indeed."

"Can I have another one?" She hesitated. "I promise I won't eat the paper this time."

"You can have a case of 'em."

Willow smiled to herself. "That's ok. Just one will do. Thanks, Chad. I'm going back to sleep now."

"Sleep on the couch; it's more comfy."

"That's your opinion," she argued. "Nothing beats nostalgia on a June morning."

She was still sleeping as Chad pulled slowly into the yard. He pushed his door shut gently, grabbed the grocery bags from the back of the truck, and crept past her to the back door and into the house. He set the table with bowls, spoons, and a gallon of milk. He filled glasses of orange juice, fried bacon in a pan on the stove in the summer kitchen, and then crept out the front door to wake her.

"Willow, breakfast's ready."

"Wha—"

"I brought home breakfast. Come on, the bacon is getting

98

cold!" He shook her shoulder glancing at the empty glass of water. At least she'd taken hydration seriously.

She dragged herself off the swing and followed him clumsily into the kitchen. "I am so tired."

Chad looked at her sharply. Dark circles beneath her eyes made her look as though she hadn't slept in days. "You look it."

"Ever the flatterer—what is this?"

"Cereal smorgasbord! I bought all of my favorite kinds and the one Mom likes."

"Frosted Mini-Wheats, Cocoa Puffs, Lucky Charms, Fruit Loops, Cap'n Crunch Berries, and Wheaties? Let me guess, your mom likes Wheaties. They just sound closer to real food."

He shook his head. "Nope, she likes Cap'n Crunch. I think it's gross, myself. I got the berries because I think it makes them more edible."

"What's with the milk? We have plenty—"

"Well, your milk is good, for goat's milk that is, but cold cereal was *designed* for cow's milk. It's like eating pizza without the sauce."

As he spoke, Chad filled his bowl with Cocoa Puffs and smothered it in milk. She reached for the first box, poured a tiny bit in the bowl, poured milk over it and took a bite. As she chewed, she read the box ingredients, glanced over the packaging, and then closed it. "Lucky Charms are gross. Tri-sodium phosphate? I use that to clean."

"Then your insides will be clean."

She picked up the Fruit Loops box and repeated the scenario. At the end of her buffet of cereals, she pronounced Wheaties the winner with Frosted Mini-Wheats a close second. "The orange juice was really good too."

She rinsed her glass and poured half a glass of milk as she reached for a cold slice of bacon. "I love bacon. Mother would bring it home sometimes, and the butcher usually brought us a pound of it with the cow if Mother remembered to ask."

She took a drink of milk and nearly choked. Chad's expression was priceless. "What's wrong?"

"It's awful! It tastes like— like, some kind of chemical. I

99

don't know how to explain it but it's almost dusty tasting or something. Ew."

Chad quickly poured him a glass and took a large swallow. "Tastes great to me."

"Oh, that is just—ew." She watched fascinated as he guzzled the rest of his drink and then poured the rest of hers into his glass. "Here, finish mine then."

She stared at the boxes of cereal on the table. "Do you realize how many boxes we have? It'll take forever to eat all of this!"

Chad grinned. "But think of the fun we'll have."

As much as she wished she felt the same, Willow was dismayed to think of many more breakfasts with cold and dry cereal growing soggy before she could get to the final bites. She shuddered inwardly just thinking about it. Carrying the boxes to the pantry, she set them on a shelf at eye level so she wouldn't forget about them. It'd be wasteful to let them get stale and inedible no matter how appealing the idea seemed.

She sank into her chair and reached for her glass. Willow sighed as she realized she'd have to rinse it again before she could fill it with water. Chad noticed, and took it to the sink rinsing well, and then brought it back. "Keep drinking. I want to see those circles gone from under your eyes."

"I need another nap. I think I'll go back upstairs."

As she disappeared from the kitchen, Chad stared at the empty doorway. She acted so pregnant! The test said no, but she was tired, she'd been so sick, and the dizziness all seemed like symptoms he'd heard over the years. Uncertain of what else to do, he dialed home.

"Mom?"

"Chaddie! I've been going crazy! What did the test say?"

"Test was negative, Mom but she's still acting so weird. She is sleeping so much, she has dark circles under her eyes, she's gotten dizzy a couple of times, and milk tastes funny to her."

"Well, her milk tastes funny to me too but—"

"No mom," Chad interrupted impatiently. "I brought home *real* milk to put on cold cereal—did you know she's never had cold cereal?"

"Did you get her Cap'n Crunch?"

"She didn't like it any more than the others I bought. She hardly commented on it at all, which tells me she's still sick. Willow never keeps her opinions to herself with me."

"So maybe it's just too early. If she doesn't start in a few days, have her take another one."

"But if she's too early to show up on a test, wouldn't she be too early to get sick?"

"Well, for most women, yes. But who knows with her? Maybe she's one of those women who gets sick within a few hours. I've heard of women who start vomiting within minutes, but I admit that it's rare."

Chad thought about that. "Oh Mom, we can't have her that sick. There is too much here for me to do myself, and she was totally incapacitated."

"So you'll buy canned tomatoes and peaches and whatever else she does. The gal who buys from the garden can do her own picking, and when you're working, that boy can come feed and milk. It'll work."

His mother's words, while logical and practical, were not encouraging. "I hope this is just some kind of stomach bug. Maybe she ate something fishy in Rockland during her deposition."

"This being 'just a bug' isn't going to erase the possibility of a difficult pregnancy, Chad. You have to..."

"To what mom?"

"Well, I just thought of something. Did Kari keep journals that far back?"

"Yes. She has journals from her college days."

Marianne added, "I'd find the right months and look and see how she reacted to pregnancy. See if she mentions getting sick, how bad, and that kind of stuff. Willow might remember, but I'd look it up myself. That must be hard—"

"Willow hasn't ever read them and therefore; neither have I. She just skipped to the one when she was about to give birth and ignored the rest."

"Read it, son," Marianne urged. "It can only help. If her mother was this sick this early, you've got a better idea of what might be happening. It doesn't mean anything if she wasn't, but it's a starting place."

Before he could say another word, the horrible sounds of

101

retching reached him. "Gotta go, Mom, there she goes again."

"Sick?"

"Yeah," he groaned, rushing to dampen a washcloth as he tried to extricate himself from the conversation.

"Praying." The phone clicked.

Willow sat up in bed looking tiny, miserable, and confused. "I thought I was done, but—" Another heave sent the rest of her breakfast from her stomach. "I guess not."

Chad glanced at the clock. It was nearly ten and he had to be at work by two. They had to get to the bottom of this and soon. He laid the cloth across her forehead and told her to lie back and rest. Fighting the urge to lose his own breakfast, he dumped and scrubbed—again.

"I'm sorry, Chad. I don't know what is wrong with me..."

"You're sick. Either with a stomach bug, some kind of food poisoning, or possibly a baby or two."

"Two?"

"Mom said something about twins maybe being why everything was so bad so fast if you are pregnant." Chad remembered the sinking feeling he had trying to imagine two babies at once and how it had mingled with a momentary feeling of excitement. Two! He couldn't let himself think about it.

"I guess twice the children, twice the misery makes sense."

He laughed. "That's encouraging. Hey, she also suggested we check your mother's journals from during that time. She thought maybe if your mom got sick quickly, maybe it's genetic or something."

"You do it. I tried to read them once, and I haven't tried again. It was horrible. If they don't say anything, maybe Grandmother Finley would know if it's a family thing."

As though she'd finished her job of talking, Willow grabbed the blanket, pulled it over her shoulder, curled into a ball around the bucket, and promptly fell asleep. Chad stood in the doorway, hands stuffed in his jeans and shook his head as she slept. She was so fragile-looking and the words fragile and Willow didn't belong in the same thought.

He went into Kari's old room, looked at the shelf between the closet and bedroom doors, and then glanced around the

102

rest of the room. They weren't in there. He checked the spare and craft rooms, the shelf in the living room, and finally found them on the top shelf of the closet in the library. He pulled the three volumes from the shelf and stared curiously at them. Three volumes for less than nine months of life. She'd been—prolific in recording her thoughts, dreams, and fears.

He set his cellphone to ring at one-thirty and sank into the couch already dreading the words to come. As an officer, even the thought of what Kari had endured made him livid. Why should the wealthy get away with crimes like that? How could Steven Solari even think his money could salve the pain his son inflicted on a young woman?

October—

I have the check. I don't know what to do with it. I took it because I thought I'd take it to the police for proof of who it was, but I'm scared. It's my word against Steve's. Mr. Solari can simply say that he didn't want nasty lies spread about their family and paying me off was easier than going through a scandal to prove their innocence.

I could keep it, save it, and if someone else came forward then I could maybe use it to show them that she wasn't the only one. Maybe that's what I'll do.

I'm afraid of him. Steven Solari isn't like his son. Steve was just an uncontrolled brute, but Mr. Solari is a very controlled and very powerful man. I wonder why he hasn't just had me killed? He could easily do that. I wonder if he's waiting for me to cash the check.

November—

I took a pregnancy test today. I was sure the stress of everything was just making me late, but I thought I'd take it just so I could sleep knowing that one thing in my life was fine.

It's not. The little test tube and dropper thing was so frustrating. It warned me not to jostle it and it took forever for the results but if this thing is to be believed, I am pregnant. I don't know what I'll do now.

November—

103

I cashed the check, bought a house, walked out of my apartment and left my car door open in the campus parking lot. I found a financial guy who set it up so that some kind of corporation bought the house and has the utilities, so no one will find me. I hated leaving without saying goodbye. I couldn't take anything with me—not even my purse. Mr. Barnes is taking care of everything for me. He says in a couple of years, I can probably request a new driver's license and Social Security card, and no one will be looking for me anymore.

I added the time and I'm six weeks pregnant. The baby will be here in mid-July. From the books I have, I should be getting sick anytime now. Lord, I'm so scared.

Chad read through December and January but saw nothing but occasional glimpses of nausea and no vomiting. From the sheer volume of work that Kari seemed to accomplish, he assumed that fatigue wasn't a problem. Her journals told much and confirmed nothing.

One passage from January ripped at his heart. Kari's words echoed in his mind as he stared at the journal. *"... why did he ask me out? Why didn't I hide in the bathroom when he got so drunk? Why didn't I call a cab? Why am I so stupid? Why?"*

CHAPTER 115

"Lass? You ok?"

Willow's arms wrapped around his neck as she stood behind the couch and laid her cheek on his head. "Yes. I think it was the milk. It tasted so funny and my stomach is still sensitive."

"But the milk was fine."

"It didn't taste fine. Maybe I'm just not used to cow's milk or maybe it's the plastic. I don't know, but it was the milk. Next time I'll just use Ditto's."

"I think you need that BRAT diet. I'll call mom and ask what is in it."

Before Willow could ask, Chad was on the phone with his mother. She slowly climbed the stairs and stood before her mirror examining herself from every angle. She didn't look bigger. In fact, she looked thinner as though she'd lost weight. Why was he worried about putting her on a diet? Did she really look that bad?

"Mom says banana, rice, applesauce, and dry toast."

She nodded. "I have applesauce and toast."

"What are you doing up here?"

"Just looking. Do I really look that bad?"

"You look a little peaked, but once your stomach recovers and you can eat normally again, you'll be fine. Put back on the pounds you lost."

The confusion on her face was priceless. "You want to put me on a diet so that I can *gain* weight?"

"What diet?"

"The BRAT one that you had to get from your mom."

He took her hand leading her downstairs laughing as he went. "No silly, it's a 'diet' in that it's a prescribed regimen of food. It's what people eat for a day or two after they've had a stomach bug to make it easy on their stomach." He handed her a glass of water and opened the front door. "Ride to town with me. It'll be good for you."

"As long as you don't expect me to go in anywhere. I need a shower."

Her stomach rumbled along with the wheels on her way to town. "I guess I'm hungry."

"I'll have a banana for you in no time. Do you like them still slightly green, very yellow, or a little overripe?"

She stared at him dumbstruck. "How am I supposed to know? I can count on one hand the number of times I've had a banana. We didn't grow them. As far as I know, they don't grow very well here."

He laughed. "Sarcasm. You're back." Her indignant snort prompted him to add, "Do you remember if they had green on them or spots?"

"I remember they existed. They were good. Sweet but not too sweet like some things."

"I'll get you a basic ripe banana. And rice. White or brown- never mind, I think I remember mom telling Cheri to do white back when we were in high school. Something about not as nutritious but easier on the stomach."

Willow waited in the truck as Chad crossed the street, waving at nearly everyone and disappeared into the market. A memory flashed through her mind of the first time she remembered coming to town. Based upon her dress, Willow assumed she'd been around four or five years old. She saw the way her mother kept her hat pulled so that it hid most of her face and wondered what others had thought of the strange woman and child that came to town once or twice a year.

"Mother, why are the houses so close together?"

The ever-patient voice of her mother answered as she wove through the streets, avoiding the eyes of those who tried to be friendly. "Because some people like to live on top of each

106

other."

"But there's no room for gardens or animals. How do they eat?"

"See that store?" Her mother paused and stooped down to the child's level. "See where the lady in the purple shirt is going in? That's a grocery store. People buy all the food they need in there."

"That store isn't big enough to grow enough food for all of these people! Our garden is almost as big as that store and where do they keep the animals? These cars would kill chickens."

Familiar chuckles made the child feel secure and foolish at the same time. She knew what those chuckles meant. It meant that she'd said something silly and that her mother didn't see how smart she really was for thinking of these things. The child thought her mother didn't always appreciate her intelligence.

"Willow, the store only keeps enough food for a few days or a week or so. They have food brought from everywhere. By bringing it so often, they ensure that everything is fresh. People just go get what they need for a week or two and then come back."

Willow's next words surprised the mother. "How sad. I'm sorry for them."

"Why sorry?"

"They don't get to see things grow. They don't get to know that the tomato they're eating is the one they picked 'specially for them. They have to take whatever someone else gives them."

Mother laughed. "Want to know a secret?" she whispered in the child's ear. "The food isn't as good either. They have to pick it too soon so that it doesn't spoil before they get it to the stores."

"I will pray for them. Those poor, poor people. Someone should tell them—"

"They know, Willow. They know."

"That's just foolish." The emphatic tone of the child's voice amused a passer-by.

"They would say that working so hard for enough to eat and a way to stay warm and dry is foolish. Everyone makes

their choices."

"*But some people make foolish ones,*" *Willow added with finality.* "*I'm glad God gave me to a Mother who makes smart choices for us.*"

"*Oh, Willow.*"

Arms around her startled her. "Wha—"

"What's wrong, Lass? Do you feel worse?"

She realized that tears were streaming down her face. "I was remembering a trip with Mother. I didn't even know I was crying."

"You should write those memories down. Our children will treasure them." He reached for the box of Kleenex he kept in the glove compartment. "Here."

"Did you get bananas and rice?"

Chad pulled out a box of fruit popsicles. "And popsicles. It's almost as medicinal for a stomach bug as chicken soup is for a cold or the flu."

Willow pulled the stick from the wrapper and bit off the end of it. "Oooh!"

Laughing Chad grabbed another Kleenex and handed it to her. "Spit it out if you need to. It's cold."

"I should have expected it, but I didn't," she said surprised.

"Nibble or suck on it. It'll soothe your throat too. Let's get you home and if you keep that down, I'll give you a banana."

"But this isn't part of the BRAT thing. Popsicle wasn't in there." She looked at it warily. Another bout of vomiting was not what she had in mind for her afternoon.

"This counts as a liquid. Liquids don't count for the BRAT so you're ok."

She glanced his way and sighed. "I think BRAT is a double entendre. I think it also stands for the state of mind of people who are too weak to protest but too hungry not to."

Late that night, Chad noticed Willow's journal on the coffee table and opened it hesitantly. She'd assured him that he was welcome to read them at any time, but it seemed like such an invasion of her privacy. Willow had given up so much of her life to make him a part of it that he felt like any more intrusion was almost criminal.

This time, however, he opened it. Curiosity triumphed over his unnecessary scruples and he sprawled out on the couch, munched on his sandwich, and flipped to the first page. The first words surprised him.

March—

It seems that nothing I do in this new life of mine is right. One moment I think I have the hang of things and the next I've unwittingly stomped on more toes. I have wondered at times if stepping away from Mother's isolation was the best choice for me, but even if it wasn't, I couldn't go back now. Life without Marianne and Libby—without Cheri and Chuck, it's a sad thought. Life without Chad? Inconceivable!

On the other hand, I do see that our life made us selfish. We did what we wanted, when we wanted, and with little regard for anyone but ourselves because our way of life encouraged it. If Mother wanted to take up weaving, she did it. She didn't wonder if maybe the noise of the loom would hurt my head or if I thought the thing was ugly sitting in the living room night after night. I may have found it obnoxious, but we each respected the other's 'right' to be obnoxious I guess. She, hated the idea of sheep, but I could have bought them at any time. We both knew that if I wanted them badly enough, I would have just done it, and Mother wouldn't have said a word. It's just how we did things. It worked for us but rarely did we have to die to self.

He skipped a few months and read from mid-April.

I decided what to give Chad for a wedding gift. Once he mentioned that he'd be giving me one, I realized that it was an opportunity for me to step out in faith. I'll move his things into my room and pray for the strength and the courage to trust. I know I can trust Chad to treat me well, but I need the faith to trust the Lord that what He created as good is truly good. Mother left no doubt in my mind that the things of

109

marriage are horrible and to be avoided. Mother wasn't a liar. How do I reconcile what she said with what God and the Tesdalls and my Chad say?

Chad swallowed hard. He hadn't realized how torn she'd been. He reread it once more smiling in spite of himself. She'd called him "her" Chad. She was fond of him. He'd known it for some time, but seeing that unintentional possessiveness meant a lot to him. At times, he'd felt very alone. He'd finally accepted that she might never love him as he loved her, and though it hurt to acknowledge it, it had also strengthened his resolve to love her as unconditionally as he possibly could.

He slowly climbed the stairs, crept into their room, and ran the backs of his fingers across the top of her head as she slept. The second banana peel lay on the nightstand next to a pile of popsicle sticks. From the looks of it, she'd eaten every single one in the box. He sighed, kissed her cheek, and left whispering, "Love you, lass."

CHAPTER 116

The trees swayed in the breeze as the morning crawled past. Willow leaned against her favorite tree, held her fishing pole, and wished Chad was with her. She had work to do but was so distracted that she'd given up after uprooting too many undersized plants instead of weeds. Instead, she had grabbed her tackle box, fishing pole, bucket, and lunch, and took off to her favorite fishing spot.

She glanced at her cellphone. Nine forty-five. Court was in session. Willow tried to remember how to send a text message but her unsettled mind made her fumble until she gave up in disgust. Lynne Solari faced the death penalty, and Chad's testimony would likely be several nails in that coffin. She had always thought she believed in capital punishment, but the idea of putting someone to death and ending the chance for salvation was repugnant to her.

The look on Chad's face when she'd said it still hovered in her memory. *"Willow, she has had forty or fifty years of opportunities. It isn't like we killed her before she had a chance to consider her actions. We don't deserve a chance at salvation; we're given one, and most of us throw it away."* His words made sense, she understood them, but her heart constricted at the idea that man killed to avenge murder, and in the process, stripped who knew how many years of opportunities to yield.

The fish weren't biting—to her immense relief. Willow didn't really want to catch any, but at least the possibility absolved some of the guilt of a wasted day. She slid open the phone and forced herself to concentrate on how to send a message. Finally, she sent two short sentences. PRAYING FOR YOU. MISS YOU.

The sun was too far on the side of the west before she realized she'd forgotten to eat. She munched on her sandwich and stared at the cellphone. He hadn't called. Court recessed for lunch over two hours earlier, but he hadn't returned her call. She tried again but no answer. The phone said it was after four in the afternoon. He should be home in an hour or two, unless they wanted him for tomorrow and at that point, he would get a hotel room.

She stood, put away her gear, gathered her things, and trudged back toward home. Illogically, every step seemed to go nowhere, but eventually she stashed her things in the barn and put a pan of water on the stove to boil. It was early, but she just felt like getting the work done and out of the way.

Every minute that she raked, milked, fed, and watered, she prayed and felt lonelier than she'd felt since those horrible days after her mother's death. Chad had accustomed her to companionship again, and not hearing from him hurt. As she finished, she wandered with Portia out to the tree by her mother's grave and sat curled there, her phone open in the grass and waited to hear.

"He's testifying against that family, Mother. We have an advocate. Well, I know we've always had *the* Advocate, but we have a nice human one too. He's very good to us—works so hard to help make everything here run smoothly." Willow dropped her head to her knees. "He loves me, Mother. Not just cares about me like he does about his sister. Not anymore. He loves me. Sometimes I feel like I'm failing him that way, but he doesn't seem to be upset."

Cars whizzed by, Portia chased the sticks she threw, and the sun sank slowly toward the horizon. Still Willow sat, thought, prayed, and rambled to her mother about everything from the state of the garden to the progress she was making on spinning. She jumped to her feet and called Portia to her side.

"Girl, I'm being immature. I don't care if he's gone all day working and then helping someone or off to see his mom—or Todd—but he gets stuck in Rockland with that trial, and I act like it's the end of the world. I'm going to make some dinner, play that movie on the laptop, bring in the charger since I've run this battery down, and spin until I'm exhausted. There's a storm coming. It sounds cozy."

Suddenly, she felt energized. She heated soup, made a salad and another sandwich, flipped on the house electricity, and set up her movie. Eagerly she raced to the barn for the phone charger and carefully plugged it into the kitchen outlet where she could hear it. With everything ready, she clicked the play button on the laptop, sat at the spinning wheel, and began the slow steady treadle as she worked to get her rhythm.

The wool twisted into a thin cord and eventually she managed to keep it reasonably even. There was something extremely satisfying about spinning as she watched the mill workers in the old cotton mills of northern England. The first raindrops hit the windows as she finished the first bobbin.

Thunder flashed, the wind picked up and rattled the windows, but she continued to spin and watch, almost unaware of the storm raging outside. Eventually, her calf muscle protested. It took longer each time she sat at the wheel, and a call to her physical therapist had assured her that she should push it until it threatened to go from sore to painful and then stop. Pain had already arrived.

Disappointed, Willow turned up the volume on the movie, moved the spinning wheel back into the corner by the chaise, and limped back to the couch. Her muscle cream was upstairs in the bathroom, and the idea of climbing the stairs frustrated her. Perhaps she should just go to bed. There was no way she would come back down and then return to bed. She'd fall asleep on the couch and wake up stiff and cramped.

A new idea occurred to her, making Willow feel ridiculously modern and decadent. She grabbed the laptop and cord, crawled up the stairs, plugged it into the outlet behind Chad's bed table and sat it on his side of the bed. Excitedly, she brushed her teeth, re-braided her hair, and grabbed the muscle cream before crawling into bed and restarting the movie. Movies in bed. What would Mother think?

The first witness in Lynne Solari's trial was Robert Beiler of the Rockland Chronicle. Chad felt his hands tighten into fists as the man took the stand, swore to tell the truth, and took his seat. He described his meeting with Steven Solari as an awkward tension-riddled conversation where he'd been drilled for information. "I couldn't tell where I'd learned about who Miss Finley's—" he glanced in Chad's direction. "I mean Mrs. Tesdall's father was. I thought he'd see right through me, but he seemed satisfied."

"And why," the prosecutor continued, "couldn't you tell him?"

"Because Mrs. Solari told me I couldn't. She gave me the information on Willow Finley."

Robert went on to describe a meeting with Lynne Solari where the woman gave all the information necessary to write his article. "She'd discovered Willow's existence through some contact with the ME's office. Finley was a name she had flagged."

"Are you saying that Lynne Solari paid someone in the coroner's office to let her know if anyone by the name of Finley came through?"

"That's what she said. The way she said it implied that Finley was one of many names, but—"

"Objection, assuming facts not in evidence." The defense attorney rarely spoke. He hardly seemed to pay attention much less bother to object to any line of questioning.

"Can you tell us what she said exactly?"

"No," Robert began, "But almost. She said, 'I have a contact at the ME's office who lets me know when someone comes through that I am interested in. I never expected to hear Finley, but she came through in May.' It wasn't those exact words in that order but really close to them and the exact meaning."

Chad was dumbstruck. Of all the scenarios he'd run through his mind, Lynne wasn't even in the running. She'd left them with the impression that she knew nothing of Steve's payoff or Kari Finley at all. This testimony implied otherwise. He missed the final questions as his mind whirled with possibilities.

"I call Officer Chadwick Tesdall to the stand."

The first questions were simple. His name, occupation, how he met Willow, and finally when he'd met Lynne Solari. Chad felt the phone vibrate in his pocket, but he ignored it as he answered the question. "That is correct. She'd disabled her own car in order to have an excuse to come to the house."

The defense attorney in a bored tone said, "Objection, conjecture."

"Is it conjecture if she admitted it to us?" Chad used the opportunity to share the information by asking his question.

He pulled out his phone and glanced at the name on the screen. Willow. Thankful they hadn't confiscated phones, he slipped it back into his pocket and answered the next question. "She said it was because she'd seen the article in the paper."

Time passed with agonizing slowness as he answered all of the prosecutor's questions and endured a rigorous cross-examination. He sighed, relieved as he was excused. His phone vibrated again just as a crowd of reporters surrounded him, and he impatiently shoved it back into his pocket as he hurried down the courthouse steps. The last thing he wanted to do is let Willow hear the questions fired at him one after another.

Everything changed in an instant. The A.D.A. left the building seconds after Chad, sending the flock of reporters away from Chad. He reached for his cellphone to call his wife and watched it shatter as a bullet ripped through it, before tearing through his body. Fire. His hand felt as though on fire. As he fought waves of nausea from the pain, he stared at the pieces of his phone and then crumpled to the steps.

People screamed. The A.D.A. dove for cover, whipping out her cellphone to call for help, while a court officer raced to Chad's assistance. Pandemonium reigned, but Chad became unaware of his surroundings. The burning in his chest and hand made it impossible to think or concentrate. He felt sweat trickle down his face in several places and wiped it away. His hand, streaked with blood, told him that his face was cut—probably in several places.

By the time the ambulance arrived, the entire courthouse was cordoned off and police crawled everywhere. As the paramedics loaded him into the ambulance, Chad insisted on speaking to the A.D.A. but the paramedic couldn't comply. "Sorry, they've got her under protection.

Chad closed his eyes and grabbed the paramedic's arm. "Tell her…" He swallowed hard. "Tell her I said do *not* call my wife."

"Man, she's gonna—"

"Do *not* call Willow. We have a good lawyer. I'll use her."

"Mr. Tesdall?" The face above Chad's head swayed drunkenly.

"Have you been drinking, sir?" Chad's voice sounded strange to his own ears.

"No, but you've been medicated."

He struggled to sit up and then sank back against the pillows. "I was shot. I can't believe I was shot. I remember now."

"It was a through and through. Not sure how it missed your heart and arteries, but it did pierce the lungs, break a rib, and your hand took the full impact of the phone. I've never seen one like it."

As the doctor explained his injuries, Chad struggled to remember something he needed to ask. "Did anyone call my wife?"

"I knew the EMT got it wrong. He said you refused."

"I did. So no one called?"

The doctor nodded eyeing Chad curiously. "Mind telling me why you don't want her to know? You can't hide an injury like this."

"I have an unusual wife. She'd rather hear it from me. Just trust me on that. I need to speak to my parents immediately. If they see it on the news, they'll call and—"

The longer Chad spoke, the more clear his thinking became. "Man, what do you have me on?"

"Your PCA has morphine if you need a boost."

"I have to avoid it as much as possible. I need to be able

to drive tomorrow."

"Well, you're not going anywhere tomorrow. The surgeon has more work to do on that hand, and we can't risk infection or pneumonia. The EMT managed to prevent a pneum—" the doctor altered his explanation at the sight of Chad's confusion. "—um collapsed lung."

Chad wanted to ask more questions, but drowsiness overtook him. Before he could speak, he slept.

CHAPTER 117

Rain still poured down on the farm the next morning. The thunder and lightning had abated, but in their place a steady rain drummed on the roof—rain that the farms nearby needed and Willow dreaded. Work was always so messy in the rain and usually meant the need for scrubbing floors. The one job she truly hated was scrubbing floors. She'd scrub the toilet, wash walls and windows, or beat carpets but floors...

Ditto protested her stall in the barn, but Willow was unmoved despite several attempts to butt her out of the way. The chickens protested as well, but Willow opened side panels to allow fresh air and left the birds in the dry coop. Nothing was more pathetic looking to her than a drenched chicken. The sheep and cow had plenty of fresh rainwater and seemed uninterested in crossing the pasture to say hi.

A new thought occurred to her as she stepped up on the porch. She did not want to drip muddy water all over the house as she entered. She did *not* want to scrub those floors. No one was home, there was no reason not to simply drop her clothing out the back door and take it to the barn that evening. Just to be certain that no one had arrived while she wasn't looking, Willow walked around to the front of the house, nodded in satisfaction, and hurried to the back porch again.

Giggling gleefully, she raced through the house, upstairs, into her room and grabbed her most comfortable shorts and halter-top. Even with the rain, it was very warm and her favorite cool clothes sounded like the epitome of comfort. She stood for an indecent amount of time in the shower allowing the hot water to pound her muscles and then slowly turned it to cold, cooling her off again.

Before she hurried downstairs to make herself something for breakfast, Willow grabbed a wrap dress she'd made the previous summer. Now that Chad lived there, people stopped by sometimes. Not often, but how embarrassing it would be to be caught running around in clothes that covered so little. It was one thing for her to wear them for herself or even while Chad was sleeping but quite another when others were around. The dress would look lumpy but she'd be covered.

She remembered a wedding gift that Marianne had been so excited about. *"Just put your meat and vegetables in it, add a little water, turn it on low, and let it cook all day. It's perfect for hot summers in your house."*

At the back of the pantry on the top right corner shelf, she pulled down her four and a half quart crock-pot and carried it to the kitchen counter. Carefully, she slit the tape open and pulled the appliance from its protective Styrofoam blocks. An instruction manual sent her to the chaise as she read every word before trying to use it.

She stepped onto the back porch to take it to the summer kitchen and paused. The yard was full of mud she'd be drenched and filthy by the time she got back to the house. The sight of the floodlight on the barn reminded her that the electricity was on in the house. She could use it and stay indoors. Chad would be amazed to come home to a meal cooked with an appliance inside the *house*!

The clock chimed nine by the time she had her food arranged in the pot and it turned on in the corner of the counter. She glanced at the phone charger and saw her phone was fully charged again. No messages. It must have been an exhausting day. Poor Chad, he'd be worn out by the time he got home.

Willow filled a bowl with Wheaties, poured her own milk over it, and took a bite. "Now that is good," she murmured to herself and shuddered remembering the horrible taste of the milk Chad preferred over Ditto's contribution.

Mother's particularity for neatness was a blessing now. A kitchen cleaned as it is used is easy to polish when you're done using it. The house needed little work done, but Willow remembered Chad mentioning his dislike for hotel beds and decided to change the sheets and blankets for him. He'd sleep better in fresh linens and with clean blankets.

Automatically, she reached for the sheets they'd always used but paused. A set of unused and silky soft cotton sheets caught her eye. They'd been a gift from her Uncle Kyle and his family for the wedding, and she'd washed, dried, and folded them with the rest of the linens without expecting to use them for some time, but now she ran her fingers over them again. They were so buttery feeling. Perhaps—

With a happy smile on her face, she grabbed the sheets and went to strip her bed. Her mattress pad looked limp and the sight of it sent her back to the linen closet where she pulled her mother's from the top shelf. Sniffing it carefully, she nodded with satisfaction; there wasn't a trace of dust or mustiness.

Singing as she worked, Willow made the bed, adding her favorite lightweight summer blankets and her lightweight quilted coverlet. She loved the beauty of quilts, but even the lightest weight batting was often too warm in summer so she'd made one with only a layer of low thread-count muslin as a batting one year It was perfect for hot summer nights.

Scooping up the pile of laundry, she dumped the bathroom hamper into the heap and carried it all downstairs to the back porch. Portia would probably have a lovely time sleeping on her blankets, but right at that moment, Willow didn't care. She refused to go near the barn unless absolutely necessary.

The phone stood forlorn on the counter. No flashing lights announced a message. She picked it up called to leave a voicemail. "I just wanted to see how you were doing and ask you to call or send a note. Everything is good here except that you're not. Here that is. Anyway, praying for you... bye..."

He'd warned her that things were uncertain during trials. Anything could delay things, the judge could require them to turn in their cellphones and all kinds of electronic gadgets before entering the courtroom, or he could be required to stay for another day. Willow, not really expecting it to be an issue, had assured him she'd see him when he got home and not to worry about her. She'd never imagined that she'd begin to worry about him.

"You're being ridiculous. Just because the last time he didn't answer the phone was a nightmare doesn't mean it always is. Go read a book or make something."

By nine o'clock, she'd given up hope that he'd be home that night. The roast, cooked until it fell apart at the touch, was delicious and hardly touched. Sitting in the icebox and waiting to be reheated, it was a testimony to an ingenious invention, the crock-pot, and to the sadness of one person eating it alone.

The coffee table was covered with a layer of handmade note cards and a stack of matching envelopes stood waiting to be paired with a card. She carefully replaced her supplies in their basket before returning it to the craft room and snapping off the light. In her room, she pulled a silky set of shorts and camisole from her drawers and examined it. Would the fabric breathe and be cool or would it be uncomfortable? It looked cool and felt so luxurious that she decided to try it. One glance at the bed sent a wave of disappointment over her. It wouldn't be fresh anymore by tomorrow night and with the rain and her day off, she didn't have time to do extra laundry to do it all over again.

Willow wandered through the house straightening little things and feeling lost. She was tired but antsy. The cards on her table were finally dry so she stacked them and set them on the bookshelf until she felt like matching them with envelopes. Finally, she stepped outside carrying her favorite couch pillow and curled into the porch swing to watch the stars, listen to the cicadas' song, and reconnect with her Lord.

The pain intensified, seemingly with every passing

nanosecond. He stared at the little button that could help alleviate some of the misery he was in and hesitated. Which was better—keeping off the medication so he could drive sooner, or ensuring that he stayed on top of it long enough to heal enough to be able to drive in the first place. For the first time, Chad was grateful that they'd talked him out of the manual transmission. With his throbbing, bandaged hand, he would never have been able to operate a gearshift.

A nurse entered the room. "So, we're awake. Time for some pain medication?"

"I can't decide which is better—less so it's out of my system sooner or more so that I don't get overwhelmed."

"Use the PCA. You can wait until you think it'll override you, but if your body has to fight pain and fight infection, it'll take you longer to heal."

With the next level of pain, Chad pushed the button. Twice. The clock said two-thirty. In seven hours, his parents would arrive, and by then, perhaps he'd feel better. He had to get sleep to heal. The phone next to his bed taunted him. She'd answer, even at this time of night, and though Willow wouldn't worry, she would be confused.

He slowly awoke to the sounds of whispering and the feeling of losing all blood flow to his arm. "He's been sleeping since I got on shift," a masculine voice whispered. "The chart says he's checking himself out after his next surgery even if it is AMA."

"AMA?" The voice belonged to his mother.

"Against medical advice."

"Probably has something to do with why he didn't want us to call Willow, Marianne."

A few minutes later, the sound of retreating footsteps and the continued whispers of his parents jarred him back to consciousness. "Is he worried about her safety, do you think?"

Pop's voice sounded strained as he tried to reassure his mom. "It's possible. Maybe he doesn't want to lead someone out there, but I'd think it'd be less safe with her out there alone."

"She has a gun, and she did take down the last person who tried to hurt her..."

Chad fought to speak, his eyes still unwilling to open.

123

"She'll want to come in if she knows. Coming in is a sure way to stress her out. She isn't handling this trial very well. I tried to get her to come and stay at the hotel—make it fun, you know? She didn't want to have anything to do with it."

"You're awake."

"Barely," he admitted.

Marianne kissed his temple and murmured, "But when you don't call—"

"Mom, she'll just think my battery died or something. She'll wonder, but she won't really worry. I could be wrong, but I don't think so. And Dad's right, we need to keep her out of town. If that shot was a trap to lure her into town by someone who doesn't know where we live, I don't want to risk it."

Marianne's eyes widened. "Do you really think that's even possible?"

"Why aim for my heart instead of my head? I don't understand it unless he just wanted to take me out of testifying for now or if it was all bait."

"Maybe it wasn't either of those. Maybe it was a warning to others who are on the witness list."

Christopher's point was something Chad hadn't considered. "It's possible. I really don't know. I don't want her out there alone, but I think I trust her more to take care of herself out there than I trust her ability to do it in town."

"So you're going to go home tomorrow regardless of how you feel?"

"After the surgery, once the anesthesia and meds are out of my system—"

"But what about getting well!" Marianne's voice grew louder with each word.

"I'll go to the clinic in Fairbury at the first sign of anything off. They have a few overnight rooms even. I have to get home."

"You could call. Tell her the trial is taking more from you than you expected. Tell her your phone isn't working, but you'll be home tomorrow and everything will be just fine."

"I'm not going to lie, Mom."

"Chad," Marianne protested quickly, "I didn't mean for you to lie. All of that is true—it's just ambiguous enough to

124

keep her from worrying and to keep you in this bed."

"Your mother has a point. Resting that lung—" The doctor stopped himself abruptly as Chad struggled to sit upright.

"If I called, I'd tell her everything. But if you called…"

"What do you want me to say?"

As she fed the chickens, the distinct sound of the French horns in Tchaikovsky's 1812 Overture erupted from her jeans. "What!" She fished the phone from her pocket and flipped it open at the sight of Marianne's name. "Oh Mom, my phone is playing music! I almost had a heart attack."

"What is it playing?"

"The 1812 Overture—the part with the French horns? You know, da de da de da de da—da da."

"Chad must have done it. Um, speaking of Chad, he asked me to call you."

Willow's voice grew wary. "About what? Why didn't *he* call?"

"Well, his phone is broken for one thing. He needs to get a new one. Anyway, he asked me to tell you that he's been detained here in town for a few more days."

"Why?"

Marianne continued as though Willow hadn't spoken. "— and he probably won't be able to call. If he does, it'll be very late at night."

"Mom, what's going on? Is there trouble with the trial?"

"Willow," Marianne said as though dreading the coming discussion, "that's all he told me to tell you except that he wants you to trust him. He'll explain everything when he gets home."

The protest that formed died on her lips as Marianne said "trust." "Can you tell me if he's ok?"

"He's ok—now. He'll be home as soon as he can."

"Should I be praying?" Willow whispered nervously.

Marianne's cheerful voice wiped away the final traces of concern from Willow's voice as she assured Willow that prayer never hurts. Willow stared at the phone for several seconds after her mother-in-law disconnected and wondered just how long it'd be before he came home. She'd heard of sequestered juries—did they sequester witnesses too?

Thursday afternoon, a detective arrived to take his statement regarding the shooting. "Officer Tesdall?"

Chad turned and glanced up at the detective expectantly. "Yes?"

"I'm detective Haunsel with the Rockland PD. I have some questions if you're up to it."

"I now understand, in a way I never could before, why victims and witnesses are so unreliable. I didn't see it coming. I can only imagine that you found through the trajectory where the sniper was..."

"We found it. We found the guy on video..." The detective pulled out glossy eight by ten print outs of the building across the street, the fourth floor, and almost a full shot of a man's face. "Do any of these look familiar to you?"

Carefully, Chad examined each one clearly. Finally, he shoved them across his legs. "I don't trust my memory on this. He looks familiar, but I could have seen him or someone that resembles him, anywhere." A thought occurred to him. "Have you checked cameras from inside the courthouse? Was he in the courtroom?"

"They're still going over those tapes. Can you tell us why he chose you?"

"I can only assume that it has something to do with my testimony... maybe he thought I was coming back after the recess but I wasn't. I was excused."

Detective Haunsel nodded thoughtfully. "What does the doctor say?"

"Gonna have to learn to shoot with my other hand. Even if they get this thing fully functional," Chad waved his bandaged hand impatiently, "they say the muscles won't be completely reliable. It'll always be a little stiff."

"Ouch. Tough luck... at least you live in Fairbury. You probably haven't drawn your gun since you've worked there."

Chad hated the implication that work in Fairbury wasn't

126

real. "I want to know that the next time a stalker breaks into my house to terrorize my wife, I'll be able to pull the trigger before he does." The man's face showed surprise and he started to speak, but Chad continued. "Sorry if that ruins your Mayberry ideal of Fairbury, but between the Plagiarist Killer and the Solari influence, we've had more crime in Fairbury in the past few years than the town has had in the past fifty. Rockland is encroaching, and I want to be able to do my part to push it back. We don't want your crime."

Marianne watched as they wheeled her son into surgery and wondered just how successful it would be. Christopher jogged up to her side. "Sorry I'm late. What's going on?"

"They just wheeled him in. The surgeon talked to me while they were taking him in. He's confident it'll be successful, but the degree of success is what is in question."

Christopher sank into a nearby chair. "My son—all he ever wanted to do was be a cop and now—"

Chad's mother wrapped her arms around her husband and hushed him. "He'll shoot with his other hand. He'll be fine."

"I think it just hit me. My son was shot. A man took careful aim and shot him, and if Chad hadn't moved at just the right moment, he probably would be dead."

"So how long until everything is out of my system? How soon before I am chemically safe to drive?"

Saturday morning, Chad bombarded the doctor with questions as he inspected Chad's sutures, chart, and checked the wound in Chad's chest. He'd fought the use of the PCA as much as possible, but the throbbing had kept him awake most of the night until he'd given in and allowed himself a few hours of pain relief. His goal was to leave that night.

"You're determined to leave tonight then?"

Chad nodded. "I have to get home. I know I'll have to

sign, but I need to get home."

The doctor called the nurse to rewrap Chad's hand and said goodbye. "I'll leave care instructions with the nurses. Try to stay as long as possible. The longer you're here, the more likely a problem happens here than at home." He hesitated. "Will you promise me one thing?"

"What?"

"If you relapse at all before you leave, will you please reconsider and stay another night?"

Chad nodded. "I'm not trying to get myself killed—" he winked at his mother. "Contrary to popular belief."

With the doctor gone, Chad tried to apologize for worrying his mother, but he didn't get far. "I understand, Chaddie. I do. I want to help, but I couldn't live with myself if—"

"It's ok, Mom. Really. Can you do something for me though?" He knew the only way his mother would quit worrying was if she had a way to help him.

"I'd need clothes whether I left right now or next week. Can you bring me sweats and a buttoned down shirt?"

"That's kind of a strange combination, son."

Chad grinned. "I'm a fashion mystery." At her disgusted look, he sighed. "Ok, so maybe I just want something easy to get on and off again."

At five o'clock, Todd arrived with a bag of clothes from Chad's mother. "Hey, man, how are you feeling?"

"Miserable but I'll do."

"You sure you want to leave?"

Groaning, Chad made a slicing motion across his neck. "Not you too..."

"I had to ask! Your mom wouldn't give me these clothes until I promised to follow you home. I won't come up to the house or anything, but I will follow you as far as the drive."

"Thanks. I thought about asking but decided I was being paranoid. Everyone around here seems to be operating under the delusion that I *want* to leave." Chad's voice sounded weary.

128

"Did you take some acetaminophen at four?"

"Four-thirty. I'll pull over at the rest stop for a refill or just take them a bit early."

Todd nodded and pulled out the latest Patterson novel. "I'll read. You sleep."

"What, no Hartfield? I'm crushed."

"I've read 'em all."

Chad grinned and tried to roll onto his side. "Seven-thirty. No later."

Todd acted as a guard for the next two and a half hours. The nurses came in now and then to check on him, offer him medication, and bring him dinner, but Todd shooed them back out, insisting that they would be responsible for Chad's relapse if they didn't let him sleep. The doctor arrived just as Todd shook Chad awake.

"It's time to get up, man. Gotta get on the road."

He tried to respond, but the doctor interrupted. "Still determined to leave?"

"Have to. I'm sorry."

"Let's check your temperature." Ignoring the nurse who stood ready to do her job, the doctor checked all vital signs, inspected Chad's wounds, and helped Chad out of bed, watching him walk around the room. "Well, I'd be more comfortable with another night or three, but as long as you keep a close eye on the wounds and your temperature, unofficially speaking, you should be good. I can't release you though. Liability and all."

"I understand. Give me the forms or whatever, and let's get this show on the road."

It took Chad longer to dress to leave the hospital than he'd ever spent getting ready for anything. As much as he despised flip-flops, he was grateful that his mother had considered the easiest thing to put on his feet and sent them. Todd drove Chad to his truck and drove from the city, each keeping an eye out for anyone who might be following.

The temptation to speed had rarely been stronger. By the time he was out of the city and onto the highway, Chad was ready to lie back down and go to sleep. As he passed the rest stop, Chad struggled to open the packet of Tylenol and failed. He pulled over, wrenched it open wincing at the sharp pain it send through his chest, coughed, and downed the pills before Todd could reach his side.

"You ok, man?" Todd had his door open before he could nod.

"I'm fine! I just couldn't get the packet open without pulling over."

"Well, if you hadn't had your phone shot into you, you could have called."

Chad groaned. "Oh man, I'm going to need a new phone."

"I'll take care of it. Just get me your info and I'll go in. I'll come out on Monday with it. You can't leave the house again before then anyway."

By the time they entered Fairbury, Chad shook with exhaustion. Each mile from Fairbury to home seemed like ten. He flashed his lights at Todd just before he turned into the driveway and then let the truck coast down the first part of the drive until it reached the climb up into the yard.

Late Sunday night, Willow once more sat on her porch swing wearing another camisole set and feeling cool and refreshed. Her hair was wet as she brushed the tangles from it and braided it into her familiar braid. One bare foot pushed the swing back and forth, as she swayed in the night air. Portia lay with her head resting on Willow's belly, and Willow scratched behind her ears, singing her favorite Argosy Junction songs softly.

The past few days had been strange. Despite years of living alone, she had become accustomed to having Chad stop by, calling, having half the small chores done before she got up in the morning and leaving her free to do other things. Without him, it felt lonely—empty. She missed his arm around her as she slept and hearing his heart beat when they curled on the couch together. She missed hearing about Aiden Cox's latest prank or a strange serenade from one of the transports to Brunswick.

More than anything, however, she missed hearing him praise her. The giant tomato in her greenhouse was gone now—taken away by Jill. Chad would never hold it and tell her how amazing it was. She had yarn ready to dye, but she'd waited for him to bring the Kool-Aid that her instructions called for. She needed to hear that what she was doing was appreciated.

Just as she stood to go upstairs and try to sleep, headlights turned into the driveway from the highway. She walked slowly to the first step and wrapped an arm around the porch post straining to see into the night. The headlights were gone now. In a few seconds, they'd flash over the top of the hill just before they illuminated the house and yard.

It was Chad's truck. He was home. Everything would be back to normal now. Willow smiled as she skipped down the steps to greet him as he shut the truck door behind him.

CHAPTER 118

As Chad climbed gingerly from his truck, Willow skipped down the steps, forgetful of the camisole and shorts that, while cool and comfortable, covered little. He watched her hurry toward him and laughed as she raced to hug him. When she realized how little she wore, she'd be mortified.

Unexpectedly, she flung herself into his arms kissing his cheek. "I missed you! I can't believe how much I missed you. I mope—" His sharp intake of breath and the way he clung to her stopped her mid-sentence. "What's wrong?"

"Just help me inside, lass. I've got quite a story to tell you, but I need some water and my head feels fuzzy."

"Chad! You're really—" His wince as she wrapped her arm around his back stopped her. "Is there anywhere I *can* touch you?" The moon moved from behind a cloud, lighting Chad's face. "What happened to you? Your mother just said that you'd been detained."

"That's all I let her say. Get me inside and ignore my pain will ya."

Willow brought him pillows, a glass of water, and remembering how much he liked Sprite when he was sick, she hurried out to the summer kitchen where she'd stashed a few cans the last time she'd been at the store. He laughed as she brought him a glass of icy cold Sprite, groaning at the pain that laughter caused.

"I knew I'd be better off at home. In the truck, there's a plastic bag on the floorboard. I need the bottle in it please." In

Willow's eyes, he looked horrible as he clenched his hand tightly around the end of a pillow as though holding on with everything he had.

Willow found the bag and a stack of discharge papers that looked similar to the ones she'd brought home from the hospital the previous summer. With both in hand, she hurried inside opening the bottle of painkillers as she did. She read the instructions carefully and then handed him one tablet. "It says take with water."

He swallowed his pill and dutifully drank the water she shoved at him before sinking back into the pillows, exhausted. "I really didn't think it'd be that hard to drive home. The traffic wasn't anything to speak of; the highway was reasonably empty. I don't know why I'm so beat."

Willow bit her lip. She wanted to demand that he tell her what happened and why his face held several stitches, one close to the corner of his eye. However, the memory of his wince as she'd hugged him, the pain etched in his face, and the bandaged hand tinged with fresh blood near the thumb stopped her. She'd have to learn a little patience.

"Where are the questions, lass? I've been waiting for you to pounce."

"I thought you might like to rest. You'll tell me when you're ready. I don't want to be a pest or worse, that dripping wife of Proverbs."

He found her hand with his good one, squeezing it gently and then reaching carefully to pull her closer to him. "Aw, Willow, but that's what I love about you. Yes, you drive me crazy sometimes, but I love that you're just you. What you see is what you get. There's no guessing if you're seething inside or miserable, because you let it all out, and I like that."

"Even when I get stubborn and refuse to do things everyone else's way just because it's everyone else's way? I seem to remember school being an issue, wedding choices being problems, and—"

"Even then. It's what makes you, you. You could be less obstinate about things perhaps, I won't complain about that, but I'd miss your input if you quit giving it—or demanding it." He winked at her over the top of her head.

"So," Willow began now unable to contain her curiosity

134

any longer. "Just what happened?"

"Well, first of all, I know who told that reporter about Steve Solari."

"Robert Beiler? Who?"

Chad nodded, toying with Willow's braid as he talked and moaning that he wished the horrible throbbing in his hand would go away. "Lynne Solari herself. Robert mentioned something about an ME with the coroner's office who kept an eye out for certain names, and your mom's was one. So, they did some digging, found that ME, and from what we can put together, Lynne knew about the rape before Steve. She either didn't tell Steve Jr. what she knew, or they made the plan together for him to go to his father and 'hide' it from Lynne." He hesitated, searching her eyes for something before he added, "There is an evidence trail that inches in the direction of Lynne being the one to order the hit on Steve Jr."

"She killed her own son?"

"Not right away of course, but when he just got worse and worse, suddenly he dies in a knife fight when Steve Jr. had never owned any kind of weapon. He liked his fists."

Willow swallowed hard, pain filling her until she pursed her lips, trying not to let them tremble. "He certainly used them on Mother."

"I thought I read about bruising so I assumed..."

"I saw the pictures she took of herself. They're horrible."

Chad stared at her, shock masking the pain that had covered his face. "I didn't know about the pictures."

"I saw them once as a child. They're in the attic in a box of papers in a sealed envelope. I was looking for some kind of picture of grandparents or aunts and uncles—I wanted to know more, and Mother had no more to share, so I spent an afternoon when she was in town going through all of the boxes I could find."

"What did you find?"

Sadness wove through her voice, choking her. "Those pictures. Once I found them, I put them away and quit looking. If that was the kind of thing I was going to find, I didn't want to know. I understood why she'd chosen our life, and I think that was the day I fully embraced it for myself." She took a deep breath exhaling slowly. "I'd always loved

135

living here, but seeing that made me reject the outside world much as Mother already had."

"But you didn't. You asked us to come back and on that very first day. How—"

Her hand crept up by her neck where he toyed with her braid and curled it around his fingers. "I don't really know. I just saw you three going out the door and felt so terribly alone. You were all so nice to me. It seemed like maybe the police were safe." A sob caught in her throat. "In just those brief few seconds, I imagined day after day without hearing another person's voice, without ever getting a hug or laughing with someone, and I panicked."

"Aw, lass. Make a guy feel guilty why don't you. When I think how I resented you..."

The pain of those days threatened to strangle her further. Desperate to avoid it, she changed the subject. "Well, to be a deliberate pest then, what happened to you? I'm trying to be patient, but if you could see yourself—"

"I have. I look like Frankenstein." He tried to remember the days that blurred together in his mind. "Wednesday at around two o'clock they let me out. You rang just as I left the building. When I got away from reporters, I pulled out my phone, and just at that instant, a bullet came from across the street, went through the phone, and then through me."

"So you fell and scraped yourself up?" Her face was turned to Chad's looking at the scratches and stitches that made him look like he'd been attacked by a weed-whacker.

"No, the phone did that. Shattered on impact and forced pieces of plastic flying into my hand, my face, my neck..."

She glanced at his hand concern etched in her features. "How bad is your hand?"

"I'll be learning to shoot with my left hand, most likely. I've got at least one or two more surgeries on it coming."

"Why did they let you come home if they have to do more work?"

Chad had the grace to blush. "Actually, they didn't. I checked myself out AMA."

"AMA?"

"Against medical advice. I needed to get home." He felt her stiffen.

"Wait—they didn't want you to leave?"

"No. I've got instructions for getting to a hospital and when. I'll be fine, but I just really needed to see you and make sure you knew I was ok."

She struggled from his grasp and climbed the stairs without any kind of response. In the bathroom, she washed and dried her face, all the while praying for a balance between her desire to blast him and respect for his right to make his own decisions. She needed to hurry back down and have the right thing to say… she looked at herself in the mirror and groaned. She'd go back down *after* she found something to cover herself with.

Chad laughed as she came back down the stairs wearing a summer robe, trying not to look as thoroughly embarrassed as she was. "I wondered how long it'd take you to figure it out."

She started to take a seat on the other couch so he could stretch out but he motioned her back to him. "Come on, I've been gone forever." Once she curled against him again, he whispered, "And you didn't need to put that on. You looked just fine—"

"I bet I did. I'll put it back on next time I walk to town."

"Over my dead body."

The conversation switched subjects with that line. "That's what I'm afraid of."

"I had to get back to you. I didn't want you to worry."

"And you think I'm not going to worry about you as you lay here when you need medical attention that I can't give you? What happens if something goes wrong? I don't know how to drive. It's a fifteen minute round trip—minimum, if I call an ambulance, and who knows if the clinic can help you, or if you'll need a rush trip to Rockland. I can't believe you did this to me!"

A weak but definite edge of anger entered Chad's tone. "To you? I did this *for* you. I imagined you here—"

Frustrated, she jumped up and spun to face him. "You want to do something for me? Fine. Get back to the hospital until they think it's safe for you to leave." Tears filled her eyes. "I cannot lose you. I'm not ready for that. I can't believe you'd do that to me."

137

"Willow—"

"This is horrible. You came home and I was so excited to see you. My stomach got all floppy on me, and I felt so happy and now I'm just sick. You're going to get yourself killed. You're going to let *her* win!"

"Willow," Chad began again. "If I went back, you'd have to stay here. You can't go near Rockland until the trial is over."

This was it. She needed to make her point and then drop it but her natural desire for her own way made her fight for the exact words that would make him listen to her and return to the hospital. "Chad, you said you wanted me to tell you what I think so here's what I think. I think that for someone who has harped on how selfish I am about stuff, you've topped it all. I stayed in that hospital, against my own preference, I went to those stupid physical therapy sessions because you insisted they were best for me. I think it's time you listen to your own advice and get back where you kept me and for a much less serious injury."

"Um, lass?" Chad's voice sounded weak and confused.

"What?" She instantly regretted the snap in her response.

"Can you call Todd and get him to come back? I think you're right, and I'd almost kill for more morphine right now."

"Under one condition."

"Anything."

She retrieved her phone before replying, "You call me this time?"

"I'll call. I didn't want you to hear the pages for doctors..." It was as though knowing he was returning took all of his remaining strength.

Willow punched the numbers he gave her and waited for Todd to answer. "Hey, this is Willow. I have a husband who is ready to return to the hospital."

"I thought you would. I'm parked at the end of the driveway. I'll be right there." The laughter in Todd's voice made her smile as she snapped the phone shut.

"He's coming up the drive as we speak."

Chad grinned wanly. "Come here then..."

CHAPTER 119

Marianne called out for Willow as she roamed through the house. As she neared the kitchen, she heard Willow call out, "I'm back here, Mom!"

She found her daughter-in-law hanging clothes on the line, snapping each item from the basket briskly with a practiced flick of the wrist, before another clothespin appeared from the apron around her waist and attached it to the line. At the sight of a row of cloth pads, she winced inwardly. Willow had a beautiful life on her little farm, but that sight killed the romance of it for Marianne. Some things were just too earthy for people like her to handle.

"I brought today's headline. I thought you'd want to see it for yourself."

Willow reached for the paper and carried it to the back step. "Sniper Caught," she read aloud to herself. "'On Tuesday afternoon after a state-wide manhunt, the sniper who gunned down a Fairbury police officer on the courthouse steps last Wednesday was apprehended as he tried to leave the country out of O'Hare Airport in Chicago. Authorities credit having a picture at every terminal in every airport in the tri-state area with the success of catching thirty-nine year old Terrance Malcomb. 'His passport was flawless,' said airport security chief, Dean Tomlin. 'If we hadn't had that picture, he'd be out of reach by now.' Mr. Malcomb is being transported to Rockland to answer charges of the attempted murder of Chadwick Tesdall of the Fairbury police who testified against his wife's grandmother, Lynne Solari, just minutes before he was shot. A plea bargain is expected.'"

She looked up at her mother-in-law. "What does it all mean? I've never understood plea bargains."

"He'll get a lesser sentence for shooting Chad by testifying against Lynne Solari. With his testimony—especially if she's the one who paid him to do it, there's no way they won't find her guilty."

"So basically, he gets fewer spankings if he tattles."

"Well," Marianne conceded laughing, "that's one way to put it."

"Why can't they just make him talk like they said they would me? Why—"

"The fifth amendment doesn't allow it. Besides, he's going to jail anyway. The only incentive they can give him is less time so they do it to ensure that they get the person behind it all." Even as she spoke, Marianne knew it was fruitless. There was no way that Willow would understand the idea of a reduced sentence for cooperation. Right was right, wrong was wrong, and there was no gray area.

"But this is good, right? I mean, no one is trying to kill him or me or any of us anymore?"

"As far as we know."

Willow squealed, hugged Marianne, and raced inside calling, "I've got to call Chad. Maybe I can come in to see him now."

Marianne shook her head and reached for another shirt in the basket. She shook it out, attached it to the line, and reached for another. It was a satisfying feeling. The breeze flapped half-dry things around her as she worked, and by the time Willow raced outside carrying her purse and calling someone on her phone, Marianne had finished the job. It felt good. It felt very good.

"Mom, can you take me to him? Chad says I can come. They're going to let him leave tomorrow anyway, so I'm staying overnight if I can get Ryder to take care of things."

"Get your helper out here. I'll go pack you a bag. You'll need more than a purse to stay overnight, silly."

Two hours later, Willow asked for directions to Chad's room. The nurse at the station eyed her cautiously and then nodded. "You must be Willow. He's in room 204. I cannot tell you how glad we are that you're here."

"Why?"

"Because your husband is driving us all nuts. He's just cranky enough to make us want to kill him and charming enough to make it impossible. How do you live with that man?"

She shrugged, asked for help in finding 204 again, and this time, the nurse understood her and pointed to the correct corridor. "On the right. Two doors down."

The curtain was drawn around Chad's bed, and some woman on TV interviewed a college student caught writing papers for half the campus at an Oregon university. "Chad?"

"Oh you're finally here. I thought Mom must have decided to push the car here."

"The nurse was right."

"How's that?"

Willow's grin was wicked. "You are grumpy."

"I've hardly seen you for a whole week. What do you expect?"

Willow's eyes filled with tears of relief. "It's so good to see you. It's been—" she hesitated. "Lonely."

"Aw, lass, I missed you too. We'll be home tomorrow. It's going to be back to normal." Chad's eyes drooped sleepily. "I think they've got me on some kind of sleeping meds. I keep falling asleep."

"Rest, Chad. I'll go find something to eat. I skipped lunch getting ready to come here." She didn't want to go. The idea of leaving him just as she got there bothered her, but he obviously needed sleep.

"Just don't stay away too long. You smell like home. I want to go home."

Outside the door, Willow leaned against the wall and took a deep breath. Chad looked terrible. His normally tan skin tone looked jaundiced and pale. The strength in his voice was gone, and she could see the pain in his eyes. It was time to get him home where there was fresh air, good food, and uninterrupted sleep. Willow remembered how little she'd slept during her hospital stay.

"Mrs. Tesdall? Willow?"

She forced her eyelids upward and met the kindest eyes she'd ever seen. "Yes?"

"I'm Dr. Shaiver. I'm very glad to see you here. We tried to get Chad to let you come, but he didn't think it was wise."

"I think he's crazy. My grandmother isn't out to kill me. I'm not a threat, but Chad sees it differently."

"Well, having you here will probably help his recovery immensely. He's been quite down." The doctor's smile was as sympathetic as his eyes were kind.

"Well, I think once I get him home tomorrow, he'll do better."

"I'm afraid not." Regret filled Dr. Shaiver's voice. "I just got the x-rays back. His lungs are trying to fill with fluid and his hand has a displaced bone. We're not sure how that happened, but it has to be corrected."

Something in the doctor's tone bothered Willow. "Can you tell me if I should be concerned about him? Is he going to be all right?"

"He's not doing as well as I hoped for. I want to blame it on his checking himself out early, but I think that just set him back a bit. I don't think it actually caused him any further injury." He rested his hand on her arm comfortingly. "I truly think it would be best if you could stay. His concern for you and how much he misses you is impeding his progress."

"Then I'll stay."

Dr. Shaiver turned to answer a page and then did an abrupt about face. "That man sure loves you."

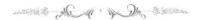

Willow spent the next hour arranging for Ryder and Caleb to take over the farm while she was gone. Todd Blankenship agreed to stay there to keep Portia company, learn how to do things to help out the boys, as well as shuttle Willow back and forth every couple of days. By the time Chad awoke, she had it all arranged.

"So, he wakes."

"Oh, thought I'd dreamed it. I'm so glad you're here."

The doctor's last words filled her mind once more. An unfamiliar warmth flooded her heart. Sitting beside his bed, she remembered the hours he'd sat with her in the same hospital. The work he'd done on his few free hours in order to save her crops, and the way he'd come back, against her wishes, proving himself a friend to someone who had pushed him away—it choked her. It was both amazing and terrifying, and the pressure in her chest felt wonderfully smothering. It made no sense. She couldn't breathe but was so happy; she truly didn't care. Chad loved her.

Tears spilled from her eyes as emotion overflowed and spilled onto her cheeks. An overwhelming sense of love and affection welled inside her as she realized that he'd loved her long before he knew or admitted it to himself. Willow brushed away silly tears as the realization struck her that she too loved her husband just as any husband should be loved by the one whom they promise to cherish for the rest of their lives.

"I'm in love," she whispered. "Wow."

Chad stirred. A weight on his uninjured hand felt odd, and he started to struggle but the weight moved. One eye crept open and then a smile broke over his face. The bed rail was down, a stool pushed up next to the bed, and Willow half laid over him holding his hand in both of hers as she slept.

Clumsily, he stroked her hair with his bandaged hand. He slowly shifted to lie on his "good" side and watched her face as she slept. The stirring of her hair gave him occasional whiffs of lavender making him want home more than ever. The past week had been packed with surgeries, nurses' interruptions, a constant flow of visitors, and he was exhausted from all of it. All he wanted was to go home, curl up in his own bed, and sleep for a month.

Willow looked so young to him. How was it that someone so confident, so wise, could look like a child when she slept? Every second that passed felt like a pound lifted from him just having her there. Nothing would help him more than having Willow looking out for him.

143

"Hey," he whispered as the one eye he could see opened. "I fell asleep on you. I'm sorry."

"You needed your rest." Emotion welled in her eyes, crumpling her features until tears flowed again—again. Had she cried when she arrived? He couldn't remember it, but why had he thought—again?

"Hey, hey, shhh... what's wrong?"

Willow tried to fight back the tears but every attempt was swallowed by a fresh burst of weeping. Her shoulders shook and deep wracking sobs erupted, sending Chad into a confused panic; his attempts to soothe her only made it worse. "I'm sorry— I don't know—"

"Shhh... it's ok. It's going to be fine," she choked.

"I missed you—" but a fresh round of weeping cut off her words.

Not knowing what else to say, Chad soothed her and whispered, "Just cry it out. You'll feel better. I'm so sorry—"

"No, I'm not sad!" The sobs made her words sound ludicrous, and she snorted a chuckle before collapsing once more. Tears soaked the bed, his hand, and her arm, until Chad reached for a Kleenex and stuffed it under the mound of hair that now hid her face from him.

"Aw, what is it?"

Several minutes passed. A nurse passing by stepped in to see what was wrong, but Chad sent her out without a word. Still, the torrent of tears continued unabated until she finally sobbed out whatever had hurt her so deeply.

Finally, she held her hand out for a fresh wad of Kleenex and raised her head. "I'm sorry. How silly of me."

"Are you ok?" Chad's hand cupped her face tenderly and tried to read some reason for her meltdown in her expression.

"I was just so happy to see you again. I missed you more than I realized." She kissed his hand absently as she spoke. She blushed.

"I don't understand—"

"I'm beginning to—finally," she whispered, almost as if more to herself than him.

"Care to share?"

Willow smiled into Chad's eyes, kissed him, and then whispered, "I love you."

144

CHAPTER 120

Fabrics lay all over the rolling table by Chad's bed. As he slept, she sketched, but nothing appealed to her. Idea after idea crossed off the list before she tried again. The nurse stepped in and peeked over her shoulder. "What's wrong with those? They're cute."

"They look like—" How did you tell someone that what they just called "cute" was ugly? "I just think they look like I put a bunch of interesting elements together rather than designed a nice outfit."

The woman, Jade, nodded. "Ok, I can see your point. I mean, I still think they're cute, but if you have to create several looks, then you're right. It won't work—no cohesion."

"Thank you! That's the word I was looking for."

Jade pointed at Chad. "How many times has he been up walking this afternoon?"

"Twice. I couldn't get him up the last time. After this surgery, his hand seems worse than ever."

"Good. Maybe they got it then." Jade pointed to the scar across Chad's cheek. "You really should let them do something about that while they can."

She shook her head. "No. Chad wants to leave. If he doesn't mind the scar, I sure don't." Willow smiled to herself. "I think it's kind of attractive—makes him look almost dangerous in a—way."

"Sexy is the word, I believe. Yeah, he pulls it off."

Irritation crept into her heart, and it took great self-control not to tell the woman to keep her eyes off Chad if that's how she was going to think of him. "I think so."

Jade recorded whatever she needed to and turned to leave. "He needs to walk more when he wakes up. He should be out of here by now."

"That's what we keep telling the doctor."

"Well, if he'd quit getting these infections..."

Willow sighed. Surgery, pneumonia, infection—it all hit Chad one after another. He'd been in the hospital for three weeks—three. She just wanted him home. Before she could think of some way to respond without antagonizing a woman who did try to help, Jade pointed to her sketchbook.

"Hey, maybe you need a theme. You know, retro-fifties or Woodstock, or something international like Nordic or something."

"Theme..." Willow stared at the page, trying to imagine what she could do with themes. "Ok... hmm... thanks."

Her pencil scratched over the page. She crossed out even more outfits than ever, but she could feel it—success loomed. Second after second passed, new ideas flowing and failing faster with each one until she thought she'd go crazy. The Nordic idea was too wintery for a spring line, so she'd tried Swiss, German, Irish—and then snickered when she realized that everything she tried had a lederhosen feel to it. All wrong for spring in Rockland.

What made Boho Chic such a popular store? As she thought about it, she realized that she had been working backwards. The fabric should dictate some of the design anyway. Setting her sketchpad aside, she rearranged pieces until she liked the combinations. The solids and prints that would match everything she set aside. Those would do for separates to go with the others. Spring and summer. One fabric seemed to beg for a dressy ensemble. She chose a dress for that one and held it, allowing the fabric to drape, hang—ripple as she waved it in the air. The sketch took little time at all. When Jade stepped back into the room with a new IV bag, she nodded approvingly. "If that goes with that fabric, it's perfect. I want one for my niece. Where do I buy one?"

"Boho Deux—next spring. I'm almost caught up—once I get done with these."

"You're *that* Willow? I saw the article about you!"

"I'm going to design them all around this one. It's almost a thirties influence, don't you think? Clean lines, little feminine touches, but not fussy. With those fabrics..."

"Like I said. I want that one for sure."

It took her an hour to sketch out two skirts, another dress, and a semi-skort that had a fun twist she wanted to try for herself. She sketched a couple of simple tops with small details to separate them from generic clothes from a department store and surveyed the line. It needed two or three more bottoms and another dress. Willow smiled. She could start drawing patterns if Todd would bring her basket and roll of interfacing. A glance at Chad, still sleeping, was all the encouragement she needed.

As she stepped out of the room, Jade's head snapped up. "Is everything ok?"

"Great. I just need to make a call—didn't want to wake him up."

Taillights blinked in the afternoon sun as Christopher and Marianne drove away from the farm, back to Westbury. Willow watched, Portia's tail thumping rhythmically against her leg, until the occasional blink of the brakes disappeared over the hill at the curve. A new appreciation for the amazing institution of family welled in her heart. She would never have imagined how difficult it would be to get Chad into the house and up the stairs. Her eyes swept the landscape as a lump swelled in her throat. In two weeks, home had somehow become dearer to her than ever.

She pulled out her phone and called the boys, assuring them that she had everything covered. She wanted nothing more than to feed chickens, milk goats—ok, goat—and check the garden. Weeds, tomato worms, zucchini. She strolled toward the back of the house and stared down at her shoes and skirt. Change first, work later.

Chad's light snore encouraged her as Willow crept into their room. He hadn't snored once at the hospital. In fact, he hadn't stirred since they'd dragged him up the stairs and settled him in bed. She grabbed shorts, blouse, and socks.

The garden looked amazing. She wandered through the rows, admiring Ryder's work. Weeds—there were none. Tomato worms—not a single one. Almost a year since her own injury kept her from working—how had she forgotten the gratitude she felt for all Chad's help?

Chickens, however—chickens needed food. She scattered the scratch across the yard, delighting in the squawks and clucks—the percussion of the soundtrack of her childhood. "Dinner, the cow wonder," lowed as she dumped the trough and refilled it with fresh—just because she could. Sheep bleated, but Ditto sang the final song.

Milk filled the refrigerator—soap time. After two weeks of nothing but hospital rooms, bland food, and contaminated, recirculated stale air, home and all the work it entailed never felt better. She reached for a basket, but her cellphone rang—a new song blasting from her pocket with a man singing how he just wanted to go home. Had to be Chad.

"Hey... you're supposed to be sleeping."

"I know. I just woke up, and I'm starving."

"You need good food." She snatched the basket and ran for the greenhouse, Portia loping beside her.. "I'll make a salad for you to munch on while I find something to fix."

"Sandwich is fine."

"No bread. I'll bake some just as soon as I get you some food. Hey, what about breakfast? Eggs, pancakes, sausage, hash browns? I could do biscuits and gravy too."

"Do that and skip the salad—but don't do it all. I can't eat all that."

A lump filled her throat. It was true. He couldn't. "My job is to get you back to where you can. I'll be up in a few."

She dropped the lettuce she'd picked into the basket and hurried back to the summer kitchen, telling Portia all about the great dinner she had planned. "He won't eat enough—not now. You'll have a good dinner tonight, girl."

Sausage patties sizzled on the stove, defrosting as they cooked, while Willow went to get eggs, tomatoes, onions, and a bell pepper. In the house, she mixed biscuits and set them on the cookie sheet before carrying them out to the summer kitchen—no need to heat up the house while Chad was trying to rest. Was it hot up there now? Maybe he would like a fan. She'd ask.

Portia nearly went crazy as she carried two plates from the kitchen, across the yard, and into the house. She took the stairs two at a time, the forks rattling against the plate, and opened the door to their room, feeling very much like a waitress with one in the crook of her arm and one in hand. "Breakfast for two?"

"That is the first food that has smelled good in so long—so long." He winked at her. "I could even drink Ditto milk."

"Good, because it's that or water. Don't have anything else—wait. I do have Sprite..."

"Gross."

She stared at him. Setting down the plates, her hand reached for his forehead, but it felt fine. Chad laughed and pulled her close. "I'm not delirious, lass. I just don't like the idea of Sprite with eggs."

Her nose wrinkled. "Smart man." He kissed her, lingering longer than either had allowed themselves in the hospital. "Scruffy one too," she whispered.

"I'll shave the minute I get a full night's sleep. Even if I have to get you to bring my cordless here and do it from bed."

"You'll be fine. You have to stand and walk. Doctor's orders. You are not going back to that hospital." She thrust the plate into his hands. "You had us worried, Chad. You were there over two weeks longer than necessary." Overcome with repressed emotion, she choked and kissed his forehead before adding, "Now eat."

"Yes'm."

"Now he learns respect."

One third of his omelet, one biscuit sopped in gravy, one-half of a sausage link, and three gulps of milk with hardly a wince. She considered it good. Chad apologized. "Wasted your time and that good food—"

"Portia appreciates it."

Perspiration on his upper lip answered the question of over-warmth. She set her plate on the end of the bed, grabbed his, and carried it downstairs. The breaker was already on, so she hurried back upstairs and plugged in the fan, moving it to the foot of the bed where it would blow directly on him. "That better?"

"How'd you know?"

"A wife does not reveal her secrets."

"Mom has been reading those marriage books again."

"How did you know?"

"That sounded like some psychobabble thing—not like my lass."

Willow laughed. "She kept sharing her 'nuggets' with me. You wouldn't believe some of the things in them. One of them said that if a woman wants her husband to feel respected, she should find something to admire in everything he says or does—no matter how ridiculous."

"Well, he might feel his ego stroked, but how is that respect?"

"Exactly! I told your mom that the author's advice would damage a good marriage and destroy a bad one. She didn't get it until Dad said, 'She's right. Most men are smart enough to know when they're being patronized. It's an insult.'"

"I can't believe Mom bought that garbage."

"I finally got it out of her," Willow said, polishing off the last of her sausage and wishing she hadn't given Chad's to the dog. "I think she saw it as finding something good to appreciate but not to hide the bad. It was just worded in a way that sounded like you only acknowledge the tiny bit of good and let the bad damage the family."

His eyes had already glazed over. "I don't follow. Why would my mom—"

"Let's say you decided we were butchering all the animals for fertilizer."

"Nauseating."

"Agreed," she conceded. "But I saw the book as saying to praise your wisdom in seeing that the crops needed to be fertilized while ignoring the ridiculous idea you have."

"And Mom..."

"Mom said that she thought it was saying to praise your wisdom in seeing that the crops needed to be fertilized before adding that I would prefer you research to be sure that animal carcasses are appropriate and affordable fertilizer choices because my understanding is that manure and organic compost is more effective and more economical."

Chad nodded. "Cushion the blow. It would be a bit easier to swallow than, 'Look, you idiot, you're not killing the animals when we can use their excrement and have the animals too.'"

Willow snickered. "I'd say that, wouldn't I?"

"Maybe not the idiot part—"

Snickers turned to guffaws as she shook her head. "I'd say that first and you know it."

"Positive thinking?"

"Positively *not* thinking." Willow winked, grabbing her plate. "Get some more sleep."

CHAPTER 121

August—

He's home. I cannot believe he was gone for so long. The final surgery was successful. The doctor says he'll have full use of his hand, but that it'll take work to make it strong again. He's been target shooting with both hands and is determined to get back on track. He can't go back to work until mid-September according to Chief Varney. Even then, he's going to have to run some kind of obstacle course first. Chad called it a PAT which he says stands for Physical Agility Test. The way he said it, I can't decide if it was a joke or if that's what it is really called. He said he had it "down PAT," so I can't tell.

The first two weeks at home were enough to drive us both crazy, but now he is working on some kind of strange project. I'm not allowed to go out front, and anything that needs to be done out there he does. I don't really know what is going on, but he's happy, and that's such a nice relief that I am trying not to be frustrated with covering my eyes whenever we go somewhere or come home. Oh, and I miss seeing my flowers.

In June, and now this month, he watched the calendar closely, and he was disappointed each time I pull out the basket of monthly pads. I cannot decide, however, if the disappointment is because it's another week "apart" or if it is because it means no baby. Either way, I find it kind of cute and very funny.

I think I need to suggest some kind of party. Maybe we can do something the first weekend of October if he has it off as kind of a "celebrate going back to work and all the fruits of our hard work around here" kind of thing. We could have roasted corn, and he could grill those hamburgers he loves so much. (And I can have one without hearing, "told you.")

I hear him calling me. It's an amazing thing. For so long I had no one who called me to see what they were doing or to help them with something. Now I have that again, but it's even better now. Now just hearing him call for me gives me such a warm feeling in my heart. That might be why I'm still writing and not running to make sure he hasn't cut off his other hand...

"I'm coming!"

Chad's voice boomed up the stairs, "You're not coming fast enough, woman! I'm finally done!"

At the bottom of the stairs, Willow sat on the last step, crossed her arms, and looked up at him. "Make me."

He stormed out the door, charged down the front steps, and disappeared. Seconds later, he stood in front of the screen with hose pouring water all over the porch and grinned. "Get out here, or I douse you and half the house."

"You wouldn't!"

He reached for the screen handle, but Willow jumped and raced to beat him. "You win!" She stopped at the screen and stared at the hose. "Toss the hose, buster."

Chad leaned closer letting the hose touch the wooden accents of the screen door and then flung it behind him. "Come on, lass. I'm finally done with your gift."

"Gift?" She pressed her nose to the screen trying to see outside. "What you've been doing is a gift for me?"

"I missed your birthday."

"You were in the hospital! Of course, you missed my birthday," she protested.

"Better late than never?" He swung the door open and waited for her to step out on the porch. She glanced around the yard, into the pasture, checked the paint, and finally turned to him and shrugged.

"I don't get it."

154

"Look again. Your favorite place out here."

Her eyes immediately sought the porch swing and almost glanced away again, but something wasn't right. She took another step and then giggled. "Oh my word. You didn't." A fresh set of giggles erupted as she stepped closer to the porch swing. "How on earth?"

"I thought it should be more comfortable for you on your late-night snoozes."

"But we can't sit on it!" The swing-bed was amazing, but dismay filled her heart as she imagined sitting with her legs stuck out in front of her awkwardly.

"Oh, but look!" Chad hurried to the swing, pushed back two brackets, and the new portion of the swing hung free. "I only added fifteen inches and it'll need a new pad..."

"That's amazing!" Willow lifted the "leaf" of her swing, pulled the slides forward to support the new base, and grinned. "I love it!" She threw her arms around him knocking him into the window.

"If I'd have known I'd get attacked again, I would have given you one of Wayne's daisies."

She laughed, shaking her head. "Nope. Not true. You would have built it faster..."

The Friday before Labor Day, Chad woke up, shaking Willow excitedly. "I have a great idea!"

"What? Huh? Are you okay?" The dark sky outside her window told her it was still very early.

"I want to go somewhere. I have two more weeks of time off. I've gotten good enough at shooting to pass the PAT. Let's go somewhere!"

Willow struggled to sit up and clear her head. She pulled her hair from the braid and reached for a brush as she tried to follow Chad's early morning ramblings. "Go where?"

"I don't know—somewhere different. We could go to Jamaica, or hmm... maybe Hawaii since you probably don't have a passport."

She gave him an incredulous look. "You've got to be kidding me. Passport?"

"Right. Hawaii—or better yet, California! California is really diverse. They have the ocean...you've never seen the ocean."

"No, I've never seen the ocean; that's true."

"And the mountains, and desert... they're all like an hour or two apart. You go from ocean, to mountain to desert. It's amazing. We could fly out, rent a car, and just tour the state. All those missions..."

Willow dropped her brush. It hit her knee, causing an immediate reflex kick. "Are you serious? You want to go to California just like that? What about the animals and—"

"Can't we get Caleb to sleep out here for two weeks? He did great while you were in the city..."

As she considered his suggestion, Willow played with the brush. Work wasn't something you just delayed or ignored so that you could enjoy a two-week whim in another state. There was so much to do before winter. The idea that they could just pack up and go seemed absurd and yet... She glanced in his eyes and saw the excitement—the eagerness. He wanted to go so badly, and if there was one thing Chad never did, he never asked anything of her. He gave and gave until she forgot how much of his old life he'd left behind him when he joined her on the farm.

"So how long would we be gone and when would we leave?"

"You'll go?" He shook his head. "Wow. I—I was sure you'd say no. I just kept thinking of you in the ocean, hiking in the mountains, chasing lizards—you would definitely chase lizards."

"Of course, I would. Who wouldn't? You really want to go?"

He paused before murmuring, "More than anything."

"If I can get them to come get Ditto and take away Dinner... it'd be too much to deal with all of it when I got back. I doubt I'd enjoy the trip if I knew I had that to do when I got home, but I could butcher the chickens today, and if they could come get the animals by Tuesday we could go on Wednesday. I think."

"I'll make reservations, find suitcases, and..."

Willow didn't hear much else he said; her mind was

already planning phone calls, clothing, and replanting in order to leave on time. By the time breakfast was over, she'd made a list of things to do and calls to make and wrote another one of all necessary items for a trip. Chad drove to town to use the library's internet to order tickets. He arrived home by lunch with tickets and luggage and the biggest grin she'd ever seen on his face.

"What'd you get done?"

"They're coming for Ditto this afternoon. I guess they had a delivery later today anyway and had to drive right by. I'm glad I called early. Mr. McFarland can't come until Tuesday afternoon, and Lily said Caleb could stay out here if Ryder could stay too." She hesitated. "I think she's afraid that grandmother Solari will hire someone to kill me at my house, and he'll somehow be mistaken for me."

"Well, he looks so much like you. I mean, take away six inches, forty pounds, and a head full of hair and you'd be twins—almost."

Chad passed their itineraries across the kitchen table. Willow reached for them tentatively and then glanced up at him. "We're really going?"

"The money is spent now, we have to go."

"Aww... isn't that too bad? What rotten luck." Willow winked and passed him a sandwich.

Why Chad didn't think about Willow's reaction to air travel was something he pondered for years to come. He was used to thinking about her reactions to new and unusual things—well, unusual to her. However, perhaps due to lingering effects of various drugs and anesthesia in his system, the lack of sufficient exercise, or because he'd gotten word that the trial was almost over and would probably have a verdict sometime while they were gone, Chad entered the airport blissfully clueless of her trepidation. He did not prepare her for security checks, baggage checks, and long waits in lines. He did not prepare himself for her reaction to them.

Receiving their boarding passes was a simple process

that unfortunately kept the warning bells from sounding. However, the line through security solved that problem. The airport was packed and the lines long. Bored passengers stood in their own little worlds, some talking on cellphones, others checking their watches or phones as though the minutes would magically convert to seconds by sheer ocular suggestion. Willow took it all in wordlessly.

As they neared the checkpoint, Willow's eyes widened as a woman was escorted aside and patted down thoroughly. "What are they doing to her? Someone needs to stop them!" Her voice grew louder with each word. The other passengers stared in amazement as she nudged Chad insisting that he go to the woman's rescue. "You're an officer, *do* something."

Chad cringed as a TSA agent tossed a dirty look in their direction before waving his wand over the body of a teenager with more spikes in her body than a campground of tents. "Shhh. Willow, it's what they do. It's their job. It's for our safety."

Willow apparently did not appreciate being shushed. "You are telling me that in the United States of America, *our* citizens are hauled off and physically manhandled under the guise of safety! What are we being protected *from* I'd like to know!"

"What planet is *she* from," the man behind them muttered, annoyed.

"It's because of 9/11, now shhh."

"Why shhh?" Willow's voice scaled higher and then froze mid-sentence as she saw Chad unlace his shoes and dump them in a bin. He emptied his pockets, removed his belt, and dumped it all in a basket before sending it through the conveyor belt. From the front of his suitcase, he pulled a zip-lock bag and laid it on top before it went through the scanner.

To her horror, an alarm screamed as he stepped through a door-less doorway. Chad looked confused for a moment, patted himself down slightly and then groaned. "Oh man, I meant to drop this off at the station." He sheepishly pulled his badge from his front shirt pocket and dumped it in the basket. He shrugged at the TSA officer and shrugged. "Too excited to get going, I guess."

A second pass with wands showed him clear, but the

158

woman receiving his bag shook her head in disgust as she pulled a large tube of toothpaste, shampoo-conditioner mixed bottle, and the brand new bottle of after-shave he'd brought home but not packed. Chad's eyes widened. "That's not my stuff."

"It was on your case, mister."

"It's yours Chad."

"But that's not what I packed!"

"I repacked it. Those tiny things you had in there wouldn't last you two weeks!" Her eyes grew wide as the officer removed the items from the bag and tossed them in a bin at her feet. "What are you doing? You can't just take people's property!"

"Um, yes I can. And shoes off."

The stubborn look on her face made Chad nearly crazy with frustration. "Just do it, Willow." Her eyes told him no before her mouth could follow, but she stopped short when he added, "Trust me." He turned to the officer who waited and said, "She's never flown before, and I didn't think to prepare her."

"Do I have to pull out my toiletries too?"

"Absolutely."

Impatiently, Willow unzipped her suitcase, pulled out her glass jelly jars of tooth powder, deodorant powder, shampoo, and conditioner. A bar of soap came next followed by a cosmetic bag. "Do I leave the stuff in the bag or dump it in the basket?"

The woman stared slack-jawed for a moment and then tossed all of the jars, approved the soap, but removed face cleanser, toner, and moisturizer from the cosmetic basket and dumped those in the bin at her feet as well. As she stepped through the scanner, Willow found perverse pleasure in seeing that the overhead scanner didn't make a peep, but her triumph was short-lived.

"Step over there please."

Chad groaned. With all of her protests, he hadn't been surprised but he'd hoped. Willow's immediate retort sent new waves of nervousness through him. "Do I have the right to refuse?"

"No."

159

"Am I under arrest for anything?"

The woman gave her a scathing look. "Should you be?"

"I don't know, my grandmother is on trial for murder here in this town, maybe I'm guilty by association? Why do you want me to step aside?"

With an expression that Chad found unreadable, the woman said, "Because it's my job to ensure that no one else gets on a plane and flies it into a building anywhere."

"Like that could ever happen."

The woman looked at Chad, her expression priceless. "Is she for real?"

"She's for real. Just think of her as an Amish woman flying for the first time. She's clueless, and I wasn't thinking." Chad pleaded with Willow, "You need to go over there and let them do their jobs." His tone became stern—the same one he used with Aiden Cox half a dozen times a week.

Willow's mortification over being physically patted down, twice, made Chad wince inwardly. She wasn't going to be happy about that. As if on cue, the moment they stepped away from security and started toward their gate, Willow's questions flew. "What just happened back there?"

"They checked to make sure that we brought nothing on the plane that could be used as a weapon."

"What about my knitting needles," she protested. "Aren't those a weapon?"

"I've never understood that. Maybe because they're wooden and in your bag."

"They took my scissors!"

"They were the size of Rhode Island!"

Her frustration boiled over. "So are those knitting needles if you compare sizes!"

As they waited to board their plane, Chad explained the two planes that had flown in to New York's World Trade Center, flattening the towers in the process. His voice choked as he described the plane downed at the Pentagon. "I just wanted to get there and help—but so did half the country. He told of United flight 93 and the courageous men who determined to avoid another major loss of life. "We don't know for sure if they made it and prevented it or if they just convinced the men to take it down before they got there, but

160

most of us like to think they got those—" He stopped and took a deep breath. "Americans have been willing to give up a little of their rights and freedoms since then in order to prevent another chance of that happening. When someone fights it, it makes them look guilty."

"I thought we were innocent until *proven* guilty in this country."

Feeling weary, Chad nodded. "In regards to a crime, you are. If you're accused of a specific crime, you're innocent until proven guilty. However," he continued as a look of triumph entered her eyes, "that doesn't mean that when a man wants to bring something onto a plane that could be used to control the pilot, we have to let it happen. Especially if that man, or woman, happens to be protesting a bit too much. I'm pretty sure your beloved Shakespeare commented along those lines."

"But it's a violation of my rights to tell me what I can and cannot take on a plane. How can they get away with that, constitutionally speaking? I'd call what just happened back there 'unlawful search and seizure.'"

"It's not a right to ride on the plane, though. That right isn't guaranteed by the Constitution. These are private planes owned by private companies, and they can make any rules they want about who can and cannot fly on them and what they can bring."

"Oh! I misunderstood. I thought this was some kind of law. If you chose to fly on a plane with these rules, then no, we can't complain."

Oh how he wanted to let her think it. The temptation to drop the subject there was so great that Chad nearly offered to bring her a coffee even if it would make her jittery. However, his conscience wouldn't let him. "It is Federal Law."

"Then it is still a violation of many people's rights. The airline doesn't have jurisdiction over their own property. They're forced to follow these laws—"

"And what about the rights of the people on the ground? Should they be endangered because an airline decides they'll let anyone with five hundred dollars and an ID fly on their planes?" He sighed rubbing his temple. "We won't agree on this, Willow. Not right now. How about we table it for some cold winter's night—after I show you footage from the 9/11

161

attacks."

One disaster averted, Chad was relieved when their flight was called to board. Willow followed him onto the plane, down the aisle, and to their seats. He hefted their luggage over his head and into the stowaway bins above their heads "I got you the window," he said smiling. "I thought you might like to see the clouds up close and personal."

"You can see the clouds?" She frowned. "I thought that was just poetic license in books."

A derisive snort from behind them sent Chad's blood pressure up a notch but he chose to ignore it. "Yep. My favorite is when we are just going up. You can see all the farms and roads down there. It really does look like a patchwork quilt of fields."

She waited expectantly. After what seemed like hours, the flight attendants rose and began their normal spiel regarding smoking, oxygen masks, and exit routes. Willow sat quietly, hanging on every word as though it meant life or death.

As the plane taxied down the runway, her hand grabbed his in a vice-like grip. He knew the exact moment her stomach lurched by the way she reached for the complimentary vomit bag in the back of the seat ahead of her. A glance at her told him she was missing the best part of the take-off.

"Look down there."

With obvious hesitation, Willow opened one eye and glanced out the window. Chad need not have worried. One glance at the ground, the skies, and the sun glistening on the wing behind them was all she needed to overcome the momentary fear in her heart.

"We're really going!" she whispered awed. Remembering something Marianne had shared once, she turned back to him and smiled. "Are we there yet?"

CHAPTER 122

LAX bustled with activity, a homogeny of languages, cultures, and Willow found them all extremely fascinating. While Chad searched for their rental agency, Willow engaged in the age-old practice of people watching. The languages fascinated her most. Heavy accents made even English-speaking people sound exotic and from another world.

"Come on, let's go. I got us a cool Mitsubishi Spyder! We'll tour the coast and let the wind whip through our—" he pause grinning. "Well, *your* hair anyway."

In the car, Willow handed him an envelope with the dozens of printouts that he'd brought home from work. The envelope made him laugh. Palm trees, Route 66 signs, cacti, mountains, and surfboards covered the outside of it. When had she had time to decorate an envelope for his MapQuest printouts? "You're amazing."

"What?"

"It's pretty. You even made an envelope for directions- pretty. Who does that?"

Willow shrugged and accepted the envelope back sans directions to the hotel. "I do. Who wants a boring gold envelope for everything?"

The sheer volume of cars that spilled from the airport in constant streams overwhelmed Willow immediately. "I thought Rockland was busy, but—"

"Well, this is the airport and we came straight to it from Fairbury so we missed the traffic, but yeah, LA has amazing traffic."

"Ok, after I merge onto CA-1N, what do I do?"

Willow read the directions carefully. "Turn left on Pico Boulevard and then—"

"That's enough. I just needed to know if I needed the right or left lane when I got to the 1 north."

As they pulled up to the hotel, Willow gave him an odd look. "Seriously, *Hotel California*? You're joking right?"

"Cool isn't it?"

"Unoriginal is more like it."

"Come on, Willow—the Eagles song? It's cool!"

She shrugged and grabbed her tote. "Are we going in, or are we going to sit out here and contemplate the beauty of the décor?"

Once they stepped into their room, Willow became entranced. She stood, suitcase handle in one hand, tote bag in the other, and stared out the window at the rolling surf. "It's so—big! Look—it goes forever and it's loud! I can hear it all the way up here."

Chad grabbed her hand and tugged. "Come on, let's go see."

Willow found herself following him down steps, onto the sand, and stumbling as they raced through it to the water's edge. Swiftly, she kicked off her sandals, stepped onto the cool, wet sand, and waited for the waves to crash over her feet. "Oooh. It's cold!"

Her feet danced backwards. Chad, still rolling his pant legs up mocked her for being a wimp. "Come on, just a little cold water and you run!"

"I didn't expect it to be so cold. It's beautiful out here, but that water is *cold*."

"Want to learn how to find a sand crab?"

His excitement was infectious. Chad waited for the next wave, dug near the edge of the water, and pulled the tiny crab from the hole where it tried to burrow deeper into the sand. Immediately, Willow began digging as a new wave crashed over her feet. "I got one! Oh, it's so tiny and cute. Do they get any bigger?"

"I've only seen them about this size, but the males are a little smaller I think."

"I can't believe how you can actually smell the salt in the air. I always thought that was just an example of literary imagery. I never dreamed it was salty enough to smell."

"Check out the pier." Chad pointed to the famous Santa Monica pier with its Ferris wheel towering over the nearby shops and restaurants. "That Ferris wheel is even taller than the roller coaster."

"I've always wanted to ride a Ferris wheel."

This was surprising. Of all the things Willow might have ever wanted to do, something involving heights was the last thing he'd imagined. "I can't believe you want to be up that high. I distinctly remember you hating the heights of the buildings in Rockland."

"I've gotten used to them," she protested. "I don't think I ever realized how tall a Ferris wheel would have to be, but I still think I want to try it."

"Really?" If she was willing to try the Ferris wheel, maybe the roller coaster wasn't such a pipe dream after all.

"But don't expect me to get on that other thing. It looks *fast*."

"Well, it probably is, but it's just a ride. Hundreds of people probably ride that thing every day. Maybe thousands."

"And the first time I saw a movie," she reminded him ruefully, "I lost my dinner because the screen spun too much. How do you think I'd do if something was actually spinning?"

"You have a point. Maybe on an empty stomach and with your eyes closed?"

Scrutiny was an understatement compared to the examination Willow gave Chad. Did he really want her to try something so crazy? "Are you going on it?"

"Oh, without a doubt."

"Hmmph. We'll see. I might feel more daring tomorrow. I'm hungry."

The switch in topics took Chad several seconds to process. "Well, there are places on the pier I'm sure..."

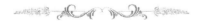

"You ready?"

Willow nodded nervously and stepped into the car. Chad

helped her fasten herself in securely and wrapped an arm around her shoulder. "Remember, if you feel sick, don't look, or just stare at the seat ahead of us or something."

"Ok." Her voice sounded small, even to her own ears.

The coaster made the slow ascent making Willow wonder why she'd ever thought it'd be frightening. "This is as slow as the Ferris wheel."

"Not for long!"

The ride whipped them into a spiral, before dashing in a curve that looked like it'd send them straight into the ocean. Several more dips and climbs followed before they zipped into the boarding area much more quickly than she'd ever imagined and with her stomach intact. She climbed from the car feeling weak-kneed but fine.

"Well?"

"It was exhilarating!"

"Want to go again?" Chad wasn't about to let an opportunity like that pass.

"Not yet." Willow paused, waiting to see if she fell apart. "I want to make sure it doesn't have some kind of delayed reaction. I'd hate to get sick and have it all blow back into my face. I didn't think of that."

"I did. I haven't prayed so hard about anything so frivolous in years."

She stared at him, stunned. "And you went anyway?"

"Yep."

"What," she began curiously, "Did you pray about last time you prayed so hard for something so frivolous?"

"Lass, there's no way I'm tellin'. Let's play some arcade games."

"What games?"

"Skeeball. It's my favorite. C'mon!" Chad pulled her to the arcade place he'd spotted the previous evening. "You'll love it."

Waves crashed against the shore, cool breezes whipped her sweater collar against her cheek, but Willow sat calmly and marveled at the beauty of the moon across the water.

Footsteps behind her brought a smile to her face. How differently footsteps sounded when heard in the sand instead of on a floor or over grass or dirt. It sounded closer to snow than she would have ever imagined.

"Willow?"

"I'm fine, Chad. Just listening to the waves."

His arms wrapped around her waist as he knelt behind her. His head rested on her shoulder and he whispered, "This isn't Fairbury, lass. It might not be safe out here."

"I'm fine; you're fine; we're fine."

"He, she, it is fine." He kissed her cheek laughing. "See, I can conjugate too."

Willow's arm stretched in front of her pointing at something she didn't think he saw. "Look at the moonlight. You know how books talk about it being a bridge across water? It really does look like that, doesn't it?"

"What books?"

Chad probably thought she was crazy. "*The Harvester* for one. Ruth appears to walk across the whole lake in a bridge like that."

"Never read it."

Willow struggled to her feet using his shoulders as a balance. "This winter. I'll put it on the coffee table for you."

Her mind wrote the journal entry as she lived it. *Moonlight on the ocean, salt air in the breeze, sand between your toes—I've never experienced anything more romantic and stirring than kissing Chad on California's beaches. I didn't want to leave. I didn't want it to end. Ever.*

"Lass?"

"Hmm?" Willow hardly noticed the tone that she'd soon learn meant Chad was in one of his thoughtful moods.

"Do you have any idea how utterly happy I am?"

167

CHAPTER 123

They drove from Santa Monica to San Diego after three days at the beach. Hungry, they decided to try to find a restaurant. When two exits produced nothing of interest, Willow insisted he stop at a shopping center. While Chad waited in the car, she strolled into the first business, returning minutes later and waving a sheet of paper with directions to the 'best fish taco in the San Diego area.' "She said we wouldn't regret it."

"I already do," he muttered under his breath, revolted at the idea of fish in tacos. "I hope they have other tacos too."

"Oh come on, have some sense of adventure—turn left."

"How far away is this place?"

Willow sighed impatiently. "She said two or three miles. Turn left at the next street."

"I can't believe you asked total strangers where to go for food."

Willow had not yet been inducted into the not-so-secret society of wives with husbands who cannot fathom the concept of asking for directions. Now, she sat staring at him as though he was insane. "You're kidding me, right? People ask you directions to places every day and you're surprised that I asked someone?"

"I'm a cop. People ask cops. They don't ask strangers on the street."

"But you're still a stranger! You're an officer, but you're still a stranger."

Chad didn't know how to make her understand why people should and do trust officers over the average Joe on the street. As they pulled up to the restaurant, Chad had to drive half a block to park. "I can't believe we're eating at a hole in the wall like this. It's insane."

Willow finally stopped in the center of the sidewalk and waited for him to look at her. "Do you not want to eat here? I thought you were joking, but if you really don't want this, then let's find something you do want."

"This is fine."

"Is it?" she demanded. "It doesn't sound like it's okay. It sounds like it's a problem."

"I just didn't expect lunch at a greasy spoon, but I'm sure it'll be fine."

"I think," Willow said after several seconds' reflection, "I think I'd rather skip it. It's not worth it. There's that pizza place we saw. Let's go back there."

Chad knew he'd been a jerk. Willow had decided she was hungry, didn't want fast food, found another alternative without expecting him to know what to do in a strange place, and he'd done nothing but complain because the idea of fish tacos made his stomach churn. There was no reason not to go have a normal beef or chicken taco and let her enjoy her disgusting choice. Even as he chastised himself for his behavior, he realized that he was still being a twit.

"Willow, will you do me a favor?"

"Sure."

Her attitude surprised him. He'd expected a bit of sulking in the least. "Will you go order a fish taco and whatever else you want in there and pretend I wasn't a first-class jerk right now?"

She grinned. "You're sure?"

Even as she said it, Chad felt even more stupid than ever. Since when had Willow ever sulked? "I'm more than sure. You eat fish. I'll get carne or something."

The relish with which she dispatched the revolting tacos almost destroyed his appetite. Her plans to try to recreate them at home with trout from the stream polished off what little appetite he had left. However, her suggestion that they visit the San Diego Mission next redeemed the afternoon for

170

him. Stomach growling within minutes of leaving the restaurant, they took off in the direction advised by the man who served them their lunch. To Chad's surprise, Willow was a storehouse of information about the San Diego Mission. She stood outside the mission looking up to see the bells. As she pointed to the different once, she showed how to tell which was original, and explained about how the other large bell had been made from remnants of the original bells. She described when they had been commissioned and why and the one day a year that all five bells ring at the same time.

"How do you know so much about this mission?"

"I loved the idea of the missions as a child, so Mother bought several books on them. This was the first mission in modern California, so I studied it as extensively as I could. When I think of those priests and how they came evangelize— it just amazes me what a wonderful thing that was."

"Wonderful? Willow, they enslaved those Indians— Native Americans—whatever. They were cruel and forced Christianity on them. How can that be wonderful?"

"I didn't say," she began patiently, "that how they evangelized was wonderful. I think that they did evangelize was. They came in and did what they thought was right. Their hearts were in the right place, even if their actions weren't the right actions."

"The heart is deceitful and wicked, and what those priests did was too."

Impatiently, she climbed the steps. At the top, she turned to Chad and sighed. "I am not justifying all of their actions, but if you read their writings, their motives were to teach the lost about Jesus. They cared about the souls of those Indians. That is what I find wonderful."

As she described the different aspects of life in the mission—the chapel, the gardens—Chad listened, amazed. She spoke with genuine interest and attention to detail. Several other tourists followed them listening and occasionally asking questions. When one tourist commented about how the Native Americans had been forced to live at the missions, Willow shook her head emphatically.

"The primary source documents of the time say otherwise. They only had room at the mission for about half of

171

the natives to live here at a time, and there is no evidence that they could not come and go at will between rotations. The mission was just too poor to feed and shelter all of them."

"Lass?"

Willow's shoulders drooped. "Hmm?"

"Next time I want to learn something, remind me to ask you to read up on it."

Everywhere they went, people they talked to asked if they'd eaten at In-n-Out Burger. The trip north to the mountains found them at a shopping center with the bright yellow arrow pointing to the restaurant. "Want to try it?"

"Can we say we've experienced California without it?"

Chad grinned. She wanted a burger but didn't want to sound too eager. She loved her burgers even if she wouldn't admit it. He pulled into the parking lot and glanced at the tables. "Out here or in there?"

"You choose. I'm good either way. You're the hot one."

He couldn't let that one slide. "Thanks. You're pretty ho—"

She swatted at his arm. "If we were home, I'd cool you off with the hose."

"Then I guess I'm glad we're not home." He held open the door and the cool air made up his mind for him. "We eat in here. This feels great."

Willow scanned the menu above the registers. "Um, I hope you want a hamburger."

"Why?" Chad glanced up, following her eyes.

"Because you can buy burgers, drinks, fries, and shakes. That's it."

"Well, they are famous for their burgers."

"Are they?" She frowned. "How do you know?"

"Because everyone we meet suggests them?"

After ordering their meals, Chad and Willow waited at the front of the store and watched the employees as they cut fries, put fresh meat on the grill, and literally toasted the buns. By the time their number was called, Willow insisted on buying Chad a t-shirt as a souvenir. "I can just see you

172

milking the next goat or giving the new dinner cow water while wearing that shirt," she giggled as she spoke.

Chad bit into his burger almost before he seated himself. "Well, I have to admit, they're good. They're really good."

Willow nodded her agreement and examined her burger wrapper closely. "Look! Remember that woman who said there were Bible verses on the packaging? This must be what she was talking about. Nahum 1:7 is printed right there!"

"The verse?" Chad looked at his wrapper but didn't find it. Finally, he saw the reference. "I wish I had my Bible."

"It's um...oh, man. The one about the Lord being helpful in trouble and that He knows who trusts in Him."

Chad examined his cup. He lifted the lid and glanced inside, checked the seam, and finally lifted it to look under it. "This one has Proverbs 3:5."

"Trust in the Lord with all thine heart and lean not unto thine own understanding."

"Impressive."

"Isn't it!" Willow was thrilled. "I can't imagine what made them do it but it's brilliant. You put it out there without preaching and trust that it won't return void."

Laughing, Chad swallowed hard and tried to get a drink after choking on his burger. The shake didn't work. "Get-Coke," he begged.

Willow raced to buy a drink, filled the cup they handed her, and hurried back. "This one says John 3:16."

After a few gulps. Chad took a deep breath. "So, with this packaging, they're ready in season... or is that seasoning."

"Are you ok?"

"I'm fine. There's nothing on the fry thing that I can see." Chad looked disappointed.

"I never thought I'd read wrappers so carefully. I wonder how many people actually look up the reference." Unaware of Chad's amusement at her expense, Willow glanced around the restaurant, trying to see if anyone noticed the little words that meant so much to her.

As he watched, delighted with her perspective on life, free of the cynical thoughts he had about the effectiveness of a tiny Bible reference that few would see and even fewer would read, Chad took a deep breath and sighed. "Lass…"

"Hmm?" She didn't even look his way.

"I love you."

A slow smile spread across her face as she turned to see what prompted his latest reminder. "That is really nice to hear."

The climb into the mountains began almost immediately after they left the restaurant. Tight winding roads wound around the mountain on a slow climb dotted with occasional turnouts. Willow, of course, wanted to stop, take in the view, while Chad, in typical male fashion, was on a mission to conquer the destination in as little time as possible. Her eyes widened as he snapped for her to sit down when she tried to rise onto her knees to see the view below them.

"What is wrong with you?"

"If we got in an accident, you'd be thrown out and killed. Get down."

"Then pull over!"

"There'll be views when we get there. We just got started again." The irritation hadn't left his voice.

Willow sank into her seat, correcting the seatbelt and staring at Chad in shock, hurt, and dismay. "What is the rush? I don't understand."

"We just got back on the road, and you want to pull over already."

"And I ask again," she repeated very slowly, "What is the rush? So what if we just got back on the road? I thought the idea was to see California, not to whiz past it as quickly as possible."

"And I'll say again, why do you want to stop when we just got going again!"

"Because I want to see!"

Chad swerved into the turnout, slamming on his brakes as he did. "There. Have at it."

Lost as to why Chad was being so grumpy, Willow grabbed their camera and left the car, feeling half-abandoned. So far, he'd been interested when she wanted to see new things, but she knew instinctively that he didn't plan to move from his seat. Two cars passed before she could jog across the road and lean against the railing that helped keep cars from tumbling down the hill if they slid off the pavement.

The view was unlike anything she'd ever seen. Trees slowly gave way to dirt and then buildings rose up from the ground. Cars zipped to unknown places, and while the air was crisp and clean from her vantage point, she could see a brownish-gray haze over the valley below her. "Chad—that haze down there—is that pollution?" she called curiously

"Yes." His answer was curt.

"Wow, you can see it! I can sense it in Rockland sometimes. It feels like I can't get enough air, but I've never *seen* it like this."

Ignoring his grunt, she snapped a few pictures and walked across the road. The car door was stuck with the seatbelt trapped into it. Chad irritably kicked it from the inside while she lifted on the handle and then stumbled back against the mountain at the force of the door flying open. "Ooof."

The moment she was buckled, Chad shot out onto the highway again. They drove up the mountain, the wind flying through their hair, what of it Chad kept on his head. Willow watched the trees fly by, amazed as she saw houses packed together and set into the side of the mountain. Eventually, Chad pulled into the parking lot of Johnnie's Market and General Store, grabbing his printouts and grumbling over them.

"What's wrong?"

"This isn't right. We should be in Arrowhead by now, but that sign I just saw says Lake Gregory, which..." he turned the papers as if they'd tell him something different. "According to this, is the opposite direction from Lake Arrowhead."

"Well, let's ask someone."

"I'll figure it out," he groused.

A dark green Suburban pulled up beside their car. A cute teenager jumped out with a bright smile on her face. "Cool car!"

"Thank you," Willow answered smiling. "Can you tell us

175

how to get to Lake Arrowhead?"

Another voice broke in before the girl could answer. "It's only about ten miles back down the road. You take Lake to Hwy 18 to Hwy 189. Where are you going in Arrowhead?"

Willow smiled at a sweet looking woman with an adorable baby on her hip. "I don't remember, what's the name of that inn Chad?"

"Lakeview Lodge."

"Oh, you'll like that—"

A child's voice interrupted her. "I want to see the car! Can I see the car?"

Before the mother could ask, the young woman dashed around to help her little brother and sister from their seats. Small children swarmed the convertible. The boy gave Chad a serious expression and asked, "Where are you going in that car?"

"We're trying to find some place to sleep."

"You don't have a house?"

Chad laughed. "Not in California, but back where we live, we have a little farm with sheep, a cow, a dog, and a goat."

"We have goats!" The boy's eyes lit up excitedly. "The mama is going to have babies."

"That sounds very exciting."

"Are you going fishing?"

With mock sorrow, Chad shook his head. "I wish I could, but we didn't bring our fishing gear."

"My daddy has fishing poles and a boat and everything. You could go fishing with him."

"Si, let's go in now."

"I was telling him—I was telling him how to go fishing."

Chad and Willow watched as the family disappeared into the store, and then Willow sighed. "Wasn't he adorable?"

"Yeah. Did you see that baby?"

"She was so cute!"

He took a deep breath and laced his fingers through hers. "Sorry, Lass. I was being a bear."

"I still don't understand."

"I don't either. I think it's genetically wired into men to focus on a destination, and any obstacle to that destination

176

must be eradicated at all costs."

"Huh?"

"I don't know, but I remember when I was a kid. I hated it when Dad refused to stop. He'd be zipping past all the best places, while we all begged him to stop. When did I become my dad?"

"I don't know," Willow answered, shrugging her shoulders, "but usually I'd say that was a good thing. Just not in this one. I want to enjoy this trip."

"I'm going to do it again."

Willow grinned. "I know."

"This is a mountain lodge?"

The door to their cabin stood open revealing a shabby chic and Victorian dream. The room was beautiful; she would not argue that. However, there was nothing like the mountain lodge they'd anticipated. Their imaginations had conjured ideas of log furniture, pine trees, boats, bears, and similar things but instead, they found roses, wreaths, antiques, and the delicate scent of floral candles.

"Well, it's pretty," Chad commented carefully.

"Well, yes. It is. The bed looks comfortable. It's huge!"

"It's quiet up here," he tried again.

Chad waved at her and then pointed to the suitcases. "So, you want to try hiking around?"

"I'm starving."

"Ok, change, food, water for hiking. In that order."

Within the hour, Chad parked at the north shore campground, and they took off up hiking trails. Willow was fascinated with the nature around them. She listened for birds, watched squirrels darting to the campsites before racing back to their homes. She dropped her water bottle, and started to retrieve it but Chad grabbed her hand. "What are you doing?"

"Getting my bottle?"

"That's poison oak!"

She stared at it with a disgusted look. "Oh. Mother hated that stuff."

177

"You've never seen it? The woods around Rockland are full of it!"

"Mother killed it. By the time I was nine or ten, it was gone. She didn't let me anywhere near where it was. I think," Willow confessed, giggling, "Mother had a bad experience with it."

"How do you kill all the poison ivy and oak in such a big area?"

"Diligence. Mother was nothing if not diligent."

Half an hour later, she had learned to identify and ignore all poison ivy and oak thanks to Chad's careful training. "We'll have to read what Mother did to kill that on our land so we can kill it from the land we bought from Adric," Willow mused absently as they climbed.

"Do you have any idea how amazing it is that we have that record? I mean, it's just so rare know so much about your parents' day-to-day lives these days. I have no idea how Mom learned to cook, or to rear children or anything like that. I can ask, but I don't have a ready reference at my fingertips like you do."

"We do."

Arms around his wife, he looked out over the tree-covered mountains and agreed quietly. "*We* do."

Willow took a deep breath, her lungs filling with the fresh pine-scented air. "I could live here, I think. I liked the other places we visited, but I could live here."

CHAPTER 124

The spiraling descent from the mountains was a study in contrasts. Slowly the lush greenery gave way to trees, then rolling hills and finally on the highway, they whizzed into the barren brush-dotted desert. As they passed large housing tracts, complete with back yards not large enough for a volleyball game, Willow shook her head.

"There's all this land... why is everyone so packed together?"

"I don't know. You'd think land would be cheap when its unfit for growing and so far from the ocean."

Willow consulted her map and shook her head. "It's just over a hundred miles to the ocean. That's not that far. That's a trip to Rockland and back."

Eventually the traffic along the narrow highway thinned, the stoplights disappeared, and they zipped along the road occasionally passed by an SUV or trapped behind a slow moving truck. The land rose and fell from valley to valley, but the road seemed straight as it sliced through the landscape. Odd spiky trees with branches that looked like a medieval mace stood alone against the landscape and occasionally in mini "forests."

At one corner, traffic converged between highways, but Chad continued straight ahead. Fields of solar panels flanked them on the left in direct opposition to the blank canvas of scrubby nothingness on their right. After a steep climb, a strange cluster of buildings, one with a gigantic "ping-pong

179

ball" on top, appeared on their left. The sign, as they rolled past slower than before, identified it as a closed federal penitentiary.

"Are you sure this is the way to Death Valley?"

"We're going to Ridgecrest first. It's called the 'Gateway to Death Valley,' but I just really wanted to go that way because it is mentioned in one of Ted Dekker's books, and I want to see it."

"I think this is so amazing. There are a million colors of brown and green that I've never seen before!" Willow's eyes never stopped roaming the countryside as she pointed out trails, motorcyclists, and the occasional jackrabbit.

A huge sign that read, "Ridgecrest, Gateway to Death" with the word Valley blackened out loomed in the distance. Around the curve, after turning onto a new road, the car sped up a slight hill and slowly showed the valley below them. "That's Ridgecrest."

"Down there?"

"Yep."

"But, there's no ridge. That's a valley!"

"Look at the papers in the envelope. I think that valley is called the Indian Wells Valley."

"Why did they—"

Chad interrupted her laughing. "I don't know! Maybe ask someone in the town. I just know the name."

"The name is stupid."

"That," he commented, still laughing, "I'll agree with."

Willow couldn't get over the strange little city surrounded by nothing but mountains. As they pulled into a museum parking lot, she pointed to a nearby park. "That looks interesting."

"It's a park."

"Well, it looks interesting. I mean, look behind it—all brown and gray and then that park is all green and trees. It's weird."

Once inside, Willow wandered through the exhibits while Chad asked directions to a good hotel and restaurant. Within minutes, she returned to his side, pulling him to see one of the exhibits and giggling. "Look. They have a Navy base here."

"Okaaay... and your point?"

"This is the desert. It's China Lake. In the middle of a valley, where there is no water, and they have a Navy base— in a place they call Ridgecrest." A new fit of giggles overtook her.

Chad pulled her toward the door, thanking the ladies who had made suggestions. "I think I need to get her out of the heat. It's frying her brain."

She protested all the way to the car, across the town, and even a few times as they rode the short elevator to their room. "I'm not crazy—they are! I've never heard anything that made less sense."

"It is a name. It doesn't have to make sense."

"But it should!" Chad started to respond, but Willow preempted him. "Promise me you won't try to make me name a redheaded girl something like Raven or anything like that."

"I'd never try."

She dragged her suitcase into the hotel room and flopped onto the bed. "Whew." A moment later, she sat up, glaring at him. "You wouldn't try because you think it'd be a waste of your time."

"Wouldn't it be?"

Her hands dug into her purse for her brush and a hair tie, and she sighed. "Yeah."

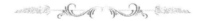

Around midnight, Chad reached for her. It took several long seconds—as much as a minute or two—before he woke up enough to realize she wasn't there. "Lass?"

No answer.

Chad dragged himself from bed and snapped on the light. She was not near the window where rain pelted it with enormous drops. He checked the bathroom and then glanced around for her shoes. Gone.

He dressed, pulling his jeans on over his sleep shorts and digging a shirt from his suitcase. He stuffed his sockless feet into his shoes and grabbed the keycard to the room. The hotel was silent. Vending machines hummed as he passed, but Willow wouldn't have used them for anything, so he moved along, checking the ice machine, the stairwells, and finally rode the elevator downstairs.

The lobby was empty, but the night clerk recognized him. "She's out front—seems to like the rain."

"You're kidding me." Chad shook his head, muttering as he strode toward the front doors, "Travel almost two thousand miles to the desert, and she stands out there and stares at rain—rain!"

However, the moment he stepped through the doors, Chad knew exactly what drew her. There was no thunder, no lightning—nothing spectacular to draw you to it—nothing except the scent. A hint of sage filled the air, but there was more—something stronger. Willow stood under the portico but out of the rain.

"Hey, lass. You all right?"

She turned, smiling. "Isn't this place a living irony? Can anything else happen that is so unexpected for it? Rain! I came all this way to see rain in the desert—to *smell* rain in the desert. I wish I could bottle this. I'd wash my clothes in it."

"What about your lavender?"

"I think I'd take this over that."

As much as he liked the scent around them, Chad couldn't agree. Life wouldn't be the same without the subtle whiffs of lavender at the oddest moments at home. "Maybe just some things."

"I wish our rain smelled like this. What is it?"

He shrugged. "I don't know. I think I smell sage, but there's more to it than that." He tugged at her. "C'mon. Let's go inside. I'll even ask."

"Go ahead. I want to smell this a little longer. I'll ask when I go in."

Chad wrapped his arms around her waist, leaning his chin on her shoulder, "I never thought I'd fly and drive all this way to see you staring out at rain."

"I'm not watching rain. I'm smelling it. This is just intoxicating." She tilted her head back. "I keep waiting for thunder and lightning."

"I know they get it sometimes. I've seen post cards with showers of lightning behind cacti."

182

Willow sighed. "You're not going to go back to bed, are you?"

"Not without you."

Ninety-eight miles from Ridgecrest, Chad and Willow pulled up to the famous "Scotty's Castle" and marveled at the beauty of the desert villa before ever exiting the car. The sun shone hot overhead as if the skies had not emptied the previous night. Although they'd enjoyed the top down on their convertible for most of their California trip, the mountains and deserts were both too cool and too warm to be comfortable. A castle tour started only five minutes after they arrived, and as they wandered through the rooms with original furniture and clothing they were serenaded by the massive pipe organ. Immediately following, they wandered the quarter mile of tunnels and learned about the alternate power options.

"Why don't they finish the pool?" Willow couldn't comprehend storing thousands of tiles for almost a hundred years instead of completing the project.

"The depression hit and the funds weren't there. It isn't your typical swimming pool. It's quite elaborate," the tour guide answered lazily.

"All this room for two people," Willow commented to Chad as they wandered the grounds. "They have staff housing. Who needs staff when you have nothing else to do?"

"Maybe they wanted to spend all day playing that organ."

"Or building the pool," she quipped, laughing. "I can't imagine all this space and time and what you'd do with yourself if you didn't have work to do."

"So in the immortal words of Carroll O'Connor in *Return to Me*, 'I'm blessed with work.'"

"What's *Return to Me*?"

Chad laughed. "A movie I'll let my mom know you haven't seen. You'll love it."

Before she could respond, a strange looking creature darted across the desert floor and Willow chased after it. She shouted for Chad to head it off on the left and then pounced like a cat. "I got it! What is it?"

Snickering, Chad poked at the little thing and said, "Horned toad. It's a kind of lizard, I think."

"Oh it's cute. I wonder if it could live in Fairbury?"

"Probably not, and even if it could, the airline wouldn't let him come."

Disappointed, Willow put the critter back on the ground and watched him skitter away again. "He was so unique!"

"Let's get pictures of this. I want our children to see what amazing places we visited." Chad tugged at her hand leading her away from the bush.

By the time they returned to LAX, Willow had seen the highest and lowest spots in the continental United States. She'd walked through vineyards in Napa, toured the capitol building, ridden over the Golden Gate Bridge, and stood on a low cliff overlooking the sea at Carmel. Out of spirits, she hardly wrinkled her nose as the TSA agent sent her through the metal detector and waved the wand over her. Chad watched, concerned, until he could pull her aside.

"What's wrong?"

"Nothing—not really."

"Okay, then, what is not wrong?" He slipped his fingers between hers and tugged her toward seats set apart from the others.

"Is it crazy that I want to be home so badly that I am going crazy for the time to pass?"

"Not crazy at all." He swallowed hard, fighting to hide his disappointment. She had seemed to enjoy the trip, but now he was not quite as certain.

"Then is it crazy that I also don't want to leave?"

Without releasing her hand, he pulled her into a one-armed hug. "You have no idea how much I needed to hear that right now."

"Does that mean it's not crazy or that it is?"

"That means that I was starting to doubt if this trip was a good idea."

"So," she added after seconds ticked into a minute or more, "would it be too expensive to come back some winter? Can you see a baby playing at the shore like that?"

"I think we'd have to go to Florida in winter. I think their water is warmer."

She grinned up at him, kissing his cheek. "Then maybe Florida next time—when there's a baby to play in the sand."

Chad closed his eyes, absorbing her words. Next time. She expected to have a next time. After being certain she would never agree to leave the farm again, hoping for a next time wasn't so crazy after all. "We'll do that. I'll take you to Disney World."

"What's that?"

A boy of about ten walked past and overheard her. "Dude. Disney World? Who doesn't know about Disney World?"

"I don't. What is it?" Willow's smile seemed to disarm the boy.

"Wow."

CHAPTER 125

October—

Well, Chad has been back to work for almost six weeks. He spends much time with target practice when he's off work. He has all kinds of hand exercises that he does. I think he's concerned that as it grows cold, his hand will grow stiffer. I just don't know sometimes if he'll be able to keep working. At what point, will his hand fail him, and will it be in the worst instance possible?

The harvest is finally over, we are settled in for winter, and I've been spending the past week trying to make our staples order. We need salt, oils, spices, baking powder and soda, paraffin, and things like candle wicking. I didn't buy those things last year, and it shows. I actually had to have Chad buy me some salt from the store. How strange.

The packaging on food products still astounds me. I have a dream of running a store where there are no packages. People bring their container, and I fill it up with whatever they're purchasing. Then I weigh it and charge by the ounce or something. Can you imagine the waste that could be prevented? Chad says that the people who make their living by creating and producing that packaging would be out of work. I wonder what they would do, those people. Would they decide to live a dream they put on the back burner, or is their packaging job their dream? Is it arrogant and rude of me to find that a horrifying thought? Probably. Most of my thoughts like that appear to be.

I am getting better at the dulcimer. I bought a book that explains how to read music and a book of music, but I find that I prefer to learn, as Chad calls it, "by ear." I think this is what Mother warned against—this dependency on what I hear rather than knowing how to read and know at sight what to do. I won't quit, though. I love sitting in my rocking chair by the kitchen stove and playing music while something bakes. Chad loves it too. He doesn't think I know it, but he comes in the front door, leans against the wall opposite me, and listens. I can see him standing there as if he was in sight. I know he leans against the wall, he crosses his arms, tilts his head back, and closes his arms. If footprints are any indication, he also rests one foot against the wall.

Winter will soon be here. The greenhouse seems to defy that. I am always amazed at how well things grow in there. I start a fire whenever I'm in there, and it seems to keep the plants happy. They don't grow as lush when it's cold, but they do grow amazingly well—if a bit smaller. I have much more food growing than I need, and that was the idea.

On that idea, I have decided to follow Chad's idea and build a vegetable stand. I'll be open Monday through Thursday and let Jill have what produce I don't sell for her Farmer's Market. I'm moving the garden to the alfalfa field next year and will plant alfalfa in the garden spot as well as on some of the land that we bought from Adric—crop rotation! Us! We've been planning the fields, and I think it's going to work.

I am also buying more sheep. I ordered a dozen lambs for next June. We thought about breeding the sheep, but I'm not ready for that yet. I love the work, and I'm ready to take on the spinning and eventually the shearing, but I just don't want to deal with pregnant sheep and new lambs. Not yet. Caleb thinks I'm crazy, and Ryder is thrilled. It amazes me how much Caleb loves the animals and how Ryder is only interested in the plants. If I ran a full-scale operation, I'd hire them both fulltime to manage each aspect of the farm, but we're too small for that.

Chad read the entry in late October and smiled. So, she knew about his trysts behind the wall as she learned to play.

188

It amazed him how perceptive she was. It also amazed him how often she asked him to go look up something she'd written in her journal. His experience with Cheri for a sister had taught him that not all women like others—especially men—reading their journals.

He gazed down at her, wondering once more if five months were five months too soon to be bothered by a lack of pregnancy. Then again, they'd lost much of July. For what seemed an incalculable number of times, Chad stuffed down his disappointment. He'd been so sure that they would have a special souvenir of their trip. The basket of "monthlies" in the bathroom that morning told him there wasn't.

It didn't seem to bother her—not yet. He tried to keep his eagerness at bay. After all, six months ago, she'd still been struggling to accept the one part of marriage that she'd feared most. A slow smile formed around his lips. He knew the exact moment that fear died. *Lord, thank you for wedding gowns that lace up the back,* he mused as he crawled into his side of the bed, trying not to wake her.

She curled up against him, murmuring something about whether he'd eaten and if he had seen his mail. "I'm good, lass. Sleep."

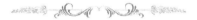

The door slammed as Willow stormed out into the yard, but Chad didn't follow. He sat in Mother's rocker, seething. *Lord, of all the stubborn—*

The door jerked open again. "—forgot to tell you that Luke called while you were sleeping." She hesitated before biting out, "Love you—you irritating jerk."

His lips twitched as he finished his frustrated prayer. *—unreasonable women, why did I think marrying that one would be a good idea?*

The recent calls list on his phone proved the veracity of her words—as if he needed such proof. He punched Luke's number and waited for his cousin to answer. "You rang?"

"Found a piece of marble at a salvage yard. It's perfect, but it won't last long. Got time to go look, or do you want me to just get it, or do you want to pick out something yourself and pay retail?"

"Get it."

Luke's relief told Chad he'd already bought it before he said, "Whew."

"You bought it before you even called, didn't you?"

"It was only fifty bucks!"

Chad grinned. "I bet it'll be perfect."

A few seconds of silence told him that Luke had something else to say. "Um, Chad?"

"Yeah?"

"You sound irritated."

That surprised him. How did Luke know that? "Had a blow up with Willow."

"And you're talking to me instead of to her?"

"Letting her think through it. She's being ridiculous."

"And wherever she is," Luke insisted, "she's thinking the same thing about you."

"Well she shouldn't be."

Luke tried again, that slow, quiet tenacity of his reminding Chad a little of Willow. "Did she sin?"

It killed him to answer truthfully. "No."

"Did you?"

"No—I don't think." Chad sighed. "Look, she got mad at me, so I tried to comfort her, and she got all ticked off."

"Comfort her?" Luke chuckled. "You mean you tried to solve her frustration in bed."

"Well—" How did Luke always know what he didn't say? "I wasn't trying to solve anything, really. I just thought she'd—"

"Respond to irritation and angst like a man."

"Huh?"

"Look, Chad. If there's one thing I've learned, it's that women—at least in my limited experience—get angrier when we try to make them feel better by bringing sex into it. Aggie says it made her feel cheap and used."

A cold wave of dread washed over his heart. "No way."

Luke sighed. "Looks like Willow and Aggie were cut from the same opposite cloth from the Tesdall-Sullivans. Call your dad. He'll know what to say or do. At times like this, Uncle Christopher is the best thing you could hope for."

"You call Dad for advice?"

"Or Uncle Zeke, sure. Who else would I call?"

Chad laughed. "Man, you just rocked my world. I can't imagine you needing to call anyone for advice on anything."

"Where do you think I get the nuggets I pass on to you?"

Minutes later, Chad stared at the phone, his father's number the most recent on the recently called list. He grinned at the apology still ringing in his ears. *"—sorry, son. I didn't give you the same talk I gave Luke before his wedding. I figured you wouldn't be needing it and it might make what you were going to be missing cut even more. When you called the next day and made it plain that your wedding night wasn't cuddling up with ice packs after all, I meant to take you out fishing and share a few things I've learned the hard way. I just forgot."*

He had to talk to her, but pride still niggled. *She could at least have tried to see it from my point of view. I just wanted to make it up to her—make her feel better and she—*the thought died at those words, pride popping and zipping away like a balloon. If he wanted to make her feel better—if making her feel better is what *really* mattered to him—then he wouldn't be offended when she didn't appreciate the manner in which he did. "Or at least I wouldn't be as offended," he muttered to himself.

Outside, Portia and Willow had vanished. Summer kitchen—empty. Front porch, back yard, chickens, goats, sheep, cow, and greenhouse—not there. He glanced across the fields to the lone oak by the highway, but unless she had deliberately hid behind it, she wasn't out there. Left without any other ideas, he strode across the pastures toward the pool. She couldn't be fishing, but maybe she had gone there to think—pray—come to her senses.

She wasn't there, but she had been. He followed the stream, around the bend, and found her examining plants—poison oak. "Lass?"

"Go away, Chad. I'm still mad."

"I talked to Luke and my dad."

"You dragged two other men into our bedroom?" Her eyes flashed. "Are you really that stupid or just that cruel?"

He couldn't help chuckling. A weak attempt at humor

191

flopped before he even spoke. "Willow, we didn't go into the bedroom..." Her indignant glare amused him. "I learned something from them."

"What? That you're a jerk? I told you that."

"I learned that men and women are different."

Her fury fizzled. "I could have told you that."

He stood, hands stuffed in his pockets, staring at their shoes. "Lass, I did what would make me feel better. I tried. I didn't know how it would make you feel. I still don't understand it, but I'm sorry."

"You dismissed my opinion as uneducated and immature and then tried to placate me with sex. Really, Chad? You didn't think that would make me angry?"

"I—"

"I don't understand you."

Tentatively, he reached out and brushed her cheek with his hand. "I know. I don't understand you either. So, let's agree to disagree and then agree on something else."

"Agree on what?" She glared at him again, suspicious.

"I won't ever try to apologize like that again if you promise to remember that if I'm ticked off at you, and you want to try to bridge a gap I've refused to cross..."

"Putting a bow on your pillow might be a good starting place?"

He grinned. "It'd be a really good starting place. It won't fix it. We still have to talk, but it will take the edge off my angst."

Chad ached to hug her, but he wasn't sure anymore. Would she misunderstand that too? He shoved his fist back in his pocket and tried to hold her gaze. Willow stepped closer. "You want to hold me."

"Mmm hmm."

"You're afraid to try."

"Afraid might be a bit strong, but I'm wary."

"Note to Chad: His wife will never refuse a hug as long as she doesn't feel like he's only doing it to get something more."

"Gotcha."

They strolled back to the house, hand in hand, Chad amazed again at how similar and different his wife was from nearly every woman he'd ever known. At the back door, Willow glanced at him. "Do you really think I'm that ignorant?"

"Not in general, no. I just think you need to see the full picture of why 9/11 made people willing to lose freedoms in exchange for safety. In that area, I think you are working from a theoretical knowledge that ignores a reality that couldn't have existed at the time the ideology was invented."

"I almost don't know what you just said."

He frowned. "I just mean—"

"You can repeat yourself all you want, but I'm not going to be able to hear it." A smile, one she only gave him at the most intimate moments, slowly formed on her lips. "Someone gave me other ideas, and I really can't think clearly anymore."

She winked, turned, and dashed into the house. Chad grinned and rolled his eyes heavenward. "I guess that's why I thought marrying her was a good idea, eh?"

CHAPTER 126

November—

We're killing the poison ivy and oak. It took us a while to find Mother's references to how she did it, but now that we have, we're succeeding. So far, we've kept ourselves free from contamination, but it isn't an easy job. Come spring, we'll have to walk the entire length of land every other week to eradicate any new growth, but if we're vigilant, we shouldn't have to worry about it. Chad did find a new growth of ivy on our land where the trees start to thin close to Adric's old property. Apparently, over time, seeds blew or something, but it's gone—at least for now.

Chad keeps an unhealthy watch on my cycles. Honestly, we've only been married for six months, but sometimes he acts like it's been six years. I kind of feel pressured to produce, but it isn't like there's much I can do about it. Mother conceived under the least promising of circumstances. From what I read, the stress of a situation like that can make it difficult to produce a child. I, on the other hand, have the best of circumstances, and yet I wait. Mom Tesdall tells me that the colder it gets, the more she expects to hear news, but I can't imagine why. I didn't know temperature had anything to do with it. I should ask Chad.

Jill has suggested that I consider raising mushrooms. I always wanted to eat the mushrooms and toadstools that grow wild in our woods, but Mother didn't know and didn't care to learn which were safe and which were poisonous. In a controlled environment, it'd be easy to do, I guess. Maybe I should order a book and see what it says. Mushrooms in our own cooking would be delightful! I loved the various kinds we had while we were in California, and the ones Chad brings home are so ridiculously expensive.

I am growing spoiled in this marriage. Where I once dreaded the idea of snores across the hallway keeping me up at night, I now find it lonesome when Chad is away from home. My workload is even lighter than it was when Mother was here, even though the amount of work we have has doubled. I wonder sometimes, what did Mother do? During the busiest times, I know she was there helping to package butchered chickens or can the garden produce. I know she did almost all of the alfalfa cutting and storage, but Chad did that this year in very little time with that machine of his.

I just can't remember what she did all day. Am I forgetting her? I can still hear her voice singing over the dishes. Mother was incredibly inefficient with time when she washed dishes. Why did I never notice that? I hear her reading me parts of commentaries. Her voice hasn't left me, but if it weren't for the thousands of pictures that I have of our life, I am afraid that I would have forgotten her face already. Even now, unless I glance at the framed picture on my dresser, I don't remember her. Is it wrong that I am growing content in her absence? Is it cold and heartless that I am thankful God sent someone else to be there for me? I'd love to see her again. I miss her almost daily, but the longer time goes on, the more I realize how much happier she is where she is. I do think that had I died as an infant, Mother wouldn't have kept going She would have given up—or worse. I see now that her only happiness in the last twenty or so years of her life was in me and in the knowledge that someday she'd be with Jesus and away from this earth.

Thanksgiving is this week. We're going to have Cheri and Chuck, Mom and Dad Tesdall, and Chris says he's bringing someone. Mom is beside herself with excitement. I had planned to cook several chickens, but apparently, one **must** have a turkey for Thanksgiving. So, I went hunting again. Mom is baking pecan pie and pumpkin pie. I'm supposed to make berry cobbler. Cheri is bringing a "green bean casserole." *Whatever that is. Chad says I'll love it or hate it. What is it about holiday foods that inspire such extreme reactions?*

Mom wants me to teach her how to knit. She's bringing "everything she needs," but I have a feeling she'll have more things than anyone would need to get started. Still, I can't wait to have them here. I'll give her some of the wool I dyed with the Kool-Aid packages she sent me. Every week or two, she sends something because she 'thought of' me. Sometimes I get packets of pretty paper for our journals, fabric, or a book. Once it was a bunch of the flavored drink packs, after she saw the yarn I dyed with the ones Chad brought me, and an article on how to combine colors for different looks.

Lily stopped by last week and asked how Chad and I are doing as a couple. She told me that we need to focus on us as a couple, but I have no idea what that means. Isn't that what we do every night when we read to each other, work on our projects, or take a walk? Isn't that what our more intimate times are all about? I wasn't sure I wanted to know what she meant, but I need to remember to ask Chad. Maybe I'm failing him someway as a wife, and I don't want to do that, but maybe we're just not supposed to look like every other marriage. Isn't it reasonable to assume that some marriages will be different than others? I think it is. Somehow, I think all the introspection into how we're "doing" could be just as damaging as never thinking about it at all. What do I know? I should ask Chad. Why do I get the feeling that he'll just laugh at me and roll his eyes at Lily?

Chad's laughter brought Willow jogging upstairs. He held up the journal and asked, "Did Lily really ask how we're doing as a couple?"

"Yep. After I wrote that, I wondered if maybe since I am not pregnant yet, she assumed you still lived in the other bedroom or something."

"Possible. You know, I didn't mean to make you feel pressured about pregnancy."

She pushed him out of the way and pulled open her sock drawer. "My feet are frozen." As she passed him on her way downstairs, she quipped. "There could be worse things." At the top of the stairs, he heard her mutter in stage tones for his benefit, "Perhaps that is exactly what we need."

CHAPTER 127

The spinning wheel whirled as Willow slowly fed tufts of wool into it, demonstrating the technique she'd mastered in the past few months. Marianne sat on the couch next to her, casting on stitches slowly and painfully as she struggled to hold the needles comfortably. Occasionally, Cheri would look up from her pile of skeins that Marianne had brought, and as she wound them into balls, complain about her aching hands.

The men, on the other hand, not having the television to shout at, played "keep away" football in the front pasture, until Cheri and Chris' girlfriend went crazy from wool overload and escaped to join them. Shouts and complaints occasionally seeped in through window cracks until Willow and Marianne glanced at each other and raced for their coats.

They played guys against girls, married against single, and mixed teams until the cold and exhaustion drove them inside. Willow watched, concerned, and Christopher watched her, as Chad stood next to the kitchen stove flexing his right hand and allowing the heat to help work out the painful muscle spasms. From the other side of the room, Christopher sipped his coffee and prayed silently for his son. "Chad, can you fill me a fresh cup of coffee?"

The request was ludicrous considering Christopher's cup was over half full but he swallowed a large gulp and forced himself not to wince as the hot liquid burned his throat on the way down. However, it worked. Chad immediately poured himself a fresh cup of coffee and wrapped his cold aching hand around it.

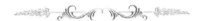

"So what now?" Chuck was like an adolescent with ADD.

"Pictionary?" Marianne's voice didn't sound very enthused.

"Apples to Apples?" Cheri sounded only a little more interested in her suggestion than her mother's.

"Poker?" A shrug and an evil glint in his eye was Chris' only response to Emily's playful slug at his suggestion.

"Mother and I often read the *Courtship of Miles Standish* on Thanksgiving," Willow suggested helpfully.

Amused glances flitted around the room while Willow waited to see if she should retrieve their volume of Longfellow's poetry. Chad, knowing his wife was clueless at the internal laughter at her expense, decided to play a joke on Willow and his family at the same time. "I know, let's play 'stump Willow with Shakespeare.'"

"Okaaaayyy." Though the entire room glared at Chuck's lack of tact, he echoed the minds of everyone but Chad and Willow.

Chad, on the other hand, was excited. This would be good. He passed out the three-volume set of Shakespeare from the library and told them to pick a quote, any quote and the game was family vs. Willow. "First to ten points wins."

Willow won, with only one error, in five minutes flat. Immediately, she took the books from the table, flipping through one carefully for a couple of minutes and then stared at her husband. "I was not wrong! *That was Much Ado about Nothing!*"

At the guilty expression on his face, Willow raced after Chad. He grabbed his coat and burst through the front door, down the steps, and jumped the fence into the pasture with Willow hot on his heels. The family stood around the large picture window and watched as she finally dove for his ankles toppling him. To their surprise, she pounded him. Her fists flew and his head jerked with each blow until Marianne demanded that Chris go put a stop to it. A minute later, Chris and Willow both pummeled Chad until everyone was sure he'd be unconscious.

After a couple of minutes, Chad jumped to his feet and took a bow, clearly untouched by his "beating." Chris and Willow, doubled over in laughter and panting exhaustedly, waved with one hand while resting the other on their other knees. Christopher gave Marianne a strange look and sighed. "I think our family has corrupted her—or vice versa."

"How can you stand it when he leaves at all hours?" Emily sat curled on Willow's couch, the rest of the family sleeping in various rooms.

"Probably because it's all I've ever known. I guess maybe it should bother me, but it doesn't."

"Wouldn't he be able to help you more if he had normal hours?"

"Actually," Willow mused thoughtfully. "Just the opposite. Because he's awake and home during light hours sometimes, Chad can help with more than if he worked from seven to six every night."

"But weekends..."

"Maybe. We don't do much work on Sunday, though." Willow shrugged. "Not usually anyway."

"Does it take all day? I mean, I saw you out there splitting logs, and Chad was milking cows—"

"Goat. Milking the goat—just one."

Emily's nose wrinkled in disgust. "How can you stand all that work just to get a glass of milk? He had to boil stuff and pour it through the cloth and then mark the jar... it was just an awful lot of work. Why not just buy a gallon at the store?"

"Because I don't want to have to spend the money; I don't want to walk five miles to get it and then have to walk five miles home every few days. I don't want the pasteurization and homogenization to take away some of the nutrients from the milk. I want it as close as to how God designed it as possible. Milk is such an amazing food."

"How long have you lived like this?"

"All my life. I don't know any different. Before last year, I'd never spoken to anyone except my mother, our financial advisor, and a couple of delivery people and even then, rarely."

"You're kidding!"

She shook her head smiling. "Outside Bill our advisor, I could count on both hands the number of conversations I can remember having with anyone but Mother before she died."

"I don't know how you do it. I just don't know how you can stand it!"

Rather than defend her lifestyle against the unjust prejudice, Willow shrugged. "I understand that. I remember how flabbergasted I was when I saw how others live. The money they spend on things that they will replace next year because it is 'obsolete,' the dependency on what others provide as to the choices available..." She gave Emily an embarrassed look. "I was so revolted by the lack of space around homes, and the artificial things like treadmills to simulate a walk. I was fascinated by it. I spent a long time on my friend's treadmill because it was a novel thing to me, but when I thought about what it represented, I was appalled. People manufacturing a simple task like walking didn't make sense."

"Marianne thinks you walk on water and generate electricity while you do it."

"Mom likes playing house out here for a few days at a time every now and then, but when it comes down to it, she's happy to return to her mechanical servants and her stores."

"Did you ever consider leaving when—" Emily stumbled over the word die and its synonyms. "It happened?" she ended lamely.

"My financial advisor wanted me to take a job offered to me at a store in Rockland."

"Boho. Cheri told me about your children's designs."

"Right. Bill wanted me to come and then get to know him better..." Willow didn't feel like explaining.

"And you just said no?"

"Emily, I would have suffocated in the city. I need fresh air, meaningful work, and I need to decide what I want and don't want to do. If there weren't people like me, vegetables would be obscenely expensive. Without people like you, when people like me slice through their leg with an old-fashioned scythe, they'd die. We need different people to do different things. I couldn't stand your world and you're not interested in mine. That's okay." She softened her words with another smile. "It's really okay."

A dim light shone in the living room window as Chad arrived home at two o'clock that morning. He had no doubt that Willow would be waiting for him, a sandwich ready and the living room fire blazing to warm him. Her internal alarm seemed to know exactly when to wake half the time, and the rest of the time, he knew she needed her sleep. Their life, almost from the time he met her, had slowly developed a perfect rhythm and harmony to which nothing he'd ever seen could possibly compare.

"I was wrong. I expected a sandwich, not stew," he said as he entered the back door.

"I thought after all that turkey at dinner, you might want something different, but I can—"

As soon as Willow started to pour the stew back in the pan, Chad stole it, planting a kiss at her temple. "You are downright feisty."

"And you like me that way, so quit fussing and eat."

"How'd it go tonight?"

"Well, I found out Emily won't be trying to move in with us." His laughter erupted loudly enough to make her clamp her hand over his mouth. "Shh."

"Not fond of farm life, eh?"

"You could say that. She finds the mud, manure, sweat, and unsterile environment revolting."

"It's so much more picturesque in one of those country life magazines, isn't it?"

"I don't know," she admitted as she led the way to the couch. "Our magazines were never picturesque. They were realistic."

"Well, the country magazines mom always got showed pretty stables with perfectly groomed horses and polished hooves. Kitchens that never saw berry canning or soap making. Just a nice Sunday dinner and cookies and milk on a school afternoon."

Willow curled against him sleepily. "Well, she won't be

buying any goats anytime soon, that's for sure."

"Are Dad and Chris still planning to make it to the sales?"

"As far as I know. They'll probably be up about the time you leave. Good buy—"

"Best Buy," he corrected, amused.

"Whatever—they're going there to buy some kind of camera..."

"Got it. Okay. I've got a list..." Chad fumbled through his pocket and handed it to her. "Give this to Dad, *and don't open it.*"

"I take it you're not making me that skein winder I asked for?"

As Chad drove back down the driveway on his way back to work, Willow heard the sounds of the men waking up and poured cups of coffee for them. Christopher entered the kitchen first and found Willow waiting for him. She passed him a piece of paper. "Chad's list. I'm not supposed to look. I didn't. Make sure he knows that."

Chad crawled into bed at six-thirty—full, exhausted, and hoping his father was successful with the list. Willow's journal lay open where she'd left it before she crawled into bed.

Black Friday,

This is what they call this day. While the country recuperates from overindulgence, they overindulge in other areas as well. In some ways, it seems to indicate excess in all forms of American society. Why else would it take until one month before the end of the year for some businesses to turn a profit? I cannot comprehend that.

However, when I see the excitement in Chad's face, the grand elaborate schemes for hiding their plans from each other right under the very noses that they're deceiving. It all has a delightful air of mystery about it. I don't think it'd ever be my "thing," but I love seeing the camaraderie between the men as they sally forth to slay the gift dragon in their quest to

204

please a loved one. It's almost gallant in a strange sort of way.

I spoke with Emily about our life here. I spoke confidently, and I hope, compassionately. I know I had—well, have—reallystrong opinions about the average American lifestyle. So much of it seems lazy and self-centered to me, but as Chad has pointed out numerous times, I'm just as self-centered in my own way.

It did make me wonder, however. Just how many of Chad's dreams and preferences did he give up to marry me? Am I holding him back from... something? Did he choose this farm because that's what it meant if he chose me, or did he choose me and got a blessing with the farm? Is it the blessing to him that it is to me? He never complains. He works just as hard as I do, and yet, why?

What did he give up to marry me, and would I have given up something that great and wonderful to marry him, whatever it was? I know he loves reading about my childhood, but did he really think about what it meant to choose the life that produced it? I think I am beginning to see just what an amazing man I have married. Even if this life was his first choice, he chose me to share it with him.

Me, with all my stubbornness, my... oh my. Wow. This man loves me. I know this, and when I think of it, does he have any idea how much I truly love him?

Mother prepared me for everything I could ever face in this life- except for how to share it with someone like Chad. The one area I need the most help in now is the one I am sure to fail. Lord please don't let me fail him. Lord please give me the courage to ask about what **he** *wants for* **his** *life- for* **our** *life. Prepare me for the answer I just maybe don't want to hear.*

Chad's face settled into a lazy smile as he slid between fresh sheets that smelled faintly of lavender. His head sank into the softest pillow he'd ever used, and he pulled quilts and blankets over him that he knew had been made by his wife's hands. His sweats and t-shirt appeared like clockwork in his drawers, always fresh and clean. The scent of the family's breakfast slowly wafted up the staircase, but Chad's stomach was already full and happy having come home to a breakfast

205

he'd never get anywhere else.

"What do I want Lord? Remind me to tell her I want exactly what I have. Right here. Right now." As he drifted off to sleep, Chad added one more thought. "Unless you wanted to add a baby or three into that mix. That'd be just about exactly right."

CHAPTER 128

The long driveway home greeted him with artificial pine swags tied with red bows and lit with twinkle lights—she'd taken his advice and used the extension cord to the barn. Candles in the windowsill and lanterns along the porch lit the house making it look warm and welcoming. The upstairs windows had candles in lanterns like beacons on a hill. In all, it was a festive picture worthy of Currier and Ives. The only thing it lacked was a horse drawn sleigh rushing down the "lane."

Chad loved nights like this. Off at six, dinner waiting with a house smelling like Christmas personified, and a bath towel hung by the upstairs woodstove, waiting for him to step out of the shower—the perfect recipe of domestic happiness. He remembered his first winter in Fairbury, the bare apartment, the boxed and canned foods, and the sheets he now realized probably were changed only once that whole season, were things of the past—a past he hoped never to see again.

He climbed from his truck wearily. It had been a long hard day. Fairbury rarely had more than a speeding or drunk tourist, but a domestic dispute that had gone south, a baby who had died of SIDS, and strung-out teenagers from Rockland who tried to rob the Fox theatre gave the Fairbury police enough drama to last them until the New Year. He wanted nothing more than to take a shower, relax, and let the stress from his job melt away in the haven of his home.

Unlike his co-workers, tonight he wouldn't flip on a television and see the ugliness of the world in his own living room as well. This had bothered him at first, but after months of news-free living, Chad was happy to get a recap of world events at work without all of the sensationalized local bits and bizarre horrors that punctuated the nightly news.

Willow sent him upstairs the moment he entered the house. The towel already hung from the towel rack Willow had installed as soon as cool weather set in. Fresh clothes waited for him on the closed hamper lid, and his favorite CD waited in a player, ready for him to escape for a few minutes. By the time Chad jogged down the stairs, the stress and grime of the day was washed down the drain, and Chad was ready to enjoy the next two days off.

"So, what do we need to do for Christmas?"

"It's still two weeks away."

"Ten days," Chad corrected, "but who's counting?"

"Your mother's quilt is almost done; I just have to finish the binding. Cheri's sweater is finished, Chris' sweater is done, and your father's afghan needs a lot more work, but it'll be done in time."

"What about my present? Are you done with it?"

"It's wrapped, stored, and out of the way so you can't peek." She gave him a sly smile. "Is my skein winder done?"

"A skein whater?" He laughed at her mock indignation. The winder had been done for two months. What she didn't know about was the hoosier Luke was making for her. There was a perfect place for it where the hutch was and the hutch would look wonderful on the wall next to the dining table. He couldn't wait to bring it home.

"Hey, we can do whatever we want for the next couple of days, so what sounds good?"

"We should go snowshoeing one afternoon. The snow is so thick this year. I had to shovel the roof this morning."

"Was it that bad?" Chad had never seen anyone have to shovel a roof in his life. He'd always assumed that was something reserved for Alaska or was an urban legend.

"Mother was adamant. If the snow was over fifteen inches and lasted more than a week, it had to go."

"You could have fallen off of there!"

"Chad," she began with forced patience in her tone, "I've done this my whole life. I think I know how to keep myself from crashing to the ground."

"I guess you do. Now that the roof is clear, what do you want to do?"

"We could make Christmas cookies..."

"How about you bake, I eat?"

Willow tossed him a sassy glare. "I had a crazy impression that you wanted to do something new, but that'll work too."

"We could go into town and watch a movie..."

Shaking her head, Willow carried the dirty dishes to the sink. "Not interested."

"We could go bowling..."

"I could teach you to knit and you could make scarves for all of Luke's children."

"Did I tell you?" Chad hesitated. "Aggie's pregnant."

Willow's eyes lit up excitedly. "Really? Oh I bet she's so excited! When—how far—"

"March."

"Oh baby clothes! I've got to start making baby clothes! I need flannel and s—Wait. March? That means she's been pregnant for..."

"Several months. Mom didn't want to tell you, but I finally told her at Thanksgiving that I was telling you before Christmas if she or Aggie didn't do it first."

Confused, Willow shook her head. "I don't understand. Why wouldn't she tell me?"

"I think she was afraid you'd take it hard."

Willow dropped the last dish in the drain, banked the kitchen stove, grabbed a plate of cookies from the shelf above the stove, and carried it into the living room, visibly trying to repress her irritation. "All this time I could have been excited for her, praying for her, sewing and knitting for her, but I'm supposed to take it hard, so I don't get to know. I feel gypped."

"We'll go to the city tomorrow and buy all the yarn and fabric and anything else you could possibly need. You were busy with harvest and everything else anyway."

"I guess so. I'll write Aggie a note tonight, though. I bet she thinks I'm the worst cousin-in-law ever known to mankind." She took a deep breath and met Chad's eyes. "Don't keep something like that from me again. It is a little insulting, but primarily I feel like you deceived me; you hid something from me because you or someone else thought the worst of me. I know," she continued quickly seeing the objection on his lips, "it was meant for a kindness, but it still says that I'm petty enough after only six months of marriage, to be too full of my own disappointment in not being pregnant that I cannot rejoice with someone who is. That isn't who I am, and I thought you knew that of me."

December—

Aggie is pregnant but no one told me. Apparently, I am supposed to "take it hard" when a wonderful thing happens to someone else. I could understand if I'd been married for five years with no signs of children, and it was bothering me... maybe then... but I don't understand why now. We haven't even been married a year. Of course, I was surprised when Mother was pregnant after one horrible encounter, and yet with much, um, practice, I am still waiting. I don't feel barren though—not yet.

How do I convey my disappointment to Chad? I feel betrayed by him listening to his mother on this. Mother's lessons didn't cover how to tell a husband—wow. I feel silly. No, mother didn't tell me how to handle a husband, but Chad's a person too. I keep treating him as though husband is the only facet to his personality. He's a person, and when people disappoint us we confront it, forgive, and move on. I sort of confronted it. I need to forgive and move on. Two lessons in one. I feel quite educated this morning.

Chad is milking and feeding the animals. The chickens are racing around the yard like crazy. I don't think they'll be out there for long. I should have shot a turkey for Christmas. It's too late to shoot one now and I don't have anything for Christmas dinner except for roast. How can I make roast different and festive? Maybe we should raise a few turkeys as well. I'm not doing a pig though. That was disgusting.

Chad's main Christmas present gets here this afternoon.

He keeps trying to "do something," but we can't leave or we'll miss delivery. I think I'll send him to town for something- maybe dinner. I can "forget" dinner. I am so excited. If there is any one thing that Chad wants for this farm, I think I've found it. I hope it's the right choice.

Baby gifts. Tomorrow we're going to Rockland and buying all kinds of wonderful things for me to make little sweaters and booties and diaper sets... I have all the patterns mother bought but didn't use for me. I can do it! It'll be good practice for... someday.

At four fifteen, Chad bounced along the road with orders to bring home lasagna from Marcello's. Willow loved lasagna but rarely asked for it and refused to try to make it. *"Some things are perfection as they are."*

While Chad ran several errands, including shipping a box of scarves to Aggie's children, Willow helped the deliveryman put his gift into the barn. She couldn't wait to see what Chad thought of it! It was the most exciting gift she'd ever purchased.

Chad found her in the kitchen practicing "Away in a Manger" on her dulcimer. "Dinner's here. Let's eat."

"Can you get me more milk from the barn while I cut?"

He rezipped his jacket and stepped back outside. Willow set the lasagna on the warming shelf of the stove, and pulled on her jacket, and stepped outside the second Chad's body disappeared into the barn. He slammed into her just as she reached the door. "Whoa. Merry Christmas."

"I can't believe you bought me a horse!"

"You keep saying that a horse is the only thing keeping this from being a 'real farm,' so..."

He grabbed her hand and pulled her over to the horse's stall. "He's—"

"She... Lacey."

Chad nodded. "She's beautiful. What—"

"She's two years old, a quarter horse and done whatever that means."

"Dun. It's her color."

"They change colors for a while?" Willow was confused.

"You didn't go through the horse stage when you were a

211

girl, did you?" D-u-n. Dun. It's the name of the color." As he explained, Chad smoothed the horse's neck, patted her face, and ran a hand along her back. "She's just beautiful."

"As I said, Merry Christmas. You have to buy your own tacks though."

"Tack. I'll look tomorrow while you're buying up baby supplies."

Reluctantly, Chad followed Willow to the house several minutes later. "Where did you find her?"

"I asked Terry over at the feed store if he could find me a good horse. He asked around and found Lacey."

"This is going to make that skein winder seem awfully inadequate."

"Of course it won't!" Willow grinned, thinking she'd trapped him into admitting her gift. "It's exactly what I asked for. What better gift could you get me than that?"

"I don't know but I am going to feel pretty guilty come Christmas morning."

She passed him a plate of lasagna. "Eat your dinner. Your horse might want a walk around the yard before you go to bed."

"And then I think it's time you learned a new game."

"What game?"

Chad grinned. "Chess."

"Why do I have the feeling that you are very good at it? Mother never liked it so we didn't play it."

"Well, I'm no Chris. *He* was the chess master. I was just his practice partner, but once in a while I'd win and I don't *think* it's because he let me."

As he went back out to the barn, Chad dropped a box and rule sheet in her lap. "Read through that a couple of times, and I'll be back."

"Do you want some hot chocolate?"

"I'll make it when I come back in. You read."

Willow grinned as the back door shut behind him and opened the chess set setting up the pieces quickly. When Chad arrived, she grabbed the rules and forced herself to look engrossed in them as he brought steaming cups of hot chocolate. "Well, I'm ready to try, it but you're probably going to have to help me..."

212

"So if you and Mother never played, how did you beat me two games out of three?"

"Beginner's luck?"

"Who did you play?"

Willow winked as she set the pieces back into their places. "Me."

"You would."

CHAPTER 129

"Let's get it in the house first, and then I'll take you out to meet Lacey. I'm going to have to take her over to Brant's Corners and get Uncle Zeke's friend to outfit her."

"I can't believe she just bought you a horse."

Chad beamed. "Oh man, wait'll you see her. She's gorgeous, very good temperament and everything, but..."

"What's wrong?"

"Willow is terrified of her."

Luke's jaw dropped along with the tailgate to his truck. "You're kidding. Willow? She's used to animals—big ones like cows even."

"Not big ones that want to be friendly."

The men tried not to chuckle as they stumbled through the yard with the hoosier. Every few feet they stopped, set it down, and then hoisted it once more. The steps were a bit difficult, but once through the door, the hoosier sat beautifully in the place Chad had planned for it.

"That is just perfect. I can't believe you got the flour hopper and everything. She's going to love that!" As he spoke, Chad tied a huge red bow around the hopper and jerked his thumb at the corner. "Will you get me some tape from that drawer?"

By the time Willow arrived back home after an afternoon of shopping with Cheri, Chad and Luke were walking Lacey around the yard on her lead. Cheri raced to hug the horse, but Willow just leaned against the porch and watched delightedly as everyone admired Miss Lacey. "Come on, Willow," Cheri called as she led the horse closer to the house.

"Let me get her a carrot." Willow practically ran into the house as Cheri led the horse closer and closed the "safe" gap that Willow had painstakingly created.

"She really does hate the horse," Cheri remarked, as Willow disappeared into the kitchen. "What on earth?"

"I don't know but she will barely feed the poor thing." Chad's words were meant for Luke and Cheri, but his voice spoke to Lacey.

Willow came outside with a handful of carrots and waggled one to catch Lacey's attention. "There, girl!" With a powerful throw, Willow sent the carrot flying toward the pasture. Chad barely had time to let go of Lacey's lead rope as the horse chased after the carrot.

"What—I've never heard of a horse playing fetch!" Luke stared at the horse awestruck. "Then again," he added, "there really is no reason why a horse wouldn't if I'd ever thought of it."

"Well, she doesn't fetch really. She just chases it."

Once Lacy knew where the carrots were, she hurried back to Willow, but Willow was ready. She tossed another carrot and the horse made an arc in the snow and raced after it. Chad watched as his horse, time after time, raced to the pasture to snag the carrot before trotting back for another one. When the last carrot was gone, she hurried to Willow wanting more.

"No Lacey, they're all gone. I don't have any more! Lacey!" Willow backed away from the horse until she tripped over the back steps. Luke and Cheri erupted in fits of laughter, but Chad followed as she stumbled up the steps and escaped inside, Lacey standing with two hooves on the first step whinnying for her to bring out more.

He pushed his way past the horse, and burst into the kitchen. "She won't hurt you, lass."

"My head knows that, but my heart sends me running before my head screams loud enough to be heard." She started to say more but the sight of a hoosier with a bright red bow stopped her. "What—"

"Merry Christmas."

216

"Did you and Luke—"

He shook his head. "No, just Luke. I didn't see how I could go work on it without you knowing."

To Chad's surprise, Willow jerked open the kitchen window shouting, "Thanks, Luke!" before she turned around and threw her arms around him. "And thank you! I love it. Mother always talked about building one and putting it right there, but she never got around to it."

"I wish I'd had the tools and the time, but by the time I thought of it…"

"It's perfect." She jerked her thumb at the back door. "Get out there with your family. I'll make some hot chocolate and pull out the cookies."

Chad stepped out of the door and then popped his head back in to suggest that she make a few sandwiches and saw her running her hands over the smooth surface of the wood. Abandoning the sandwich idea, Chad slipped out the door smiling to himself. "I think that was a good idea," he muttered as he hurried to return his horse to her stall.

New Year's Eve—

Another year, another Christmas without Mother. It amazes me how things all stay the same even when they're so very different. Mom Tesdall gave Chad and me the oddest looks when she saw our gifts for each other. I finally asked her what bothered her, and she commented that she didn't know how we'd afford to keep giving each other such expensive gifts. At first, I was confused. I couldn't think of what I had said or done that might give anyone the impression that I would always spend so much. This year, I spent what I'd earned with the garden surplus. It felt wonderful because I knew I was buying Chad's gift with money I'd earned rather than Steve Solari's money. But it turns out that it was another one of those things where I am weird again. Apparently, if you give someone a gift that costs fifty dollars this year, then next year you're expected to keep the cost similar. I don't understand that at all. I mean, what if the best gift for that person isn't something you can buy?

What if it is just something you can make and doesn't cost much? Do you put an envelope in with it covering the monetary difference? It seems absurd. Chad says that his mom doesn't understand how I think, but that I should just be me and not worry about it. People will always be happy with what I give them. I hope he's right. I certainly don't want to be rude. It's amazing what is rude. I would have thought any expectations of a gift or its value would be rude.

I spoke to Mom about the Aggie situation. I think I embarrassed her, and it made me feel badly, but at least she understands now that even if I had been disappointed that Aggie was pregnant when I am not (it still sounds so juvenile to write that!), it is worse to know that others hid their joy from me. Chad knows how I feel about how he listened to his mother, and he agrees that it put a distance between us that almost damaged our relationship. I was angry about it, but Chad reminded me that he's never been married before either and only had his mother's (usually good) advice to follow, so he did without thinking. Looking back it is easier for him to see why I was bothered. We both learned lessons on that one.

Lacey is fitting in nicely with our other animals. I think she has decided that I am beneath her notice, which is fine by me. Chad still teases me about my fear of her, but that is one big, overly-friendly-if-she-likes-you animal! Her teeth are huge! So, we seem to have come to a truce. She won't come near me, and I give her lots of alfalfa, carrots, and apples and even oats, but Chad says too many oats aren't good for horses. I always thought they were, but I guess not. He stirs blackstrap molasses and cod liver oil and I don't know what else into the mix every few days. He rides her a few times a week and brushes her often. He keeps asking me to try brushing her, but I'm not going near her. Chad says I'm shooting myself in the foot, because soon she won't listen to me. He thinks it'll make it difficult for me ever to become "friends" with her. I don't want to be friends with her, so that suits me just fine. I think Lacey and I have an understanding, though, so we're good.

Chad suggested that we build "roads" across the land from field to field and pasture etcetera, so that he can drive tools and things from place to place, and so that me dragging the cart around will be easier than going through grasses and things. I'm not sure how necessary it is, but if it makes it easier on Chad, I think it's worth it. The work this year is going to leave less leisure time. I'm going to have to schedule things carefully and make sure I schedule occasional afternoons off. I am concerned about pregnancy. I mean, with the work we have planned, what happens if I get pregnant and am as sick as Chad says some people get? Even if I don't, I could need clothes at just the time I won't have time to make them or something like that. I have to plan for it all, even if it might not happen. I found plans for more strawberries in one of mother's journals. She never did the berry hills that she'd planned, but I think I will do it this year. If I could sell enough to pay for the time invested in the plants... I think I'll start seedlings tomorrow in the greenhouse if Chad can find seeds at the Feed and Seed.

"Willow?" Chad's voice broke through her reverie as she entered her thoughts into her journal.

"Hmm?"

"It's almost midnight and you're drooping."

"But I wanted to stay up until midnight like you said." Her petulant tone told him she was exhausted.

"You will. I've got a surprise, though. Come on."

Chad led her downstairs, insisted she put on her jacket, and then led her to the porch. "Cover your eyes and count with me. Open them at one."

A minute ticked by. Seconds. Finally, Chad's voice started counting down from ten. "Five... four... three... two... one..."

Willow's eyes flew open and stared at Chad expectantly. Then, a burst of fireworks rose from the center of the yard and exploded into the sky. Colors reflected on the snow and sparks showered downward, fizzling as they touched the snow. A boyish delight in Chad's eyes amused her as he watched her reaction to the relatively small display of pyrotechnics.

"Happy New Year, lass!" he shouted from the yard.

Laughing, she scooped a huge handful of snow from the porch railing and formed a snowball. As she tossed it at him, she screamed at the top of her lungs, "Happy New Year World's Greatest Husband Ever!"

CHAPTER 130

March—

We've had a thaw but it won't last. It is unseasonably warm and that means mud. Things try to grow and die because they think they're ready to weather life above ground, but as always, they'll get a rude awakening. Chad just read that and laughed at me, but he'll see that I'm right. Every time nature tries to blossom too early, storms, snow, frost, or something will come along and kill the tender plants. If only they would wait for their time. If, rather than rushing to pop out of the ground and be noticed for their early arrival, the plants waited for the dangerous times to pass, they would grow stronger, brighter, and smell sweeter than ever.

Chad says that is a good analogy for some of the little girls at church. They try so hard to be "grown up," and look the part, but in the end, there is nothing to look forward to. It is truly heartbreaking how jaded many little eleven-year-old girls are about relationships and life in general. I guess Chad is right. It is a good analogy. As breathtaking as a single red tulip is surrounded by snow, it is much more vulnerable to plucking than it would be had it waited for its sisters to bloom with it.

Valentine's Day was full of fun and surprises. Chad had flowers delivered to the house. I guess I never realized that Wayne at the Pettler would deliver flowers for me. What a fascinating business. Apparently, the other officers teased Chad about being cheap and unromantic because he didn't send red roses. Who knew that is customary for every "romantic" occasion. Chad knows me well. The gerbera daisies he sent were bright and colorful, and I'm planning on growing a bunch myself now.

Speaking of growing flowers, I sold a huge bunch of lavender to a woman from Brant's Corners. Aggie called and said the woman wanted it for crafting and offered me much more than I would have imagined it is worth. That reminded me that we'd planned on the lavender rows along the driveway so I've started plants in the greenhouse for that. Chad says as soon as I give the word, he'll plant them for me. How is it possible that Chad works for the police department, isn't home half of his waking hours, and yet he manages to cut my workload significantly? I do much less work now than I did when Mother was alive and it's not because Chad works non-stop or anything. Chad says I already wrote that in another journal entry. Well, it's true!

Portia is a big girl now. She works hard to keep everyone, including Chad and me, rounded up into nicely huddled masses, and of course, fails miserably when it comes to the human population. The barn cats have tried to subdue her, but alas, she tries to keep them in line anyway.

I avoid what is truly on my heart. I need to get it out and deal with it, but I fear hurting those closest to me. It's odd, in less than two years my thoughts have changed drastically. I would never have thought twice about reigning in my thoughts or words when it was just Mother and me, but as Chad likes to say in a tone that sounds broken hearted, I've been "civilized." So here goes. I am not pregnant. I've been married for nearly a year and there is no sign of a baby on the horizon. The real problem is that, to me, this isn't a problem. However, everyone around us seems to see it as something horrible. Well, those who want to see us with child. Another group—just as vocal—thinks it's best that we wait a few years before starting a family. I don't quite understand why either side is so concerned. Either we have a baby or we don't.

I was quite content to wait until it just happened, but even Chad is making noises like something is terribly wrong. He brought home several printed pages of articles on "infertility" and "trying to conceive," and has been reading them diligently. From what I've read, I think everything in my body is working fine. I checked the temperatures, checked the gunk it told me to (revolting, by the way—I get Mother now), and basically, there's no reason that I can see as far as the body goes, for me not to be pregnant so I think perhaps it's just not time yet. God knows what He's doing, and while Chad agrees, he's not so sure we know what we're doing. In the famous words of the local tween-agers. What. Ever.

Willow shifted nervously in her seat as she filled line after line after line of what she considered increasingly evasive information. Much of it she couldn't answer. She didn't know if there was a family history of cardiac trouble, diabetes, cancer, or depression, but she did know that her mother died of an aneurysm, she'd had a tetanus shot within the past 10 years, and was not allergic to general anesthesia.

This, however, was nothing compared to the abject misery induced by five innocent words spoken by the nurse when she called Willow's name. "Willow Tesdall? This way, please."

From that moment on, Willow's first visit to the gynecologist nearly became her last. From the backless paper gown, to the instruments of torture attached to the paper-covered table, to the ice-cold stethoscope that the doctor pressed against her chest through the paper, the invasion grew to epic proportions. Her eyes widened, her words grew more and more clipped and stilted until finally the doctor sat on the rolling stool next to her shoulder and patted her arm.

"Are you always this tense Mrs. Tesdall?"

"Willow. Please just call me Willow, and what do you mean?"

"Well," the doctor smiled reassuringly at Willow as he tried to make her more relaxed and comfortable. "You jump at any attempt to touch you—like I said, very tense—and I don't know how I'll manage to get a decent pap smear if this keeps up so—"

"What's a pap smear and why do I need it?"

Dr. Walston pushed his chair back and stared at the nurse. After a few seconds, he glanced at Willow again and asked, "Is this your first gynecological visit?"

"I think so. I've only been to the doctor for stitches once, when I sliced open my leg and got surgery, and I think that's it. I was at the dentist once, though."

With a look at his nurse that spoke volumes, the doctor excused himself for a few minutes, while Anne explained the processes of an exam, what each test was for, and what the doctor would be doing. The fact that Willow did not grab her clothing and run is a great testimony to her love for Chad and her desire to understand if there was truly anything wrong with her. Although she was content to wait many years to see if God blessed them with children, Chad, somewhat pressured by family she suspected, was nervous about "wasting time" in not correcting anything that might need correction.

Despite Nurse Anne's very helpful preparation, Willow found the entire exam to be humiliating, invasive, and painful. She cried through the pap, the internal, and the chest exam. Dr. Walston tried to be as gentle as possible, but eventually seemed to opt for speed over comfort, once Willow assured him she'd prefer it to end the ordeal.

In his office, Dr. Walston asked several questions that she could see he assumed Willow wouldn't know, but to his surprise, she was prepared. From within her ever-present tote bag, she pulled a month's worth of fertility information— enough to make any regular charter proud. He read everything carefully and then smiled.

"You've done your homework."

"My husband is concerned."

"Well from the looks of this, he doesn't need to be— everything seems well enough for now. I am going to send home a few ovulation predictor kits, and I want you to use them according to directions. If you have any questions at all, call the nurse's desk. Those ladies are pros at making everything clear. Once you have a predictor, I want you to come in and we'll do an ultrasound on your ovaries and see what's happening."

"And that should fix it if there's anything wrong?"

"No, that should tell us if anything's wrong."

Willow looked at him curiously. "What could be wrong that this super-sound thing will show?"

"Well," the doctor's mustache twitched with amusement

224

at Willow's skepticism, "it'll show if your ovaries are working properly, if they're releasing the eggs, and if necessary, we'll order a dye test to see if the egg can get through the fallopian tubes."

"And if, say, the tube is too small or something? What happens to the egg?"

For the next half hour, Dr. Walston explained more about the reproductive cycle than Willow imagined most people wanted to know. She thanked him for his time, paid for the visit at the front desk, and left with a bag full of boxes that were to become her closest companions in the next month. The whole idea seemed like a waste of time and money to her, until she thought again of how excited Chad would be when she told him everything worked fine and they just needed to be patient.

She jumped on the bus to Fairbury, unlocked her bicycle from the rack behind the Fox, dumped her paraphernalia in the baskets, and strapped on her helmet. Through the streets she rode, hoping to avoid Chad and the questions he'd be sure to ask, and barely remembered to stop at the feed and seed for the roll of fencing she'd planned to use as an excuse for her ride to town. Chad called her name just as she passed Center Street. She waved cheerfully calling, "I got the fencing! I'll see you at four!"

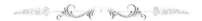

To her amazement, the next three weeks crawled past. They planted their garden, increased their sheep flock by twenty new lambs, and exponentially grew their chicken production. People had been begging for fresh eggs, free-range chicken meat, and Willow was determined to provide top quality products for those ready to pay. It required inspections by health boards and the FDA—even for their little farm—but they passed without a problem, and the result was more work than ever. Willow loved it.

Chad tilled fields and planted grain and alfalfa, while Willow created even more berry, melon, and flower patches. The work was hard but satisfying. When Brad Waverly needed an extra day's work to fund one of his many hobbies,

225

Chad gave it willingly and spent the day working on one of the many projects that Willow devised.

Two days after their first anniversary, the ovulation kit told her what Dr. Walston had been waiting to hear. She was ovulating—or about to. The "ferns" showed plainly on the mini microscope included in the kit, and the nurse at Dr. Walston's office arranged an appointment for ten o'clock the next morning. It was time to discover if everything "worked in that department." What strange ways they had of describing things.

Having been to the office already was helpful, but nothing could have prepared her for the horrible invasion of the ultrasound wand. While the doctor examined her organs and how well they were or weren't operating, Willow closed her eyes and whispered repeatedly to herself, "this is for Chad, this is for Chad, this is for Chad. He's worth it. I think."

The results were inconclusive, but the doctor showed the swollen ovary where the egg would burst forth at any time in the next twenty-four hours. "Come back tomorrow morning, and let's see what we see. How about eight?"

Willow left the office in a daze. She was tired, sore, and mentally drained. She took a cab and directed him to the hub, but as they passed the Rockland Towers, she begged him to pull into the portico. "I'll get out here. Thank you."

In less than an hour, Willow curled comfortably in a hotel bed, sleeping peacefully.

Portia raced to greet Chad as he climbed from the truck. He absently patted the dog's head as he hurried into the house. He'd seen Willow's call, but a fight at the high school was more important at the time it came through, so he'd planned to call her back. He hadn't planned for a dead battery. Again. It was time to buy a new cell battery—or maybe a cellphone.

The house was empty. The barn, nearby pastures, and greenhouse were empty as well. Unsure what else to do, Chad plugged in his phone and punched quick dial, waiting impatiently for her to answer. She didn't. However, she had left a voice message that he listened to curiously.

"Chad. I'm in Rockland—no, I won't tell you why; it's a surprise. Anyway, it's taking longer than I thought it would, so I won't be home until tomorrow. Call when you can. Oh, and will you check the black-faced lamb? I think she hurt her leg yesterday. I love you."

To his amusement, there was the same familiar hesitancy after signing off as if she either didn't know how or didn't want to disconnect the call. A surprise for him huh? Well, whatever it was, it would give him time on Lacey in the morning before work. That horse seemed to love the early morning rides across pastures and through trees almost as much as he did. He'd go eat in town, come home, go to bed early, and then get up for a morning rendezvous with Lacey. It all sounded wonderful, but he felt as though he'd lost his last friend. "She's not coming home, girl," he whispered to Portia on the way to the house.

CHAPTER 131

Lacey plodded through the damp grasses of the pasture early the next morning. The muffled *plop* of her hoof occasionally became overshadowed by the sound of the same hoof pulling free of mud with a sickening suction sound that belonged in dental offices rather than peaceful fields just after dawn. Hardly conscious of where the horse picked her footing, Chad rode along, dreaming of more sheep, horses, cattle, and of course, afternoons fishing for trout on a lazy summer day.

He'd tried to avoid all thoughts of Willow and what she might be doing. Chad's mother had called looking for her just after supper the night before, and Chad had to admit she wasn't home. Marianne wanted to race over to Willow's hotel to find out whatever the secret might be, but Chad refused to say where Willow was staying and begged his mom not to ruin Willow's surprise. As a safety measure, he'd called Willow and suggested she turn off her phone.

Maybe she was pregnant. Could you find out so soon after a cycle? He knew, more than most men, he imagined, every nuance of her bodily functions after watching so carefully for any evidence that his wife might finally carry their child. Would Willow run straight to a doctor for confirmation? The moment the thought crossed his mind, he rejected it as unlikely at best. Willow had a surprise and she'd share it when it was time. He could go looking for clues...

"Lacey, I'm pathetic. Did you know that, girl?"

The horse tossed her head as though disgusted with him,

but Portia, jogging happily at his side, gave a sympathetic whimper. "I guess you did," he laughed as he gently tugged the reigns to turn the animal around once more.

By nine o'clock, he had milked the goat, moved the sheep to another pasture, and let out the chickens for their daily foray into seed and worms. Chad wandered into the barn with the last load of eggs and realized that they'd need a larger barn at this rate. There wasn't room for more cows in the winter, the sheep pens weren't nearly large enough, and to move the chickens in as they'd discussed, would mean a bigger mess than either one of them cared to contemplate. It was time to make some major plans—immediately. Well, after calling their egg customers to let them know their eggs were ready and could be retrieved—from either the farm or the back of Chad's truck while he was at work.

While Chad planned bigger and better barn like your typical male, Willow, in her own typical feminine fashion, slipped on a new skirt, blouse, and braided her hair before rushing downstairs for breakfast. By eight o'clock, she sat waiting in the waiting room anxious to see what the doctor would find today yet dreading the process. "Lord, if I was of a scientific bent, I'd design a less intrusive way to examine one's innards."

"Excuse me?"

Willow glanced up to see the nurse standing there ready to take her into the room. "I was just informing the Lord that someone needs to reinvent your machine to be less invasive. I dread this."

Once ushered into the office and given the thin, drafty gown to don once again, the nurse disappeared into the hallway and peals of laughter followed. "Glad I'm amusing," she muttered to herself as she piled her clothing on the chair and lowered herself to the paper covered table. "Oh this stickiness is only slightly less disgusting than that goo they glop on that thing..."

"Morning, Willow. How did you feel last night?"

"Should I have felt anything?" Confusion flooded her features.

"Some women feel pinching on the side that is ovulating... for you it'd be your right side."

230

"Well, I felt a dull ache for a while last night, but it felt better after I ate so I just assumed..."

Dr. Walston and his nurse exchanged glances that seemed to mean something, but Willow didn't know what. The screen—oddly colored and three-dimensional—fascinated Willow this time. Watching the changing pictures of the inside of her body helped override some of her discomfort. "So, do you see what you're looking for?"

"I see what I expected. I'd like to do another one in a couple of hours, but I think I've seen enough to know what I think I want to try first."

She stared at Dr. Walston, waiting for him to elaborate. "And that is?"

"Well, it doesn't look like your egg is releasing. The ovary is trying, but it swells and then reduces."

"Can you do anything to make it release?"

"We have a drug we'd like you to try next month, starting five days after your cycle. Then you'll use the same ovulation kits, and when you see that you're ovulating, come in. Don't bother with an appointment; just come. I want to see if it looks like an egg released."

Willow stared at the screen and then raised her eyes to the doctor's face. "It sure seems like a lot of hassle. I mean, my mother, in less than ideal circumstances, was pregnant with the only chance she ever had to get pregnant, and look at me." She sat up and wrapped the paper "gown" around her tighter. "Is it right to play round with this stuff?"

Dr. Walston took her hand and waited for her to finish. "You don't have to do anything with this information. It might not do this every month, and yet it might. We don't know. I understand why some people have problems with in-vitro or other procedures, but if your thyroid doesn't work, we give it the right treatment to fix it. I personally don't see any difference between making one this of your body work and making another work."

"Do I want to know what in-veto is?"

He barely stifled a laugh. "Vitro. In vitro fertilization. I don't think you want to know."

"Good. I'll just trust you on that. So I take these pills and it makes the egg drop?"

231

"You make it sound like soup, but yes. That's exactly what you do."

A look crossed her face that made the doctor pause before he left the room. Finally, Willow picked at her cuticles and whispered, "Is it wrong not to say anything to my husband until we know?"

"Why wouldn't you?"

"He'll get his hopes up. What if it doesn't work?" Willow looked miserable.

"Well, I don't usually recommend keeping things from your spouse, but waiting a month before you say anything so you have something concrete is understandable. If you feel guilt, I'd tell him. If you are just concerned about doing what is right, perhaps you can talk to your pastor or priest."

"So where's my surprise?" Chad wrapped his arms around his wife as she climbed off the bicycle.

"They said it'd be at least a month, but hopefully it's all 'ordered' and ready to go."

"A month! I'll have the new barn built by then!"

Whirling in place, Willow stared at him slack-jawed before she laughed. "You had me going there for a minute."

"No, I'm serious. We're going to need more room for animals next winter, and I think we should consider a larger and warmer hen house."

They walked to the house discussing Chad's plans and Willow's idea for getting broody hens. "I don't know why Mother never found a source for them. I think it'd be a much better way to keep new generations of chickens arriving on a regular basis."

"Wouldn't it get bad to have such close interbreeding?"

"I read an article once—kept it too. It was about how there are co-ops that swap hens on a regular basis and with different people each time in order to keep the bloodlines 'fresh'. It was really interesting. There's one for this area and one near Chicago. Between the two of them, we should be able to keep a fresh genetic pool at all times."

"So," Chad began again teasing, "what *can* you tell me

about this surprise?"

"Absolutely nothing. And, if you keep bugging me about it, I'll call and cancel. If you knew what I had to go through to make this happen, you'd feel guilty right about now."

The scent of venison stew hit her the moment she opened the kitchen door. Chad didn't cook much, especially on the woodstove, but he'd managed to perfect stew in the two years he'd known Willow, and he'd also learned that she loved nothing more than coming home to the scent of a simmering pot of it. Bread warmed on the warming shelf and the coffee table was "set," with windows opened to send the heat out of the kitchen and draw the cooler evening air through the house. She still felt awkward eating on the couch, but when the kitchen was too warm for Chad's taste, he always moved them into the living room, and Willow didn't have the heart to complain.

"That smells heavenly."

"It does, doesn't it? I remembered the turnips this time." Chad winked at Willow's mock surprise. "Hey, I'm not that pathetic."

"So, tell me about this barn idea..."

"Mom, I think she's pregnant."

"You said that two weeks after you got married."

Laughing, Chad described her two trips to Rockland. "The last time, she stayed overnight. She didn't tell me she went the first time, but I was talking to Ben who runs the shuttle between Rockland and Fairbury, and he mentioned it."

"So what about that makes her pregnant?" Marianne didn't quite understand her son's logic.

"I think she's going to a doctor to see."

"Well it doesn't take two trips and an overnight to get a positive test, Chad."

"No, but with such a long wait, she might decide to have him check with an ultrasound or something after the test. Maybe that's why she stayed overnight. She went for the test, then went back a few weeks later to make sure baby was still

233

fine, but they had to schedule the ultrasound and fit her in the next day."

"Maybe, but I think most offices have them in the rooms now. I don't think she'd have to come back."

"She's so frugal though," Chad protested doggedly. "I think she probably found the cheapest guy in town, and he probably works with the hospital lab or something."

His reasoning did make sense. "Did you check the credit card statements or the account online?"

"I wasn't sure if that was fair. I mean, where do you draw the line?" How he wanted her to say on the other side of checking the accounts.

"I would."

"Even if she said it was a surprise?"

Marianne's protest could be heard throughout the—he glanced around and saw no one—empty police station. "This is my grandchild we're talking about. I want to know if she exists!"

"She?"

"I'm a grandmother. I have an intuition into this kind of thing, and we're having a girl first. Go check and call me back."

Chad told her to hold a minute. "Ok, I've logged in. Let's see..."

For the next few minutes, Chad scrolled through the very few credit card transactions, the bank cash transactions, and finally found a check to a Dr. Walston for several hundred dollars. "Bingo. Dr. Walston. I Googled, and he's in a 'Woman's Center' over on Telegraph."

"That's a very well respected center." Marianne's voice was excited. "I just looked up gynecologists and obstetricians, and he's listed!"

Chad grinned. This was it. His wife was finally pregnant. Who knew, just two short years ago, that he'd be chomping at the bit to be a father? Who knew that he'd be sitting at work doing detective work on his wife, rather than the creep who was writing bad checks all over town? Who knew he'd be surfing the web for cradle kits?

"So are you going to be a papa, or what?"

Joe's voice startled Chad, and he closed out the window

of various cradle options. "Officially, I have not been informed of any such thing."

Joe laughed. "Congratulations, man."

"Seriously, Joe. You know this town. Don't let anyone *think* you think that, much less *hear* you say it. You'll have to sit on suspicion until my wife actually deigns to tell me."

"And I thought you had it bad when you were falling for *her*. This is worse."

"Just pray she isn't sick. This'd be a bad time for her to be bedridden."

"Oh, my word." Judith broke in disgustedly. You've become Mr. Farmer."

"I thought this place was empty," he growled as he hurried out the door.

CHAPTER 132

The next six weeks dragged by for both Chad and Willow. Chad waited daily for Willow's announcement, and Willow followed orders for medication, testing, and of course, the obvious. He hinted about his surprise, but nothing he said or did tempted her to reveal her secret. She acted utterly normal almost every minute of every day, which drove him nearly insane. While he watched for any sign of morning sickness, swelling feet, or odd cravings, Willow worked her farm, followed doctor's orders, and waited for the magic date.

The day before her birthday, she had orders to take a pregnancy test, and if it wasn't positive, start testing her ovulation again. Chad, finally realizing that her birthday had arrived once again, decided she must be waiting for her birthday to tell him. His mother called every few days until Christopher heard of it and put a stop to it. She called one afternoon, apologetic and repentant saying, "When it comes to babies and Willow, I don't think I'm very rational. Just keep me out of it until it's a definite thing, okay?"

July twenty-second arrived raining, pouring rather, and dreary. Willow had no doubt that the stick dipped into a cup of urine would be a waste of time, money, and hopes, but she followed orders to the letter. After a second look at the stick, she flipped open her phone and called the doctor's answering service, insisting he call her back immediately. The call came five minutes later.

"So I'm looking at the stick and it looks wrong. There's

the bright blue line and then this faint pink one."

"It worked. I guess I'm glad I canceled the ultrasound of your last ovulation."

"What worked?"

"Willow, you're pregnant." Amusement filled Dr. Walston's voice. "Wasn't that the idea?"

"Seriously? One little pill for seven days and I'm pregnant?"

"Well," the doctor hedged, "I think you should come in for a blood test, but yes, you're probably pregnant."

"When can I come in?" The eagerness in her voice delighted him.

"This is why I chose this specialty. Nothing is more exciting than to see someone finally get pregnant after months and sometimes years of waiting."

"So that means what time?"

Dr. Walston laughed. "We'll fit you in whenever you get in town. Come today. I'll have Holly draw you."

"Draw me why? What does that do?"

"Blood, Willow. Holly will draw blood, give it to the lab, and we'll find out if Clomid was a 'cure.'"

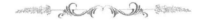

July 23—

I'm twenty-four today. It's an amazing day for me. I've spent the last twenty-four hours (two twenty-fours, how interesting) trying to think of the best way to tell Chad that we're going to have a baby. At first, I thought I'd do something with the test I took, but seriously, a stick full of urine? That's just revolting. So then, I thought about knitting booties at the speed of lightning but I don't really have any yarn soft enough for a baby.

I thought about telling Mom. After all, it might be kind of funny for her to tell him, but then I realized that I'd have to tell her first and that just seems a bit out of order. I know; I'm good at stating the obvious.

So instead, I'm debating between mailing a card, sending him a baby bouquet, or... oh, I have an idea. I'm just going to wait to see how long it takes him to read this. He'd better not take forever, or I'll go crazy.

Meanwhile, Chad and Bill have spent the past two weeks discussing the expansion of the farm, the new barn, the necessary inspections, and such. I don't understand half of what they're talking about sometimes, but it feels really good when they have a question and I have the answer. I may not understand what they're doing with my information, but at least I have the information we need. I feel less ignorant when I remember that.

July 24—

Oh, and in case Chad missed that part up there about the baby, I'm due in April. The doctor says around tax day. He called the baby "our little tax deduction." I tried not to be insulted.

July 25—

Perhaps I should put this on the kitchen table. Open. With the entry underlined.

July 26—

And circled.

July 27—

Highlighted? Seriously, I know it doesn't usually take him this long to read my journals. He does it every other day or so. Chad... knock, knock? Are you in there? Read July 23. Read it twice if you need to. Oh, and if I was snappish earlier—ok, I was—it's not pregnancy hormones. It's just thwarted surprise irritation.

Chad awoke shortly after midnight and found Willow gone. A glance at the clock told him it'd go off in an hour for his next shift. He tried to turn over and go back to sleep but failed. Finally, he crawled out of bed and jogged downstairs.

Her journal lay open on her chest as she slept on the front porch swing. He smiled at the widened seat. That had been a stroke of genius, even if he did think so himself. Habitually, he pulled the journal from her arms and glanced at the last page open. Circled? What?

He read the next one. It made less sense so he flipped the page back one and read July twenty-fourth. Due? Baby? He flipped another page back and read about her plans for telling him. Chad laughed. She stirred, smiled in her sleep, and rolled over, her pen falling to the floor.

Chad hardly noticed. Grinning at the words on the page, he waffled between shouting for joy and shaking her for not telling him immediately. Finally, he pulled the summer quilt over her shoulders, whistled softly for Portia, and pointed at the swing when the dog climbed the steps.

"Watch, girl. Take care of her for me," he whispered.

With a second, and then a third, glance back at her, Chad slipped back into the house and climbed the stairs. He didn't sleep. Rather than catching the last hour of slumber before he had to get up and go to work, Chad lay in bed, staring at the half-illuminated ceiling and imagined pigtails and scuffed knees, buzz cuts in summer and pink snowsuits in winter. The fact that the faceless child changed genders faster than he could keep up with them didn't matter to him—a baby.

Christopher answered the phone quickly. The last thing he wanted to do was let it wake Marianne prematurely. She'd just gotten over a nasty summer cold and had seemed out of sorts—not returning to her usually chipper self.

"Yes?"

"Dad? It's me."

"Chad? Isn't it kind of early son?"

Laughing, Chad turned right onto the highway and headed toward home. "I've been watching the clock since just after midnight. I consider myself having nearly infinite patience."

"What's up?"

"Willow is pregnant. I just found out last night."

It was Christopher's turn to laugh. "Let me guess; you found out sometime just after midnight last night?"

"Elementary, my dear father."

"Any idea when this baby is coming?" Christopher didn't

know whether to shout for joy or groan with the realization of coming estrogen-induced shopping trips, magazine purchases, and the incessant, if his years of parenthood were any indication, discussion of possible names.

"April."

"You've got a name covered if it's a girl then."

"I'm not naming my daughter April!" The disgust in Chad's voice was almost comical.

"I happen to like the name, but as long as you don't call her Beech, Oak, Aspen, or Sycamore, I'll be good."

"Very funny. *Grandpa.* Tell mom to call Willow, will ya?"

"I have a better idea. Send that wife of yours to the door today wearing a large t-shirt and a pillow underneath, but be handy."

"For what?" Chad was turning into the driveway and his mind somewhat distracted.

"To catch her if she faints."

"Will do. Don't tell her. We'll leave after I get off work."

"Can you get someone to handle night chores?"

After a moment of thoughtful silence, Chad answered. "Mmm hmm. I think so, why?"

"Plan to stay. Your mother is going to be over the moon, and she is not going to want to see you turn around and go home after just a couple of hours. Stop by the store on the way, and I'll have a box of books, catalogs, and magazines to keep her happy for a while."

"Your store carries books, catalogs, and magazines on babies?"

"Not all, no, but Fran will go get what I need for me if I buy her lunch." Christopher checked his wallet as he spoke and added more cash from the cookie jar on the counter. This would be expensive, but worth it.

"Ok. Will do. I'm off to find my wife. I haven't told her I read it yet."

"Huh?" The question never crossed the airwaves.

While Christopher stared at the phone, wondering what his son meant, Chad practically leapt from the cruiser and rushed into the summer kitchen where he expected to find, and did find, Willow straining the milk. "So, I hear our taxes get more complicated next year."

241

Willow jumped at the sound of his voice, spilling milk all over the counter. "You hear?"

"Ok, I read. I can't believe you've known since the day before your birthday and didn't tell me."

Soaked in milk, Willow cleaned the counter without a word. She sat the strained jars of milk in the fridge and scalded the pail. Once the rinse water cooled in the bucket by the back door, she stripped off her soaked clothes, dumped them on the washing machine, and peeked around the corner. With only the cruiser in sight, she dashed across the yard in her underwear and into the house. Chad followed, laughing.

"That's what you get for holding out on me," he called up the stairs. She'd skipped up them two at a time, but Chad took his time. He was still tired from interrupted sleep, excited about baby news, and trying to pretend to be affronted by her lack of shared information. "Are you sure about your dates?"

"Why?" Willow appeared in her favorite cropped shorts and the halter he loved now that he was free to enjoy it. Two summers ago, it'd had been an awkward moment or two when he'd arrived to find her half-dressed as she worked around the farm.

"Because you started going out of town two months ago. I assume you went to a doctor?"

"Yes, but I wasn't pregnant two months ago. I've been pregnant for almost three weeks he said."

"Sooooo," Chad drawled as he tried to make sense of her sentences, "what were you doing at the doctor's before that?"

"I went to see if anything was wrong with me."

"By yourself! Why didn't you tell me?" Though he knew he sounded irritated, Chad was truly just surprised.

"Because, I didn't need more pressure to produce offspring." Chad heard the strain in her voice and sighed.

"Can I do anything right?"

"What?" Willow didn't seem to understand him. "I thought you'd be happy about it."

"I'm thrilled, but I feel like a heel. I didn't realize you still felt pressured to get pregnant."

All angst diffused from the conversation as Willow laughed. "There isn't another man alive who knows more about his wife's body's inner workings than you do mine."

"That sentence is a bit tough to follow, but you're probably right."

She grabbed his sleeve and pulled Chad down the stairs behind her. "You need to eat your breakfast sandwich. It's ready for you."

"I called Dad."

She spun on the step ,nearly falling as she did. "Already?"

"Well, mom has been anxious—" Her sigh was almost too quiet for him to hear. "What?"

"You know I love your mother, right?"

"Right." He didn't like how this started.

"It's been difficult in regards to the baby thing. She was so excited when you thought I was pregnant before. Then she called every once in a while trying to ask, but not asking... and then there was Aggie's pregnancy thing." The dismayed look on Chad's face made her hasten to reassure him. "No, Chad. I'm not angry. It's just so much pressure. What if I was more infertile than I am—was? It makes me wonder if she would see me as some kind of failure."

"It's partly my fault," Chad confessed. "I called when I thought you were pregnant. She finally called and asked me not to share information, because she knew she was being pushy."

"When did you think I was pregnant?" Willow turned to get his food for him in the kitchen.

"When Ben said he took you to Rockland... and then you said you had a surprise and stayed overnight... well..."

She sat his plate in front of him and poured him a glass of milk. "Why do I have a feeling there's more to it?"

"I checked the bank account online to confirm my suspicion. That's why I think your dates are off. If you went in June..."

"I went to find out why I wasn't conceiving. I saw Dr. Walston—"

"The obstetrician."

"The infertility specialist."

Nothing she could have said would have surprised him more. "You went to a specialist?"

243

"You brought home all that stuff about what might be wrong, so I thought it was important to you." The bite of breakfast sandwich stuck in her throat as she said it.

"Lass, why didn't you tell me? I could have gone with you."

She attempted a chuckle but it sounded like a whimper. "Chad, you would have decked that doctor."

"Why?"

"Let's just say the things they have to do to find out what is going on..."

"Ahh..." he nodded understanding. "Pap smear and all of that?"

"You—" She bit off another large piece of sandwich and chewed furiously. "You knew they'd do that, and you let me—"

"Let you!" Chad was laughing now. "You went without telling me! How on earth did you expect me to warn you of anything?"

"Well, you do have a point..."

After several bites in silence, he asked, "So it was an infertility specialist. What did he find wrong? Endometriosis? Acidic environment? Short—"

"According to Dr. Walston, my body didn't cooperate in making soup."

"Making soup?"

"The egg didn't drop."

244

CHAPTER 133

The ride to Chad's parents' house started out with excited discussions of the birth in April, their plans for expansion, and how a baby would or wouldn't alter those plans, and, much to Chad's amusement, Willow's insistence that they stop at her favorite yarn store for baby yarn to start a supply of booties and "soakers." Half of what she said went over his head, but Chad good naturedly followed her into the store and watched as she chose the softest white yarns he'd ever felt. The other yarn she purchased seemed coarse in comparison.

"What is the difference?"

"This," Willow answered rubbing the soft skein against her face, "Is for sweaters and booties and all that wonderful stuff next to the skin."

"And that?" Chad poked at the other yarn thinking it was gravely inferior.

"Soakers. To cover the diapers. It has to be one hundred percent wool so the diaper doesn't soak through."

"Soak through? That is the diaper?"

"No, diaper cover."

"Diapers leak?" Chad was confused. "I would have thought they'd design them better."

"Mother started with plastic covers for mine, but then *Mother Earth News* had an article about making soakers out of felted old sweaters. I just thought I'd knit them and felt them instead of trying to find enough old sweaters."

"But I know Aggie doesn't have leaking problems with hers. Maybe diapers when we were little were unreliable, but these new ones seem to be better."

Understanding dawned as Chad spoke. She grabbed the bag full of yarn and led him to the door. "I'm talking about washable diapers—not disposable. We can't burn disposable ones, Chad."

"Cloth diapers?" Why the idea surprised him, he didn't know. If she washed her monthly pads, of course she'd use washable diapers. "I don't like the idea of diaper pins. It's horrifying. Truly horrifying."

"I'll think of something. Maybe snaps or Velcro or even buttons..."

As they drove through the streets of Rockland, Willow saw the street to the Women's Center. "Dr. Walston's office is down there. When we have the next ultrasound, you should come and meet him."

Suddenly, the impact of all that Willow had done assaulted Chad. "I still can't believe you went by yourself."

"It didn't make sense to get your hopes up again—"

"I'd think that was my choice."

"For over a year, I've been pressured by nearly everyone I've met to either be pregnant or to avoid it like the plague. Everyone seems to expect me to want a baby more than life itself or to insist that it's too soon. Maybe if I'd been married for five or ten years and still hadn't gotten pregnant—maybe then it'd make sense, but this is obviously another instance of 'Willow is too backward to be normal about this stuff.'" She glanced at him briefly. "Frankly, I'm sick of it."

"You're not the only one involved here. What was I supposed to think when you didn't come home that time— when Ray said he'd taken you to town..." Chad ground his teeth together in frustration. "When you said you had a surprise for me!"

"Has it really gotten to the place where the only surprise you wanted from me was a positive pregnancy stick? You're kidding me, right?"

Shaking his head, Chad turned onto the main street in Westbury and wove sharply around a creeping car. "That's not what I said."

"It's sure what it sounds like. I'm sorry that I wasn't able to hand you a urine soaked, plastic covered, proof that you've passed on your genetic material. I'm sorry that I didn't follow yet another conventional 'norm' and disappointed you. Again."

"You're being unreasonable, Willow! It was a logical assumption on my part—"

Willow cut him off mid-sentence. "And I think it was logical to find out what's wrong before I dash all your paternal dreams. What if I'd been declared infertile? Would this argument be about what a failure I am in that area instead?"

"Oh, don't be ridiculous. If I'd had the choice, which was removed from me thank-you-very-much, I would have liked to be there with you. What if they *had* said you were infertile? What if that hit you harder than you anticipated?" She made a gesture of protest, but Chad kept going. "I know, *if* you were so human as to have a weak moment of discouragement most women I've ever met—"

"And here we go again. One more dig about how I'm just abnormal. Why did you marry me, Chad? You knew me—that apparently I'm different. Why did you suddenly decide that you wanted me to become what you could have had in every other woman you've ever met? Why?"

For a brief moment, guilt struggled to bore a hole in Chad's heart. He heard tears in her voice and saw the firm set of her jaw so familiar to him. Anytime she struggled to avoid crying, her normally oval face looked nearly square as her jaw became prominent with tension, and now it looked like the image of Steve Solari. The impatient swipe at the tears in the corners of her eyes told him she'd be pulling out her claws next. Willow despised angry tears.

"I married you because I love you. Just you. Nobody else but you. Boop boop de doop."

"What?" Willow glanced at him alarmed. "What are you talking about?"

Chad turned onto his parents' street and pulled up in front of their house. "It's an old song. Stupid one too." He wiped a remaining tear from her eyelashes. "But it's true. I'd be miserable with an ordinary woman. Don't get me wrong, it might be easier," he teased, "but it'd be boring. I like who you are, and I don't want you to be any different, but it's hard to

247

predict when you're going to be like everyone else, and when you're off in your own world. Sometimes, I'm thrown off guard."

They sat in his truck, gazing at each other, saying nothing, but every word necessary travelling between them— unspoken. At last, Willow nodded. "So, we've both been kind of ridiculous; is that what you mean?"

"Can you define ridiculous?" Chad wasn't about to open the doors for further angst.

"Well, I felt pressured to put my order in for a stork delivery, and you felt left out when I made arrangements to get the stork out of prison without you."

Laughing, Chad jogged around the truck and opened the door. "Something like that. Can we start this over?"

"Done."

He handed her a pillow and said, "Stick it under—quick! Before Mom sees."

Chad opened the door calling, "Knock, knock," as he always did, and as always, Willow cringed. It seemed so rude to enter a house without waiting to be invited.

"You're here! I—" Marianne paused, shocked. "Does this mean what I think?"

The sight of Marianne jumping up and down amused them. "Does this mean you're in the 'I approve' camp on the baby question?"

"People don't approve?" Marianne looked scandalized.

"Some don't."

"I have to tell your father—" Chad's mother began.

"I told him this morning. I was supposed to go get magazines and such—"

"But I knew you'd forget them," a voice came through the door.

"Christopher! You knew about this and didn't tell me? I can't believe you went to work and let me think this was just an average get-together."

Christopher set a stack of magazines on the kitchen bar and poured a glass of iced tea. "I tried to get here in time to see your reaction, but I left without those stupid magazines..."

For the next half hour, the women worked together in

the kitchen making sandwiches, pasta salad, and lemon bars for dessert. The men discussed cradles, life insurance, and the quality of Fairbury's little league, while the Willow and Marianne created imaginary wardrobes, blankets, quilts, and toys for the anticipated child. Marianne was just as certain that it was a girl as Christopher was about a boy. Chad and Willow listened to their animated repartee with amused smiles, until Willow mentioned the ultrasound.

"Already? I thought they didn't do those until sixteen or twenty weeks. Teresa Mallory's girl was twenty weeks, I'm sure."

"Willow had some testing done, so they wanted to see how everything went."

Silence hung awkwardly over the table. Marianne and Christopher held a rapid conversation with their eyes and facial expressions, until Chad finally dropped his fork and threw up his hands. "What! Just spill it. Do you have any idea how much we hated when you guys did that when we were kids?"

"Well, when you spring this testing on us... Is the baby ok?"

"Mom, the baby's fine. Willow knew how eager we were for her to get pregnant, and when the pressure got high, she just decided to find out if there was anything wrong with her that might prevent a baby."

"Prevent a baby? Something was wrong? What did the doctor say?"

Chad looked at Willow to explain. All he knew was they'd discovered incomplete ovulation and given her something to help. The discussion had been interrupted so many times that he still hadn't heard how they'd fixed it. Willow told the story of the ovulation kits, the ultrasounds, and how one dose of Clomid had solved the problem.

"Clomid? Are you serious! How could you let her Chad? That stuff is so dangerous! She could be carrying a litter—"

Willow's jaw dropped, and it was instantly obvious that she was unaware that it still held partially masticated sandwich. After a second or two, she swallowed and took a long drink of her lemonade. "A litter? Chad, what is she talking about?"

"Sometimes Clomid has the side effect of releasing several eggs instead of just one or two. It's rare, but it happens. That family in Iowa was one..."

"So does that mean triplets or even quadruplets?" Willow looked stunned.

"The McCaugheys had septuplets." Christopher didn't like the look on Willow's face. She was clearly stunned, but anger filled her eyes.

"Seven babies. At once? Are you kidding me?"

"I can't believe Chad agreed to it," Marianne began.

Willow cut her off abruptly. "He didn't. I made the decision on my own."

"Didn't the doctor mention the risk of multiples?" Chad hadn't expected Willow's surprise. As careful as she was to ask questions about everything, and with medical disclosure laws, surely the doctor mentioned the possibility.

"He mentioned multiples, but it sounded like twins. I never realized—"

"You did ask him Chad?" Marianne had obviously missed the part where Willow didn't inform her husband of her decision.

"I didn't know, Mom. Willow went alone."

"She what!" Shocked, Chad's mother turned to Willow, indignation clouding her features, eyes, and unfortunately, her judgment. "What were you thinking?"

"I was thinking," Willow began as she stood and tossed her napkin on the chair. "I was thinking that I was sick and tired of the pressure. Everyone, and yes that includes you and Chad—Dad was probably the only exclusion—kept hinting, asking, pushing..." She swallowed hard and raised her eyes to the shocked faces at the table. "I was sick of feeling like I'd failed this family, my friends, and my husband. He brought home page after page of what could be wrong, what we should try to make it 'work'..." She choked down tears. "I felt like a breeder filly. It was horrible and I just wanted it over."

Before they could respond, Willow turned and rushed from the room, the front door slamming shut behind her. Christopher stood calmly and shook his head as Marianne began to protest. "She's right, Mari and you know it." He stepped around the table and leaned down murmuring into his son's ear. "It's time to put your mother back in her rightful place as mother, not confidante and buddy. You brought another woman into your marriage, son, and you brought the last woman most women are confident competing with. No woman wants to feel like his mother has a place in their bedroom."

Chad and his mother stared after Christopher as he left to find Willow.

"Um Mom—"

"Your father's right. I never thought I was interfering that much. I didn't say anything about all the physical labor, the adding more and more work... I didn't say anything about a lot of things because I knew it wasn't any of my business, but the baby..."

"I brought it up. I sensed that she didn't want to talk about it all the time. I assumed it was because she was as disappointed as I was. She wasn't, Mom. She has this faith."

Chad dropped his head into his hands. Marianne didn't know what to do to comfort her son. Torn by her contribution to the miserable ending of what should have been the best lunch of the year, she patted his hand and dabbed at her eyes, smearing mayonnaise across her cheek as she did. What she didn't expect, was Chad's admission of fury.

"I'm just so angry, Mom. She left me out of this. She went through that examination alone; she made medical decisions that could have caused complications, and I wouldn't have known to tell the doctors. She does this and—" he groaned. "She goes off half-cocked and makes these decisions without any kind of thought to others who are involved or will be. It's so infuriating."

At first, Marianne was tempted to agree. She wanted to commiserate, justify, and advise, but Christopher's admonition pricked her heart. "I'm not the one to talk about this with, Chad. I've already caused enough problems. I had no idea but—" She swallowed, choking back emotion. "You're right. Dad's right. We all put a lot of pressure on her. Because we weren't saying, 'why aren't you pregnant yet,' we didn't think we were, but I can see now why she felt that way." Marianne stood, hugged her son, and turned to leave the room. "I'm very sorry. I'm new at this mother-in-law thing,

251

and I failed miserably. Please forgive me."

"Willow! Wait up."

She whirled to see Christopher jogging down the sidewalk after her. "What—"

"I want to talk to you."

"Please, Dad, I don't think I can take any more scolding right now."

Smiling, he took her hand and led her around the block and down the street to a small park with a shaded bench. "I didn't intend to scold. I wanted to see if you were okay."

"I'm a bit ashamed of myself. I can't believe I spoke to Mom like that."

"My Marianne is not usually a meddling woman. This has been a very unusual thing for me to watch." Willow started to respond, but Christopher stopped her. "No, wait. Listen to me. We're all learning how this works. I've only been a father to children I've raised. I drove Chad away from me for years, and thanks to you, I have him back again. I don't know how to be a father-in-law. I don't know how to give the kind of counsel that I know my son still needs without seeming to interfere in his family. And, as is my normal behavior, I withdraw and wait for it all to smooth over. Marianne is the fixer. While I stood back and waited for my children to get over their hurts and difficulties, praying like crazy for them, Mari was in there talking to them, listening to them, and keeping those lines of communication open."

Nodding, Willow agreed. "I can understand that."

"I have a feeling that this wasn't all about Marianne's surprise at you going to the doctor alone."

"It wasn't. Chad and I had an ugly argument on the way over here."

"About the same subject?" Christopher could, with incredible accuracy, predict what each had said and why. Unlike his wife, he wasn't emotionally swayed by the situation. He saw the strengths of each side of each argument and the weaknesses as well. Using what he considered simple logic, he picked apart Chad's defense, Willow's offense, and left her dumfounded when he finished.

252

"It was wrong to go alone?"

"You and Chad are not individuals anymore. Not in areas like this. You are an individual in your personal likes and dislikes. You don't have to prefer blue just because Chad does. He doesn't have to like roses over snapdragons just because you do—"

"Actually, that'd be the other way around..."

Christopher laughed. "You like denim and he likes lace or vice versa. Those are personal preferences and as an individual, you don't have to be a clone of each other; that's not what I'm saying. However, in marriage, there are areas that you must be one—of one mind. You must think and act as one when it comes to your family, and I'd say that increasing that family counts."

"I thought I was. He wants children, and I wanted to do that for him. I wanted to stop the constant pressure, yes. That's why I went alone. I didn't know what would happen, and it would only upset him until he knew answers."

"And it would save you grief while you were waiting for those answers," Christopher finished, an understanding tone to his words.

"Basically."

"You denied him the right to help carry this burden, Willow. You took from him the chance to see his child at the earliest stage of development. You took from him, the opportunity to pray for you, to hold your hand during the examination, to protect you from what could have been a very unscrupulous doctor. You stole those from him."

"I did?" The confusion on Willow's face combined with the pain in her eyes nearly broke Christopher's heart. He loved his daughter-in-law, and hated that he had to hurt her by speaking the truth.

"You did. I know you didn't mean to. Somehow, I think your mother left you alone in your decisions unless they directly involved her."

"She did."

"I think," her father-in-law continued, standing and taking her hand again as he led her toward home, "I think I understand. I'll talk to Chad."

"He'll forgive me," she said simply. "He always does.

253

When will he tire of always having to do that?"

"My son was wrong too, Willow. Chad put you in a terrible position. You didn't act out of selfishness or indifference. You acted out of love and self-preservation. While your actions were wrong, I think you might have made other choices had you not felt backed into a corner."

As he spoke, Willow shook her head. "I don't know. I might have, but then again, I might not. I'm used to thinking and doing for myself. I don't know if I would have thought that fixing my body was Chad's territory too. I remember finding it weird and a little annoying when he brought home all that information about what might help or might be wrong."

"I think," Christopher tried again seeing that his meaning wasn't clear, "had the lines of communication not been 'pressure sealed,' the subject might have come up naturally. You would have seen where Chad was going with things and why you might want him with you. No one is faultless here, Willow." Christopher paused in front of his home. "But neither is anyone fully to blame. You both made mistakes. Marianne made mistakes." He swallowed. "And I made the same mistakes I always do. I hid my head in the sand and waited for the storm to pass. Please forgive me."

CHAPTER 134

August—

    The exhaustion is overwhelming. My doctor warned me of the nausea, but I've hardly noticed any. However, the sleepiness... I have never been so sleepy. I wake up and make food, milk the goats, and then I take a nap. I get up, drink some water, rush to the bathroom, and check the plants and sheep before I go to bed again. Later I wake up and finish some work, putter around with Chad or wait for him to get home, and fall asleep again. The doctor says it's normal. I feel terribly lazy, but when I can't work anymore, I assume I need the sleep so I sleep.

    The doctor showed us the little TV screen today. On the screen were two ovals. Two separate ovals. My plans to find a midwife and stay home like Mother are over. I carry twins. Two babies. Chad will not agree to my staying home to give birth—especially with the apparent risks that people assume with two children. I am not sure why, but with the doctor and nurses squawking and clucking like my chickens, it was easier just to agree. Dr. Walston has referred me to Dr. Weisenburg in Fairbury. It makes the doctor visits less of a nuisance I guess. They want me in there every four weeks!

    Meanwhile, although I shouldn't be "showing" yet, there is a definite change in my physique. My favorite summer shorts, much to Chad's disappointment, do not fit. I've stashed them in the drawer for next year, but Mom says that I probably won't fit into them ever again—especially after twins. I've made me two high-waisted dresses already—just to get the band away from my stomach. I think Chad is sick of them. He asked me twice this week if I didn't think we should go shopping and get me some new clothes or at least some maternity patterns.

Oh the maternity patterns—they're horrible. I cannot stand them. Everything is either too revealing or too much like wearing a sacque. Yuck. So, I'll be designing something for me, but I don't know what yet. Aggie said that she wants a copy of every one of my patterns for their next child. She also recommends I find a way to make a few pretty things "nurseable." She says most nursing clothes—I didn't know they had special clothes for nursing—are just as awful as maternity. Oh boy. A whole new design realm.

And, on that topic, I'm excited about the spring line for Boho. I really love what we came up with, and now that they're almost done, I'll be able to get started on my own clothes. There are fifteen pieces this year. I had a hard time balancing separates and one-piece items, but once I looked at everything together, it looked great. I think any little girl would have fun wearing clothes that are both cute and practical. That practical side is harder to achieve than the cute, though.

It's time for another nap. Another one. How will I survive nine months of sleeping? Will Chad get tired of filling in for me? He's already working on the new barn, he's ordered the new chickens, and he's got a dozen more ideas. Our lives are busier and more complicated than ever, and now two babies are going to need our attention. I can't carry both on my back all day like Mother did with me. Even Chad can't— not with him gone half the time. Somehow, I'll have to find a way to make that work. Somehow.

Willow loaded Jill's truck with produce, soap, candles, and strawberry preserves that were canned in their now heath department-approved kitchen. Chad, caught up in the excitement of dollars and cents, suggested that they sell all the strawberry preserves and buy jam at the store for half the cost and bank the difference. Willow nodded, said it was worth considering, and the next time she went to town, brought home a jar of strawberry preserves from the store. The following morning, she spread each half of a piece of toast with the two options and asked Chad to choose which they'd serve at their table.

He knew the difference immediately and as tempting as it was to save face and money, Chad pointed to Willow's jar. "I like that one best, and you know it."

"I didn't know it, but I do now."

"Sometimes a guy has to taste it for himself. Night and day really..." Chad's words drifted into nothingness as he watched Willow.

A new manila envelope and her coloring pencils sat next to her plate. As she ate, she carefully wrote "Boho Spring Line-3" in the center near the top and then shadowed the words making them bold. He could predict, having seen the process a dozen times over the past two years exactly what she'd do next. First, she'd draw brackets around the words connecting them at the corners, then she'd color in the area around the words... yep, there she went.

"Why do you do that?"

"Do what?" Her tongue stuck out of the corner of her mouth as she carefully connected the corners.

"Decorate the envelopes? Do they need to be decorated? With all you have to do and want to do, do envelopes for Boho need the designs on them?"

Willow looked up at him. "Does it bother you? We've always tried to make them more attractive..."

"I thought it was just a way to fill the time."

Laughter rang throughout the kitchen. "Oh, Chad, surely you didn't?"

"Well, yeah..." He felt foolish. Why else would they so painstakingly decorate something that was usually hidden in a box unseen?

"You've lived here for a year and half-lived here for nearly twice that, and you think we need things to fill our time?"

Even as she spoke, Chad realized most women would have been insulted. "Yeah—that was dumb. So why then?"

"Because it's pretty... and relaxing."

"But no one sees them. Why not make things to relax you

that you can actually enjoy all the time?"

Willow shrugged looking around the kitchen curiously. "Where would I put them? I don't have room for pictures on the walls or stuff on shelves. We make what we can use, and since we have to have the envelope anyway, we might as well make it pretty."

The simple logic made him smile. Most of the things his mother or aunts made were proudly displayed somewhere or given as gifts. Willow was happy knowing she'd made it, and every time—all three or four of them—that she had to pull out that envelope of fabric swatches, design sketches, and pattern pieces, she'd smile at the beauty in a simple manila folder.

"You should buy white folders. They'd give you a cleaner palate."

Willow nodded absently as she finished the title area of her envelope. Then, she replaced her pencils in the paper covered soup can probably left over from Kari's first days in the house, and set them on the window ledge. The envelope tucked behind it and waited for another few minutes of rest and doodling. A thought occurred to her and she pulled the envelope back to her staring at the top curiously.

"No. The tops wouldn't match. There's a fine ridge of that manila colored paper at the top of the envelopes. White would stand out and look awkward. We've always colored over it but it wears away at that top fold."

"I have two days off. What do you want to do?"

"Finish the barn. We need that done."

"Well, we can't finish in two days..."

"We can make some serious headway."

"I've been thinking about that," Chad began hesitantly. He knew Willow was still uncomfortable with changes, and with half the town and family warning him that at any moment she was going to erupt into hormonal tirades, he'd been walking on eggshells in anticipation.

"Oh?"

"Well I thought maybe Luke and Laird could help. We have that new guy in town too..."

"What new guy?"

"Charlie Janovick. He moved here from Brant's Corners

a couple of months ago. He kept getting calls for repairs on things or small remodeling jobs and decided to move. He's actually living in Joe's old place."

"I've never seen him at church..."

"He came once, but he's been driving back to Brant's Corners. This winter he'll make the switch I think."

"So you want to hire these men to come help us build the barn?"

Chad nodded. "We need it done before it snows, and the way things are going, I'm not going to make it with just Ryder and Caleb stopping by every now and then."

"Too bad they don't do 'barn raisings' around here. We could invite the whole church to help."

"So you don't mind?"

"Why would I mind? We have to get it done, and I'm barely able to put up a sheet of plywood per day. I'll never be able to help with the upper ones the way I'm going."

Chad pulled out his phone as she talked. He called Luke and arranged for his cousin and 'nephew' to come immediately. Charlie couldn't come before four but he promised to try to clear the next day to help as well. In ten minutes, Chad had lined up a full two days' worth of work.

Willow stood as Chad made the first call and started to set enough yeast for a few loaves of bread. She pulled out her baking table and started measuring absently as she hummed something indiscernible quietly under her breath. While Chad made notes, calls, and finished his breakfast, he watched his wife mix dough, knead it, and plop it back into bowls to rise. To his surprise, she dropped a kiss on his forehead and went straight to the couch, a minute timer in hand.

Before he could rinse his plate and follow, she was asleep, beads of perspiration already forming on her upper lip and forehead. He couldn't stand it. August was miserably hot in the Finley house, and while Chad had acclimated somewhat, he couldn't handle seeing his wife trying to sleep through the stifling heat. From inside the library closet, he pulled an oscillating fan and dragged it into the living room. He plugged it in and then went to flip on the circuit breaker box.

The bread timer went off all too soon. Willow dragged

259

herself from the couch and stared incoherently at the fan for a moment, until she realized what Chad had done. In the kitchen, a note was pinned to the cloth covering the bread bowls. "Lass, I'm out at the new barn with Luke and Laird. It's too hot in here to bake in the stove. Please take it out to the summer kitchen. Oh, and stop by the barn. I've got something for you."

As her hands plowed into the bread kneading it, dusting again with flower, kneading some more, Willow smiled remembering other summer mornings when her mother had come in to find Willow working on the week's bread and saying, "Why don't you just bake it in the barn today. The house is hot enough without making it one huge oven."

By the time Willow finished with the bread, took it to the summer kitchen, and found the men at the barn, Portia was a nervous mess. The minute Willow set foot out the back door with her loaves of bread in their pans, the dog had tried in vain to lead her to the new barn. She circled, dashed away, and returned, whimpering for Willow to follow. However, Willow, being the uncooperative mistress, chose to ignore the dog in favor of ensuring there was enough defrosted ham, turkey, and baked bread to feed a crew of workers.

At the barn, the men, drenched in sweat, were putting the outside plywood on the walls. Willow called out immediately, Hey, need a hand?" She knew they'd say no, and of course, a chorus of 'we've got its' followed in quick succession.

Chad jumped from the pile of boards he'd been using as a riser and dragged her around the side of the barn. "You sleep ok?"

"Like a baby."

"Well, you're sleeping for three right now..."

Willow punched him softly and shook her head. "You said you had something for me?"

Her husband's kiss surprised her. "Mom said she'd come and bring Aunt Libby if you want company."

"Will they come next month when I have to do the canning instead?"

"What about the beans..."

"I'll fall asleep on them. I know I will. I'd love the

260

company, and I could use the help, but I'd fall asleep and they'd have wasted a trip."

Chad nodded. "I'll see if mom will come for a week next month. What about Cheri? She has a month before school starts. Want me to see if she can come for a week next week and keep whatever you get started going if you drift off?"

The idea sounded promising. "Only if she wants to come. Don't guilt her into it, Chad. Don't do it."

She glanced up at the barn. "You guys already have this side mostly done. How'd you get those big sheets up so high so fast?"

She watched for a while and then hurried to check on her bread. By the time it was done, the turkey and ham were nearly defrosted, fresh lettuce, tomatoes, and onions washed, sliced, and ready to go on sandwiches, and the last of her cheese decorated a very small saucer. "Time to make cheese, I guess," she muttered absently, as she put it all on a tray and carried it to the house. Mint tea was next. She started a glass gallon jar of tea in the sun and then had idea. Checking the clock, Willow decided she had time before lunch and left Chad a note.

"Chaddie-my-laddie,
I decided to ride my bicycle to town and buy some lemons for lemonade, or maybe I'll by the bottle of lemon juice Mother bought sometimes. It'll save all that work you like to talk about. I thought about seeing if you needed anything before I go, but then I decided I'll just call. You'd try to drive me if I talk to you first, and you're busy. Just leaving a note in case you try to find me, and I'm not here."

Joe watched as Willow Tesdall rode down the street, deposited her helmet in the front basket of her bicycle, and then parked it outside Fairbury Market. What was she doing riding her bicycle to town in this weather? The bank's digital temperature reading said 98 degrees. Willow chugged a bottle of water and it made him smile. He'd expected a canteen or something. As she disappeared into the cool market, Joe pulled out his phone. He pointed meaningfully at Aiden Cox as the boy rode by, his helmet dangling from his wrist. Again.

"Hey man, don't you have the day off?" Chad's affirmative sent Joe into a lecture. "What are you doing letting your wife ride to town in this weather. The woman is beet red and beat. B-E-A-T."

Chad's groan of surprise made Joe backpedal. "Sorry Chad. I thought you knew…"

Unaware that Joe was inadvertently tattling on her, Willow picked out a large bottle of lemon juice, a pineapple, and for Chad, a package of the disgusting "American" cheese that he loved. He could ruin his sandwich with it if he wanted. It took half a dozen tries to find the only package the store sold that said "processed American Cheese" rather than "cheese product" or "cheese food." Had Chad not showed her, she would never have known.

Just as she reached the cash registers, her phone rang. True to her personal dislike of public phone use, Willow turned it off and waited until she returned to her bicycle to return Chad's call. "Guess you found my note."

"Got a call from Joe. He saw you ride up and thought you looked beat. Why didn't you tell me? I'd have taken—"

"That's why. You guys are busy, and I just wanted to satisfy a whim."

"A whim?" Chad's voice sounded unimpressed.

"Yes. I wanted you guys to have lemonade. It just sounded so refreshing."

"You're something else, lass. Did you know that?" He hesitated but couldn't resist. "Want me to run in and get you?"

"No. Work on the barn. Us chatting isn't getting more walls up. I'll be home in thirty minutes or so."

Halfway home, Willow almost regretted the decision. Hot, sweat dripped from every pore in her body, and her water was gone. The next wave of sleepiness descended faster than she could ride. Her legs dropped wearily against the pedals barely pushing them down, and the resistance of the other leg being pushed up brought the speed of the bicycle to a slow crawl. She wobbled, before pulling the bicycle off the shoulder of the road and stared down the highway. She had

262

another three miles to go—at least. Her eyes begged to close. The oppressive heat added further weariness, until she wheeled the bicycle across the highway, down the ditch, and leaned it against a tree a few dozen yards from the road.

Seconds later, she lay beneath the tree, her tote bag for a pillow, and slept.

CHAPTER 135

"She should have been home an hour ago even if she walked all the way home with a flat."

"It's awfully hot out there, Chad," Luke agreed. "Why don't you go find her? I'll bet she's got a flat and is walking really slowly."

"I can't figure out why she isn't answering the cell." Even as he said it, Chad realized why. She'd been in the store and had instinctively switched it off when he called. The desire to bang his head against the wall became strangely appealing.

"Go, Chad. We'll make sandwiches and kick back on your porch."

"The electric is on. Feel free to pull the fan out there to cool off."

Without waiting for a reply, Chad rushed to the truck and whipped it around, sending dust clouds everywhere. Three times he drove back and forth between town and his house before he saw Willow's bicycle leaning against a tree about a hundred yards from the road. He pulled into an outlet fifty feet away and turned off the truck. He didn't see Willow, but as he reached the bicycle, he saw her lying on the ground half-hidden by summer grasses. Before Chad woke her, he carried her bicycle to the truck and stowed it in the bed.

Kneeling beside her, he brushed the tendrils away from her forehead and whispered, "Lass... let's get you home."

She barely stirred. A few more whispered words did little to rouse her. However, Willow did manage to wrap her arms around his leg, holding it close to her cheek. Stifling a laugh, Chad tried again, this time lifting her head onto his knee as he settled down next to her. "Willow? Come on now, you're going to be eaten by bugs. Let's get you home."

Her eyes blinked uncomprehendingly at him several times. "Chad? Is everything ok?"

"Well, now that I found you—"

"I was lost?"

He nodded. "But now you're found."

"I'm not blind though—I see just fine." She sat up and looked around her somewhat dazed. "What are we doing here?"

"I was hoping you'd tell me that. When you didn't come home by lunch, I went looking for you. Your phone's off."

"I forgot to turn it on after the store. I don't remember coming over here."

"What do you remember?" He hadn't expected her not to remember.

"I remember riding home. It was hot and my legs didn't want to keep riding. I stopped on the road..." She thought for a moment and then shrugged. "After that, I just don't remember."

"I think you got overtired. How do you feel?"

"Thirsty."

Chad led her to his truck, slammed the door shut behind her, and looked heavenward. *"Lord, what am I supposed to do with her?"*

"Did you say it was lunch time?"

Nodding, Chad made a U-turn and zipped toward home. "Yep. Half an hour ago or so. That's when I noticed you weren't home."

"The guys must be starving. I'm so sorry."

"They're making sandwiches and relaxing on the porch as we speak."

She glanced at her hands. "I'm hungry. Where's the stuff I bought?"

"In the back of the truck with your bike." Chad drummed the steering wheel with his thumb as he carried on a private inward debate. "Will you do something for me, Lass?"

"Sure."

266

"No more trips to town, especially in this heat, until your exhaustion is past? It bothers me that you don't remember walking to the side of the road."

She nodded as he pulled into the driveway. "I'm just not used to having to think about whether I can make it home or not. It's such an easy ride that—"

"You're riding for three. Maybe that's why."

Willow groaned as she climbed from the cab of the truck. "Chad my dear, that is going to get very old, very quickly."

"Go lay down. I'll bring you water and a sandwich."

"That, however," she continued grinning, "will not get old for a long time."

September—

I'm still sleeping more than usual but not quite as much as I was. At ten weeks, my body seems to have adjusted to things much more than they were at first. I occasionally feel a bit peaked in the evening but resting, the cooler weather, and lemonade really seem to help. I drink a lot of lemonade these days. Chad says I'm going to have children with very sour dispositions.

The bulk of the canning is over now. I'm working on pumpkin, apples, and some of the fruit that we froze until I had time to can it. Odd way to do things but it's working. I planted my first set of fall crops in the greenhouse. As of today, the entire thing is being utilized to its fullest potential, with the exception of hanging planters. Chad was planning to build me some, but with the rush to finish the barn, it looks like we'll be ordering them instead. The manufacturer of our kit makes great accessories that are, in my opinion, ridiculously expensive, but Chad assures me they're worth the investment. He says what I've made in produce sales this year has already paid for half the cost of the greenhouse and its installation, so I guess it really will be worth it.

We realized last night that we forgot to tell Grandmother and Grandfather Finley about the babies. I've written them a letter and enclosed it in a special "announcement card" that I made. I said that babies are twice as nice when they come in double portions. Chad said it was cheesy, but he couldn't keep that giant grin off his face as he said it, so I know he was pleased.

I wonder why I find it so difficult to include Mother's family in my life. I keep trying, but I forget. I know they feel rejected by me. Grandmother has said as much. I never know how to answer. It is never deliberate, but how can I argue with the facts? I do ignore them. I do forget them. When I do think of them, it is at the most inopportune times like in the middle of making candles or butchering chickens. It's not like I can just stop and pick up the phone. And, I really don't like the phone anyway. I do need to do better about it. I don't know how but I do.

Chad is making two cradles from kits he bought online. He says one will go on each side of the bed. I'm glad I have a big room. I think I'll be removing the bed tables when the time comes so that the babies are in easy reach. Oh, and he's hysterical with the diaper snaps. I bought a tool for hammering snaps onto the diapers to make them pin-less, and it is Chad's job to "install" them. He loves pounding those things into place. Who knew? Thus far, we have two half-finished cradles and two dozen diapers. I have a feeling that might get us through one or two days of diapering maximum. I'll be making a few dozen more. Mom says to make sure I make the next two sizes now while I have time, because I won't once the babies arrive.

Mom is here now. She's been here for a week. Cheri came for a week last month, and we got the rest of the late tomatoes, the peaches and most of the berries canned. She worked hard, and as much as she grumbled at first, I think she liked it. She's learned to spin as well as I can, but she has absolutely no interest in doing anything with the wool, no matter how much I try to teach her.

We've been making clothes for me. I need them already. Mom said she didn't show until her sixth month with Chris, but she said that he was a small baby anyway, and of course, there was just Chris growing. I love what we've made so far, and she found me several pairs of flannel lined maternity overalls for winter. They're going to be great.

Dr. Weisenberg says that everything—babies, placenta,

my belly—is growing on schedule. I don't have to have another ultrasound in November, but he does want one in December. He says we'll be able to tell if they're boys, girls, or one of each. I'm hoping for one of each myself, but I expect two boys. Chad wants us to find out. I am so excited that I can plan this! It's so amazing that they can see inside!

Willow pushed the journal away from her. Marianne was sleeping, the animals were all happy outdoors, and Chad was at work. It was a perfect night for fishing. She grabbed her phone and called Chad. "I want to go fishing."

"So go."

"You wouldn't mind?"

"As long as someone knows where to find you if you decide to sleepover with the fishes—not sleep with the fishes, that's out of the question—but if you want a sleepover, I want to know about it." Chad's joke fell flat even as he made it.

"I don't get it."

"Just have fun and bring home dinner."

Willow stuffed the phone in her pocket and grabbed a piece of paper. She wrote a note, grabbed her sweater and outdoor blanket, and slipped out the back door. Unlike most her previous dogs, Portia was content to lie quietly beside her as she fished. With rod and tackle box in hand, Willow whistled for her dog and took off toward her favorite fishing hole, the moon lighting her path as though shining just to make the walk pleasant for her.

Retracing steps she'd made hundreds of times before, Willow slowly regained a natural rhythm of walking, praying, and just being with the Lord. However, by the time she arrived at her favorite tree, Willow had new thoughts swirling in her mind. Had her mother walked to the pool while carrying her? Did she fish back then? Her memory of Kari's journals didn't find answers to her questions, but the first year's journals were much less prolific than subsequent years. Did her mother love the night air, the cool breezes, and the sound of water splashing over rocks a little ways downstream?

For the next hour, Willow pounded heaven with questions about her mother that she'd never thought to ask before the news of her pregnancy. She prayed for wisdom, strength, and courage. Eventually, her prayers disappeared into daydreams until she curled up on the blanket, smiling as she pictured Chad teaching a little boy how to milk a goat or burn the trash. Her mind took her into the future with pictures of him explaining rainbows and why things are the colors they are. Small hands folded in earnest prayer for "daddy's safety at work" tugged at blossoming maternal heartstrings, until Willow thought she'd go crazy waiting for the next thirty weeks to pass.

Memories of little Ian nestled in her arms, his little fist curled around her finger, assaulted her emotions until it seemed nearly unbearable to wait. She chuckled at her own foolishness. Clearly, the hormonal excesses she'd been warned about were real. She felt like a crazed woman. The babies would come sooner than she'd be ready for them.

Somewhere between her plans for a double crib and her last sip of water, Willow fell asleep. She dreamed of walking to town in a thunderstorm to give birth to two babies the size of toddlers. Chad drove as fast as he could behind her but never caught up to her, until she reached the doors of the hospital. Babies with teeth grinned at her from their bassinettes, while everyone commented on how tiny they were but reassuring her, it was "to be expected with twins."

Chad saw the note on the kitchen table and climbed the stairs to see if Willow was home yet or not. Seeing their empty bed, he made a quick sandwich and started off for the pool. He'd spent many nights out under the stars with Willow, fishing, talking, and sometimes sleeping. He'd find her under her favorite tree, curled on the blanket, and if experience taught him anything, with Portia standing—well most likely laying—guard over her.

"She called Lord. She remembered. Maybe our little Mrs. Independence has finally gotten a handle on life with responsibilities toward other people." He paused, hating how his words sounded aloud. "And I need to remember that someone who has spent most of her life alone needs that freedom from time to time. I'll squash who she is if I keep expecting her to fit into the mold of my experience."

At the top of the hill before the descent to the stream, Chad paused. There, nestled beneath trees that had protected her for most of her life, Willow slept, Portia lying beside her as expected. The dog's head rose at the sound of his movement and his scent on the breeze. She glanced in Chad's direction and then laid her head back on her paws as though to say, "Well, you didn't think I'd let anything happen to her, did you?"

Chad nudged his wife. "Willow. Hey, lass, it's time to wake up. You'll sleep better in your bed."

She sat up blinking. "I guess I fell asleep."

"Catch anything?"

Willow pointed to the bucket in the stream. "Half a dozen." She glanced around. "Is it two already?"

"Two-thirty." He pulled her to her feet. "This is becoming a habit with us."

"What?" Willow grabbed her tackle box.

"Finding you sleeping under a tree. It feels like it should be some kind of fairy tale."

"Sleeping Mommy."

CHAPTER 136

December—

    Christmas is coming but we aren't fattening any geese around Walden Farm. I think I'm doing all the fattening that is necessary. I'm huge. Seriously, I am amazingly rotund. Ok, I'm immensely rotund. At five months pregnant, my doctor says I am approximately the size of a woman who is around thirty-three weeks pregnant, even though I am only twenty-two weeks along.

    We saw the babies. They have fingers and toes, and you can see them on the screen. Oh was I relieved to have an ultrasound without that awful thing inside me. It was nice for Chad too. The doctor is certain that one of the babies is a boy. The other he thinks is a girl, but he isn't sure. We were going to stay with Dr. Weisenberg, but he suggested we go to Dr. Kline in Brunswick. He didn't feel comfortable with handling a twin birth with his current workload. I don't know what that means exactly, but I assume he knows his business.

    Until I heard "a boy and a girl," I hadn't even imagined having one. Yes, I thought it might be nice, but I assumed that I'd have the two boys I'd always pictured and just brushed off the idea of a girl. Now... I picture a miniature version of my mother and Mom—Marianne—and I want her. I've made a few little feminine day gowns. Mom brought patterns for them, and I've been sewing and embroidering... Chad says I can't put his son in a gown. I can't imagine why (that was sarcasm for my captive audience of one). So, for little guy, I've been making "onesies" and using appliqués and such to feed my need to sew for my son as well. So far, Chad hasn't been affronted by my creations. I'm working on baby quilts next. I think I'll do a pink, a blue, and a green. If baby two isn't a girl, I'll have a quilt for him and a pink baby gift. If it is a she, then I'll have green for either boy or girl—gift speaking again. Perfect.

Chad laughs at how much white I'm sewing. He says that it'll all be stained and ugly immediately, but I reminded him that bleach is the righter of all stained wrongs. I love white little baby things. I have white blankets, diapers, gowns, sleepers, and even "nursing gowns," courtesy of Mom who seems to bring me a new gift every time she comes. The babies have toys, clothes, and books to please a dozen children. I have maternity clothes, nursing clothes, patterns, fabric, snacks, and things to pamper myself with like lotions, creams, and such. She visits me once a week for an afternoon, and we work on making baby scrapbooks, ready to insert pictures at will. It makes her happy, and all of the stress that had tried to root into our relationship has been ripped out. We're back to who we were, and I love it. Mom is a wonderful woman and it feels like I have her back again.

The babies move constantly—or so it seems. Honestly, I sit sometimes and stare at the way my stomach rolls one way or another. I eat and drink constantly. I can't put much in me at one time so instead, I "graze," as Chad puts it. Dr. Kline says that my weight gain is phenomenal. I thought that meant a lot, but apparently it means that I'm gaining exactly what is necessary to give these little tykes a good start and nothing more. He is optimistic about my ability to return to close to pre-pregnancy weight. I think I'm supposed to care a lot about that, but frankly, I'm too busy to worry if my backside is wider or my chest needs another increase in support. And it does. If I wasn't unbalanced with the babies sitting in front, I would be by their bottles above. Oh, my word it's amazing. Chad laughs. I can't wait until I have some milk flowing and can squirt him in the eye. That'll teach him.

We did have a bit of an upset over the whole milk thing. He'd forgotten that Mother had supply problems, and I didn't thrive at first. When I mentioned getting another goat around *the time of the birth just in case, he came unhinged. Unglued. Flipped out. Freaked out. Lost it. Ummm, I know Cheri used more phrases but I've forgotten them. He brought home a can of formula and explained why we'd be using that instead. I opened it, poured it into a cup, took a sip, and spat it out across the room. Oh boy did we have a lovely argument that time...*

Chad, reading the journal, laughed at the recollection of Willow's disgusted and indignant face. *"I will not feed my child this nasty stuff until you are willing to drink it too. I can't believe you'd even suggest it. Smell it!"* she'd demanded thrusting the glass under his nose. He knew he'd lost the argument the moment he gagged at the smell.

"I can't feed my babies goat's milk. I just can't do it. It's not—"

"It's good enough for me... and it was for me as a baby... it's good enough for you... but it is bad for the babies?" Her voice had been full of surprise at that moment.

"It's just," Chad remembered saying, as though he watched the scene all over again, *"that we don't boil the milk, we don't—"*

"It doesn't need to have all the vitamins and minerals boiled out of it. Why would we do that?"

"But they're just little babies, Willow! What if—"

"I thrived on that stuff, Chad. Thrived. Do you think I want to risk my babies? Do you think I'd do anything to hurt them? Do you think Mother didn't study everything she could to make the very best decision? Do we not live daily with the wisdom of those decisions?"

He hadn't liked to admit the strength and validity of her argument. After all, he was constantly telling people how wise Kari was, how knowledgeable, and how their success was largely dependent upon all the research she'd done for them over the years she'd lived on the farm. However, the idea of feeding his babies raw goat's milk just seemed irresponsible. He chalked it up to a lifetime of indoctrination regarding things of that nature and promised to discuss it with the pediatrician.

This sent them off into a whole new discussion that

275

they'd never considered. Doctor visits, well baby check-ups, and vaccinations became hotly debated topics until they both exhausted. Finally, Willow made an appointment with a pediatrician that both Dr. Kline and Dr. Weisenberg recommended, and the resulting consultation left both Willow and Chad confused, uncertain, and a bit chagrined. Dr. Wesley, a tiny woman with bright red hair and the greenest eyes either of them had ever seen, assured Chad that many pediatricians recognized goat's milk as an excellent food for babies over six weeks old, and discussed what she considered to be the biggest flaws in formula. Happy to hear Willow planned to nurse her babies as long as humanly possible, she assured both parents that whether they supplemented with nothing, with goat's milk, or with formula, as long as the babies could digest what was fed, developed no sensitivities to it, and thrived, she would approve any of the three choices.

Chad was relieved. Somehow, a doctor's validation of Kari's research made him more willing to endure what he knew would be a cry of protest if the necessity ever arose. His family simply wouldn't understand. However, his concerns about well-baby checks were also validated. Willow considered them unnecessary and asking for trouble. She was concerned about constant exposure to germs in a doctor's office where sick children waited in the same room as well children, were seen in the same rooms as well children, and for what? Measurements? Weight gain? Willow was certain she could handle any of those things at home.

Dr. Wesley disagreed. She discussed the tendency of one twin to be smaller, of slightly increased speech and motor skill delays and assured Willow that she'd be happy to take the twins as the first children of the day on their visits if germs were a concern. Chad had sighed in relief when Willow nodded and said, *"As long as we can leave through the back door, I guess."*

They were still at an impasse in regards to vaccinations. Chad insisted on none at birth. When he heard of the Hepatitis B vaccine at birth, he was adamantly opposed to it giving Willow the false impression that he'd be opposed to most of the shots suggested. She'd endured the Rubella shot when the titer came back negative for antibodies for the sake of the babies, but she saw no reason for them to have the shots while their immune systems were still developing. Chad disagreed. He was, however, adamant that there be no shots before age four months. When asked why, he couldn't give a coherent answer, but to Willow's way of thinking, it just gave her that many more months to convince him to avoid them all together.

They filled evenings with debates on car seats, scheduled feeding, and diapers. Often one of them took the role of devil's advocate for the sheer joy of the discussion finally admitting that they were in full agreement with the other. Chad was waiting for Willow to return from her fourth trip to the bathroom since supper before he brought up the next topic of debate. He was sure she wasn't expecting it and she wouldn't like it but on this one, Chad was determined. There wasn't an option in his mind.

Willow waddled down the stairs, her favorite top stretched taught across her immense, in his opinion anyway, belly. Already she had to put her foot up on a chair to tie her shoes, but the babies had hardly slowed her down at all. She worked from sun up till sundown, slept like a log, and rose the next morning fresh and eager for more. Dr. Kline had warned him that by the end of February, she'd be slowing down much more than she thought she would.

"Beating up the bladder tonight are they?"

"Yep. If I didn't need the water so badly, I'd quit drinking it and save myself the trouble." She sank into the couch awkwardly and then put her feet up on the arm leaning into his chest with her back. "Ahhh that feels good. Hey, I had an idea about names."

"What's that?"

"I think we should choose boy and girl names with the same initials. That way, I can monogram their clothing and if they look a lot alike, we won't mix them up."

"You want to monogram their clothing?" Only Willow would think of it. "Isn't that a bit- um... formal?"

"Oh, I wouldn't make it look like those towels we got for the wedding... I was thinking about cute little letters that looks babyish or fits the style of the outfit. Just a little monogram on the pocket or the bottom of the feet."

"Well, it would help," Chad teased, "in reducing the options of names anyway. Did you have any idea of initials you wanted to use?"

"I was thinking one could be CWT and the other WCT. Chad and Willow. Cute?"

"I like, it but I wanted to name a girl after our mothers and you."

"Since when?" For the past six weeks, he'd been throwing out every name under the planet and not one was a family name.

"I thought of it yesterday. We could name her Karianne Olivia after you, Mother, Mom, and Aunt Libby—I just thought of the Aunt Libby part."

"I like that..."

"What were you thinking boy wise? There could be two boys in there you know..."

"But Dr. Kline said he thought the other one was a girl." Willow was confused.

"Well, ultrasounds are more accurate than they used to be, but they're only as accurate as they can see. He's certain one is a boy, but he's guessing on the girl because he didn't see um—" Chad winked at her flushing face, "evidence of a boy."

"I wish I knew for sure."

"I think it's funny that you want to know. I was sure I'd have to bribe you with a few hundred sheep or something to get you to let them look at all."

Willow shook her head. "Why not know! We can make clothes, buy toys, pick names... I think it's amazing that we have the technology, and I love being able to plan it all."

"Plan. I should have thought of that. The only thing the Finley woman love more than doing things the old fashioned way is to plan out their every step."

"Sue me." Willow reached for her water, grimaced, and took a swig. "And here starts the ten o'clock tramp to the necessary."

"I've got another thing to bring up that you're not going to like."

"Then don't!" Her wicked grin prompted a fresh burst of chuckles from Chad.

278

"Sorry, no can do."

"So, what won't I like?"

"We have to buy another car." Even as he said it, Chad felt like a coward. He'd left out the worst of it and he'd done it deliberately— stalling.

"Soooo why will that bother me? We can't get the babies home in the truck. I know that. Well," she thought for a moment and shrugged. "You could always get Mom to take us home."

"And how would we all go to church, visit my parents, or go to the babies' checkups?"

"That's one way to avoid them..."

"Not happening. You agreed."

She threw up her hands in mock despair. "Don't shoot! I'll surrender. So, you buy a car. Do the accounts have enough money? What's the problem?"

"Well, buying the car isn't the biggest problem." Chad took a deep breath. "The big problem is that you're going to have to learn to drive."

"Not happening."

"Not an option," he countered quietly. Before she could mount her offense, Chad clamped a hand over her mouth, trying to make it playful rather than offensive. "Just listen. I promised not to lead you anywhere you weren't ready to go unless I had to. This is my first deviation. Like it or not, you must learn. Period."

"Why?" The lack of belligerence in her tone relieved him.

"Because you never know what could happen to those babies. They get sick. They need help. Croup, pneumonia, RSV, there's all kinds of stuff that babies get, and I might not be able to get to you in time to get them where they need to be. One could start learning to crawl and fall down the stairs. They could cut themselves on something—anything. Your mother managed not to need an ambulance and I commend her for that but—"

"But you're not willing to take that risk."

Chad shook his head. "No. I'm not. I have been praying that you'd understand. I'm not asking you to drive everywhere. If you want to stroll to town with them, so be it. If you never leave the farm except when I'm driving—that's fine. But I want you able to do it if they need you to."

"Do I have to get a license?"

"I think it'd be smart..."

"If it was a true emergency, couldn't they just give me a ticket for driving without one and we pay it? I don't want a license."

"But you'll learn to drive." It wasn't a question.

Willow nodded. "You teach me how, and I'll make sure that in an emergency, I can safely get us medical attention."

"I won't pretend I wouldn't prefer you had a license. I want you to pray about it—think about it—reconsider. But for now, as long as you learn how to drive, I'll be content."

They sat discussing names until Willow yawned the third time. For Chad, that was his clue that she needed bed. Now. He practically pushed her upstairs and demanded that she brush her teeth, before he hurried downstairs to blow out the Christmas candles. From just outside the library, he shoved the wise men along the edge of the table a little closer to the tree.

As they crawled into bed, Willow holding her unwieldy stomach until she rolled over comfortably, Chad debated asking the question that had confused him for weeks. He'd known she wouldn't want a license. Instinctively, he'd predicted her exact response. He'd avoided asking the question, but here, resting comfortably in their bed as he listened to the crackle of the wood in the stove outside their bedroom door, he was ready to ask.

"Why don't you want a license, Willow? Having it doesn't mean you *have* to drive..."

"It's silly really, but—"

"Come on, I'm curious."

She rolled over to face him, slowly releasing her supporting hands from around her belly once again. "I don't want the temptation. Just as Mother needed to turn off the electricity to avoid the things that would drag her from the life she wanted to live, I need to avoid the one thing that I think would tempt me away from the one I want to live. I don't want to become lazy, and I think I would."

"That's absurd! Willow, you're the least lazy—"

"And I have safeguards in my life that help keep me that

280

way. Remember how I forgot to order staples until I ran out of salt? It's already easy to do those things, knowing you can just bring them home for me. What'll happen if I can run to town for a piece of fabric instead of taking the time to make it myself? Little outfits like Cari's and Lorna's won't happen."

"But you loved making that fabric—surely you'd do it again in the same instance."

"I don't know," she said thoughtfully. "I'd like to think I wouldn't, but I love to look at fabric ideas that others have as well. Who is to say I wouldn't be tempted to shop for it? It's not wrong to shop for it, but I don't want to wake up twenty years from now and regret that I lost my ingenuity and creativity due to my own laziness."

"I am having trouble imagining you as lazy."

She laid her hand on his cheek, smiling. "Chad, you have a hard time remembering that I'm imperfect except when we happen to disagree. It's sweet, but if you really think about it you'll remember just what I pill I really am."

"Should I say something sappy like, 'if you're a pill, then I'll take my medicine happily?'"

"Um, no. That's just... um... no."

Laughing, Chad waved her over and began kneading her shoulders and back as he did every evening when he was home at bedtime. Within seconds, she was asleep and he at peace. Knowing his children wouldn't be at the mercy of an ambulance for medical care if needed reassured him. "Four more month's Lord... just four more months..."

CHAPTER 137

"I-I-I tried to-to- tell him b-b-but he w-wouldn't listen."

"And now the barn roof needs to be replaced already?" Willow stared at Charlie Janovick in dismay.

"Yes."

"And you think the metal is the best option?"

"Yes."

Willow nodded. "I see. Ok. Give me a list to do, and I'll take care of it."

"I-I-I'm sorry W-W-Willow. I-I-I should have b-b-been more p-p-persuasive."

"He was in a hurry and heard what he wanted to hear. I probably would have done the same thing." She dished out a bowl of stew from the stove and handed it to the handyman. "Eat. And while you're at it, tell me if you want to do the work yourself or if you think I should find a contractor."

"C-c-contractor. D-d-definitely. I-I-I would d-do it, b-b-but time..."

"You think it's more important to get it done quickly and a contractor can do it faster than one man alone?"

Nodding, Charlie swallowed his first bite, and nodded at the bowl appreciatively before saying, "I-if I-I-I wasn't so b-b-usy, I-I-I might have t-t-time b-b-but..."

"Well, I won't pretend that I wouldn't prefer to have you do it. You're a genius with your hands, but if you find me a good contractor who can do it before the next snow, I'll consider myself blessed."

"G-g-got the m-man for you. I-I-I'll s-send h-him out."

The next morning, a middle-aged man with a spread around his middle to match knocked on her door. Willow grabbed her coat and stepped outside. "Sorry, my husband is sleeping. He just got in at six so I'm trying not to wake him."

"Charlie told me what's going on up there and what needs to be done. I'll take a look, but I suspect if Charlie says it, then it's so. He hasn't been wrong yet."

"And your name is?" Willow liked the man already. Anyone who recognized Charlie as a treasure was all right in her book.

"Sorry—Paul Plummer."

"The roofer."

"You don't know how often I get people trying to convince me I know how to fix their pipes. Not only do I not know, I don't want to learn," the man joked as he grabbed his ladder from his truck. "I'll just climb up there and give it a once-over."

Minutes later, he climbed down shaking his head. "Charlie's right. You've got ice between your shingles and some are already tearing. I don't know what went wrong up there—didn't take the time to look—but outside the fact that I use this product because I believe in it, I think it's the only one safe to install this quickly and in this weather."

"Can you have it done by Friday?"

"I'd have to charge quite a bit extra..." The man seemed embarrassed to say it.

"I don't care. We can't afford to add more work onto what we're already doing." As she spoke, Willow clutched her stomach and sucked in her breath.

"You ok, ma'am?"

"Yep. I've just got a kicker in here, and sometimes he really gets me."

"You due soon?"

"Two months."

Before the man could express his surprise, a car pulled into the yard next to his truck. Carol Finley stepped out of it, waving at Willow excitedly. "Wait'll you see what I brought!"

"My grandmother is here. I need to go, but thank you. I'll sign whatever paperwork you want. Just please try to get that roof on before the next snow. If we like your work, I'll see what Chad says about replacing our other roofs to match. I know Mother planned to replace the old barn roof next year anyway."

Leaving the man, Willow waddled through the snow rubbing her belly briskly and wishing she'd not decided that a maternity coat was a waste of time and money. "Grandmother!"

From the trunk, Carol Finley pulled a large box. "It's a jogger stroller. It's meant for use on the roads, so you could walk to town with the babies and it'd be a comfortable ride. The wheels have shocks and everything." Before Willow could respond, Carol pulled out a large department store bag. "And, one of the ladies at church gave this to me for you. Her daughter had twins last winter and found this coat..."

The women chatted as they dragged the box onto the porch and then went inside. Willow tried on the coat and was excited to see that not only did it button, it would still button for at least a couple of more weeks. "This is so thoughtful! I'll take good care of it for her."

"Oh no, it's yours. She's not having any more children, so she doesn't want it back." Carol pointed at the truck retreating down the driveway. "Who was that?"

"Something's wrong with the barn roof, and apparently it's serious enough that it has to be replaced immediately."

"Storm's coming Friday. We were worried. They said they expect a lot of power outages in the outer lying towns."

"Considering we hardly use power, we're not concerned for us, but I made extra candles yesterday, and Chad took them to town in case people need them. He's going to haul wood today too."

One last glance out the window showed the new minivan parked beneath the awning Chad had erected. "I see you bought the car."

"I'm learning to drive it too. So far, I haven't hit anything, but I have come close."

The women talked over tea and cookies, Carol sharing stories of her own pregnancies and Willow laughing at the antics of her unborn mother in utero. As Willow hemmed summer blankets, Carol worked slowly on the afghan she was

285

crocheting under Willow's patient tutelage and talked about impending baby shower. "I didn't come to your bridal shower—I wish I would have..."

"You weren't ready. I understood that."

"We kept you at arm's length because of Kari's decisions. That was wrong, Willow."

Willow shook her head and snipped the embroidery floss. "No. It wasn't. Family ties aren't created at birth simply because of the birth. They're slowly interwoven as time and relationships emerge. You can't just wake up one morning, find out you have a grandchild of twenty-two, and expect to have a close, personal relationship. I had more connection with you because Mother was careful to teach me all about you." She corrected a stitch and added, "When you add to it, all the pain of Mother's disappearance, I'm amazed you ever speak to me."

Chad burst through the door grinning. "Fran sent this package home. I think I know what it is, but I'm not sure." Dropping the box on the couch next to Willow, he raced into the kitchen. "Where are those batteries I bought?"

"In the cellar. Top shelf to the right of the door next to the candles," Willow called back stifling a giggle as she struggled from the couch. "He'll stare right at them and never see them... this time."

"Visual learner?"

"Yeah... the vision of my immense belly reminds him that he can use his eyes just as well as I can use mine."

Carol's laughter followed as Willow waddled through the kitchen and down the cellar steps. "Did you find them?"

"Top shelf where—oh Willow, you didn't have to come in here. Now you have to climb back up again."

"I can stand the climb better than the shout. Here." She passed him the box of batteries. "What do you need with them?"

"Power is out in town. I'm going to keep them in the car for when people need them."

"But the storm hasn't hit yet!" Willow's surprise was arrested by a swift kick to her bladder. "Ow!"

"Don't you dare go into labor now, woman."

"I'm not due yet! It's—oof—just a kick. I want you to

286

have a talk with your son when he gets here. I am not putting up with this kind of treatment."

To her amusement, Chad laid both hands on her belly gently sliding them around until he found the offensive foot. He sank down on his heels and pressed his cheek against her stomach where the baby had started moving again. "Hey, little guy," the movement stopped. "Be nice. Your mama's tired and those kicks hurt. You can move, but take it easy ok?"

The foot stretched again, but Chad massaged it until it disappeared from the surface. "How do you do that? I try it and get a punch to the rib in addition to the kicks."

"They know authority when they hear it."

"I think you have a future in hostage negotiation."

Exhausted, Chad crawled from the covers and shuffled downstairs. Sitting in her mother's rocker, Willow's eyes were closed, and she rocked slowly. "Can't sleep, lass?"

"I could sleep fine if little feet weren't running relays."

"Relays huh?" He stood behind her kneading her shoulders with his hands. "How do you know it isn't all one very rambunctious child while his sibling is the victim of false accusations?"

"How do you know the rambunctious one is a he?" She leaned her head back and grinned into Chad's sleepy eyes. "Besides, I can tell where the movements are coming from. Either they're doing the tango in there or they're running relays. One baby can't be in all places at once. Not even yours."

"What do you have to do tomorrow?"

"Just a bit of tomato picking for Jill and cooking for the work crew."

He marveled at this wife of his. "You know, lass, you don't have to make them a hot lunch every day. It's not expected, much less required."

"They're out there working, in the freezing cold, to protect my barn and get it done before the storm. The least I could do is cook them a hot meal." She smiled thoughtfully. "I

287

guess it's good I didn't need to relieve any more angst, or we wouldn't have had enough dishes."

"Missing Mother these days?" His hands found the knots beneath her shoulder blades and worked diligently to release them.

"I'm missing her, but it's not the same. I have family in my life now. I've read her thoughts and fears that I never really understood before she died. I'm more ready to accept that she's exactly where she'd wanted to be since that horrible day that changed her life. She's content. I miss her, but I no longer resent her for leaving or God for taking her."

They stayed there for some time without speaking— Willow rocking, Chad rubbing the aches and kinks from her very swollen body. Finally, Willow caught his hands in hers. "Go back to bed, Chad. With Brad sick, they could call you in anytime. Get some sleep. I'll be fine." She smiled at his protest and shook her head. "I've got to get used to it anyway. Your mother assures me I won't get a decent night's sleep for the first year."

Reluctantly, Chad climbed the stairs and crawled under the covers. Now awake, he lit the oil lamp beside their bed and reached for her journal. He hadn't read it in a week. As busy as they were, it was a nice way to make sure he was in tune with his wife's thoughts.

February—

Time flies. I never understood that concept as a child or even when Mother was alive. Before the strangeness with the Solaris, not much had changed around here, and I rarely looked back, wondering where the time had gone, but the longer I'm married and the closer these babies get to birth, the faster the days seem to fall from the calendar.

Dr. Kline is very happy with how our little tykes are growing, how I'm stretching, and how I don't seem to be gaining too much. I'm finding it impossible to keep food down now. If I accidentally overeat— just one extra bite will send me running for a bucket, so I now carefully planning every single bite to ensure I don't eat too much or too little. It is a nuisance of epic proportions, but I'll survive. I told Chad the first thing he must do after the babies are born is go get me

288

something, anything, that I can fill my stomach with.

Grandmother Finley and I have forged a tentative relationship. As time goes by, we become more comfortable with each other and remember to seek out time together. My life is busy—too busy to make new friends, so it wasn't a priority to call, write, or visit. I'm not proud of that, but Chad reminded me that mail, phones, and roads work both ways. The full responsibility of keeping touch wasn't mine—we shared it. Now, we seem to take turns. At first, once a month to six weeks one of us would call, send a letter, or if nearby, stop to visit for a few minutes. Then it became every four weeks almost to the day alternating between us. After Christmas, it seemed as though every other week we'd find ourselves chatting, writing, or visiting, and now a week doesn't go by without me seeing or hearing from her and receiving a letter or two.

Mother's journaling bug has hit Grandmother. She's not up to keeping them pretty, so I cover them, add embellishments inside from place to place, and give them to her whenever she says she's getting low. She's become quite prolific, and she says she keeps all of my letters protected in clear plastic sleeves in a binder. I need to cover one of those for her too. I think she'd like it.

I will now confess that I am becoming nervous about motherhood. Mom brings books and articles to help "prepare" me for the baby. They tell me how to deal with cracked nipples, afterbirth pains, colic, reflux, how to avoid SIDS, and how to keep my marriage intact after the little adorable invaders that apparently want to do nothing but ruin our time together and ensure they have no siblings. Considering I have zero experience with children and babies, I don't know just how much to take to heart and how much to file away for "just in case."

Chad stared at the words before he made a decision. This needed to stop. Now. His mother would be horrified to know she was creating anxiety in Willow. He turned out the lamp, rolled over, and tried to decide whether he should tell Willow to put the stuff away until she needed it for reference or tell his mother to be ready to help whenever something came up.

The stairs creaked. She was coming back to bed. He waited. The closet door opened. He heard her take something from the shelf and wondered what she was doing. The water came on in the bathroom and then silence. Creak. Surely she wasn't. Creak. It was softer this time. A minute or two later, he saw her shadow enter the bathroom, exit, and the closet door came open again.

"Steps creaking again?"

"Yep."

"Did you oil it or what?"

"Oil? The step? Of course not! Powder. Sweep it into the cracks and voila. Stops the creaks."

He shook his head. "You're absolutely amazing, lass. Amazing."

"What are you doing awake?" Willow rolled into the bed laid her head on her husband's chest.

"I was reading."

"What did I say this time?" Drat—she recognized his tone.

"Well, apparently my mom is causing a bit of stress—"

"Oh no, Chad. It's not like that at all! She's being really helpful!"

He laced his fingers through hers and smiled as a light kick bumped against his side. "Mom would be so upset if she knew you were taking these things to heart. She's trying to build you a reference library, not give you a coronary. Just take what she brings, put it on a shelf, and don't worry about it until you need it."

"Yes, dear."

"Don't patronize me, woman!"

"Why not, you matronize me all the time."

He pretended to growl. "Do you want me to tell that child to start kicking again?"

"I'll be good, oh wise and wonderful husband of mine. I'll be good."

"Thought so."

CHAPTER 138

The storm raged outside. Half the woodpile sat in the middle of her kitchen and stacked next to Kari's old bed. The chickens were snug in the barn, and Willow had orders not to even consider stepping outside for any reason other than labor or fire. The new barn roof was finished just in time for the storm of the century.

Willow, on the other hand, was going a little stir crazy. She'd finished every project on her list, cleaned the house from top to bottom, purged every room of anything extraneous, and then sat in her mother's rocker until she felt like there was simply nothing to do. She'd read every book in the house so many times she knew her favorite passages by page number. Her journal was littered with inane comments left every few hours over the past twenty-four hours.

Finally, she opted for Christmas presents. Considering that she might just be a bit busy over the next few months, Willow took out a fresh composition notebook, covered it with paper, decorated it with paper holly, ribbons, and buttons for berries and opened it. On the first page, she wrote the names of everyone in Chad's family from Mom and Dad Tesdall down to Aggie and Luke's new baby. Page after page of friends, loved ones, and even acquaintances that she wanted to remember appeared beneath her pen.

Chad found her, notebook in hand, and sobbing an hour or two later. Concerned, he shrugged out of his coat leaving it on the floor by the door, dumped his belt, and hurried to the couch where she sat cross-legged, her belly covering her ankles. "What is it? What's wrong?"

"Look at that!"

Page after page of names and gift ideas, mostly jellies and baked goods, turned beneath his fingers. "You don't have to do all this. Alexa Hartfield doesn't expect two hundred origami birds for a Christmas gift!" He glanced at the next page. "No wonder you're so emotional. I'd be overwhelmed too. That's a lot of work—"

"That's not why I'm overwhelmed! Since when does a little work stop me? Look at this list of friends, relatives, countrymen!" She winked at him as she spoke the last word. "Two years ago, I could name on one hand the number of people I'd been introduced to in my life. Now, I'm afraid I won't remember them all." A ragged sob caught in her throat for a second before a fresh bout of weeping began.

"Oh, lass..." He didn't know what to say. The aloneness that had kept him coming to the farm in the first place was something he didn't miss. He remembered the first time he read of Kari's birth all alone, in a storm, no way to call for help; it still wrenched his heart thinking about it. The sight of Willow standing alone on her porch, Othello at her side as he drove away that first afternoon had never left his mind. He never wanted to see any human so alone and disconnected from mankind again.

"God has been so good. I can't stop thinking of that scripture in the Psalms that says 'He sets the solitary in families...' He did that for me. He gave me a family and then from that family, He created a whole new branch in our family. I am so blessed."

Chad didn't understand why the weeping. As fresh tears flowed soaking his shirt and great sobs shook her shoulders, Chad patted her back ineffectively and murmured hushing noises in between his futile attempts to staunch the flow of tears. Seconds passed. Minutes. Each one seemed longer than the last until finally, he lost all patience.

"Willow please. It's going to be ok. You won't be alone again, I promise. Even if something horrible happened to me—"

Her shoulders shook even harder. Ready to slap her in

hopes of stopping what seemed to be hysteria, Chad's eyes widened as he realized the sound coming from behind his wife's hands wasn't weeping anymore. She was laughing.

"What—"

"You just sound so sweet and funny as if tears always mean something bad. I'm happy."

"You're crying because you're happy that you know a lot of people that you feel obligated to give gifts to and overwork yourself into early labor." He paused. "Wait. That's it, isn't it? You're trying to have these kids too soon so you don't have to wait anymore. That's why you've been sewing and cleaning and going through every possession as though you were putting your affairs in order."

Willow tried to speak, but he continued for a minute or two recounting every activity she'd attempted recently until finally he jumped to his feet, whirled to face her, and pointing her finger in her face accused, "You're nesting!"

His eyes saw his finger thrust almost between her eyes and a slow flush crept up his neck and burned his ears. Sheepishly, Chad pulled his hands back into his pocket and stared down at his wife. Her face was nearly purple with repressed laughter. Eyes bulging, watering freely from the strain, she looked ready to explode. "Just let it out. I deserve it."

She flopped over on her side and howled. For several minutes Chad and Willow laughed until even Chad found himself wiping tears of hilarity from his eyes. "I needed that," he confessed when they finally regained composure.

"Me too. I was feeling a little sorry for myself with nothing to do, and then I started making a list—I mean, most of that is already made—"

"How?"

"I'll give extra jars of preserves, jams, and jellies to most of them. I just want a little something that says, 'I appreciate having you in my life.'"

"And then you saw just how many people were in your life and got all weepy on me?"

"No, I got weepy before you ever came home. You interrupted my tears of thanksgiving. It was my party, and you weren't invited."

"So do you want to tell me why you were planning Christmas presents in February?"

"I was bored."

He stared at her slack-jawed. "Will wonders never cease?"

March—

That's it. I am ready to be done with this business of gestating. Is it terrible that I can't imagine ever wanting to do this again? Chad already speaks of "next time" as though it was a given, but knowing what I now know of the medication I used to help me ovulate, I'm not sure I'm willing to risk having half a dozen children all at once. Our lives here would be over. I know people have done it and have probably handled it beautifully, but for me, I see it as a very frightening prospect. How would I keep my sanity, be a wife, run a farm, and still manage to give my children adequate care? I don't know that I could. Two at once is overwhelming enough to imagine. Four or five at once... Now that I know it is possible (well, not just possible but that it has actually happened), I don't think I care to risk it.

However, Dr. Kline assures me that sometimes, all the body needs is a pregnancy to properly regulate hormones and "prime the pump," as he put it. He says that it is entirely possible that I will have no trouble ovulating in the future. He warns us not to get our hopes up, but that we also should not automatically assume that because I was infertile (how strange it seems to say that as I sit here leaning so far over to reach the table comfortably) I will continue to be so.

Each day I grow a little weaker. It's hard to keep up my workload when I'm carrying thirty-five extra pounds across my midsection. It's hard to get enough food in me, so I've taken to focusing on the highest quality food I can find. I cook a steak for breakfast and keep it on the warming shelf of the stove until I finally nibble through it. Then I go for a glass of milk, followed by whatever fresh vegetables I've managed to pick the day before. The greenhouse is invaluable. I keep a new quart of fruit on the counter every day and eat from it

294

every time I walk by. It helps to keep my blood sugar levels stable. I wasn't careful for a week there, and I found myself feeling faint quite often. Hard-boiled eggs are in the icebox for whenever I need them, and Chad brings home some kind of new fruit every day or two. I've been eating oranges especially. Oh, they are so good.

Each night I go to bed after a tiny snack of oatmeal and milk and I sleep like a baby—well, like I hope these babies will sleep. It seems as though the minute I go to bed, they're ready to get up and play. Chad says it is because I rock them to sleep all day, but when I lie down, I quit rocking them. I didn't have the heart to tell him that they move most of the day too.

Dr. Kline wants me to make it to March fifteenth. After that, he says I can work myself into labor if I choose, but until then, my job is to keep eating, keep my feet up as often as possible, and keep these babies growing inside me. I can't decide if I want them to come as quickly after the fifteenth as possible or if I want more time. We're almost to the end of just Chad and me time, and while I never thought much of it when people were pushing for us to wait for children, I now see their point. Our marriage will never be the same. That's not a bad thing—I'm not saying that, but it will be different and I like how things are. I want to enjoy it while I have it. Mother's biggest goal in the life she created for us here was that we enjoy each and every day to its fullest. We don't look back on our days wishing we'd appreciated them more because we took the time to do it while we lived it. I want that for this area too.

Chad, however, is ready to be a papa. He sings to the children, reads them the Word (I never imagined him volunteering to read anything aloud, but he does it frequently now), and spends hours "brainwashing" them as I call it. He reminds them to obey Mama, treat each other kindly, remember to do their jobs diligently, and so many other little admonitions of good and proper behavior. It's quite endearing, and I wonder if it'll make any difference, but even if it doesn't, I have wonderful memories of it to comfort me as I try to train all that into them.

Names have become a bone of contention between us. I

295

have this slight feeling of panic not knowing our children's names. I can't imagine the pressure of choosing while in the hospital, but Chad says if he can't name an animal without seeing its eyes, how is he supposed to name his child without holding him, looking into his little face, and sensing his personality. I think it's an excuse to avoid the fact that I don't want to name them Adoniram and Brainard or Isobel. Those were his last options. He's on a missionary kick or something. The good news is that he has agreed to consider Christopher and Chadwick for middle names if we have boys. Truthfully, I think a girl will be Karianne Olivia. He mentioned it once, and while he has been talking about Elisabeth, Amy, and Isobel lately (I have prayed he wouldn't mention Gladys), he doesn't seem as enamored with them as he is the men.

Mom bought us a baby name book, and I went through it and highlighted every name I liked with a pink or blue colored pencil. There were many lovely names in the book that I'd never heard of, and they were tempting. I could tell Chad liked some, but others didn't appeal to him. He said he can't understand how I can love a name like Margaret and then suggest Windsor in the next breath. Of course, he likes Margaret and despises Windsor. I thought it sounded interesting. He says why not Westminster? I said Westminster sounded like a boy's name, but it'd be fun to have twins Windsor and Westminster. His utter silence I took for a "no."

Grandfather Finley came by to see me this week. He was on his way back from Brunswick and took the Fairbury route in order to come here. It was a nice visit, but I can tell it is still difficult for him to see where Mother lived, see her pictures on the wall and the end tables and know that she was so close and yet out of his reach. He hasn't read most of the journals. He says they are too difficult to handle. I think he got to the part about the nightmares or maybe my birth and couldn't see that it got better. I assure him that we were happy, that she missed and loved them, and that I never doubted how much she admired them and hated what she'd done to them. I don't know how much he enjoyed his stay; he seemed a little uncomfortable. But he says he has to come back in a week and a half, so perhaps it wasn't too awkward

296

for him.

Every time I see him or Grandmother, they have some kind of gift for me. This time, he brought me a very expensive camera. I don't quite know how to accept it, but Chad says they have lived for so many years unable to give to their daughter or granddaughter, so I should let them have their fun. Chad has spent hours on his Internet at work researching lenses for this camera and finally ordered three. From what I understand, he spent many times more just on those lenses than Grandfather must have on the camera. Those are some amazingly expensive lenses! However, I've been practicing, and it does take some amazing pictures. I've even gotten a couple that feel a little like Wes Hartfield's style. I wasn't sure I'd like this computerized camera, but I do. Chad was right. I can take two hundred pictures and "throw away" all but five, and it didn't cost me any more than if I just took those five. How amazing! So much of modern technology seems wasteful to me, but I have to say, that one thing alone must save a fortune in bad pictures and wasted paper.

The babies are restless. I think I'll walk again. My ankles seem less swollen now. It's a delicate balance between being on my feet too much and not enough. If I am not careful, either one will give me elephant ankles—in other words, none.

CHAPTER 139

"I have three and a half more weeks."

David Finley looked at his granddaughter and wondered how she could possibly hold out another minute, much less another twenty-four days. "Are you comfortable?"

Even as he spoke, Willow shifted in her seat, trying to give her lungs any kind of relief from the constant pressure. "When I'm standing I can breathe, but I get tired quickly. When I'm sitting I don't feel like I'm about to tip over and my back doesn't ache, but then I feel as though I'm drowning out of water."

"Have you considered asking them to induce your labor?"

She shook her head. "The doctor mentioned it when Chad was concerned about my feet swelling, but we all agreed that as long as I'm healthy and the babies aren't in any kind of distress, the longer they're in there, the better in the long run."

Eager to show him her progress in learning the camera, Willow pulled Chad's laptop from the bookshelf in the library and brought it to the coffee table, swaying a bit as she stood upright again. "Oh I hate it when I get off balance. It feels so weird," she muttered as she punched the button for the screen to come on.

"It is very strange to be watching a laptop boot up by candlelight," David remarked amused.

"I guess it is. I hadn't thought of that."

"You wouldn't, I suppose," he agreed, smiling. His

granddaughter looked so much like his mother, and yet he'd seen pictures of Lynne Solari and the resemblance between them was uncanny. How could two women who looked nothing alike have a granddaughter that clearly resembled both of them?

"How is Grandmother? Is she over the flu yet?"

"Just a slight residual cough. This is the first time she's gotten the flu from the shot, but she says it isn't as bad as getting it without one so I guess we'll keep getting them."

"Well, I'm glad she's better. I could have these babies any time and she promised to sit with Mom and hold them while I sleep. I plan to get lots of sleep when I get half a chance."

"She's all ready to go. Has a bag packed as if she was having the babies herself. She even has one of those journals you made her all ready to write down her first thoughts as a great grandmother." He paused. "You know, she's been writing down everything she can remember that has happened since we lost your mother. She wrote about Kyle's graduation, his marriage, the grandchildren, everything. It has been amazing to see all that has happened in our lives."

"You read it?"

He blushed. "Well, she said I could…"

"Chad reads mine several times a week. It's a great way for us to make sure that he knows what is going on around here. His hours mean that sometimes things happen that I thought I told him and then wham, nope. I didn't." She blushed. "Like yesterday. He came home ready to butcher the chickens, but I'd already done them. Boy was he relieved."

"He doesn't like butchering?"

"Not chickens!"

Something didn't make sense to David. "What, not that I'm not interested mind you, but what does that have to do with the journals?"

"Oh, I keep doing that," she muttered exasperatedly. "He came in to ask me about it, but I was sleeping so he opened my animal journal and saw how many I butchered, how I prepared them, and who we should call to have them come get them. He made calls instead, which is fine by me. I really do not like the phone."

"Carol mentioned something about that the other day."

"I didn't realize I'd told her. I didn't mean to. It's the easiest way to keep in touch."

"Oh she just said that you always seemed more at ease in your letters or when she visits."

"I feel guilty sometimes," Willow confessed, "for not coming more often. She must get tired of the drive."

"Actually, I think she enjoys it."

He watched helplessly as Willow struggled to pull herself to a standing position and adjust her center of gravity. She shuffled to the woodstove, opened the door, and peeked in. The coals, after a little adjustment, made a perfect bed for a new log, before Willow slammed the door shut on it once more. David followed her to the kitchen where he watched the process all over again.

"It's work just keeping the house warm, isn't it?"

"It's a good work. It feels good to accomplish something so important with such ease. I mean, I spend two minutes and our house stays warm and toasty for a couple of hours. It's really quite amazing. I'll be back down in a minute. It's time to light the upstairs stove."

Watching her climb the stairs was more painful than he could have imagined. She looked like she was twelve months pregnant and carrying triplets—both. She'd given up trying to wear anything remotely attractive and settled for house gowns that hung from the shoulders and covered her.

These visits were hard for him. He came because it was right and because he loved his daughter. Whatever mistakes she'd made, she'd done it to spare them. She'd sacrificed her happiness and ease in order to protect them, and he worked hard to remember that, but unlike his wife, Willow wasn't a link to Kari, she was the thing that had ultimately torn Kari from them. Though he truly didn't blame Willow, he did find it hard to connect with her across the chasm that Kari's disappearance created.

He glanced at his watch. Twenty-five minutes. Surely he could leave in another twenty minutes. After all, he was just stopping in after a business meeting. A quick visit... She wouldn't expect him to stay for dinner. Would she?

Suddenly, her cry sent David flying up the stairs faster than he'd imagined he could move. The sight of her leaning

301

against the woodstove, her palms flat against the metal alarmed him, until he realized the door was open and there were no flames inside. "Are you ok?"

"Towel," she gasped. "Please. Cupboard behind me."

He grabbed a fluffy white towel and passed it to her. "What's wrong?"

"Can you call Chad? I need him to come home." Her knees buckled for a moment before sheer willpower forced them straight again. "Now," she growled before a low moan escaped.

"Where do I call? What's his number?"

She stared at him blankly as if the question made no sense before she wailed, "I don't know. Station. Call the station."

Within minutes, David was informed that Chad was in court and his cell phone off, but they would send someone in to get him. "He'll come soon, Willow. What can I do?"

"Help me downstairs. Please. I don't think I can do it by myself."

The trip downstairs was slow and tedious. Every step left her gasping and panting for air, until David was certain she'd give birth in the living room. Once she reached the bottom, Willow sent him back upstairs for fresh towels to sit on. Every errand, no matter how small, sent him racing to help, until there was nothing left for him to do but wait for Chad to arrive. All ideas of leaving were gone now. He could never leave her alone like this. His daughter had been alone in labor, but his granddaughter would be spared that pain at least.

She whimpered with another pain causing his heart to contract with it. "Would it help if I rubbed your shoulders?"

Willow shook her head and then hesitated. "Um—"

"What, sweetheart. What can I do? I want to help if I can."

"My lower back. It's what really hurts. Would you rub that?"

One hand pushed stray tendrils away from her damp forehead while the other rubbed her lower back until he thought it would go numb. Somehow, he managed to apply firm pressure to just the right spot.

"Oh that feels good."

"When this hand gets tired, I'll move to your other side and use the other one." He passed her the glass. "Drink. You need your strength."

"I can't," she gasped as a new pain began. "I can't until I'm on my way to the hospital. I can't get back up those stairs to use the bathroom."

"You need another one down here."

"That's what Chad keeps saying. Like I've got time to clean two of them." The edge in her voice told him she was nearing the peak of the contraction.

"Would you like me to get you a wet wash cloth for your forehead?"

She nodded, whimpered, and slumped over the couch pillow clutched to her chest. "Thank you."

For thirty minutes, he held her, rocked her, sang the songs he'd sang to Kari as a little girl, and wiped the perspiration from her face. For thirty minutes, he endured the pain from the side of one who can do nothing to alleviate it. He kissed her temples, rubbed her hands, massaged her back, and even brushed her hair when she asked.

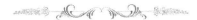

With each minute that passed, she grew more and more anxious calling—no crying—for Chad as each contraction built upon the last until she thought she'd go insane with agony. Nothing she'd ever endured prepared her for the sheer torture of those contractions. She'd read about breathing, practiced religiously, and prepared for focusing to ensure minimal discomfort in the beginning stages of labor but to no avail. Either the contractions she experienced were worse than most people's early labor, or her pain tolerance level had dropped to negative numbers. She truly didn't want to know which it was.

After what seemed like decades, she looked into her grandfather's concerned eyes and begged to be taken into the hospital. "We can call Chad, leave a note—I don't care. Please take me now. Please. I can't drive."

The trek to his car took twice as long as made any sense.

Her grandfather drove in erratic spurts, first racing down the highway and now slower. Curves he took at a near crawl, straight stretches faster until she began to feel nauseated with the change. Perhaps, instead, it was the pain of the contractions. She didn't know.

A wheelchair wheeled out from the emergency room doors and met them at the car. Willow's surprise was evident. "I called ahead and told them I was coming. I'll be right in after I park, okay? You'll be okay?" His concern touched her.

"I'll be fine." She gasped. "Thank you, Grandfather. Thank you."

"We've got to work on this title thing. Be right back."

Inside the hospital, they wheeled her down corridors, into a labor room, and onto a bed that seemed little more than the table from the doctor's office to Willow's way of thinking. From that moment on, her images of labor changed irrevocably. Starting with the IV, baby monitors, and internal checks that nearly sent her through the roof in pain, it moved to a quick ultrasound to check baby positions, Demerol for the pain, and occasional vomiting that neither she nor David understood.

He tried joking but they all fell flat. He sang until he grew hoarse, and finally wrapped a hand around hers and told her to squeeze whenever she needed relief. She nearly broke his thumb. "Sorry," she gasped as another wave hit her. "Where is Chad?"

"They said he's coming as soon as they tell him. Carol's on the way too."

"Mom Tesdall is on the contact information. Can you call her?"

He rose to go and she gripped his arm even tighter. "Where are you going?"

"Do you want me to call?"

Illogically, Willow whimpered and shook her head. "Don't leave me. I don't know how Mother did this all alone. Please—" Her words were cut short with a cry of pain.

Her nurse, Sandi, rushed into the room surprised to hear her growing louder so quickly. "You doin' ok, sweetie?"

"No." Before Willow could answer, David's answer cut the air. "Do something for her. She's the strongest, healthiest young woman I've ever seen. If she's hurting this badly, do something."

"I'll call Dr. Kline." She paused by David's side. "Have you heard from her husband?"

"No."

"How long since the contractions started?"

"Water broke at two o'clock almost on the nose. I heard the clock chime about the time I grabbed her a towel."

"Two hours. Hmmm."

"If you could call the emergency contact number—Mrs. Tesdall can get in touch with her son better than I can."

David helped Willow from the bed and hung her arms over his shoulders. Pulling the IV pole with them, he slowly backed around the room. Their shuffling traveled very little distance around the room but she seemed to like the change. Her head flopped against his chest as she struggled through another contraction. "Grandfather,"

"Oh we have to find something else for you to call me."

"Not now. You smell good. Like pine and soap."

His deep chuckle reminded her of Chad's when Chad was amused with her. "I'm glad you approve."

"I want my babies to recognize that scent with the sound of your voice and the touch of your hands. Please keep coming. They need their great-grandfather."

"As long as you don't make them call me great-grandfather. That's too much of a mouthful even for me."

"Double G-pa. How's that," she murmured before a deep groan cut off his reply.

"They're getting worse, aren't they sweetheart?"

"I don't know how Mother did it," she sniffled between tears. "I'm about to die, and they said I'm at 'four.' That means I have six more of these to go. If time is equal that's..." Confusion clouded her features and her eyes. "A lot more hours."

"My Kari was a strong woman."

"And she swore she'd never have children again." Willow retorted grumpily. "I think I get it. I don't know if I'll do this again if it's like this."

"The memories will fade, sweetheart. My wife and Sheryl both swear that after a few weeks it's just a fuzzy memory.

305

The babies—"

"Why didn't Mother have that?" she wailed. "Why did she have to keep such a vivid memory of such a horrible time?"

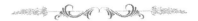

In the same soothing voice that had comforted Kari through scraped knees, bruised feelings, and a broken heart in the tenth grade, David Finley promised her he'd be there, he'd never leave her, and like Jesus, he wasn't going to forsake her. He promised that Chad was coming and that he'd be there soon. This is exactly what Willow needed to hear. Once he hit on the one thing that truly soothed her, David didn't quit. He talked about the little boy that Chad would have to stop and scold for not wearing his helmet causing Willow to smile.

"Aiden. He never learns."

Going from there, David assured Willow that Chad had to turn in the cruiser so the next officer could take his shift. "He's probably turning in the keys right now." After helping Willow to lie on her side once more, he continued with stopping at the farm, feeding and caring for the animals... "He'll probably have to push some more alfalfa down from the rafters of that big ol' barn you guys built, so the sheep don't starve while you're gone."

"Call Ryder and Caleb. He has to call them. For tomorrow. Ask."

"When he gets here, I'll make sure he did."

From washing up the dishes to changing sheets and getting the house ready, David mentioned everything he could think of to keep Willow's husband from arriving. He sent Chad back to town for a bank robbery, over to Westbury to pick up his mother, and help a kitten out of a tree for a little old lady. This made Willow snort.

"Cat's aren't worth the trouble. He has babies to help," she whined as another contraction started to build.

"You're right. They're not. But kittens are. Kittens are delightful until they become cats. Then they're disposable."

"Don't we sound horrible," Willow giggled as she realized what they were saying.

"You're smiling. I'll talk about just about anything to keep you smiling."

His hands worked on Willow's hips, back, and shoulder. Just as she murmured that maybe she'd learned to control the contractions, they grew harder sending her into deeper and more frantic cries of pain. David thought he'd go insane if he had to see her suffer any longer. "I'll be right back. I promise. Count to sixty, and I'll already be here. Ready?"

Ignoring the terror in her eyes, David dashed from the room, found the nearest nurse, and demanded they get his granddaughter relief. "She's in agony. If she's making this much noise, she's suffering ten times more than you think. I want that doctor here now or so help me—"

"What doctor?" The voice came from behind David's ear.

"Her doctor is Dr. Kline and I want him now."

"I'm Dr. Kline. How can I help?"

"Do something for Willow."

Anxious to get her some help as quickly as possible, he raced back to Willow's side wetting the cloths he'd left again and wiping her forehead. "Look at her."

Dr. Kline settled at the end of the bed, ready to check her progress. How David hated this. He wanted to be far away when his granddaughter was in that position, but instead, he focused on her eyes, told her to breathe a little slower, and squeeze his hands harder. The doctor pulled off his gloves and tossed them in the garbage can. "Well, you're at five already—"

Willow's wail pierced their ears. "I can't do this. I just can't do this," she moaned. "Cut them out of me now!"

"I'm not going to do that, Willow," Dr. Kline argued. "It's not in your or their best interests at this time. However, I am," he continued at the despairing look in the eyes of man and granddaughter, "going to order an epidural for you. You'll be able to stay on top of the pain with it."

The doctor dragged David from the room and demanded, "Where is her husband? I expected to see Chad by her side the whole way. He told me her mother went through this alone, and he's concerned about her mental stability over it so where is he?"

"We've called. He was in court with his cell phone off,

307

and they said they'd go tell him. I have no idea—it's been three hours!"

Another shriek sent David back to her side, leaving the doctor confused. A woman burst into the O.B. ward demanding to know which was Willow Tesdall's room. Seconds later, Marianne collapsed in a chair next to Willow's bed and sighed. "Finally. I'm so sorry it took me so long."

"Where's Chad?" Willow's eagerness couldn't be hidden.

"He's coming. The officer, Brad I think, who was supposed to call him was called to a barroom brawl and couldn't go to the courthouse. Everyone's in a mess, the trial is taking longer than expected, and Chad was last on the witness list. I told him to stay until dismissal, but he can't get through anyway."

David's eyes widened. "Why not?"

"Big accident. Two tractor-trailers hit each other around the bend where Chad was hit last year. The whole road is blocked off. I had to backtrack and come around through New Cheltenham."

The anesthesiologist came through the door all smiles and too chipper for anyone's comfort. "Let us be getting you some relief, mama," the man said in a deep Indian accent.

The torture of laying on her side, bending in half when there was nowhere for her upper body to bend, and all through a contraction, sent tears of pain rolling down her cheeks. Marianne mopped her face and kept eye contact, promising that it'd be better soon. David tried to slip from the room, but Willow grew hysterical as he disappeared behind the privacy curtain. He returned and laid his gentle hands on her feet, itching to get back to the other end of the bed and away from areas that might send a baby flying into his fumbling hands.

The relief from the epidural was nearly instantaneous. The anesthesiologist watched for five minutes to see if she responded well to it, and then gave her a full dose. Her eyes nearly glazed over in abject relief and gratitude. "He is my new hero. I want to name the babies after this man. What is your name?"

"Jasvinder. I am thinking you'll want to choose another name perhaps."

308

Marianne, satisfied that Willow wouldn't be splitting in half anytime soon, kissed her forehead. "I'm just going to call Christopher and tell him you're resting easier now. I'll call Chad too. He's going crazy with worry."

To David's surprise, she smiled her thanks and turned to him without a murmur. He'd expected her to come unglued as Marianne left, but she hardly noticed. "You doing better, sweetheart?" The moment his hands moved away from her, she whimpered as her eyes pleaded for him to hold her. "I'm not going anywhere, Willow. I'll stay right here until Chad comes."

"Please stay."

"I'm staying little girlie, I'm staying."

CHAPTER 140

At a quarter past seven, Chad finally burst through the emergency room door, his gun holster still strapped to his belt, his heavy jacket covered with snow, and eyes blazing with frustration. "It's a nightmare out there," he muttered as he rushed down hallways, through doorways, and finally into Willow's room.

"Hey, lass." His entire demeanor changed as he sought his wife's side. "How are you doing?"

Marianne slipped from the room, and David started to follow, but Willow's hand shot out and grabbed him. "You said you wouldn't go."

"But Chad's here now." Willow's eyes pleaded with him not to leave. David saw the pain and confusion in Chad's eyes and bent low, murmuring "Willow, you're hurting Chad. He's been trying to get to you to be here for you. I'll go call Carol, get a cup of coffee, use the restroom, and be waiting outside the door inside five minutes. All you have to do is have Chad come get me, and I'll be right back."

David's eyes met Chad's and spoke volumes. Chad, uncertain about what to do, dropped her hand and smiled. "I'll be back in two seconds. I just have to ask the nurse a question."

Outside the door, he threw David a confused look. "What's going on in there?"

"It was bad, Chad. Very, very bad. I think she just latched onto me because I was *there*."

"Well I tried to be!" Chad stuffed his hands in his pockets. "I don't understand."

"She's reliving Kari's labor—I think. She's hurting, and just now she's received a little relief." David squeezed Chad's shoulder. "She needs help. Not just physically, right now the worst of it, thanks to that epidural, is emotional. She's barely hanging in there."

Nodding, Chad hurried back into the room and seeing his uniform reflected in Willow's eyes, picked up the phone. "Hey Joe, I need you to come get my belt. I can't leave Willow, and I forgot—Oh, good idea. Thanks."

"Okay, how are we doing? What did the doctor say?"

"About thirty minutes ago or so I was halfway there." Her voice sounded weak and exhausted.

"You ok? You look so pale. I'm so sorry it took so long to get here. Brad is kicking himself for bungling this."

"Tell him it's ok. Grandfather was here. I was fine."

"You're angry with me."

"Of course not. I'm just glad you're here."

They were interrupted by Dr. Kline. "Oh, Chad. I'm very glad to see you here. So, how are you doing now, Willow?"

"Much better. Much. I feel twinges every now and then but the pain—the real pain, is gone."

Chad cringed for his wife as the doctor watched the monitor, waited for a contraction, and then did an internal check. "Well, for some people, epidurals seem to speed up labor a little, but I think you're one of the majority. Still at five. Sorry."

"At least it isn't as painful," she whispered weakly.

"I want you to try to sleep. I need you to get as much rest as humanly possible so that you are rested for pushing. We want to avoid that C-section if we can."

"Can she eat? She hasn't been able to keep much food down at a time, so I'm thinking that after five and a half hours, she must be hungry." Chad's voice sounded almost imploring, but his eyes demanded help for his wife.

"Sorry. No. There is still a very real chance of a C-section that we can't risk food in her system if we need to put her under for surgery. We can add a bit of glucose to her IV in order to keep up her strength."

312

Before Chad could say anything else, a nurse came into the room. "Officer Tesdall, there's an officer out here for you?"

"That'll be someone from Brunswick. They're going to take my gun for me. I can't believe I brought it in."

Dr. Kline watched as Chad left and then looked at Willow sternly. "I overheard him out there talking to your grandfather. He's hurting. He feels rejected. If you don't want him in here, say something now before it gets any worse."

"Of course I want him in here. I just—I need Grandfather too."

"Why?"

"He didn't get to help Mother. He had to read about her being all alone. He felt rejected and helpless. He was helping me, and he was good at it. I think he needs that."

"Tell your husband, Willow," Dr. Kline advised. "He needs to know you're not rejecting him."

Chad's entrance stopped Willow's exhausted response. "Chad?"

He hurried to do something, anything, to make her more comfortable. He'd thought about twice the pushing, twice the nursing, twice the diapers, and sleepless nights, but he hadn't imagined twice the pain. Willow had a strong threshold for pain, but according to the nurse Sandi, she'd been out of her mind with agony.

"I'm here. What can I do? Do you want your grandfather back? I can go get him."

"I do, Chad, but not before we have a few minutes alone. I missed you. I needed you."

"I'm so sorry." Chad felt like a heel. "I didn't know—"

"I just need you to know how important it is to me that you're here. I'm not asking for Grandfather because he's more important to me right now. I'm asking because helping me is important to him right now."

The light of understanding dawned in his eyes. "Of course. I'll go get him." He turned to leave, but she caught his hand. "Can't you even give me a hello kiss before you rush off to bring other men into my life?"

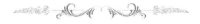

Around midnight, things grew intense. Dilation was at eight, and Willow's exhaustion was evident to everyone who entered the room. Marianne came in from time to time to brush her hair, clean her face, and give the men a chance for more coffee. Carol sat quietly in the corner, praying like she'd never prayed before, and Cheri paced outside the door like a father from the forties.

The men, however, rarely left her side. David sat next to the bed kneading her shoulders, adding pressure to her back, and whispering encouragement. Sometimes he sang; others he was silent, trying to disappear into the background so that Willow and Chad could spend this special time together. He was relieved to see the pain that had been etched in her eyes replaced with fatigue. As much as he'd love her to be at her best, tired was better than tormented in his opinion.

Chad, once he got past seeing his vibrant wife pummeled by labor, became a rock. He sat at the head of the bed and supported her as she reclined for maximum lung capacity. He talked to her about names, about plans, and about his day—anything to keep her distracted. At one point, he gently rubbed her arms. Immediately, he realized his mistake. Willow's hand involuntarily jerked upwards and gave him a lovely bloody nose in less than two seconds flat.

The nurses from then on called her slugger and joked about reporting her for spousal abuse. Chad promised to fill out the forms next time he went to work. Just before one o'clock, the new night nurse, Wanda, strolled in, and with the tact and gentleness of a back alley dentist, checked for dilation and turned to leave the room. "Can you tell us where she is?"

"She's at nine. At her rate, she'll be there for a few more hours, so get some sleep. She's got work ahead of her and then motherhood. This is her last chance to get some rest without someone interrupting it every two minutes."

Just as the woman barged through the door in search of another victim to invade, the blood pressure cuff went off automatically. "She's joking, right?" Willow's shocked expression mirrored Chad and David's.

"How is that woman still employed. She has the bedside manner of a bull in Pamplona."

"That's insulting," Willow retorted angrily.

"I call them like I see them, Willow."

"I still feel sorry for the bull."

Before the men stopped laughing, Dr. Kline came through the door. "I thought I saw Wanda leaving. I've never known her to be all that—" he paused searching for the right word. "Funny."

"She's not, but Willow is." David brushed damp tendrils from Willow's head.

"Can we request that she not be allowed in this room again?" Chad didn't even attempt to hide his fury. "I will not have that woman attacking my wife again."

"She attacked—"

"I can still feel where her fingernails raked me." Willow's whimper was barely audible, but the pain in her tone was unmistakable.

"She won't check you again. I'll talk to her. Until delivery, I'll keep her out, but I want her during pushing. She's the best delivery nurse around. If we end up in the OR, I want her there."

"OR?"

"Operating Room," the three men said simultaneously.

"Why the OR?"

"Sometimes the second baby needs to be taken cesarean. I told you that."

At one-thirty Barb the Bubbly came in and checked her, shaking her head sympathetically at their eager expressions. At two, she returned but still no progress. By three-thirty they were all growing antsy. Dr. Kline entered at four o'clock and rearranged her. She sat up a slight bit straighter, legs drawn up closer, and as the next contraction came, he gave her one last exam. "If I just do a little stretching..." He smiled at Willow and gave the men a slightly bloody thumbs up. "Dilation complete. Time to push. I can feel your body bearing down already."

"Baby is coming?" The hopefulness in Willow's voice touched the hearts of the doctor and Willow's family alike.

"Bab*ies* are coming."

315

"Come on, lass. You can do it." Chad held her hands, supported her shoulders, and found himself straining with her through each push. He'd have hemorrhoids before they were done if he wasn't careful.

The room was dimly light, a light at the end of the bed for the doctor's benefit, but the lights by Willow's head were out, and the overhead lights were off. Marianne, Carol, Cheri, David, and Christopher all stood outside the door, plastered against the wall and listening to Willow as she moaned, groaned, and screamed throughout each contraction. Chad alone sat at her side glaring between contractions at Nurse Wanda at Dr. Kline's side.

After the first ineffectual push, Dr. Kline turned down the epidural drip leaving her with more feeling and much less comfort. The pain, however bad it might have been, was nothing like her initial contractions. She handled each one as it came, stayed on top of it, and then relaxed between them, prepared for the next before it hit. It seemed as though she'd finally found her groove and was ready to take on this business of birthing babies.

By five, she'd been pushing for forty-five minutes and the head was just beginning to crown. By five-thirty, Dr. Kline was ready. "Ok, on this next one, push hard. I mean *hard*. I want you to push like your life depended on it. It doesn't. You're both fine. But push like it anyway."

The contraction began and this time, Willow felt it before Dr. Kline announced. She grabbed the rails of the bed and practically pulled herself up off it. She pushed with every ounce of strength she had, until she was sure her organs would explode out of her. A new sensation began building slowly. In her exhausted state, it took a minute to recognize what was happening but suddenly she exclaimed, "It's burning! Is it supposed to be burning?"

"Keep pushing, Willow. Don't stop now. That head is coming and…" On and on the doctor went, encouraging, urging, demanding, and consoling when the head slipped back into the canal. "It's ok. That happens sometimes. Next time it'll come through. Take a deep breath. Chad, get her some ice. Now let's get ready, because I think the next one is almost here. Come on…"

Several minutes passed as they waited through the next contraction before she pushed. Her body, exhausted, didn't have the strength to try again, but as the next contraction built, she was ready. As the contraction peaked, she bore down with everything she could and the head was born. "We've got a darling head of blonde fussy hair! Get ready for the next contraction, Willow. Take a breath—no stop pushing. Just relax until the next one."

"I feel constipated!" she shrieked. "I want it out of there!" Before the doctor could respond, she gave one more strong push and nearly sent the baby flying into the doctor's hands.

"Well? Is he, she, it ok?"

"Don't call our baby an it," Willow snapped. The next contraction was already building.

The nurse felt for the baby's head and nodded at Dr. Kline as he clamped the cord and offered for Chad to cut it. Chad shook his head violently. "You get it. Thanks."

Barb stood in the corner, working over the baby and making Chad very nervous. Dr. Kline and Wanda checked Willow's vitals, watched the monitor, and felt for the second baby's head while Barb suctioned out the first one, cleaned it up, and wrapped it in a blanket. The child's wails drove Willow nearly insane as the next contraction built. "Someone pick up my baby and comfort it!"

"It?"

Willow whacked Chad again restarting the blood flow she'd caused earlier. "Ohhhh it's coming!"

For the next few minutes, things blurred. Willow pushed, the doctor encouraged, and Chad prayed more fervently than he'd ever prayed in his life. He could see Willow's strength fading quickly, and if this baby took half as long to push out as the last...

Dr. Kline saw the sack bulge and ripped it away from the head. "Ok, there's the head. You did very well, Willow. One more push and it'll be over. You can do it. Take a deep breath, exhale. Come on, exhale. Do it again, you want to get some good air in those lungs before you start pushing again. Chad, get her some ice. Barbara, how is baby one doing?" Dr. Kline kept talking without a break, change of tone, or anything to indicate that things had changed.

317

The next contraction built and with a fraction of the effort expended to deliver the first baby, the second slipped from the birth canal into the doctor's waiting hands. The room erupted in laughter when Willow sighed, "Oh that felt good."

"Good? You've got to be kidding me! I saw your face. That was torture."

"No, not the whole thing," she gasped. "Just that last two or three seconds when the body slipped through. It felt like I'd been holding my bladder for nine months and I finally got to go. Oh man, that was almost worth the pain by itself." She looked at her stomach critically. "You know, it's a lot smaller—a lot smaller. But are you sure there isn't another baby in there?"

Contrary to Willow's concerns, there wasn't another baby in her womb. However, she did have two good-sized placentas to deliver before she was able to hold her children. As she accepted the first baby from Barb's arms, she realized she still didn't know if they had boys, girls, or one of each. "Is he a he or a she?"

"Boys. You have two very healthy boys."

"I got my boys, Chad!" Willow said, her eyes filling with tears. "I always thought I'd have two boys and I do! I have sons. I can't believe that I have sons!"

Chad, overcome by the beauty of the infant in his arms, stood, walked to the door, and beckoned the family waiting there. "Come see the lads. You've got to see them."

Wanda huffed and muttered something about visiting hours, but Dr. Kline sent her from the room. "Barb can handle it; I need you with Mrs. Pham."

"She's supposed to have a nurse for each baby, Dr. Kline."

"Bethany is on her way in. They'll call if they need help. I need you with me."

The babies were passed from grandmother to great grandmother to grand and great grandfather. Uncle Chris arrived just as Aunt Cheri picked up the first boy, gazing adoringly into his eyes. "I thought I wanted girls, but he's just so perfect. Which one is he?"

"The hospital band says. I've got baby two so you have baby one."

"They're not identical are they?" Christopher suddenly had visions of mixing the children and for some reason that bothered him immensely.

"No. Fraternal but you can't tell right now, can you? I think they look identical."

"No they don't," Willow argued. "Baby one's head is longer than two. He looks like he's wearing a stove pipe hat."

"That's just because he was in the birth canal for a longer time. It shapes the head. In a day or two it'll be fine."

Chad whispered something to Chris before taking his son back from Cheri and sitting next to Willow with him. "It seems strange to realize that he's a firstborn."

Sleepy, the babies hardly moved as the family played musical infants, passing them around until Chad realized Willow still hadn't held her second son. "Ok, Willow's turn."

David brought the second child to Willow's side and whispered something in her ear. She nodded, a grateful look in her eyes, and whispered, "Thanks. I'd appreciate it. I can't tell you—"

Once again, David whispered something in her ear causing Willow to smile. "I love you, Grandfather."

"If you love me, you'll call me anything but that. I'd even take Granddad..."

"Granddad it is. I love you. Thank you."

Chad watched amused as David Finley rounded up the inhabitants of the room and pushed them from the room, insisting that Chad and Willow needed time alone with their children. Barb did her job cleaning, adjusting Willow's medication, kneading her uterus, but somehow without intruding into the new little family's time. Chad watched as Willow counted fingers, toes, and double-checked to see for herself that she really was the proud mother of sons.

"What did your granddad say, lass?"

"He said thank you for letting him be a part of this. He said to tell you he hopes you don't feel displaced, but that it was very healing for him."

"I need to thank him for being there with you. I can't

319

imagine how horrible it would have been—you could have been alone just like your mother—"

"I would have called Lily, or Aunt Libby, or someone who could get here fast. I was in too much pain—it was bad Chad. It was the worst thing—"

"Shh... look at them. The worst brought the best. It's over and just beginning all at once."

To be continued...

Past Forward. Don't miss a single episode of this serial novel. Check for them **FREE** on Kindle.

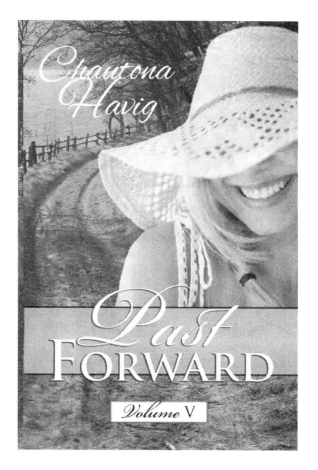

Coming Spring 2013

Made in the USA
Middletown, DE
30 June 2018